Sinking Dixie

Mussie,

Laissez les bons temps rouler !
Happy Berry Fox!

J. G. BREERWOOD

Designed and produced by:
Maine Authors Publishing
12 High Street, Thomaston, Maine
www.maineauthorspublishing.com

Printed in the United States of America

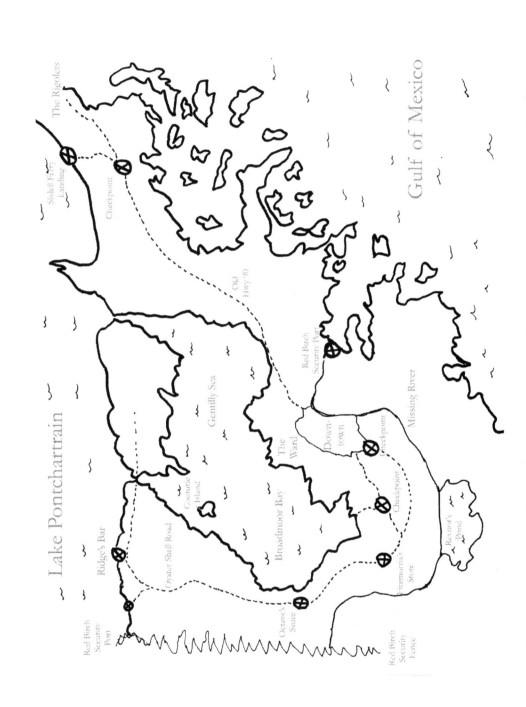

Lake Pontchartrain

The Rigolets

Skull Ferry Landing

Red Birch Security Port

Checkpoint

Old Hwy 90

Gulf of Mexico

Gentilly Sea

Couture Island

Red Birch Security Port

Ridge's Bar

Oyster Shell Road

The Ward

Broadmoor Bay

Down-town

Red Birch Security Port

Checkpoint

Checkpoint

Missing River

Octave's Store

Fitzmurris's Store

Checkpoint

Revnor's Pond

Red Birch Security Fence

Prologue

"Will you come with me?" she asked, and right then I knew it was over. Mira would accept nothing less than an answer, which was fair. I had been dodging the subject since she had received her acceptance letter. Now she needed an answer that I wasn't ready to give.

It was a slow night at Romero's, the Tex-Mex joint in Houston where I worked, and I turned on the ScrollScreen above the bar. The latest Jump-jive posts crawled up the screen in little rows, and "Domestic Strength Administration Praises Chief Security Officer for Keeping New Orleans Safe by Banning Mardi Gras" caught my eye.

I shook my head and switched the newsfeed to a baseball game. When I'd first heard of the New Orleans Restoration Act, I was elated that government had the initiative to rebuild the city after it had been obliterated by Hurricane Beckham. However, I soon learned that they intended to build something entirely different, not restore what was.

Mira entered, singing, and shut the door behind her. "Hi!"

I smiled. "Thought that was you." I poured a few knuckles worth of beer in a rocks glass.

"Well, I need to practice for the play."

"Right." I took a generous sip of beer.

"I see you're being inconspicuous."

"Yep. It's pretty good. From Massachusetts, I think. Vodka tonic?"

"Reading me again. Something wrong, Derek?"

I dropped a lime wedge into the fresh cocktail. I gently slid it down to her across the slick bar top. "It's just this whole New Orleans Restoration bullshit. I hear they don't want people to move back."

"You want to move back?"

I shrugged and sipped my beer.

"It's almost a year after Beckham. It's all gone, Derek. Your uncle's house got destroyed; we looked at the drone pictures. Remember? This music program's only three years, so maybe by then the city will be better."

"Well, I got some money saved. Now is the time to get something."

"Wait. You want to move back now?" Her eyes lost their brightness.

My eyes left hers and landed on the lime drowning in vodka.

"What would you do if you did move back?" she asked.

"I don't know. Be a part of something."

"Part of what?"

"It. I don't know. Why do you want to go off to France?"

"Because I want to reach people through music. You know that. This program is a good opportunity."

"Well, maybe I want to inspire people, too."

"I wish you would. I always have. But what are you going to do there? Most areas don't even have running water or electricity. I've heard rumors of pirates."

I perked up. "Really?" My mind started to trail off, dreaming of a romantic life of eye patches, rum, and Jolly Rogers.

Then she reached across the bar and grabbed my hands, pulling me as close as the bar allowed. Her fingernails were hard and cold, but her flesh was soft and warm. Her eyes, however, were unyielding. "Okay, Derek, if you don't want to go to France, just tell me. But don't go moving back to a disaster area just to spite me."

I looked down at the beer in front of me, avoiding her gaze. I shrugged and said, "Well, I don't want that."

She clutched my fingers tight. "What *do* you want then? I'm not asking you to be with me forever in France."

"Then what *are* you asking me?"

Mira gazed at me, her wordlessness prodding for an honest response regardless of how much it could hurt. But I swallowed it with a manly cowardice that we mistake for pride. She let go of my hands, stood, and left.

Later that night, I tiptoed into her bedroom and crawled into our citrus-scented sheets.

She rolled over. "Will you come with me?" A touch of vodka lingered on her breath.

She asked two things yet needed only one answer. She wasn't just asking me if I would follow her to France. She was also asking if I still loved her. Whatever I said, it would answer them both. I still loved her, but I wasn't going to France with her. I'd be a coward if I backed down now. How could she love a coward? I needed to prove I wasn't a coward and had some purpose of my own. I needed to move back to New Orleans.

"No." I said it like a teenager. Unsure. Cracked voice. She rolled over to the very edge of the bed and pulled the sheets over her ears, denying me the privilege of stroking her hair in the night. She didn't snore for the rest of the night, that's how I knew she pretended to sleep. Instead, she lay awake in silence. Silence was always her most effective weapon in a fight. Some men claim that they somehow enjoy the "silent treatment," but they clearly had never met Mira. You can refute words. Her silence was not a reprieve, but a cold and torturous quarantine. Even if I went back on it now, she wouldn't accept it.

We were officially over; I was certain of it then. Now that I'm writing this only three years later, I'm not so sure. Afterthought is the most productive activity in a jail cell, after all. There is little difference between the "beginning" and the "end" of anything. It's just perspective. You can tell a lot about people by whether they think something has either begun or ended. And arguing whether it's the "beginning" or the "end" is pointless. Believe me, it can almost get you killed. Instead, opportunity is the constant in the formula for progress.

If I had gone with her, this book would probably not exist. I'm sick of hearing that "everything happens for a reason." Instead, most things occur regardless of much reason at all. Things happen *because of* certain reasons, not *for* them. New Orleans wasn't destined to be destroyed by Hurricane Beckham for any reason no matter what the churchgoers preach or how much the resort developers lick their chops. Put simply, coastal erosion was the reason that New Orleans perished, and everyone had ample time to stop it. But we didn't. It stopped us.

When you remember a place that no longer exists, it is impossible to understand your life as being linear because that life no longer exists. You recall your life in timelines, not time. Time has a past, a present, and an ongoing future; however, timelines end. Hurricane Beckham severed the course of our lives and created a new one, one that our brains cannot, or will not, accept. Fractured timelines begin to weave braids in your psyche, and everything takes on two or more shapes as you unconsciously refuse to let go. When you see one thing, sensory images pulse through you. For instance, you see a past restaurant's rustic walls, you smell the catfish fillets crackling in the fryer, you hear the live band's rhythm in the corner, you taste the briny raw oysters, and you feel the lively atmosphere of not only the restaurant but also New Orleans itself, all while staring at a lifeless, moldy pile of debris.

I remember New Orleans before Beckham destroyed its physical footprint. I also remember New Orleans before the Refounders shoplifted its cultural footprint. Ill-humored historians are calling those nostalgic days the "AnteBeckham Era." A time when the Mississippi River doglegged around the city, when the historic buildings told a story of their own, when we lived day-to-day inhaling the finer things in our ears, our lungs, and our stomachs.

Then Beckham came and all was lost. Mira and I initially relocated to Houston where she could finish college. I followed her to Houston, but wouldn't follow her to France. Go figure. No one has yet to determine what to call that time period. It was a place ripe for beasts and brutes. It was a time when we all thought our collective purpose was more powerful than the juggernaut of profit. Whatever you call that era between the AnteBeckham era and the Refounding, it was a present void of any foreseeable future. Those of us who lived in the wreckage adopted nicknames that were indicative of where we had once lived, so the city would at least live through us. I became known as "Ridge" since I was born in River Ridge and later moved to the Esplanade Ridge neighborhood after my parents passed. Others took the names of the streets they lived on before Beckham. Wherever we claimed, our pride and purpose was all we had left.

But this past spring, the court had decided that the Refounders could officially take that from us, too, in order to achieve their success narrative at the cost of New Orleans itself via eminent domain. People can disagree on whether it is better for the city. It might be; however, I'd rather sit in jail than be a part of it. It's their New Orleans now.

Thus, my triple-braided psyche often confuses me, making remembering when things happened rather difficult. One's eyes, ears, and stomach can often be in three timelines at once. But no matter how big or strong a person's heart may be, it can only be invested in one.

City Hall

Mira couldn't help but think how City Hall hadn't changed much, despite it being a compound of air-conditioned shipping containers. Anyone with any authority, or any knowledge to do anything, was never there, while every employee never seemed to know anything. If they knew how to do something, they couldn't do it for some odd reason.

The temporary City of New Orleans Permits Office reeked of mildew. An AC window unit was wedged into a rectangular hole cut into the steel, and water dripped into an overflowing glass jar on the floor. A drop plopped every few seconds, soaking into the purple carpet. Goose bumps sprouted all over her legs from the cold draft from the AC. Pink insulation busted through the wall panels as if some unruly child had stuck pieces of cotton candy all over the wall. Brown boxes were haphazardly stacked to her right, up to the ceiling and to the far wall. One wrong touch could send them all tumbling down in a cardboard avalanche. A puff of insulation scratched her nape. She pulled her chair away from the wall, wedging her knees up against the secretary's particle-board desk. She adjusted her necklace.

Her Eagle buzzed on her lap. **Bloody Mary Monday at Welshy's!** Tapping the screen, she closed the reminder application. Ten thirty a.m. She had been waiting for over thirty minutes now, and a bloody Mary would sure hit the spot, she thought. She scrolled her contact list for someone who could join her later. Conveniently, it was her day off, since the city and the Catholic Church needed to save money by closing the schools on Mondays.

The metal door squeaked open and a young man entered. His eyes deep in his Eagle screen, he bumped into Mira.

"How can I help you?"

She thought to herself, I spoke with you almost thirty minutes ago. But instead she said, "I'm here to see Ms. Holden about obtaining a food services permit for a St. Joseph's Altar at Archbishop Fullerton. That's this March. March 19th, 2063."

"Ms. Holden is not who you need to see. Ms. Holden handles permits for *demonstrations*, not events."

Knowing that's not what he had said earlier, Mira said, "Well, who do I need to see then?"

"Mr. Galloway." He sat at his desk and tapped his phone's screen.

After a few moments of silence, Mira asked, "Well, where is he?"

"He's not here."

"When will he be back?"

"Anytime between twelve and three."

Mira took a deep breath. "What's his number?"

"I can leave a message for you."

"He's got to have a business card or something, sir."

"I can leave a message for you. It will be easier to leave a message with me."

"What's his extension, sir?"

"The voice mail's not set up yet. You'll have to leave a message with me."

The heat from her Eagle made her knees sweat, so she put it in her purse. She sighed. "Okay. Just tell him Mira Roche from Archbishop Fullerton High School came here and needs a food services permit for March...wait, shouldn't you write this down?"

"I'll remember it."

She grabbed a pen from his desk and wrote down what she needed and whom she needed to see on the back of her own business card.

"I would have remembered it."

She opened the door to the dusty and muggy air. The wind blew through the demolished remains of the old City Hall building, and the dump trucks carrying away debris left a trail of dust. The humid-

ity, however, was quite standard even for early February. The rows of
container offices resembled a military encampment, especially with
the surrounding barbed-wire fence. She unclipped the yellow visitor tag from her blouse and gave it to the guard at the gate. The
older man checked the code on it and stepped into a small booth.
Crowds of people hurried down Baladucci Drive, some wearing
medical masks. The Gulf Guard of America blocked all intersections
ahead, redirecting traffic down Alex Crowley Boulevard toward the
Belmont Expressway.

"What's all this?" she asked as she held out her Eagle.

He scanned the code on her screen and confirmed that her visitor tag code matched her Eagle-i profile code on the monitor. "The
Superdome. The charges were set to detonate a few minutes ago. They
must be behind schedule."

"Oh, right. That's today."

He nodded and smiled. "So you're lucky—you can still see it. You
might want to cover your mouth with your scarf there. It'll be awfully
messy afterward."

Lucky? She thought. "Have a good day, sir."

She looked down Baladucci Drive toward where the Gulf Guard's
roadblock diverted dump trucks down Alex Crowley a few blocks
ahead. Few high rises still remained along Baladucci Drive, and only
a handful were structurally sound after Hurricane Beckham. The
old One Shell Square stood stronger than most buildings, but the
developers had decided they would demo it anyway in order to cus-
tomize the future beachside Shangri-La Hotel & Casino. Half of the
abandoned Superdome peeked from behind another condemned
building in the other direction down the street. The gold-colored siding had flaked off, leaving it black and gray. The white round roof had
grown black spots and streaks from years of wind and rain. Its corporate sponsor had abandoned it, and the NFL had begun including Canadian teams, so the Saints had little choice but to ascend
to Toronto. The stadium looked like a giant rotten mushroom with
a wide stem and small, spotted cap. Barricades blocked the crowd

of spectators at Presley Avenue, about a half mile before the dome. Massive protests had taken place for months after they'd announced demolition plans. But that day, everyone just watched and waited. No one wanted to miss the once great stadium caving into itself. The actual media members, dressed in suits, accompanied cameramen on the tops of vans. The bloggers and social media reporters wore the new style of Kesh boat shoes, which were made to look dirty for high premiums, and no socks. They held up their Eagles, taking photographs and video. Mira realized that everyone in the crowd was holding up their phones to record the event.

Mira pulled out her Eagle and texted her boss. So it finally hit me. Dome's being demoed today[10:37AM]¬

She put it in her purse and turned toward the Superdome again.

Next to her, a stout woman scrolled through photographs on her own Eagle. She chuckled as she came across her young son dressed as a pirate from the Mardi Gras parade two weeks prior. When she noticed Mira looking over, she said, "Isn't he jus' precious. He wanna be a pirate."

Mira smiled. "That's cute. I once knew a boy who had a fascination with pirates."

"Ya know, I say to 'im that he ain't gonna be one, but he sure of it someday."

Mira smiled again and nodded.

"So, what he end up bein'?"

"I'm sorry, ma'am. Who?"

"That boy wishin' he was a pirate."

Mira frowned and said, "He got his wish."

The charges thundered ahead. Some yelled with excitement while others remained dead silent. The mushroom-cap roof dipped in like a deflating balloon. Then the circular walls crumbled like paper and twisted inward as dust shot up to the sky like a smokestack. A tsunami of dust raged down the street as the landmark sank into the ancient grave it stood over. Mira lifted her scarf over her mouth and closed her eyes as the concrete dust peppered her ears. Her Eagle buzzed in her purse and she took it out. The white light from the screen illuminated the dusty air around it like a car's high beams catching fog. The dust stung her eyes.

Some people applauded. Others didn't. Her Eagle buzzed incessantly. News updates flooded her Inbox.

New Orleans Superdome demo a success![10:38AM] chasethetruth

Superdome demolition safe and clean[10:38AM] Patriot Public Radio

Refounding's here and here to stay, child[10:39AM] Principal Whitman

Welshy's Pub was just a few blocks up Baladucci Drive, and she needed that bloody Mary.

Chapter 2

It's never wise to sleep with a gun in your lap, but it's easy to do. Squeals woke me. The sun broke the horizon to my left and the eastern sky was pink. In the early dawn, all moving things look either black or gray, like either shadows or ghosts. After my eyes adjusted to the darkness, I saw that a congress of feral hogs had already converted my fresh garden into their pigpen. The dawn light hid their individual coloring. Some were red, others white. Some were black, others brown. Some were all four colors, like calico cats, but cantankerous beasts, not cuddly felines.

When I lifted the revolver, they detected me and froze for a second. The leader rose from his mud throne. He must have been four feet or taller. I aimed at him and pulled the trigger. He squealed and charged through the mud toward me, but his hooves sank deep into the mud, which gave me a head start for a scrubby tree near the levee. Panic-stricken, I unloaded a few more bullets then dropped the gun to free both hands to hoist myself into the tree. It was just high enough to avoid a tusk up my ass.

Clearly, the boars had stopped being afraid of not only humans but also of guns. At one point in civilization, firearms had marked our dominion over the rest. It's surprising that the beasts didn't eat us all before then. And, in the end, they probably still will. Goddamn feral monsters. Someone brought them over from Russia, and they've been conquering us ever since. As a kid I remember them coming from over the River Ridge levee when the river got high and bulldozing my parents' tomato garden. When they weren't doing that, they were wallowing mud holes in the fairways of the nearby golf course. No surprise that they survived the storm. Immortal, like cockroaches.

After Beckham, they crept in from the surrounding wetlands and ravaged farm pigs, creating their own hybrid breed. They destroy everything in sight and enjoy every minute of it. They are the perfect organism: highly adaptive to any environment, near constant reproduction, unforgiving to any native species or habitat, and armored. If they grow large enough, their skulls and muscles can toughen enough to repel gunfire. I wouldn't have believed that either until I fired at almost point-blank range and not even a single drop of blood could be found on the ground.

I had dug rows in the land between my bar and the Lake Pontchartrain levee, and I'd planted Anaheim peppers, okra, and beets. It had rained the night before, and feral hogs sense fresh mud the same way a shark smells blood in the water. I sat and waited for them a few hours before sunrise. Fresh pork was enticing and great for bartering. You could trade a loin cut for a gallon of gasoline or a small jar of salt. Running water, electricity, salt, and food were scarce in those days. Still, some of us either refused to leave or decided to return to show those bastards they couldn't just erase our heritage. We had our pride and our purpose, and that went further than most people thought possible. If only vanity could have filled our stomachs…

Just when I thought my weight would break the branch, a dog barked on the other side of the levee. The boar ran away and led his followers into the jungle of briars and storm debris. I climbed down and picked up the gun. My grip tight on the weapon, I was ready to run for the back door. Coyotes and abandoned dogs had also interbred and roamed the territory. These wild dogs usually barked while attacking. I opened the breach of my revolver. Two bullets left. I crawled through the high wet grass up the levee for a look.

The sun barely broke the horizon, and a small boat flashed a spotlight ashore. I knew better than to shoot more than once. The first shot gives away your presence, and the second gives away your position. My third shot might as well have painted a target on my chest. Only one man and a dog were in the approaching boat. Perhaps it's a Manchac pirate, I thought. They brought in black-market tobacco, gasoline, and other commodities. They never traded black-market guns, at least not to us.

The Manchacs wouldn't use lights, though. Pirates did their best business in the dark. This guy had to be a Redsleeve. He'd surely call in a squad to investigate the gunshots. I didn't have much time. I needed my Patriot Rifle Administration proprietor's permit for the revolver. They'd ask for that and inspect the place for sure. Only one bottle of rum was left in my inventory, and they'd repossess it for "appreciation of services." But if they wanted to see the walk-in cooler, they'd find "stolen" guns that just so happened to be on the PRA's repossession list. Couldn't think of that any longer. Had to act. No telling how many would come.

The small boat was a fishing skiff, not the usual red airboats on patrol. Perhaps the Monster had some of his mercenaries going stealth. My only chance was to take him down before he called it in. I could dump his body in the lake and play dumb. On patrol, anything could happen, right? I could blame the Manchacs. Missing him was not an option, and I wasn't even sure if he was in range, but the time was right. I got down, the cold dew wet against my stomach. Sweat streamed into my eyes, stinging them like mosquitoes biting my eyeballs. I just needed to keep them open long enough to aim and fire.

The dog complicated things. The Monster only trained attack dogs because they not only saved him the cost of bullets but also protected his mercenaries from charges of brutality and murder. I had two bullets left, but couldn't kill both. I wasn't that good. If I shot the Redsleeve, the dog would jump me. If I shot the dog, the Redsleeve would shoot me. Why were they still in the boat? What were they waiting for? Let's get it over with already, I thought. I breathed heavily and clutched the revolver with both hands. Fright spared me the pain of the sharp metal grip digging into my palms. I won't let him haul me off downtown, I thought. No one ever came back. The Monster made sure of that. The dog paced the bow anxiously as they neared the bank. He had to die before his dog got close enough to leap ashore. He was almost in range. It was time. I steadied my hands atop the levee. I clenched my teeth and beaded his torso, my fingers taut on the trigger.

Chapter 3

A man pulls a trigger with his stomach, not his finger. And the hunger, the fear, and the horror brewed at my core. I closed my eyes, searching for the strength and focus to kill this man.

"R-Ridge?"

I relaxed my fingers. "Mr. Buras?"

I heard a blood-curdling cough that reassured me of his identity. Wedging my pistol between my belt and my wet chest, I walked down the levee. The wind off the lake bit through my wet pants into my thighs.

"Christ, you had me scared half shitless, Mr. Buras. Thought you had red sleeves."

"Ha-ha. B-but I do." Mr. Buras wore a red flannel shirt and a gray hat that had a yellowfin tuna and "Venice, LA" etched into it. The bill was split up the middle, and Mr. Buras had attempted to stitch it together. The old man was adamant about sticking with that old hat. He also always wore a smile, which was rare in New Orleans at that time.

His dog, Ol' Sulphur, stood by Mr. Buras's side on all three legs. He looked like a golden lab but probably wasn't. Mr. Buras had saved him as a puppy from a leg trap set for the wild dogs. Even though it was impossible for dogs to smile, he seemed to, just like his master.

Mr. Buras talked slowly so as not to cough again. "W-w-ell, what do you declare?" He stroked his upper lip and stuck out his lower jaw.

I laughed. "That's a good impression of him."

He threw me the rope, and I tied it off on a metal post that was cemented inside a tire. I pulled in his boat, and Ol' Sulphur jumped ashore. He sat back and looked up at me, panting. I rubbed behind his ears, and he panted in ecstasy.

Mr. Buras said, "W-we was near the bayou, and I heard s-some shootin'."

"Damn hog ran me up a tree. They rooted up all the seeds I planted just last night."

"Killed it?"

"Nope. Bulletproof bastards. So, where the fish at this morning?"

He pointed westward, coughing violently. He wiped the drool on his sleeve. "S-specks hittin' good o'er where the bridge was."

"Well, if you catch more than you know what to do with, come back this way. I'd love something other than grits. That's all I've eaten for, like, three weeks. Shipments haven't come in for weeks. That's why I'm trying to get this little garden started here."

"Oh? W-well, you want some a these crabs? J-just ran the traps." He pulled up a burlap blanket that revealed a hamper full of a few dozen blue crabs. Some folded their claws under them, while a few others raised their claws up at us. They all blew bubbles to cool themselves off. It looked as if they were lathered in soapsuds. "H-how's a half dozen sound?"

"Really?"

"You got season for 'em?"

"Yeah, got a li'l liquid boil and some cayenne."

"Sh-should be enough."

"What you need for 'em?"

He coughed and said, "Any tobacca?"

"Sure do." I walked up and over the levee. The orange sunrise made my rusty tin roof look coated with cinnamon. A dirt-dauber wasp civilization adorned my cinderblock walls like an arthropod pueblo. The screen door squeaked behind me, and I pulled the solid metal door of the walk-in cooler. I set the pistol alongside several shelves of pistols, shotguns, and rifles hidden behind empty beer boxes. These guns had been donated for safekeeping; however, they were "stolen" according to PRA records. I couldn't use them since I had no ammunition. The ammunition was Fitzmorris's part of the bargain. I pulled a big mason jar from one of the beer boxes but found only a few tobacco shreds inside. I needed to give him more to be fair.

My bar was rather simple. I didn't decorate the walls much, and the cinderblocks made it difficult for hanging things anyway. I'd heard that sometime after Hurricane Katrina, people salvaged trash and made it into "art." But I refused to put trash on the walls, since there was enough of that everywhere already. Only one picture of an old ship hung on the wall above the register. My favorite patron, Choppy, had donated that to me. The bar was L-shaped, where the L's bottom faced the front door. I carried a candle inside a cracked coffee cup. The register was against the wall, surrounded by empty liquor bottles. I kept the bottles on their shelves for the façade of an inventory and found a good use for them in storing drinking water.

In the register, I rummaged through batteries, matchboxes, various medicine tablets, travel-sized toothpaste tubes, thumb-sized bags of salt, and some U.S. coins. It hadn't taken very long for U.S. money to lose its value here. Paper money was mostly useless even for businesses; however, we all needed to keep some on hand to keep up the pretense of operating under the federal monetary system, but it was useful in starting fires. The coins, however, proved more useful for scouring sludge out of window frames, for grounding tarps, and for weighing fishing lures. Tobacco, on the other hand, never lost its value. Brown gold. I found some in an old grits can, and I filled an empty aspirin bottle with it. I grabbed a small ice chest inside the dusty, dry ice well.

The sun was brighter. Mr. Buras gurgled and spit a big loogie about the size of an oyster into the water. A cacao swam up and ate it.

"Will this be enough? There's about ten or twelve cigarettes' worth in there." I tossed him the aspirin bottle. "I think they're startin' to cut it now. Smoke it and see if you think it tastes a little grassier."

He wheezed and coughed. "S-so half dozen, right?" I handed him the ice chest. He reached without gloves inside the hamper. He jerked his hand up, and a crab dangled from the fleshy part between his thumb and forefinger. "Sum'bitch," he said. Getting on his knees, he stuck his hand into the water, and the crab let go as it felt the cool water. "S-sometimes 'em boys get ya," he said, reaching into the hamper again. He pulled out one crab, his thumb and forefinger clutching the flipper joint. The crab tried but couldn't reach Mr. Buras. He dropped it inside the ice chest, and the crab's legs scuttled along the sides in a circle. He set five more in the ice chest. He said, "L-little lagniappe for ya, too," as he put in a seventh crab.

"Appreciate that."

He handed me the ice chest. "Oh. If you need somethin' different, then here." He reached into a small bag and tossed me a navel orange that still had green leaves on the stem. "I brought it for the boat, but you c'n have it."

"From your tree? They're the best!"

He nodded and smiled. "Th-they okay. Not the best like down Plaq'mins. You young. Never had one a them?"

I shook my head.

Mr. Buras frowned. "I-I guess you never will. No one will." He looked up and smiled at me, but he didn't mean it this time. He snapped his fingers twice, and Ol' Sulphur jumped into the boat.

"W-well Ridge," he tipped his raggedy Venice hat, "the specks're callin' me."

"Good luck. There's my declaration for ya." I smiled, throwing him his rope.

He started his motor and went toward the Causeway Bridge ruins to catch speckled trout. The pilings of the fallen bridge spiked out of the water like nails on the western horizon. It was once the world's longest bridge. As cars drove across the horizon at night, I remember the headlights flickering through the railings, like a parade of fireflies. The distant Lakeway One ruins reflected blood-orange in the sunrise. Most of the windows had shattered, but the building's few intact windows reflected the light as if it were still alive and occupied. And, after driving back twenty-six miles, that Lakeway One highrise seemed to say, "Welcome Home," as if it were some grand monument from an ancient coastal civilization welcoming mariners after their epic voyages.

Setting the pistol at my feet, I lit a hand-rolled cigarette, and the stale taste confirmed that the Manchacs were cutting their supply with bark or dried lake grass or something not tobacco. As long as they had it, who the hell cared? For a split second, the smoke stabbed my lung walls like a million acupuncture needles, generating the type of calm that only tobacco could deliver, whether pure or cut with something else.

Downtown

M ira's father always said that whenever he couldn't understand New Orleans, he would have a drink and that helped him remember. She walked through the pedestrian tunnel that covered the banquette down Baladucci Drive. The plywood walls muffled jackhammers breaking foundations of old office buildings. Shouts in English, Greek, and Spanish added to the cadence of demolition and progress. At the intersection of Alex Crowley, a Latino worker stood wearing a neon-orange vest and a hardhat.

He held out his hand. "Wait, miss."

She stopped, and someone bumped into her from behind. Mira turned, and a man in a suit fumbled his Eagle. Mira reached out and steadied the electronic device for him.

He gripped it and said, "Thanks," without making eye contact.

She turned back to the intersection, where a line of dump trucks rumbled by entering the adjacent demolition site. One truck was loaded down with steel rebar, spiking up from the bed like a motorized porcupine. A contractor's truck followed with several European laborers sitting in the bed. Desperate Greeks were now immigrating in droves to New Orleans for demolition jobs.

"What's going on up here?" she asked the laborer.

His eyes looked from side to side. "Wait, miss."

She smiled and nodded. She took her Eagle out of her purse, opened her note page, and typed, Suggest Spanish class for curriculum¬

"Okay, miss." The worker waved at Mira and the businessman, who still hadn't looked up from his Eagle.

Mira put her device in her purse and crossed Alex Crowley. She wrapped her scarf around her face just below her eyes. A crowd of pedestrian workers—both white- and blue-collar—gathered on the far corner waiting to cross Baladucci Drive, and Mira joined them. A Gulf Guardsman wearing blue camouflage with a Gulf Guard patch with a pelican's silhouette, checked his watch. He did not appear to be fazed by the dusty wind, and his sunglasses protected his eyes. He looked across Baladucci at the other Gulf Guardsman and nodded.

"Go ahead and cross, folks," he called out to the pedestrians, waving them on.

The people crossed the street, shielding themselves from the piercing wind with their hands or bags. One-ton construction trucks, purple government sedans, concrete and steel trucks, and dump trucks waited bumper to bumper all down the street. Heavy exhaust lingered in the air.

Mira crossed in front of a brown jalopy, and a bearded man stuck his neck out of the passenger window and called out something in a language she didn't understand. The opposite Gulf Guardsman, who was short and stocky, tensed and approached the bearded man in the car. He responded in that same language, reached into the car, and pulled the man halfway out the car window by his shirt collar. They exchanged heated words before the guard tossed him back into the car. He straightened his blue camouflage uniform.

"My parents are Greek. I understood him. He's sorry for what he said, ma'am."

"Um, thanks," she smiled. "What did he say?"

"Don't you worry. Have a great day." He smiled and waved the other pedestrians across the street.

She retrieved her Eagle from her purse. Greek classes too¬

Mira dusted herself off with her scarf once she stepped into Welshy's Pub. Neon beer signs and flat screens lit up the bar. The establishment had an odd scent: body odor, sawdust, bad breath, flatulence, peanuts, beer, and burgers. *Men*, was the best way she could describe it. Almost every man in the bar stared at her, not speaking, as she entered. Young professionally dressed women were rare outside of the "New Carré," the newly established red-light district, because male laborers and contractors ruled the city's "Refounding." About ten men sat at the horseshoe bar. Two small groups of men sat at tables to her left. Three Gulf Guardsmen—two white and one black, dressed in blue camouflage fatigues—drank beer at one table, watching SportFlix updates on their Eagles. Four black men, two old and two young, drank from a pitcher and snacked on peanuts at another table. The old men wore flannel shirts crusted with concrete bits, and the younger men wore white tank tops drenched in sweat. A laborer whose arms were coated with sawdust spun his barstool around as Mira passed him. A stout man, mouth agape, sat facing her with a longneck in one hand and a bunch of bar peanuts in the other.

Don't be scared, be strong, she thought. When they sense fear, they think they're invited to either save you or take advantage of you. When they sense strength, they leave you alone. She sat at the bar. The bartender's back was toward her as he washed glasses in the sanitizing sink. He bent forward, thrusting each glass into the brushes as if he were giving CPR to someone.

He wiped the sweat off his forehead with the sink's blue water running down his forearm. "Whatcha got there, babe?"

"Bloody Mary, please."

"ID?"

She pulled out her Eagle and opened up her profile screen. The barkeep held up a laser gun and scanned her code. He walked over to the computer screen that displayed the "About" page on her Eagle-i page, which acted as both an official government identification and a marketing godsend.

After confirming her age and criminal history, he scrolled down to "Preferences" and clicked "Beverages." He returned and asked, "Spicy with Tabasco and horseradish? And extra green beans, right?"

"Exactly."

The Gulf Guardsmen laughed. The one with red hair—buzzed military style—leaned back, drinking. He slammed his empty glass on the table.

"You shoulda seen the pack we ran 'cross this morning. These weren't no mangy mutts, neither. Healthy lot. Good mix of gray and amber pelts, too."

"You think they straight breeds, yeah?"

"Hey, shut up. They're getting to it." Then all three men listened intently to their Eagles.

The bartender set a bloody Mary in front of Mira and sent a payment confirmation message. Mira wrapped her fingers around the cold glass. Artificial ice. The mark of modernized society, she thought. Three long green beans curled out from her pulpy drink like alien fingers in tomato soup. She pulled one out and sank her teeth into it, relishing the tangy zest. The spices hit the back of her throat. She leaned back on her stool and let the vodka snap between her temples.

The three Guardsmen focused on their Eagle screens and turned up the volume. A commentator announced that Met Reilly had accepted LSU's head coaching position. They shouted and cheered. The redheaded guard held up his Eagle and played "Callin' Baton Rouge."

Mira smiled. Her father used to have guests over for football games many years ago, and one of her duties was to cue this song on the stereo whenever LSU scored a touchdown. Everyone at the party would sing along and dance around just enough not to spill their beverages, though they spilled quite often anyway. When she learned to play guitar, "Callin' Baton Rouge" was one of the first songs she tried playing, since she knew the words by heart. It never sounded right without the fiddle, though, so she learned to play that, too.

Mira brought the fiddle to music practice early one Saturday at Cabrini High School the day of the Crescent City Classic race. She figured that some music would alleviate the runners' pains. She played her fiddle and sang on the curb of Esplanade Avenue. Runners streamed down the street in a steady current, and they

cheered Mira in return for the music. Most people dressed in typical running attire with shorts and a T-shirt, whereas the serious runners wore their specialized wicking shirts. And then there were the
festive runners. Frat boys running in togas. An older gentleman jog-
ging in a full tuxedo. Mario and Luigi. The Flash. Wonder Woman.
Superman with an afro wig. And there were teams that drank as
hard as they ran. They'd stop every half mile or so and do Jell-O
shots. They drank beer during the whole race, as team members
rotated pulling the beer wagons that were loaded with either ice
chests or tapped kegs. A group of runners wearing purple and gold
came into view. They suffered from a lack of training or an excess of
alcohol—or both—she thought even then.

They trudged closer. Mira played a fast fiddle tune and sang the
opening lyrics to "Callin' Baton Rouge."

Their spirits lifted instantly, and they sang along in unison as best
as they could. They all high-fived each other.

The last guy in their pack limped along and said, "Thanks. We
needed some inspiration. *Go Tigers!*"

She sneezed from the zesty smell of boiling seafood drifting
across Esplanade Avenue. An older man, playing a tambourine,
walked across the street to join her. Two runners, a young couple,
ran up to the tambourine man. He pointed across the street at a table
set with paper cups full of beer. They gave him a thumbs-up and ran
across the street. That was when she made eye contact with Derek for
the first time.

She blushed, remembering, and sipped her bloody Mary. Her father
had been right, she thought. You certainly understand New Orleans
better after a drink.

She scrolled her contact list for anyone who would appreciate a
drink with her on this late Monday morning. Many people would
enjoy one; however, there were few whom Mira wanted to spend the
time with. The one person she'd have most preferred to join her was
across the New Carré at 530 Trujillo Parkway in the temporary jail-

house. As she thumbed the names up on her screen, newsflashes popped up.

Randall McMason Commits Suicide in Anticipation of Indictment[10:44AM]¬ Patriot Public Radio

Rushed, Bias Investigation was McMason's Trigger[10:44AM]¬ chasethetruth

She gasped, nearly dropping her Eagle on the concrete floor. It took a few minutes for it to sink in: McMason the Monster had just shot himself. Other people's Eagles buzzed and chimed. The Guardsmen stopped talking LSU and removed their hats. The bartender checked his screen and then poured himself a beer. Anyone with an Eagle sat speechless. Things were changing faster than anyone had expected. All before lunch, both the Superdome and McMason had become memories. Nightmares for some.

This changes everything, Mira thought. She checked the time: 11:45 a.m. Prisoner visitation hours ended at noon. She could make it if she cut across the New Carré. Go-cups had been outlawed by the Refounders, so she slipped out the door with her drink in hand as soon as the bartender was elbow-deep in blue chemicals.

Chapter 4

Men who have ice have power over others. The crabs wouldn't keep until afternoon without ice, so I needed Fitzmorris. His store was the only place to get it, unless one wanted to go downtown into the lion's den of the Refounders and the Monster's mercenaries. I wasn't doing that. I opened my register to see what Fitzmorris could need. He loathed tobacco, and that's what I bartered with most. I'd normally trade him Nevis Single Malt Scotch, but none had come in for weeks.

My salt wasn't worth much to him considering he was my secret salt supplier. The Redsleeves had picketed the area and searched all incoming shipments. Since all bridges leading into the city were knocked out, it was easy pickings. The elevated I-10 west of the city was also damaged. Salt wasn't supposed to pass the picket line, and we had heard that McMason had an exclusive contract with a salt supplier. So we never asked Fitzmorris where he got his. If tobacco was our brown gold, salt was our white diamonds. Everything tastes better with salt, but we needed it for pickling meat and vegetables, since most of us didn't have the luxury of cold storage. Also, it helped with oral hygiene and infections.

In the register, I pushed aside a few toothpaste tubes and AA batteries. A cream-colored oval pill hid in the back corner. Bingo, I thought. A blood-pressure pill was exactly what he needed. At the bottom of the tray, a pink piece of paper read "Patriot Rifle Administration Gun Ownership Permit (BUSINESS OWNER)" in bold print at the top of the page. I folded it and put it in my back pocket in case the Redsleeves stopped me. I wedged my gun in my belt. Its weight pulled my pants below my waist. With my pocket-knife, I cut a new hole in my belt. A base diet of rice, grits, and hard liquor couldn't keep the pounds on.

Rats scurried in the vents above. I snatched Mr. Buras's orange and walked out the back door. I peeled it with my knife, and the pores sprayed oily mist each time I pulled off the white rind. Before I dug into the actual fruit, my hands were completely wet, as if citrusy liquid soap coated them. Cold juice squirted onto my hands as I pulled the sections apart. I licked the bottom of my wrists to savor every last drop. Then I ate the bitter rind, which oddly tasted a little sweet. Perhaps my body knew it needed anything it could get and lied to me about what things could taste like.

Seagulls swooped nearby, and one nearly clipped my ear. I thought of taking a shot at them, but the chances of hitting one on the wing with a single bullet were slim. I'd heard that they tasted like sea algae and feathers anyway. I threw the peels on the levee. They swarmed down, biting at each other's wings and pecking each other's eyes for the orange peel. I pulled my gun out of my belt and double-checked the chamber. Same two bullets left. I had no idea when I could afford another bullet, much less three.

Locking the deadbolt, I lifted the ice chest and carried it to my little black pickup. The crabs' sharp legs scratched the insides of the ice chest as I set it in the bed. The scratching noise always gave me the chills. My uncle Gerry took me crabbing in Lake Pontchartrain sometimes, and their scuttling made me think of a troll clawing its way through the floor. I got into my truck and took two empty whiskey bottles and three plastic juice bottles for drinking water. I started the engine and drove onto Oyster Shell Road, which was still pasty from last night's rainfall. The shells hit hard against my wheel wells. It was therapeutic, actually.

Oyster Shell Road wasn't originally a road. It was first cleared by the Gulf Guard of America in the immediate aftermath so dump trucks could haul debris out to barges on Lake Pontchartrain and from there to the Gulf. McMason had vowed to keep up the road when he relieved the GGA, but the potholes just deepened and

filled with chalky water. If I had to guess, the road ran similar to
the way Wisner and Carrolton Avenues used to—from City Park to
the Riverbend—but there was no way to be sure. Most streets and
landmarks were buried under the wreckage. On the right side of
the road, rolling hills of debris rose as high as three stories in some
places. Chunks of houses, dead oak trees, telephone poles, rusty cars,
school buses, and sailboats all blended as one homogenous blanket
of ruin. The sun stripped the coloring from everything. The overall
debris was generally brown and gray. I drove by a small oyster boat
that rested on the deck of a luxury yacht. Boats had been piled every
half mile or so. Barnacles pimpled their rusty hulls. From a distance,
the boat piles looked like chunks of concrete and steel that had been
tossed along the shores of urban lakes. The GGA had piled them up
in the hopes of at least organizing the mess and later contacting the
owners. McMason had sworn to get rid of them, yet there they stayed.

Broadmoor Bay came into view on my left. Somewhere under
the placid water rested the former neighborhoods of Mid-City, Gert
Town, Broadmoor, and Central City. It was the bottom of the geo-
graphic bowl that is New Orleans, and the waters never receded
as the lake waters leveled off through Bayou St. John and the massive breach in the Orleans Avenue Canal I-wall. The hurricane tore
down most of the buildings and telephone poles, so the bay almost
looked natural. Some tops of oak trees crested the surface, and they
looked like small household bushes peeking above the water. The distant green roofs of the former Xavier University loomed over the surface. Even though debris covered the bottom of the bay, it was easy to
envision the houses and neighborhoods intact under the dark water.
Like Atlantis. I suspected that's why Mr. Buras never liked fishing in
Broadmoor Bay. It was too close to home for him, considering he
really was from Atlantis. His native Plaquemines Parish was nothing
more than saltwater and seeping crude petroleum.

In the far distance, rows of stone crosses stood above the bay surface. Some cemeteries were as vast as neighborhoods. Any coffin that
was not sealed within a raised stone tomb eventually broke free from

the softened bottom and floated up to the surface like whales coming up for air. Choppy, one of my regular customers, said once that the coffins looked like a bunch of canoes. Since I'd moved back, I hadn't seen anything of the sort. And thank Christ for that.

The bay receded as I neared higher ground. The ground was still higher along where the river used to run, even though the river had changed its course in the wake of Beckham. I wasn't sure what the engineers were calling the Mississippi River now that it embraced the Atchafalaya. However, we called it the "Missing River."

A massive pothole nearly swallowed my truck. Avoiding it was impossible because it nearly spanned the width of the road. Pretty soon, I thought, we'll be able to scoop catfish out of these potholes. The Monster's renewed contract meant that the holes wouldn't be fixed.

Oyster Shell Road Variety Store wasn't very far after passing Broadmoor Bay. The road bent to the left, and the store was probably near where Carrolton Avenue had once met St. Charles Avenue at Riverbend. But it's all speculation, really. The high debris obscured any view of the Missing River levee, so I couldn't be sure. The business consisted of a café, a store, and a Laundromat.

There were only two cars in the shell parking lot. Usually, I had to park along the edge of the road. I went in, and the shelves were bare. A fluorescent bulb flickered from the ceiling. Fitzmorris was nowhere in sight, so I walked into the café for a coffee. Five of the six tables were empty. Huey had his back to me, wiping tabletops. Choppy sat by himself at a table by the window, holding a paper cup of coffee that was probably just lukewarm. His short white hair and stubble contrasted with his dark skin. It looked as if he had been doused in salt. He wore his blue ferryman jacket. No telling if he was on his way to work the Slidell Ferry or if he had just gotten off. His eyes met mine, and he nodded. Choppy had those deep, orange eyes that hinted at countless stories he would never tell.

"How are you, Choppy?" I walked over to his table.

He always paused before greeting people. Choppy looked me in the eyes for a few moments and then said, "Chillin', chillin'."

"Coming to the bar tonight?"

"Oh yeah, fo' sho'."

"I'll have a few boiled crabs."

"No shit, yeah? A'right, a'right. Soon, I'm gonna be startin' dat night shift, but I come in befo' dat, yeah."

Leaning over, Huey wiped a table with a wet rag in quick circles. His gray ponytail was as greasy as the kitchen walls. He cut the sleeves off of all his shirts to show off his tattoos. His arms illustrated a map of the old city like you'd find on an old tourist brochure. His right arm resembled the East Bank, and his left portrayed the West Bank. On the right arm, the Superdome looked like a flying saucer; the Crescent City Connection Bridge's peaks rose every time his elbow bent; the blue Aquarium of the Americas resembled an image from freshman geometry with its cylindrical pointed top; the white, rectangular One Shell Square towered over the skyline; the St. Louis Cathedral's three steeples and grand clock were below his right wrist. On the left: the Westbank Expressway snaked from wrist to shoulder; his left wrist marked Algiers Point; his shoulder presented the Huey P. Long Bridge. The Gretna Courthouse and ferry were at his elbow. He had once owned a coffee shop on Huey P. Long Avenue, as he frequently reminded his customers. In a way, seeing Huey's tattoos was the only way for us to see those landmarks. Whatever was left of them, anyway. Of course, some of the ruins were intact near downtown, but none of us ventured there by choice.

"Any coffee today?" I asked.

"Yeah, I got coffee." His surly tone was quite normal. His gray goatee always bothered me for some reason. I could never figure out whether he trimmed it in patches or if that was how it naturally grew.

"How much?"

"I got plenty of it."

"How much it costs, Huey?"

He leaned back and stretched his illustrated arms over his head. "Whatcha got for it?"

"All I got is seventy-five cents in U.S. coins and a little salt. I got a blood-pressure pill, but that's for Fitzmorris, as you know."

"How much salt you got?"

"About a half-thumb's worth."

"That'll work."

"Bullshit. That coffee better be straight off a Cuban boat for that price."

"Don't drink it then."

"Hue, just take the coins, for Christ's sake. You need something to give for change if just anybody comes in. Fitzmorris can get you salt whenever you need it. And also, a quarter's just about the right size to clean out the corners of the fryer."

"Okay, fine."

I sipped the lukewarm coffee from the dusty paper cup. It tasted awfully bitter.

"What kind of coffee is this?"

"Just regular stuff. Whatever I can get."

"Tastes like bark."

"'Cuz it's got bark in it. I grind it up with the beans. Stretches it out."

I shook my head. "Where's Fitzmorris at?"

"Around." He went on wiping tables.

I walked back into the store. Fitzmorris stood on a stepladder and tightened the flickering fluorescent bulb. Hearing my feet scrape the concrete floor, he glanced down at me and then went back to turning the bulb. His glasses flickered as the bulb clicked on and off as he turned it.

Fitzmorris was middle-aged, pudgy, tobacco-free, and never swore. He was just the kind of man you'd think this place would eat alive. But not Fitzmorris. He'd eat the world before it ate him. He told me one day that he preferred the world just the way he always ordered his oysters: small and raw. Fitzmorris had built this store after the wreckage, and that's all we knew of his backstory. His store kept everyone from going hungry, while I kept everyone from going crazy. At least that's what I told myself.

"Fitzmorris, I need some—"

"Wait." He rolled the bulb with precision and finesse until it emitted solid light. He watched it for a few seconds with his stubby fingers tense in the air, as if staring at it would make a difference. He wore a collared shirt and faded slacks that had become too big, like clown pants. Two bungee cords held up his pants as makeshift suspenders. The grits and rice diet was thinning us all, but he was still somehow overweight compared to the rest of us. He grunted as he stepped down. "Okay, what now?"

"Ice."

"You need it for the bar, right?" He folded the ladder and walked to the counter.

"No. I could probably use some for that, too, but I got some crabs from Mr. Buras this morning and need to put 'em on ice for now. I also could use some drinking water, if you would be so generous. I brought bottles with me."

"Ah. Good old Buras keeping at it. So you don't need much ice, then?"

"No. Just enough for a little ice chest."

"Good. The machine's been problematic. Getting a technician out here to fix it will probably be impossible." He set the stepladder behind the store counter and said, "Bring your truck around to the back." He bent down to tighten his shoelaces. The locked glass case above him was fully stocked with Marlboros, Camels, and other brands. Legal but heavily taxed. No one could afford them nationwide, much less here. Hence the booming black market.

I drove my truck around to the back, where a gutterpunk was filling jars with the water that was dripping from the air-conditioner. I could smell his B.O. at a distance. His thermal top had yellow stains on it. His meager reddish beard still didn't hide the fact that he was in his early twenties. At one point, gutterpunks had garnished their faces with silver studs and rings. They stopped wearing valuable metals on their faces when desperate people began ripping them out of their eyelids and lips to barter with, since silver and copper never lost their value.

"You ready, Ridge?" Fitzmorris held a bucket of ice just outside the warehouse door. Rusty cars and moldy refrigerators were piled up beyond the warehouse. I stepped from the truck and opened my ice chest.

"Fitzmorris, you know there's a gutterpunk loitering over there?"

He began pouring the ice over the crabs. "They're sure good-sized, aren't they? Old Buras doesn't mess around, does he? Um, yeah, I know. He's not a vagrant, though. He helps me from time to time when I need an odd job around here. I usually pay him in food or cigarettes. Depending on the job, of course."

"Then he mustn't know you give us free water. He's drinking the shit dripping from your AC."

"He does not know. I have to draw the line somewhere, Ridge. I can't have all the vagrants around here. I'm here to help, but I'm also here to run a business."

The warehouse was empty except for some dusty, broken washing machines along the back wall. I carried my bag full of bottles to his washbasin and filled them with sulphur-smelling water. When you don't have running water, it doesn't take long for a faucet to become a miracle maker.

"So, I planted those seeds."

"Oh, right?"

"Goddamn pigs already rooted it all up."

"The seeds will still grow, right? Maybe they just scattered them all around. They'll sprout up in random places. Give it some time."

"Yeah, but when they do, there'll be nothing left. You have any fencing in stock?"

"If you can find some fencing in here, you can have it."

I began filling the next bottle.

Fitzmorris adjusted his glasses and said, "So, no Nevis yet?"

"Nope. No scotch at all. I'm down to only one bottle of the rot-gut rum."

Fitzmorris sighed. "Everything I've ordered hasn't come, either. They say they sent the trucks."

Turning off the faucet, I capped a liquor bottle of water, set it in the crate, and went on filling another. I said, "Is it the Monster? You'd think he would stay away from straight-up hijacking. The media and all."

Fitzmorris waved his arms as he spoke, as if he were conducting a symphony. "Please. The media's too busy honoring him to scrutinize him. And he's mandated that all reporters be escorted by his men, for their 'protection.' So the media only sees what he wants them to see."

"Where are they hitting the supply, you think?"

"Highway 90 is the only way in or out. They rebuilt that little bridge over the Rigolets. The Manchacs trade out of there, I heard," he said. "McMason's getting enough from the taxpayers as it is, and the more desperate we get then the more we need him. He knows it, too, so he won't do anything about the pirates." He paused. He took off his glasses, breathed on the lenses, and wiped them clean on his shirt. "We need to end this before it's too late."

I looked up at him, "What do you mean, 'end this'?"

"We'll be eating out of the Monster's relief cans downtown, that's what's going to happen before long. He's been pushing for that federal food supply contract."

"Well, I could start *making* liquor. I don't know anything about that, though."

"That won't solve the problem, Ridge."

"Well, what do you want to do? Go to the Rigolets and just wait in the marsh with guns?"

"We have guns. Remember?"

I waited for him to continue.

Fitzmorris's face tensed, and his voice cracked. "There will be no free water for you if you waste it like that!" He reached over and turned off the faucet. My bottle was overflowing.

"Sorry. I'm just a little surprised by your war talk."

He grabbed my bottles and filled them himself. "We made this pact a while ago if things like this happened, right? You just keep those guns out of sight. If the Redsleeves get a hold of those, we're all toast because they can probably trace the old registrations. Just keep an eye out and spread the word." He waved his arms at the crescendo.

I filled up the two liquor bottles with water and drank heavily from one of them. I paid him with the blood-pressure pill. He cupped his hand, filled it with water, and gulped down the pill.

"So you're boiling them, right?"

"Probably just before sunset, I'll start. Hey, do you think I can maybe get a small loan?"

He pursed his lips, thinking. He turned and walked to one of the broken washing machines on the far wall. Motioning to the door, Fitzmorris waited for me to close it behind me. Once I did, he peeled the duct tape off the lid and reached inside, pulling out a plastic bag of salt that was wrapped in an old shirt. He gestured for me to walk over to him.

"How much?" He breathed hard out of his nose.

I felt his blood pressure spiking. I handed him an empty dip tin.

He scooped the tin full and capped it. "So, you're on board, right?"

"Yes. You should come by tonight. I'll give ya a crab. Gratis."

"Much obliged, but my blood pressure can't take the salt."

I actually didn't intend to put the salt in the boil. It was too valuable on its own.

He nodded and handed me the loan without any repayment discussion. I thanked him, got in my truck, and started around toward the street.

Joshua rode his bicycle up to the front door of the store. Newspapers filled his front bike basket and his backpack. I never knew how he could ride his bike and smoke cigarettes at the same time, but he always did. His puffs were repetitive like an old locomotive. He was young and clean-cut. He wore a tucked-in Oxford shirt, gray suspenders, and khaki pants every day. Every day he wore it.

He had a corporate look about him and rightfully so, considering he was his own corporation. Joshua singlehandedly ran the area's only functioning newspaper. He researched the data, interviewed people, wrote the articles, manned the printing machines, and then delivered the papers every week.

I pulled the truck up to him. He nodded at me with a Marlboro hanging from his lip. We shook hands. He had a soft face but a hard grip. My hands felt like they'd be crushed if he shook them a second longer. His fingers and palms were caked with dried ink. His eyes were sunk in, which meant he'd probably spent all night printing and all morning delivering. Rice and nicotine comprised his main diet. He puffed his cigarette and grabbed a stack of newspapers. He looked through the glass door of the store, took a long drag on his cigarette, and then ran in to drop the new issues. It wasn't ten seconds until he stormed out with the remaining previous week's copies in hand.

Fitzmorris yelled from inside, "Joshua! How many times?"

The cigarette hung from his lips and bounced around as he spoke. I focused on the cigarette, expecting it would fly out of his mouth at any moment. "Ridge, why is it I ride through areas with beasts and vagrants and mercenaries and Ward Warriors all day, and yet I'm still afraid if that fat fag catches me smoking in his place? He's worried about some cigarette smoke while the whole city's ashes. And shit, I'm the only one who buys them from him."

The gutterpunk stepped away from his mason jars and walked over to us. Joshua gave him the back issues. The bum nodded and walked back to his water jars. I raised my eyebrows at Joshua.

"He asked if he could have the back issues, so I give him what I have left. Saves me the trouble." His white shirt reflected the sun so brightly that I couldn't look at him long.

"What does he do with them?"

He took a long drag on his cigarette and blew smoke from his nostrils. "Who gives a shit?" He took one last drag on the cigarette and dropped the butt on the ground. He reached in his front pocket for a fresh one and lit it. Joshua didn't buy the black-market stuff and roll his own cigarettes like most of us did. He bought the legal stuff. The good stuff. And he chain-smoked them. I wasn't sure how he had the income, since he provided free paper distribution.

"Gin?"

"No…actually that's what I wanted to talk to you about. Fitzmorris thinks that whoever's been hijacking our supply trucks may try to resell our stuff to us. And maybe we can take some back."

He pulled the cigarette out of his mouth. "Good. Eaten nothing but plain rice for two weeks. McMason?" He put the cigarette back in his mouth. He straddled his bike and inhaled his cigarette and puffed a large plume of smoke around him.

"Maybe. Fitzmorris thinks it's the Manchacs."

"I'm gonna nail that fucker, Ridge. I am."

"You coined the nickname: McMason the Monster."

He exhaled smoke from his nose and nodded. "Stuck 'cause it's true, if what Yossarian tells me is true."

"Who?"

"Nobody," he said sternly. Joshua ditched the butt on the ground. "The Manchacs, you think?"

"You dig up anything on them?"

"Nothing major. Not yet."

"Can I get one of those?" I pointed to the newspapers in his basket. One of his good cigarettes would have cost me too much.

"Dropped off a few issues at your bar on my way here. I'll see you later tonight. Gin or not." He pedaled toward the road.

"Joshua, I said keep your eyes open. Don't write anything about this."

He smiled. "A good journalist knows what to write. A better journalist waits for the right time to write it."

The New Carré

The fastest route to the temporary jailhouse meant going through the New Carré, the newly established red-light district. Some people still called it Bourbon Street though it was a grid of many streets. Once Mayor Alex Crowley had presented the potential revenue numbers, City Hall unanimously legalized prostitution. Some people wanted to call it "Storyville" in honor of the infamous nineteenth-century red-light district just outside the old French Quarter. Either way, it was popular, bringing in people from all over the nation no matter their stance on prostitution. New Orleans had found its tourism hook.

However, not everyone approved, particularly the staunch Christian crusaders blockading the main street's entrance. Mira approached a line of men and women standing shoulder-to-shoulder to guard humanity from damnation. Their cold faces were adorned with intolerance and judgment, and their signs displayed both undying love and biblical fear. Some crusaders held tall wooden crosses. The person at the center of the shield spoke into a loudhailer, announcing the Book of Revelation and shaking a sign that read "YOU WILL ENTER HELLFIRE!!!" on a background of flames. A big man wearing a "Christ Saves" T-shirt stepped in front of Mira. When she tried to walk around him, he stepped in front of her again, like a blocker in a flag-football match. He did not want to touch her, it seemed, as if he would be poisoned with sin if he did.

Irritated, she darted around him and rolled her ankle, the sting climbing up her leg. The blockade was a few people deep, and she found herself surrounded. A middle-aged woman and her two teenagers boxed her in.

The blonde girl said, "The Lord Our God is here for you."

The boy with plague-like acne said, "He gives us victory over sin and death through our Lord Jesus Christ. Corinthians 15:57."

As the woman spoke, the big man behind her stepped backwards, bumping Mira unintentionally, and her bloody Mary spilled all over the woman. She glared at Mira as if she had just been attacked, and the teens loosened their formation. Other than in her stomach, Mira couldn't think of a better place for her leftover drink.

She extended the sign of the cross to the woman with her empty, pulpy glass the same way a priest blesses his congregation. She said, "You are hereby anointed by the Father, and the Son, and the Holy Spirit." Smirking, she pushed through the gap and joined the crowd.

The crowds were unbearable at night; however, the street was quite congested even for before noon. God would not be impressed with the crusaders' efforts, Mira thought. No matter the time of day or year, the revenue rolled in. Mayor Crowley was right, and it was probable that he was receiving a cut of it somehow.

Brand-new buildings had been built to look a century old, and cobblestones lined the pedestrian streets. The developers had planned to replicate the Spanish architecture of the old French Quarter, and the buildings' second- or third-floor balconies were garnished with extravagant stainless steelwork painted black to look like antique wrought ironwork. Along the first block on Alton Street, the businesses reflected how Bourbon Street had once looked: T-shirt and souvenir shops, daiquiri bars, and strip joints. She passed by a bar called the Man Shack. In the doorway stood a hairy-chested man wearing an eye patch, a red bandana, and a leather jock strap.

"Hey you, honey! Looks like you need a Manchaquiri for that limp!"

"No, thanks." The pain in her ankle wasn't severe, but it was bad enough for her to lean on her other foot. Cobblestones were slick from spilled cocktails, so she carefully made her way down the street. Mira had a good buzz from the vodka, and the last thing she felt she needed was a daiquiri. Especially a daiquiri named after the real-life pirates that had almost killed her boyfriend.

"It's, like, never too late to get manchacked, sweetheart!"

By the next block, women strutted the brothel balconies. The urban developers had placed the brothels a block from each entrance to the district. Now the streets smelled more like Welshy's Pub. Like lots of men. Men who fixated on the women swooning above them. Men who felt powerful from their choices over them, yet powerless to resist them. However, it was now customary that the prostitutes chose their clients from the balconies above. Mira passed the Southern Belle Café, where the women wore antebellum dresses and corsets, not daring to show their ankles so their "ladylike" reputations would not be destroyed. However, their cleavages were perfectly visible and more than acceptable to the drooling lot below. Each brothel's layout was simple. Client selection was made from the second-floor balcony. Negotiation of payment and services commenced on the first floor of the café over beverages. The second-floor dressing rooms provided the women a safe environment to dress themselves, as well as easy access to the balcony in order to promote their services. On the third floor, services were rendered.

A brunette in a peach-colored dress and a redhead wearing a green dress leaned against the steel railing of the balcony, accentuating their cleavages. They elaborately fanned themselves in the moderate weather, keeping up the act. The brunette said with a thick Georgia accent, "*Well!* Ya'll *look* like gentlemen, but which one of you actually *is* a gentleman?" Men shouted and pointed at themselves, pushing others away. The brunette shook her head in mock dismay. "Ah'm afraid there may be no more in this world, Betsy Lou."

The redhead said, "I reckon *he's* a gentleman, Anna May." She pointed to a young man in the crowd, and Anna May nodded her approval. "Why don't you come inside the café, sugar, and buy ol' Anna May a café au lait?"

Across the street, women of a wide range of skin tones stood atop the balcony of the Caribbean Queen Café. The sign under the balcony proclaimed "Puerto Ricans, Jamaicans, Cubans, Haitians, and Dominicans as beautiful as their home islands!"

A man with bronze skin and a black mustache puffed a Cuban cigar near the café entrance. He was dressed in white linen, a fedora, and white leather shoes. "Cuban cigars, rum, and women! Come celebrate the liberation of Cuba with a Cuban!"

The Mandarin Tea Room was next door; however, it had closed just after tensions between American mercenaries and the Chinese military intensified.

The Mexican Mariposa Café and the Greek Goddess Café yielded the most business in the district. Many immigrant women not fit for demolition work found lucrative work in the brothels. Homesick Mexican and Greek immigrant workers happily paid for women who spoke their mother tongues. The women worked far fewer hours and made twice the income of their male counterparts. American contractors and off-duty Gulf Guardsmen preferred these two brothels over the rest.

Mira pushed her way through the crowd in front of these three cafés. Her ankle throbbed as she stepped over the cobblestones and other people's shoes. Nearly all the men were still fixated on the women in the balconies above. She felt their breath on the back of her neck and their sweat sliding on her arms as she brushed past them.

She only had about two blocks to go when she felt someone squeeze her butt. She turned around and startled a preppy young man wearing a yellow polo shirt. He looked away.

"Seriously?"

He didn't respond, looking up at the Greek women on the balconies.

She nudged his arm. "Hey!"

He elbowed into the crowd and away from her.

Then she felt a hand reach up her skirt, and her heart leaped into her dry throat as she felt the cold fingertips creeping up her inner thigh. She swung around and tried kneeing him in the testicles, but she slipped on the cobblestones and toppled on top of him. The hollering crowd quickly surrounded them. She struggled to get off the man beneath her, but his grip on her waist kept her down on him.

The noisy crowd of onlookers was elated, hoping to witness a public sex act. Many of the men standing over her activated their Eagles' video mode, the light casting Mira's shadow on her assailant. She centered the growing panic running through her body into her fist and punched him in the nose. He then released her, reaching for his nose. She stumbled to her feet, but before she could get away, her assailant caught hold of her skirt and ripped it down the middle. Finally she escaped, leaving the laughing crowd behind her. She didn't feel the pain in her ankle anymore, but a different pain, a holistic kind of hurt, climbed up her spine and into her shoulders. She kept moving forward as the shaking zipped through her body.

She walked faster toward the blockade of crusaders on the opposite side of the New Carré. They might judge me, she thought, but at least they won't invade me. Then a firm hand clamped down on her shoulder from behind. She centered all her strength in the arches of her feet and then transferred it to her hips and all the way into her hands. She balled her fists with ready aim for the preppy guy's Adam's apple, but it wasn't her assailant, but a Gulf Guardsman.

Before she even processed what was happening, he had already cuffed her hands behind her back and sat her down on the curb. Spilled beer on the concrete soaked through the fabric of her skirt. The torn skirt parted at her thighs, revealing her polka-dotted underwear.

"Wait, Officer. I thought you were trying to assault me like the guy…"

"You know that it's a violation to solicit outside the premises?"

"Solicit? Solicit *what*?"

He pointed at her exposed crotch. "Code 475G explicitly states that entrance to the cafés must be done through the back service alleys, not the main entrances, to prevent public or personal soliciting. I smell booze on your breath, too. You know it's illegal to consume alcohol during solicitation hours?"

She took a deep breath and exhaled. "Okay. I'm a teacher, not a *hooker*. I'm passing through here…" She decided not to mention where she was heading. It seemed quite possible she'd be going to the jail anyhow, now. She explained the recent attempted assault to the officer.

The Guard waited a moment. "Who's to say you don't solicit on the side?"

"Why aren't you trying to find the attempted rapist just two blocks away?"

"What do you expect, prancing around the street half naked? You can probably make more money doing this than teaching."

"You really think it's just that easy? What school would hire a hooker? We go through background checks, and they check the brothel registration database. Probably a lot more involved than what y'all have to do to show off your guns and blue camo." Mira closed her eyes because she knew she had gone too far. That damn vodka, she thought. She shuddered at the thought of Principal Whitman, her students, and her students' parents hearing about this. "Please scan my Eagle icon, Officer. It's in my purse."

"No need for that," a different man said in a calm Irish accent.

The Guardsman turned around and backed away. Mira opened her eyes and saw Archbishop Fullerton himself in his red and purple clergy cloak, smiling. "A mere misunderstanding, my young man." He bent down and said, "How would you like a change of clothes, my dear?"

She looked down at her ripped skirt and exposed underwear, and hung her head. She closed her eyes, pushing back tears. She had been taken advantage of, wrongfully accused and blamed for her victimization, and then rescued. Mira thought that no matter how much strength she might exude, she could never budge the brute world of men off its pedestal. And that's when the shaking overtook her and she cried.

Chapter 5

I stepped on the gas and drove down Oyster Shell Road, the ice chest sliding all around in the truck bed. They'd be good by the standards of the day, but not nearly as good as Uncle Gerry's boiled crabs. He was my godfather, and I had moved to his house in Esplanade Ridge after my parents passed away. Every year, he threw a crab boil for the Crescent City Classic. Over 20,000 runners, joggers, and walkers funneled from Rampart Street toward the lake, along Esplanade and through City Park. They looked like a column of marching soldiers from our porch. Friends and family came to eat crabs, drink lots of beer, and cheer on the runners. Uncle Gerry always provided the runners with light beer in paper cups on a fold-out table. He'd play his tambourine near the beer table, and every year, more runners looked for him.

I was still in high school then and didn't know how to boil it all myself, but he showed me the process, step by step. First, bring the salt, crab boil, onions, lemons, potatoes, garlic, and cayenne pepper to a rolling boil. Then dump the crabs in. Bring back to a boil for ten minutes max. Cut the propane. Throw in frozen corncobs and andouille sausage so that they cook and cool the water enough to stop cooking the crabs. Let the crabs soak up the spices for forty-five minutes, maybe an hour. Then drain the big pot and dump it all on a table covered with newspaper. The table would be full of steaming blue crabs boiled orange, with spicy red potatoes, corn, heads of garlic, and andouille. It was a truly beautiful sight. The dead-men, or "gills," were peppered red with seasonings, but you just scraped those off. And then the quest began to finger out all the delicate lump white meat hidden inside the body cavities. The meat was always firm and seasoned just right. The males had plenty of yellow fat, and the females were full of gritty orange egg sacks. Delectable.

As I drove, my mind listed what I had for the boil. First, I ticked off the items I didn't have: onions, lemons, potatoes, carrots, garlic, andouille sausage, and corn. I had some liquid crab boil concentrate and cayenne pepper. The salt, however, was too valuable to use. The propane tank was half full, judging from its weight.

Just as my stomach growled at the thought of it, red lights flashed in the rearview mirror. I checked my speed and I wasn't going over the limit, if there was one. How could I, with all the potholes? I pulled over with Broadmoor Bay on my right. A black Hummer parked behind me. The driver got out. The sunlight bounced off his massive shaved head, and his sunglasses mirrored the oyster shells below. His uniform had a black breast and shoulders, but his long sleeves were blood-red. The other mercenary got out of the Hummer. His blond hair shone white in the sun, and his lower lip bulged from dip. He inspected the bed of my truck and spit in it, while the bald Redsleeve came up to my window. I prepared my PRA gun permit, because they'd find a gun eventually. It was best to be up front with them, I thought.

He said, "Declare your purpose." He rolled his red sleeves above his elbows. No name or badge number was visible on his uniform.

I said, "I needed ice and water from the store up the road."

"What's that pink thing in your hand? That a gun permit, son?"

"Yes, sir."

"Well, let's see it."

I handed him the paper.

"The gun also."

"Why do you—"

"Give me the goddamn gun, son."

I handed him the .38, and he checked that the permit matched the gun. He handed back the permit but not the gun.

He checked the chamber for live rounds. "Business owner. So, just ice, huh? What is it you're doing that needs ice?"

"I have some live crabs in the ice chest in the back." And it would seem obvious that a bar owner would need ice.

"Oh, you mean this little cooler back here? Let's see it," he said. He grabbed the ice chest and overturned it. The ice crashed onto the shell road, and the crabs spilled out. The blond Redsleeve laughed loudly.

"What did you just—" I made the mistake of opening my truck door.

He pointed my own gun at me, saying, "Get back in your vehicle if you ain't bulletproof, son."

Lethargic from the ice, the crabs inched along the road. They still mustered the energy to stick up their claws in self-defense.

The blond Redsleeve said, "Look at 'em. Thinking like they all big and bad." He rolled his tongue and spit his used dipping tobacco on a crab. He then tapped and opened a new can. The fresh pinch he wedged behind his lip was enormous, as if he were a parody of himself.

The bald Redsleeve said, "Let's see it." He shot and missed. The bullet ricocheted against my tailgate. He looked at the gun, aimed, and shot again. Green guts and a claw splattered on my back window. He aimed and pulled the trigger again, but the gun clicked. Six crabs remained. He and his partner took out their sidearms and shot them, laughing. He said afterwards, "Not a bad little gun there. Shoots a little to the right, though."

I held my hand out.

The bald Redsleeve said, "What is it you want?"

My temples pounded. My nostrils flared. My veins pulsed just below my ears. I'm sure he could see my anger, and it was best I didn't say anything.

He said, "You know, son, technically you ain't supposed to have this bad boy outside your place a business. You need it to protect your business. Who you need protection from out here?"

You, is what I wanted to say. He waited for his answer. I couldn't say anything about the Manchacs. The Redsleeves couldn't know that we had guns. So I said, "The vagrants."

He took off his sunglasses and peered at me with his gray eyes. "There ain't none, son. No one can survive living under all this shit everywhere. That's all bullshit talk. Now, I can see you needing protection if you were driving around that gun-crazy niggertown across the bay. I got no idea why you would, of course. Unless you getting into something you shouldn't."

"If I was a teacher, sir, maybe."

"Well, you ain't one. You look too damn stupid to be one anyway. I think I'm gonna have to check out this gun's number, son, just to make sure you ain't being a menace to the people here. There's been some shootings lately…um…and this little gun might be similar to what's been described."

"Sir, I assure you I'm no criminal." It killed me to call him "sir."

The blond Redsleeve spit inside my truck bed. His lower lip bulged with tobacco, and the brown juice oozed down his clean-shaven chin. He slurred, "Ship ya ova' ta Mass'chew'sits." He spit in the bed again.

"Shut up, Rogers. Mount up. We're done here." He put on his sunglasses and turned toward the Hummer.

"Wait," I said.

The bald Redsleeve stopped.

"My gun, sir."

"If you like, son, I can arrange a meeting with you and the captain downtown."

"Never mind," without considering calling him "sir."

"See ya around, son." They walked back to the Hummer.

The Hummer kicked up shells behind them. I got out of the truck and put the ice chest back in the bed. Yellow and green slime and crab shells covered the road and my tailgate.

At least they hadn't confiscated the salt that Fitzmorris had lent me. Except for a little rum and what items I had left in my register, I had little to barter with. The salt could carry me for a little while until my liquor orders came. *If* the shipments came. Otherwise, I would have no choice but to register for the Red Birch Food and Relief Housing Program. And I'd have preferred to collect jars of water from AC units like a vagrant before being a slave to the Monster.

St. Henriette Cathedral

"Thank you, sir. I don't know what to say. I know how this must look…"

They passed down the alley between the clergy quarters and the St. Henriette Cathedral, which was still under construction. The crowds mostly stayed away from this part of the New Carré. However, drug addicts and the homeless sat against the walls under the shade of the buildings, awaiting the daily lunch that the clergy provided. They all nodded as Mira and the archbishop passed them.

"It's against my job description to judge based on appearances." Fullerton strolled with his hands behind his back. Mira thought his Irish accent was charming.

"I was just passing through here to go to the jail before visitation hours ended."

"How's he doing? If you don't mind…"

Surprised, she asked, "How's who doing?"

Smiling, Fullerton looked up from his black shoes.

Mira remembered that Fullerton knew Derek. She wasn't sure how, however. "He's typing his story. He's been mailing me the chapters as he finishes them. But I wanted to tell him about Captain McMason."

"I'm quite certain he's heard by now. How's the school coming along?"

"Very well. We'll be fully staffed and working all five days by this summer."

"That is wonderful news. I've requested more school allocation from the Vatican. I do not foresee any problem."

Ahead in the alley, two men were on their hands and knees, vomiting. They were well dressed, most likely tourists who lacked the old New Orleans skill of pacing. Three nuns approached them with wet rags, buckets, and bottles of water.

Mira said, "We're actually having…or trying…to have a St. Joseph Day feast for the students and their families. City Hall's been dodging me, so I went down there today. No luck, of course."

Fullerton was quiet for a few moments before saying, "I'll see what I can do."

"If you can talk to someone, sir, I'd really appreciate it."

They passed the nuns who were treating the drunkards. The sisters wiped the men's sweating brows with wet towels and gave them water, then helped them stagger toward the church's "sobriety house" at the end of the alley.

The cathedral's outer wall had several confessional stalls. A few people stood in line, sobbing. Ironically, the elaborate church was located at the center of the red-light district. This way, there was little escape from sin. Refounding Czar Gibbons pitched it as being a way of salvation to appease the pious public, but the city needed to make money in order to be saved. So several indulgence mutuals, which operated like reverse ATM machines, provided sinners the opportunity for absolution without the hassle and awkwardness of speaking with an actual priest. Patrons could hand-pick the specific sins committed and the extremity level, and pay the appropriate charges in order to be absolved. Of course, the city got a small cut of that revenue as an administrative fee.

"Here we are." He pulled a set of keys from his purple cloak and opened the side door.

The corridor was new and majestic. Fine mahogany chairs, desks, and armoires made the place feel old even though it had been built just months before. Fullerton opened the armoire and took off his purple cloak, revealing his common clothes underneath—a long-sleeved oxford shirt and slacks. Mira always thought it was odd seeing priests in regular clothes, as if you were catching them in the act of being a regular person. One thing, however, struck her attention: Fullerton was carrying a sidearm. He hung up his cloak and unclipped the pistol from its holster. He took out the clip, removed the bullet in the chamber, and locked the gun and ammo in a desk drawer. Mira had gone to Catholic school most of her life, so few things surprised her when it came to the Church. But this certainly did.

"This way," said Fullerton.

As they walked through the well-lit corridor, choir music grew louder and louder.

"Are y'all having mass right now?"

"Oh, that is just our sisters' choir practicing. I frequently walk in the halls, listening. Lovely."

They walked into the donation room, and Fullerton sorted through a large bin of mostly extra-large work shirts and pants.

A young nun asked in a European accent, "Archbishop, you look for clothes?"

"Sister Matrona, this is one of our finest teachers."

"Mira Roche. Nice to meet you."

"Bless you and welcome."

Mira wasn't sure if Sister Matrona believed she was a new recruit. She didn't want to seem condescending, so Mira just smiled.

"This is one of our many new sisters from Greece. She started this program that helps the immigrants get clothes and other essentials. A true server of the Lord. And to her own people, of course."

She blushed. "Thank you, Father. I mean 'Archbishop,' pardon me."

"You can call me Father still. Are there no women's clothes left?"

"No, I'm sorry, Archbishop."

"It is good that people are getting what they need." He stared down at his shoes with his hands on his waist. He looked up and smiled. "Well, could you wear our sisters' attire? I'm afraid that's all we have that will fit you."

"Well, I'm not going out there like this." She pointed at the large rip up the center of her skirt.

"Splendid. If you visited Ri...um...Derek dressed like that, you might give him a heart attack."

"You're not lying about that, Father. Wait? How do you—"

"I used to visit Derek's pub. And you and your students brought a faith and joy to my church when it was needed most. Do you remember? I'm sure you haven't forgotten. I never will, nor will any person at mass that day. And, most certainly, the Lord has not forgotten."

"Oh my, that's right. Please forgive me, I...didn't make the connection." Mira didn't like thinking about those times. They had been dark times, she felt. "So, I still don't feel very comfortable going out there alone. So..."

"There's a walkway that will take you out. It's still under construction, but no one will bother you. I'll have Sister Matrona show you the way."

Chapter 6

Now that I had no gun to hunt with, a garden was necessary for my survival, and Octave Whitman had the last of the fencing. If he only had a few scraps left, I might be able to mold a fish trap, at least. I parked in front of his place, which was a brick building on Oyster Shell Road that had been a fire station before Beckham. Four lines of various colors marked the stages of the flood on the façade. The highest mark peaked at twelve feet as a light brown. The lines grew darker as they neared the ground, and the lowest mark was black, six inches from the ground. When he moved in, Octave had scrubbed and scrubbed to clean them off but to no avail. Any building that had survived, the flood marks could not be cleaned off, as if they were now a part of them forever. Like the way scars of war remind the next generation of the grim truth.

A wooden pirogue leaning against the bricks served as his sign. "Oyster Road Books-n-Barber" was hand-painted on the rotten bottom. A stack of *The Declaration* lay next to the sign, so I picked them up and brought them in. The place smelled of thousands of old books. It was exotic to me because I hadn't grown up with things like that. Most libraries across the nation had gone digital and downsized almost a decade ago. But there was something about the yellow paper, brown edges, and cheap adhesive, as if countless answers hibernated deep within, waiting for discovery.

Two empty barber chairs were positioned near the entrance. Along the walls, basic shelves stocked several books. Columns of books were stacked high in the corners. Boxes of books were all around, and the disorder gave the appearance that Octave was moving out. His counter was a long table with two missing legs. He had propped the table up with neat piles of hardbacks.

Octave looked up from his book. "Say, fine sir?" His gray hair curled up from his baseball cap. His eyes squinted slightly as he smiled. He wore a red Hawaiian shirt.

"Where do all these books come from?"

"Companies cleaning house. Most bookstores and publishers went strictly digital once that new government ID-Kindle-Facebook-cell phone thing came out a few months ago. What's it called again?"

I shook my head.

"Anyway, most of these books are brand-new. I think the government gave generous tax credits to whoever signed up for exclusive digital distribution. I think they also get tax write-offs for donations." Smiling, he opened up his arms to show off his collection of these "antiques."

"It must take forever to go through all of them." I set the newspapers on the table.

"Whatever Sergeant Powell leaves me, I'll get to it someday."

I nodded. "So, what you readin'?" I didn't want to start talking about the Redsleeves, especially since two had just arbitrarily confiscated my gun and killed my crabs.

"*Alas, Babylon.* Just finishing it up for the second time. I figured it would be good to read it again. You know, for being written in the 1950s during the Red Scare, it still applies to us down here. Who knows, we may actually learn some things from it. I'll give it to you once I'm done with it, if you want."

I nodded. "Thanks, Octave." That's when I realized that I had never read an actual book in my whole life. Growing up, everything was already digitized and more versatile. While reading something, I could buy movie tickets or video games if I got bored. I got bored often. Books were useful in my parents' house for propping up furniture a few inches in case of a flood.

"Mind if I read one of these in here?" I grabbed a newspaper off the top.

"I'd be glad if you did."

"Joshua must have delivered these early, before you opened."

"I was open. He doesn't come in here."

"Joshua?"

"He's never come in here."

"Why's that? I would think that our only journalist would be in here daily."

"I think he's got something against fiction books. Sometimes he asks me for books about New Orleans history. But he still won't come in."

"Maybe he just doesn't want to argue with you about reading novels."

"He enjoys that. I'm surprised he doesn't come in here for that reason. Like I said, fine sir, he's got something against books." He looked down at his book and found his place. "He doesn't come in here, and I don't read his paper. My wife tells me all I need to know, and that's more than enough."

It actually made sense after I thought about it for a while. Octave delved into literature to escape how raw the real world was, whereas Joshua refused to accept that such a raw world could create anything beautiful. And, if it was beautiful, it distracted people from the hard truths they needed to know.

I walked to an end table along the front wall and moved the chair around so that my back wouldn't face the door. I began reading:

Beyond Ghent: The Battle for New Orleans
Editorial: January 8

247 years ago, the Battle of New Orleans was fought. Granted, anyone part of that feat has either long since rotted in the ground or has been happy in the sky. That depends on your take on things. Either way, who's to say the fight for New Orleans ever ended? The Treaty of Ghent ended the War of 1812 before we even fertilized that sugar field with limey

blood. I guess Sir Pakenham never got the memo as he
landed on Ship Island. Now, the Brits are back across the
Atlantic where they belong; however, New Orleans battles
on, yet the battle here is much more complicated.

I wish all we had to do was shoot a bunch of Englishmen
to win it. Can't shoot anyone, really, seeing how our benevolent benefactor, Captain McMason, and the neocons
turned coats on their gun-loyalist base by repossessing all
registered firearms in the area (with the help of the newly
formed Patriot Rifle Administration, formerly known as the
National Rifle Association) after the riots that resulted in the
arson of the Corps of Engineers Headquarters. Of course,
it's clear that Ted Revnor blew the levee at Westwego to save
all his real estate on the East Bank, not the Corps. However,
that act was enough to convince the Feds to outsource security to Red Birch Security since they did such a "chivalrous"
job at hunting down and "neutralizing" the threats posed
by escapees from the Angola prison. According to Governor
Belmont, "Red Birch Security's contribution to this state is
unprecedented. This can mark the shift toward privatization
of all future military operations to ensure effectiveness." The
Supreme Court is set to have a decision on the New Orleans
Eminent Domain case within a few months. And, considering that Chief Justice Robert Baladucci has been a staunch
supporter of privatizing anything, it seems likely that the
odds are against the Vieux Carré Council. If the Supreme
Court favors the Refounders, all of what New Orleans has
been fighting for will be for nothing. Surely they seek to
gain tons of money. Until that decision, we continue to vol-
untarily live among the ruins, like bizarro pioneers digging
into an un-developing world.

McMason is set to give a speech next week honoring
Andrew Jackson and the Battle of New Orleans. I'm guess-
ing McMason the Monster will only use Jackson as a segue

to ingratiate himself and his brigade of thugs. To be clear, Captain Randall McMason is no General Andrew Jackson. Now, I think McMason would jump at the opportunity to relocate an entire nation of people at gunpoint and not shed a tear about how deadly it became. It's almost getting to that point here. But, love Jackson or hate him, he at least saved New Orleans from militant enterprisers. McMason, however, is the enterprising militant in this case, and he seeks to squander New Orleans, not save it. Fewer people living here makes it all the easier for the Refounders to claim their territory. The federal government is paying the Monster quite handsomely to keep people away, squeeze them out, or just simply intimidate them to leave. Less people, less problems for them to fix, and more justifiable real estate for redevelopment. Just as New Orleans began, it may also end with greed and criminals. |JT|

I looked up from the paper. "If Joshua keeps at the Monster like this, he's gonna find himself floating in the Gulf of Mexico one day."

Octave opened his mouth to reply, but the door opened. A tall Redsleeve entered. He was in his late twenties and dressed differently than the patrolmen. His uniform was mostly black except for three red stripes above his shirt cuffs.

"Good morning, Sergeant Powell," Octave said.

"Morning to you, too, Mr. Whitman." He took off his sunglasses and acknowledged me with a nod. "Our border officers reported that you got some more books today."

"Yes, sir. They're still in these boxes here."

"Good. I'll just have a look at them first."

Octave must have envisioned that his bookstore would be an outlet for education and entertainment for residents living without modern amenities or power, not a hub for censorship. In the beginning, the Gulf Guard troops helped him stock the shelves after their haircuts or shaves. Once Red Birch took over, Sergeant Powell helped Octave pull them *off* the shelves by order of McMason. Powell claimed that they were protecting everyone from potentially inciting material since this place was so volatile. Powell was no fool when it came to books, and he and Octave used to discuss specific ones in depth even when Powell repossessed them. Powell used his extensive literary and theoretical knowledge to deprive people of the opportunity to learn how to be independent and self-sufficient. Octave said that he took mainly anything that prompted one to think. Sports books, celebrity autobiographies, and romance novels were acceptable. He also approved of things like résumé guides, computer manuals, and useless exam preparation textbooks. In a strange way, Octave enjoyed Powell's visits because he rarely had anyone to talk literature with, and Powell significantly uncluttered his store.

Powell was rather stiff that day, however. He just rummaged through the books and made neat stacks on the counter. Whenever he came across one that was unfamiliar to him he would scan the barcode with the new Eagle device that Octave had blamed for the death of printed books. This new device searched the title through online publishers' inventories and analyzed it based on sales, reader comments, and scholastic relevance. Within seconds, Powell had a concise value of the book that he could reference. Typically, the higher the book's value, the more likely it was to be confiscated.

"You're taking *The Grapes of Wrath*?"

"It's pro-Communist, Mr. Whitman. You know that. And, as the Lead Civilian Content Protector, I'm responsible for any potentially dangerous content that could cause violence." Powell looked down at his watch and then to the door. He arranged the confiscated books in a separate box. "Well, that should be it. I'll be… Wait. Which one is that there?"

Octave held it up.

"That's a good one, but I'll have to take that one, too."

"I have ten pages left until the end. Can I at least finish it?"

Powell glanced at the door again and swallowed. "I'm afraid not."

"It won't take me long, Sergeant."

"No."

Octave and Powell stared at each other for a few seconds. Then Octave handed the book over.

"Thank you, Mr. Whitman. I will see you when you have another shipment."

As Sergeant Powell turned toward the door, it opened. Another man stood in the doorway, dressed similarly to the sergeant except for red front pockets and red shoulder patches. He was tall and well-built, and stroked his mustache while jutting out his lower jaw. It was Captain McMason. The Monster in the flesh.

"All done here, sir." Powell said.

McMason nodded and looked at his watch. "On second thought, Sergeant. I may stay for a shave." His voice was gruff.

"Yes, sir. But what about beating the lunch rush at Rooney's, sir?"

"I'm sure Rooney won't mind us going to the front of the line."

Octave said, "Barber shop is closed today, sir. I'm sorry."

McMason fondled his mustache some more while his protruding lower jaw showed off his yellow bottom teeth. "I only have time now. My speech is this afternoon." He sat in one of the black leather chairs.

Octave sighed, walked to the chair, and draped a sheet over him.

"And even off the mustache on the bottom."

Octave turned the chair toward the sunlit window, and I suddenly realized how fitting his nickname was. His physical features were as monstrous as his policies. Artificial hair plugs spiked out of his bald head like insect antennae. Two small rashes, one below his earlobe and the other on his temple. Skinny long nose with massive round nostrils. Jowls disproportionately large to the rest of his face, as if he was an incarnation of a Disney villain or a political cartoon.

I wanted to leave more than anything, but McMason sat between me and the door. He'd size me up and question me, most likely. My only option was to not draw attention to myself and wait for him to leave. I tried to focus on Joshua's articles but couldn't help listening in on their conversation.

"Where's your wife today?"

Octave closed his eyes while he lathered the shaving cream in his hands. "At the school."

"My mother was a school principal, too. She liked it for a while. Then the parents and the kids got out of hand. They didn't want a white woman telling them what to do anymore. She didn't want to believe it at first, but my old man and I made her see how things really were." He waited for Octave to comment.

"Mm-hm." Octave spread the shaving cream carefully, like a finger painter, around McMason's mustache.

"But your wife doesn't deal with that, does she?" He adjusted his mandible.

"I guess not." Octave wiped his hands on a towel. He pulled the straight razor out of a drawer and sharpened it on the leather strop. Slow and long strokes, back and forth.

· "I commend you, Whitman. My whole life, I always wanted to make it with a black chick. It must feel good. Not sure I'd marry one, but I'm proud of you."

The blade slipped out of his hands and hit the floor. Octave picked it up and turned around, his face as red as McMason's men's uniforms. He stared at the blade in his shaking hands.

"I've got a big speech today, Whitman. Blood is unbecoming on camera. But let's get on with it so we can get to Rooney's sometime before they close up."

Octave closed his eyes and sighed, his hand steady once again.

After he finished shaving around McMason's mustache, he said, "That will be $10, Captain."

McMason scoffed. "Mr. Whitman, I save you lots of trouble by taking these antiques off your hands. And without my protection, you'd be overrun by criminals by now. I'll accept those services as payment enough."

Octave nodded and put his razor in the drawer.

Just before he exited, the Monster looked at me reading *The Declaration*. He shook his head, stroked his mustache, stuck out his lower jaw. Then he left.

Octave glared out the window for a few moments. "Excuse me, fine sir." He left the room.

I realized then that I had forgotten to ask Octave for that fencing. I turned back to Joshua's newspaper. Those articles were the first things in print I had ever sat down and read in their entirety. As I read *The Declaration*, I felt Joshua's energy transfer into my body. The words on the page became a part of me. His articles stuck with me, as they stuck with everyone in the community. I was jealous of that kind of contribution. His role in society was much more powerful than serving drinks could ever be. He hadn't even lived here before Hurricane Beckham. I had moved back here thinking that I could change the place, but Joshua had moved down from Baltimore with the intent to move people and challenge the power structure. I'm sure McMason and his men feared Joshua's words, but they publicly ignored them. The Monster never made a statement about the newspaper, acting as if it didn't exist. That made me believe that McMason was afraid of Joshua. Even though Joshua and Octave had this strange relationship, they were quite alike in this respect: They both repudiated digital technology. They drew a line in the sand. Octave surrounded himself with old books, and Joshua used a typewriter and an outdated printing machine to produce what was probably the only printed publication in North America.

Octave hadn't returned, so I looked up at the bookshelves and grabbed one without even glancing at the title. Reading was something that could make my day go by a little faster. And I could maybe learn something, too. I figured I'd pay Octave back the next time I saw him. He probably wouldn't notice it anyway.

Archdiocese Teachers' Assisted Living

Mira awoke long before dawn in her small apartment in the Archdiocese School Dormitory and Teachers' Assisted Living Building. Even though she had bathed immediately upon returning from the cathedral, she stepped into her tiny shower. Not only did she still feel slimy from the New Carré, but she also found that a hot shower was perfect for creating lesson plans. Math and religion were her instruments of the day. Mira's official Catholic upbringing and education made her a shoe-in for the religion teacher position. She had been nervous about it at first, imagining the requirement to out-right refute evolution or other things blasphemous. That wasn't the case, however. Ironically, this Catholic school honored the Wall of Separation more than most public school boards at the time—at least it seemed so to her.

Math was straightforward. There's a specific problem with only one right answer. The tricky part, however, was teaching it in a way that the students understood the whole concept. She thought that life situations were the best way to teach math. Until students were faced with a real problem to solve, it was all just an arbitrary code of num-bers. For probability, she brought a deck of cards to class. For solving variables, the students created a monthly budget and solved for dis-posable income. For units and conversion, the students used simple recipes. Some of her students had been shadowing the construction crews on campus, and their understanding of fractions and geome-try had vastly improved while doing so.

She needed to do the same thing with religion. Religion was simple to teach at first: Ten Commandments, Beatitudes, Genesis, Exodus, the Gospels, and the parables. Pretty straightforward stuff, almost a scientific formula. However, her curriculum ran thin after the first half of the school year, and the students grew bored. Mira felt that until the kids were faced with real-life situations and decisions, it was all just an arbitrary code of behavior. She kept that belief to herself, since the Archdiocese might not be so forgiving. A plan popped into her head as she rinsed the shampoo out of her hair. It called for breaking the rules, which meant it was probably worthwhile.

She dried off and slipped into her robe. Her Eagle's battery had drained throughout the night, so she placed it in the charger atop of her nightstand. She opened the drawer and grabbed a pen and a small notebook. It would be best to write Derek a letter before she started the day's endless school preparation. A quick proofread of an assignment sheet could lead to hours of grading, printing, and reading. She found that writing an actual letter to someone was quite noble and intimate. It had a special touch that a typed message could never have. She wrote:

Dear Derek,

Captain McMason's dead. He shot himself yesterday morning. I don't know what they've told you, or if they told you. I'm not sure what's going to happen now. Since you won't be testifying, are they going to still hold up their end of the bargain? Have they said anything about that? I feel like you've spent enough time in there already. It's almost a year now. Has the food gotten any better? The school cafeteria is getting better. Principal Whitman thinks better food will help with retention, but she says that the Archdiocese and the Interim Superintendent have drastically cut the food budget.

I haven't heard from you in a while. I tried to visit you yesterday but couldn't make it before visitation ended. I got hung up in the New Carré. I'll tell you why in person later. Why couldn't they just redo that area differently like everything else? You know I never liked Bourbon Street, but seeing the balconies and the building replicas just adds insult to injury. It makes us feel nostalgic, but most of us never claimed it as being real New Orleans. Now, it's the only thing that we can relate to. Why couldn't they have a streetcar line or plant some oak trees? Whoring makes the city more money, obviously. And isn't that what this Refounding effort is all about anyway?

Anyway, I finally got through to someone about St. Joseph's. Your old friend Archbishop Fullerton. I didn't even remember that I had met him before when Principal Whitman and I brought the kids there. I feel like he's more reliable than City Hall. Stay strong in there. Does that old typewriter still work? I trust that's what's keeping you so busy. Here's a book I think you should read.

We're waiting for it. Take us with you. Love.
Mira

Smiling, Mira folded the letter neatly and placed it inside an old book titled *The Ultimate Guide to Writing and Publishing Your Literary Nonfiction*. She put the book in a big envelope and addressed it to the Corrections and Detainment Center at 530 Trujillo Parkway, New Orleans, LA.

At dawn, downtown New Orleans was silent, like a cemetery. Her housing complex was just a few blocks from Archbishop Fullerton High School, and she felt safe walking by herself because security guards were stationed around the construction sites and condemned buildings. The Refounders had problems with protestors chaining themselves inside iconic structures. A group had stayed inside the old Superdome for a few days but vacated the premises once they ran out of food. Many homeless immigrants also squatted in vacant buildings. Gulf Guard troops had to force over thirty Greeks from One Shell Square. Each security guard knew Mira by now, so they waved to her as she walked by.

You can really feel a place in its silence, she thought. In Paris, she had walked the streets at dawn when she couldn't sleep. You can make sense of a place much more without all the people in it, she realized. The holistic spirit of the city seeped from cracks in the street, from chips in the walls' mortar, from ridges of an oak's bark, from rust on an iron bridge, or from the soft clay of a riverbed like warm steam comforting the city as it slept. If you stood still long enough, you could feel the city wondering how to place you within it. And, after enough walks along the Seine River, Mira had eventually decided that she didn't have as much of a place in Paris as she had hoped. The people of Paris didn't need to be reached out to right then, and New Orleanians did more than ever, she reasoned. That's why she had moved back after one semester, just a few months before the Supreme Court approved the constitutionality of the Refounding.

But class preparation was more urgent than the churning spirit of New Orleans, and Mira's mind couldn't help but focus on the day's lesson plans. School policy forbade the use of Eagles or any kind of personal electronic device in the classroom—so of course, that just made the students crave them even more. But that might just be the edge that would recapture the students' interest in her religion class, Mira thought. Perhaps they could search the web for current events that either called for moral ethics or called them into question. Perhaps they could have a class discussion on justice. They could choose from several current events: the fall of the European Union, the Boston immigration riots, war talk with China, and the suicide of Captain McMason if they even knew about it yet. Having them looking at their Eagles would be blatantly against the rules, but Mira thought the risk was worth it.

Mira had only deliberately disobeyed Principal Whitman once before. That was a different time. A darker time. Unforgiving and indifferent. Full of hard work and little return. Full of purpose and little result. Full of importance and little recognition. Full of danger with little support. She didn't like to think in the past, much less *that* past, but it felt like a dream whenever she did. As much as Mira hated the Refounding of New Orleans, she understood that it was better for her students and their families. Of course, it would have been best if Beckham hadn't crushed the city in the first place, and she understood that there were only two options: subsidence or transformation. And the tragic truth was that for New Orleans to remain a living city, the latter was the only *viable* option.

People who hadn't been there before the Refounding had the privilege of perceiving the period between Beckham and the Refounding as romantic and noble, she felt. A steam-punk paradise of sorts. The people who'd moved to the area after it became more safe and structured bragged about living within the wreckage as if they wore a black badge of courage. But whoever was there then knew better. It was a brief, yet timeless, blur of horror and wonder, of hope and hopelessness, of ruthlessness and benevolence, and of chaos and placidness. This was a place where it made sense to strive not to care in order to preserve compassion. That way, if things got worse, you could survive the cruel world. But if things got better, you still had enough optimism left to carry you forward. Now, the educators had plenty of support and resources. The blogosphere, the politicians, the businessmen, and the Church were actually investing in the education overhaul. Now, the teachers had new educational technology. When Mira had first moved back, everyone was on their own. If it hadn't been for Principal Whitman's constant effort and her husband's bookstore, the students wouldn't have had anything. Mira felt that if this New Orleans experiment of subsidizing privatized education in the faith-based realm succeeded, the rest of the United States would follow suit. Though she didn't wish for that predicament, she had no power to stop it.

Chapter 7

Sitting on top of the levee, I read that book until I was sunburned. My head ached from the first two chapters. To my surprise, the book's cover did not match its content. The book's cover said it was an autobiography by some Hollywood actor in the early 2000s, so I thought it was rather odd when the first chapter began with D-Day. Octave had switched covers on Sergeant Powell. Instead, I was reading a fictional narrative called *Cold Chambers*, which seemed to be unfolding as an alternative history about World War II. In chapter one, all guns and bombs fail on the beaches at Normandy. Anything with gunpowder is useless. The Allies continue with the assault and eventually take the position with flamethrowers, bayonets, and rocks. In chapter two, a Polish meteorologist theorizes that the massive solar flares the night before were the reason for this situation.

There was something quite different about reading words printed on paper. They stuck with me more than all the digital crap I grew up with. I thought I was reading things when I was younger, but links, videos, texting, and chatting overwhelmed whatever I was trying to read. In the end, the actual thing I was reading became the distraction. One could really let things sink in with books, however. I pinched together the pages between my place and the front cover and felt that they were a part of me the way a fire warms your bones. How could ink and paper generate so much energy? Perhaps the printed page transferred energy *into* its reader, whereas the electronic screen consumed it. I was beginning to understand Octave and Joshua.

I set the book down on the grass and rolled a cigarette. As I struck a match, something shiny caught my eye. It came from the lakeshore and kept blinking, like a lighthouse. I walked down the levee toward it. A piece of driftwood lapped against the shore, and I lifted it out of the water. Wedged into one of its ridges was a metal necklace. I pulled it out of the wood and wiped the green algae off. Maybe it was valuable. Maybe even silver.

Of course, that was the old way of thinking. Some things will never lose their value because we, as humans, just can't let them go. Things like gold and silver are rare and nice to look at. That's about it. When it comes to versatility, they're pretty much useless metals. Things like matches, antiseptic cream, batteries, salt, and candles were much more vital for everyday survival.

Most of the men I knew here didn't wear any jewelry. I only knew two women who lived here. Tilly was the Vietnamese-American who managed Fitzmorris's Laundromat and didn't care for those things. And of course, Constance, Octave's wife, was more into tattoos than nonpermanent symbols, so even Octave probably wouldn't trade for it. I almost threw it back but thought it might be useful as a fishing lure if I could mend it.

Once, there was a woman whom I could give jewelry to. I often wondered about how Mira was doing in France. She'd probably swept a Frenchman off his feet long ago. I didn't like to think that, but I couldn't help it. Whatever she was doing, I hoped she still sang. I'd developed an addiction for her voice very early on. Her father had had to work much later in the evening after her mother passed away. After rehearsals, she'd walk over to my uncle Gerry's house and play music on the porch until her father picked her up. She'd sit on the white wicker furniture and rest her guitar on her crossed legs. She'd cock her knees up high to support the guitar, and her gray-checkered skirt would fall down her thighs slightly.

I took the final drag from my cigarette and heard men talking behind the levee near my bar. I slipped the silver necklace into my pocket and walked up to the top. A young, thin black man with dreadlocks and an older white man who had forearms like Popeye, the cartoon character looked at the hog wallow.

My hand itched. It wanted to grab the gun in my pants, but there was nothing to grab. Instead, I clutched the chunk of driftwood as my potential weapon. I stood just on the other side of the hog wallow so I could have a barrier between us.

"How are you today, sir?" The dreadlocked man asked. A tattooed tear dripped down his cheek. He held out his hand to shake mine. "Gris, and this-here is Copper."

"What do y'all want?" I didn't extend my hand.

"Looking for somewhere to get a whiskey."

"Bar's closed right now. I'm out of whiskey anyway."

They glanced at each other.

"So, is that it then, guys?" I asked.

"That depends on you, hoss?" Copper asked, walking closer to the mud pit. His forearms swayed, pulling his body from side to side, like an orangutan. He reached into his jacket.

My heart sank.

He pulled out a bottle of Elmer's Ryan whiskey.

I tried not to show my desperation. "Where'd you get that?"

Gris said, "Massachusetts."

Copper said, "You want it, or what?"

"What do you want for it?"

He leaned back and wiped the sweat off his forehead with his massive forearms. "Nothing."

"Okay. Well, what do you *really* want for it, then?"

Gris said, "We just trying to give back to y'all, ya heard me."

Copper held out the bottle. That bottle was about the same size as those forearms.

I didn't like something about them and this whole situation, but hunger typically wins. This bottle could feed me well for a few weeks. "Okay. Thanks." I nodded.

I didn't know what to make of people who willingly gave things away. I hadn't lived in a barter society for very long, but I'd learned a lot about people from what they wanted to trade. You could tell who was trading or selling to the civilized world. Barterers that trade to the locals value everyday things like food, gasoline, candles, and batteries. Things that a civilized society takes for granted. I had a strong feeling that these men were Manchac pirates. They looked like more like bums than the pirates you'd see on television. No swords. No Jolly Rogers. No eye patches. That's probably how they were before Disney plundered their image.

Copper waited for me to walk around the mud hole to them.

"Just leave it by the back door there. I need to finish up something first."

Gris rubbed his eye just above his tear tattoo. "Don't know if that real safe, ya heard."

"It'll be fine."

Copper said, "Maybe we'll come back later, and you can share some whiskey with us."

They walked around to the front of the bar. I didn't hear a car engine start after they disappeared.

I took the unsealed bottle inside the bar. As I unscrewed the top, the whiskey aroma reverberated through my nose hairs. I poured a small amount, about a quarter thumb, in a dusty glass. That woody flavor just coated my tongue, exploding in the back of my throat as I swallowed. A calmness that only a good whiskey could bring.

I needed a nap before opening the bar for the night. It had been a long day already, and it wasn't even three o'clock.

Archbishop Fullerton
Middle and High School

The armed guard at the front gate of Archbishop Fullerton greeted Mira with a smile and let her in. Thanking him, she walked to the blue mailbox near the guard's booth and dropped in the package for Derek. That book might help with his diction and pacing, she thought. He hadn't mailed her a chapter for a while, so she also thought that it might motivate him to continue writing.

Several students gathered in front of the main entrance of the school. Surprised, Mira approached. "Good morning, everyone. You're here early. Is the door locked?"

The students turned around but did not respond. This was a silence that Mira did not like. She weaved through the students toward the front door, but billboards leaned against the building's front wall. Pictures of eleven children were pasted on the board. Students set objects, such as flowers, crayons, and candy, at the base of the boards. Mira recognized several of the children's pictures. The dark past forced its way into her present. She had repurposed the pain into vigor for the students' future. But the horror, the sorrow, the helplessness, and the chaos knotted inside her stomach. Her throat went dry and sour. Though no actual allergen floated in the air, her body fought a dormant pathogen that loosened her sinuses and nauseated her. This was the kind of sickness that originated from within. From an unknown bodily system that trumped the others. It was hard to think, to breathe, to not vomit.

When she saw that someone had drawn a trumpet under a photograph of little Raymond, Mira began to cry. This was the one-year anniversary of the Ursulines Eleven massacre.

Mira knew that turning one's back on others had its consequences. In theater, Mira had learned never to turn her back to the audience, and she learned quickly that that rule also applied to teaching. Subconsciously, the audience felt disengaged or shunned, and once you lost them, there was no recovery. Her eyes never left her audience, nor her students. She liked the new screens mounted on the back walls of the classrooms. Not only did the screen prevent students from piling against the back wall, it also allowed her to see what she was pointing to—almost like a weather forecaster's blue screen. This way, a teacher didn't have to turn his or her back to write on the whiteboard or look down at a computer screen to instruct. And researchers were saying that it kept the students' attention more effectively.

Mira also felt that both the girls and the boys couldn't help eyeing her up and down. Girls studied every article of clothing intently: its designer, its suggested retail, its color pattern, its material, its fit, and how well it worked with the overall outfit, as if each article of clothing were a piece of the puzzle they wished to unravel. The boys, however, just imagined her clothes *un*raveling. It didn't matter what the ages were, Mira decided. A theater audience of adults and a classroom of middle-schoolers were all the same.

Her theater experience made her a natural in the teaching field. She had no problem with speaking in front of people. She knew how to improvise on the spot to keep people's interest. The off-stage practice hours had prepared her for the evening and weekend lesson planning and grading sessions. Her skin had toughened from countless tough crowds. There was no applause after the school day, however, and every day was a tough crowd. And the teachers were never the stars, no matter how hard some tried. They were just the stagehands.

Mira came to understand that there was one fundamental difference between performing and teaching, though. Theater was a simulation of reality and an escape from reality at the same time. Teaching, on the other hand, was far too real for its own good, and there was absolutely no escape from it.

And now, on the first anniversary of the Ursulines Eleven trag-edy, simulacrum and escapism were not viable options. Mira and her students had no choice but to confront it head-on. She had reasoned that life situations were the best way to teach both math and religion, and today was the day for contemplation.

As she walked through the hall, Mira did not hear her religion students chatting in the classroom, so she expected that most had skipped that day. To her surprise, they were all seated quietly. Even Javell Green and Tamantha Warren were in class, and they had not been to school for the last several weeks. They, like the rest of the class, were focused and serious. Not bothering to turn the screen on, she sat down on the desk. All teachers struggled with retention, but today every student was present. She smiled.

"How are you today, Ms. Roche?" asked Effervescence Brown.

Mira thought for a few seconds. "Hard to say really, Effy."

Effy Brown nodded.

Justin Henderson asked, "Why?"

Mira sighed. She dreaded questions that were not related to the curriculum. Those questions were potentially dangerous. They were usually personal. She could offend the students or their parents. She could also get distracted from the material. This blurred the defini-tive line between teacher and friend; however, Mira understood that you needed a little touch of the latter in order to excel in the former. "Well, I'm sure all of you know what today is." She waited for some-one to ask, but no one did. She continued, "Last year, our students left the school when the tragedy happened. But today, you all are here."

Tamantha Warren said, "Sometime things go wrong before they good, Ms. Teach."

Mira looked down at her knees bent at the desk's edge. She let the students run with that one.

Justin Henderson turned around and said to Tamantha, "What that mean? You sayin' it *good* that my cuz got killed?"

"I ain't sayin' dat, boy."

"What *is* you sayin' then, girl?"

And that's as far as Mira could let it go. They were about to get loud. She got to her feet and started for the door.

Effy Brown said, "She ain't sayin' that. You trippin'."

Justin Henderson's voice rose. "Oh, *I* be trippin'?"

Mira slammed the door, and the students quieted long enough for her to regain their attention. "Y'all get out your notebooks."

The students slowly complied.

"For your journal today, write your feelings about this one-year anniversary. Does it make you angry or sad? Specifically, I want you to—at some point—apply some of the things we've been learning in class, like social justice or the Law of Love. Talk about how everyone is confronting it and what that means for the future."

Most of them then wrote vigorously. Javell Green and Tamantha Warren stood and approached Mira's desk. Tamantha whispered, "We sorry for not comin' to your class. We just been dealin' with a whole lotta things at the house. Can you tell us what we missed?"

Mira knew that Tamantha and Javell were siblings despite their different last names. She handed them an assignment sheet and explained it briefly.

Javell said, "Thanks. We gonna be comin' from here on out, Ms. Mira."

As the students wrote quasi-quietly, Mira opened the classroom door for some air. The classroom had no windows, like a cave, especially during the summer when the air-conditioner blasted. Across the hall, Mr. Cooper stood in the doorway of his classroom waiting for his own students to finish their assignment. He was young, as most of the teachers were. In many classes that dealt with humanities, students wrote in journals in order to jump-start their brain activity.

He glanced into his English classroom and stepped toward Mira. "Did you hear what happened?"

"I was here when it happened."

"No, no. I know about that." He unwrapped a Mano-y-Mano Energy Bar. "I mean about what they're thinking about naming the downtown square."

"Oh, Lord. What?" She stepped into the doorway and checked in on her students.

"McMason Memorial Park."

Mira clenched her hands into a fist. As if her emotions weren't in turmoil enough today, she thought. Now, they are actually considering naming the main city square after the Monster. "Who told you this?"

"It was on Chase Quade's blog."

She pulled her Eagle out of her pocket.

McMason Memorial Park Has Nice Ring to It[9:13AM] ¬ chasethetruth

Students laughed in Mr. Cooper's room, and he nodded at Mira and went back to his class.

Mira returned to her classroom. Half the class was still writing. The other half was whispering to others but hurriedly resumed writing after Mira returned. "Everyone finish up that last thought, and we'll get started. Who can define 'justice' for me?"

After a three-second silence, she expected three of thirty students to attempt an answer.

Effy Brown said, "It's like...like when you get what you deserve. Like, say, if someone does something to you and they get caught."

Justin Henderson bluntly said, "When criminals go to jail."

Mira asked, "What happens when criminals don't go to jail? What if they get praised like heroes?"

Tamantha Warren said, "*In*justice. That what that is."

"Precisely, Ms. Warren."

Critical thinking in the classroom was always the primary objective, and preaching to the students did no good, Mira had always thought. She was about to, though. Imagining a McMason statue made her skin itch and her temples throb. She was about to tell them what a monster McMason was. Most of the students probably knew already and agreed with her, but still, it was one of her principles not to bring personal politics into the classroom. Many of her teachers had done that. She'd once had a math teacher who had ranted most of the period about President Walter Warsorio and his "socialist" policies, even though that had nothing to do with freshman algebra. Another teacher couldn't help but rant during English class about President Laura Vechnell's affront to environmental policies, which was not necessarily connected with the complicated relationship between Jay Gatsby and Daisy. Mira always thought that her classmates deserved better and vowed never to cross that line of bullshit in her own classroom. Naturally, enough bullshit came along with any curriculum, so there was no reason to add to it.

A McMason memorial pushed her limit, however. As of yesterday, Captain Randall McMason was dead and gone forever. Now he was about to be immortalized. Mira didn't know what to do other than chastise him, making sure that her students knew him for what he was: a monster.

Justin Henderson said, "Ms. Mira?"

She snapped back into reality. "Oh, yes. Injustice. Um, a colleague just informed me that they are considering naming the square 'McMason Park.' How do y'all feel about that?"

Silence for four seconds.

"McMason? Who's that?" Effy asked.

"You serious? You know that crazy-ass man," Tamantha said. "He be giving them guns to those boys."

"Now hold up," Justin said. "I, for one, will be the first person to hate on that man for what he was doing with all that. But that food program he had going on…helped me and my aunt-*tee* out."

Tamantha said, "Yeah, but that all just a strategy. To control your ass, boy."

The drone of high-pitched talking and laughing emanating from the hallway drew Mira to the doorway to investigate. About twenty students were walking through the hall, and she almost fussed at them before she saw Mr. Larson, one of the social studies teachers, walking with them.

Mr. Larson was a lifer, and teaching was his lifeblood, not his job. He had been teaching more than not throughout his life. At age sixty-eight, this was his forty-fifth year teaching, and he was just as enthusiastic and dorky as he had been in his first year. His blue oxford shirt was untucked in some places around his waist, his glasses sat crooked on the bridge of his wide nose, his gray mustache curled down his upper lip, and his pant legs were too long and bunched up atop his brown shoes. He always smiled, even when he was angry or sad.

"How are you doing there, Mira? So sorry about this minor interruption, but we'll be out of your hair in no time. We're just passing through."

"Where are y'all going?"

"We're on our way to protest the proposed commemoration of Randall McMason. I'm not sure if you heard."

"I did a minute ago."

"Well, we were discussing Homer Plessy and social action, and it just seemed natural to take this lesson to the next level and actually go out and do it ourselves." He nodded his head anxiously.

Loving the idea, Mira said, "And Whitman's okay with this?"

He shrugged. "With protesting, you're bound to break some rules along the way."

She looked into her class. "You have my class directly after this?"

He peeked in the doorway and waved at Mira's students. "Yes, ma'am, I believe so."

"And I have yours directly after this."

"Oh, do you want to come with us?"

Mira ran her tongue along the inside of her cheek, thinking.

Mr. Larson then said, "I mean, civil rights, the Law of Love, social justice, personal responsibility. It's really all the same in the end, isn't it?" He smiled, nodded anxiously, and walked down the hall with his social studies students.

Chapter 8

Survival is a funny thing. The people around you are your ultimate threat, yet they are also your ultimate support. Since ancient civilization, people have just needed a place to gather and make sense of themselves in order to survive. A place that breaks this façade we call society and shows us who, or what, we really are. A place that brings out the demons, the empathy, the hate, the truth, the lies, the camaraderie, the sorrow, and the hope. A place where people can both admire and loathe each other and themselves. A place where they can settle matters with open palms or locked fists. A place where people can decide to either survive or self-destruct. A place that serves alcohol, and I provided such a place where people could experience a human condition far more pure and ancient than any church or government: the celestial state of drunkenness. The ancient Saxons and Vikings used to call it the "dream" state when the individual, the community, and their gods became one. And that's how they survived the winter, the hunger, and the slaughter. That was my role in this community. Sure, Mr. Buras and Fitzmorris kept us fed, Joshua kept us informed, Octave kept us cultured, Constance kept us educated, Judge kept us safe from the wild hogs, and Choppy kept us from complete isolation. I, on the other hand, kept the oldest New Orleans tradition alive: drinking. And New Orleans never would have survived without it.

A door latched shut, and I leapt up from my tattered mattress on the floor. I had learned to sleep through nonhuman noises like opossums scurrying through the walls or the wooden beams creaking in the night. Even the wind can open a door, but it usually takes the precision of the human hand to close a door just right to latch. Instinctively, I reached for my revolver on the office desk in the storeroom. It wasn't there, of course. My eyes darted around for a weapon. The perpetrator would hear the creaking floorboards, so I had to remain still. The baseball bat was behind the bar. The gun was in the hands of the Redsleeves. The shovel was outside near the mud garden. My eyes settled on the jar of red cayenne pepper on the shelf. If I aimed for the eyes, I'd have enough time to disarm or disable the intruder.

I opened the storeroom door without a sound and crept low in the darkness, clutching my weapon. The sun had set, so there was complete blackness to disappear into. I crouched down between the wall and the end of the bar, listening for footsteps.

"Say, Ridge? Ya open or close?" Choppy said.

Startled but relieved, I set the pepper down. He'd been standing right above me the whole time, and I had no idea. "Yep, I'm open."

"What'n the hell you doin' down there other than lookin' like a damn fool?"

"Um, just trying to ward off the rats. You know, cayenne pepper keeps them away," I bullshitted him. I guess barrooms do reveal who we are, and a badass survivalist I was not. I was a jumpy bartender. I stood and lit a candle on the bar. "Rum?"

"Two knuckles, yeah." He held up two fingers.

I lit another candle and returned to the storeroom with it. After opening the safe, I retrieved the rum and the bourbon. I almost forgot that the Manchacs had given me that whiskey just a few hours before my nap. I realized that I was shirtless and grabbed a shirt off my pillow. The pillowcase had a deep-blue stain in it. I crouched down and rubbed at it. Maybe I should have gone with Mira, I thought. I thought that a lot lately.

When I returned to the bar, Huey had taken a seat at the opposite end of the bar with his back to the front door. He was the only person who did that. For being a middle-aged veteran from Iraq and Afghanistan, he still had much fight left in him. And he invited it.

Sometimes I thought that sitting with his back to the door was his bait for confrontation and action. I nodded to him.

"Choppy, I got this bourbon in stock today. It's a good brand."

He looked at the bottle for a few seconds. "Nah. I'm straight. I'm straight. Two knucks o' rum, yeah."

I poured the rum with my right hand and measured with my left. I stuck my finger outside of the glass and poured until the liquor was up to my second knuckle. I wrote it down on his tab.

He lifted his glass and cocked his head to the side as an unspoken thank-you.

From the end of the bar, Huey asked, "So a shipment came in, then?"

I stopped myself. I couldn't let everyone know I had accepted anything from the Manchacs. Especially Choppy and Huey. They were close with Fitzmorris. If Fitzmorris knew about it, he might cut me off from his water supply for dealing with the pirates directly. I'd have to start boiling lake water or straining silt out of the Missing River and hope not to be swallowed by the giant ravenous catfish. And Lord knows where I could get food from other than Mr. Buras's lagniappe or McMason the Monster's food supplement registry. I said instead, "No. It was just behind some boxes."

"What brand is it?"

"Elmer's Ryan."

"How much for a knuckle?"

"For you, Huey? Maybe a large breakfast and two cups of coffee. Maybe even four cups, since you cut it with fucking bark."

"Why you got to be such a dick wrinkle?"

I shrugged my shoulders and lit a candle near him.

"Okay, fine. Mark my tab for one knuck worth."

As I poured him his whiskey, Octave walked in. He wore an old flannel shirt and a Tennessee Williams Festival cap. He waved to Huey and sat at the bar next to Choppy.

"Constance done had it yet wit' them kids?"

"She's still going strong."

Putting down his rum, Choppy said, "Say, your wife's stronger than any damn one of us. Shit, if she was runnin' the show instead a dat crazy-ass man, we'd all be back, hear?"

"Thanks. I'll tell her you said that." He saw the Elmer's Ryan in my hand. "So, you finally received a delivery?"

"Nope, it was just hiding in the back."

"I haven't had Elmer's Ryan in years!"

I poured him some whiskey.

"Thanks. Can I get some ice perhaps?"

"Damn it. I forgot to get extra ice from Fitzmorris this morning. Got none." I picked up the black wooden bat behind the bar and tapped the bottom of the dry ice well with it. I dropped the bat in there.

"What did you need extra ice for?"

"Mr. Buras gave me some live crabs this morning, but…"

"Dem Reds fucked wit' ya, didn't they?"

"Yeah, well, who ain't they fucked with?"

"Fo' true. Fo' true. Just after you left the sto', I saw 'em go down yo' way." Choppy sipped his rum, sucking it through his teeth.

The door chain rattled and Joshua walked in. He was still dressed in his white oxford, suspenders, and khakis. His white shirt stuck to his torso, so he had probably been biking all day, delivering *The Declaration*. Huey eyed him with disdain as he sat next to Octave.

"Ridge." He held out his hand and I shook it. His grip cracked my pinky knuckle. "No gin?"

"No, but I do have some Elmer's Ryan."

"Just the clear rum. Don't mess with dark spirits." He took off his backpack and reached inside, pulling out a cigarette.

Mid-pour, I asked, "What are you doing?"

"Oh, come on," he said pointing to the thin red line around the butt. "There's the ATF tax ring. Plain as day."

"It attracts attention."

"Just one. Got to work the machines tonight. And I've been in the Monster's lair all day. One of these days, a Redsleeve is gonna take a shot at me, I swear."

Octave said, "What were you digging up downtown?"

"Not digging up really. Went down to the schools. Talked to your wife, in fact. About how they're trying to bring back Mardi Gras this year."

Choppy nodded, fixing his eyes on the pictures of ships on the wall before him.

Octave said, "Oh, yeah. I think it's going to happen from what she tells me."

"Yup. Involving the schools and not the krewes is key. Center it around the kids, not the rich fucks." Joshua leaned back in his barstool. He rolled up his white sleeves, put the cigarette in his mouth, and held his silver Zippo between his thumb and forefinger.

I said, "Okay, just that one."

Joshua flicked his arm loose from the tight shirt fold around his elbow and lit the flint. He clicked the metal lighter closed. He dragged on his cigarette and rolled his eyes back as he released the smoke though his nostrils.

I said, "The parade krewes weren't *all* rich people. Middle-class people paraded, too."

He exhaled the smoke from his nose and said, "Ain't a middle class anymore, Ridge. You know that. And McMason burned all the floats down in Kern's warehouse, anyway. Ain't going to admit that, though, so I'm working on proving it."

Just before the glass rim hit his lips, Choppy paused with the glass in his hand. "Say, dem Reds said dat Beckham did 'way wit' 'em. You sho' 'bout dat?"

"Got a hunch. Looking into it now. Saving that information for when it counts, though." He took a deep pull.

Huey barked across the bar, "You've just got all the answers, don't ya?"

Joshua looked over at him and exhaled the smoke from his nostrils. Grabbing his crotch, he said, "I got all your answers you need right here. How about you come get them?"

"Your parents must be proud of that mouth of yours."

Joshua paused. "Leave them out of this." He flicked his lit cigarette at Huey, who rose to his feet. Joshua also stood, and they approached each other with clenched fists. Before I could jump over the bar to stop them, Father Fullerton walked in.

Joshua and Huey breathed heavily, returning to their bar stools.

"Everything as it should be, Ridge?" Fullerton said in his charming Irish accent.

"Yes, Father," Huey said.

I said, "Come in, Father. Have yourself an Elmer's Ryan."

"Excellent. You must have got some shipments in." He sat down in one of the stools between Huey and Joshua.

I left it at that. I didn't like lying to anyone, much less a priest.

He hung his black jacket on the back of the stool and reached for the pistol in his holster. "Just checking it with you."

As he pulled out the clip, I said, "No, no, Father. I'll allow it tonight."

"Are you sure, my son?"

"Sure."

He nodded and put it back in his holster. "I will definitely take you up on your offer, however. Two knuckles of the Elmer's."

I didn't have many policies at my bar, but I didn't allow patrons to smoke and required that they must check a firearm. The no-smoking policy sometimes hurt more than it helped. Since Hurricane Beckham, the use of tobacco had skyrocketed. Hell, I'd never touched the stuff until then. It had nothing to do with customer preferences or public health laws. It had to do with suspicion. ATF agents had begun to go undercover to unearth the widespread tobacco black market. Even though Joshua's cigarettes were legal, I didn't want to attract attention, considering I actively contributed to such a black market. If customers wanted to smoke they could do so out back near the levee. However, they had to return their butts to me so that no evidence could be traced except the smoke dissipating in the air. I felt if I had allowed smoking, more customers would come. But, then again, I'd be doing business with Redsleeves and Refounders.

As far as my other policy, it was pretty obvious. Even though firearms were outlawed by McMason until the area was more stable, people still got their hands on them somehow. It would have been like the Wild West if I hadn't done something. The last thing I needed was someone dying in my bar. Usually it was easy to know who had guns. The new clergy, like Father Fullerton, were always armed, yet they probably were the most responsible with them. On the other hand, the Redsleeves had not only their company-issued duty guns but also their own personal firearms, and they were exempt from the disarmament order. If anything, it kept the off-duty Redsleeves out of my bar. I refused service until I got a bullet deposit. I usually kept the power with my own revolver, but I was rather powerless since the Redsleeves had confiscated it. That's why I let Father Fullerton keep his bullets. I trusted him. Not only did he know how to use a gun properly, but he also knew when not to use one.

The new clergy was highly trained for defensive purposes, not offensive. That was part of his vows. When the so-called War on Terror took a different turn, the Catholic Church needed to do something to protect its church members from terrorist attacks. The bombing of the Vatican had prompted the church to organize a "new clergy" of both priests and nuns who would possess the training and skills to prevent terrorist attacks. And what better place to train this new elite force than a highly volatile area with little media scrutiny and a demand for spiritual guidance like post-Beckham New Orleans?

"Oh, that's good," said Father Fullerton.

Joshua said, "Father, church doesn't give you booze?"

"Some, but not much. It is very restricted due to the…nature of our vows and training. We have to take a vow of sobriety while armed." He sipped his Elmer's Ryan bourbon. He smiled. "It's more of a guideline, really. Moderation is better than abstinence. At least in this case."

He did always have just one drink whenever he came to the bar, no matter how many drinks people offered to buy him.

The door opened, and Monty walked in dressed in mechanic's overalls. He took off his cap, revealing his shaved black head. Even in the dim candlelight, his head shined. He greeted each customer as would a campaigning politician, except his warmth was genuine. He shook everyone's hand, looking him in the eyes, smiling. "What up, my man Hue? Still cooking dem grits how I like 'em?"

Sounding confused, Huey said, "I cook them like normal."

"That's right." He nodded and moved down the bar. "Father, how dat church comin' 'long?"

"Well, it is still a construction site, but we're at least having mass in there now. Will we see you there tomorrow?"

"Oh, Father, I'm gonna try, nah. These people's cars got me all crazy busy."

He shook Joshua's hand, saying, "I got somethin' for ya. I'll talk at'cha soon 'nuff."

"Sounds good." Joshua said.

He shook Octave's hand. "Hey, I need'a come see ya."

"Oh yeah, fine sir?"

"Yeah, yeah, my hair done grown too long." He bent his slick bald head, laughing.

Monty settled into the stool next to Choppy. They shook hands and exchanged words. "Say, Ridge, what they all be drinkin'?"

"Elmer's Ryan bourbon. One of the best."

"Set me up." He opened his wallet and the old NOPD badge flipped out onto the bar top. He never took it out of his wallet, even after the New Orleans Police Department had disbanded. Out of nostalgia, mostly. He now mainly fixed people's cars and was quite comfortable with that trade.

Monty was still a cop, though, deep down. He lived across Broadmoor Bay in a neighborhood we called "the Ward," but he grew up in the Hollygrove neighborhood, which was nothing but debris and muck then. The Redsleeves, at least the white ones, derisively called the Ward "niggertown." Since the city population had plummeted, several voting districts, or wards, had been consolidated into one solitary voting district. The state government had not expected, however, that that would cause the bloodiest gang war in New Orleans history. Each ward had its gang, and each was quite protective of their turf. But when those boundaries disappeared, it all became the promised land. We referred to that as the Ward Wars. And, since Monty had been a cop for a decade and a homicide detective for several years after, he couldn't help but try and uncover just how these gang members were getting guns. Machine guns, at that. And it seemed that the Redsleeves were not enforcing disarmament in the Ward as they were in other parts of the city, almost as if they wanted the gangs to kill each other off.

Father Fullerton paid in cash and thanked me kindly. Upon exiting, he held the door open for Mr. Buras and Judge, who talked about catching jack crevalles in the Rigolets. Ol' Sulphur was at his heel, striding happily on three legs. Mr. Buras took off his Venice hat and shook Fullerton's hand. Judge nodded and spit in his dip cup. He offered Mr. Buras the vacant bar stool.

"Hey," Monty said, "you brought home that bacon or what?"

Judge smiled, "Not today." Spit. "Been out in the marshes near Sauvage all week. Gettin' some duck huntin' in while the time is right. Should be out there harvestin' dem hogs next week."

Huey said, "Our tax dollars at work. The Louisiana Wildlife and Fisheries pays you to kill as many hogs and coyotes as possible so…"

Judge ordered an Elmer's Ryan for himself and Buras. "Not according to any paperwork. So blow me." He spit and looked up at me. "I'll settle up with ya next week. Good hog spot I found. Should kill a bunch."

I poured the two bourbons. "Hell, you don't need to go way out there to find those boars. They've been tearing up my vegetable garden."

"You can't shoot 'em yourself?"

I almost told him about my gun getting confiscated. "I don't have anything big enough that can take one down."

He nodded and spit in his cup.

I said, "I'll tell ya what, Judge. You come by and kill some hogs around here, and I'll clear your tab."

His eyes widened, and he stroked his beard. "In that case, pour me an extra Elmer's. Good doing business with ya."

Mr. Buras leaned in and coughed hard. "H-how did those c-crabs turn out?"

His eyes met mine, and he was smiling ear to ear. I didn't have the heart to tell him that the Redsleeves had dumped them on Oyster Shell Road and shot them with my own gun. Instead, I said, "They were great, Mr. Buras. Thanks. I had them earlier today." I wondered when I had become such a liar. Faking the emotion is always the hardest thing, but that's what essentially sells it, not actually the lie itself.

Joshua said, "Ridge, I can have another?"

I picked up the rum bottle.

"No. Another cigarette."

I gave him a hard look.

"Oh, come on. We all know everyone in here."

Octave said, "If you need to relax, try reading something." He threw a small paperback that had been in his back pocket on the bar.

Joshua said, "Sure. Something a bored porch jockey made up when he was drunk. Or some high-society fucknut that feels he needs credit for something he never did. Just what I need. Thanks, Octave." He pulled a piece of beef jerky from his bag.

"Maybe if you looked into this city's literary culture, you would understand the situation here a little better."

"It's a different culture now, Octave. Stop cloistering yourself in that book dungeon of yours." He pulled out an issue of *The Declaration* and threw it on top of the novel. He put the cigarette in his mouth. "I wasn't bored when I wrote it. But maybe just as drunk as your boy there." He pointed at the novel.

Huey slammed his glass on the bar. "I've had it with your bullshit!"

He rose with clenched fists. Joshua did the same, the unlit cigarette still hanging from his lips. Huey walked down the bar, and

I jumped over the bar between them, holding a baseball bat. Ol' Sulphur barked.

"Out back!" I shouted. I wasn't going to hit either of them, and I think they knew it. But the person who controls alcohol yields an uncanny power over others. I had to keep a hard line when it came to fights because I wasn't calling the Redsleeves for anything. I was on my own. We all were, which meant someone had to be somewhat responsible. As far as Joshua and Huey fighting, however, I was okay with it. Quite frankly, it was overdue.

Joshua undid his suspenders, lit his cigarette, and marched outside. Huey followed him. I trusted Huey wouldn't hit him in the back of the head. Huey was an asshole, but he was a soldier. At least he still had some honor. Everyone followed them outside. Ol' Sulphur barked and Mr. Buras coughed. I asked, "You okay, Mr. Buras?"

He nodded and waved me outside.

"The battle for New Orleans is about to start." I laughed and walked out to watch the fight.

That's all it was to the rest of us: a fight. To both Huey and Joshua, it meant everything. It was on behalf of their own. Huey fought to keep New Orleans for the "born and raised" that stuck with the city in its darkest hours and made it what it was. Joshua fought for the transplants that were establishing a new life, not only for themselves, but for the community, too. Both of them, I'm sure of it, believed that the future of the city was at stake. In reality, the future of the city was being decided by nine Supreme Court justices. And the war between the natives and the newcomers was a played-out story dating back to the Choctaw nation. But an ornery war veteran and an obsessive rogue journalist thought it was all riding on them. If nothing else, it would be entertaining.

When I got outside, the air was motionless, dead. No wind off the lake. We all just watched, not like it was in high school when everyone cheered like it was a spectator sport. I didn't really care who won, really, just glad it was finally happening. Maybe after this, they'd both move on and get over themselves.

Each had already gotten a few licks on the other. Blood sprinkled Joshua's white shirt. He staggered like a wrestler trying to shoot in at the right time, whereas Huey had a wide, low stance, ready for anything. Huey's eyebrow was split, bleeding. Joshua's left eye was swollen. Joshua shot in between Huey's legs like a wrestler, knocking him on his back. Just when we thought Huey had been pinned, he wiggled out of it and got Joshua in a headlock. Their blood mixed together as they fought.

Ol' Sulphur barked incessantly from inside the bar. He sounded hoarse. A strange feeling came over me, so I walked into the bar. Mr. Buras lay on the floor, motionless. Ol' Sulphur sat down with his chin on Mr. Buras's back, whimpering.

I yelled, "Mr. Buras?"

Everyone came running in to help, but Mr. Buras was already dead.

Place d'Armes

She had approximately two hours before her students had Mr. Cooper for English. If they went through the New Carré, it would be a ten-minute walk, but both Mira and Mr. Larson decided not to take that route. They were pushing it as it was, and bringing sixty high school freshmen into the heart of regulated sin was not the best way for them to learn a valuable lesson. So they paraded down Alex Crowley Boulevard and would turn down Trujillo Parkway, going around the red-light district. On the right side of Alex Crowley, progress was apparent, given the construction materials, cement trucks, and the Greek and Mexican laborers. The left side, however, was just as it had been after Hurricane Beckham: raw, resting carnage. Rats scurried under rotten wooden beams, rusted vehicles, and brick chunks from old buildings. The smells from both sides of the street wafted together. Hot tar, cigarette smoke, coffee, and fresh-cut lumber blended with black mold and the putrid odor from a cracked refrigerator.

Justin Henderson asked, "Why they ain't doing anything with this?"

"Don't know. They should, shouldn't they?" Mira said. She noticed Javell Green and some other boys lagging behind and looking in the direction of the New Carré and its brothels. The boys licked their lips.

"There's nothing over there. At least not for boys your age." They knew what was over there. There was no need to lie to them at this point, she figured.

When they turned at Trujillo Parkway, the distant jailhouse came into view. It was actually the old location of the historic U.S. Mint building, which retained much of its structural integrity after the hurricane. Its red stones stood out from the Tyvek-covered buildings that were being built on the right side. On the left side of this street, debris from Beckham remained in what was once the Faubourg Marigny. The eerie silence from the former center of the local music scene could agonize any musician. It was odd that the Refounders had not done anything with the old Treme and Marigny, Mira realized.

They approached the Corrections and Detainment Center, which shared the building with the Financing Department. An exterior fence had been added to the original black iron fence. Fleurs-de-lis had been placed there originally for decor, but now they proved useful as spikes to deter prisoners from escaping.

Mr. Larson turned around to the group of students, who showed signs of fatigue from the long walk. He pushed up his thick glasses and announced, "Ladies and gentlemen, it won't be much longer. We're nearly there. I do want to point out a few things about this building here. It was a once a mint, where they made money. This shows you how this city was relevant in days of yore. During the Civil War, the state of Louisiana seized it when they seceded from the Union, only to have it taken back by the Union two years later upon capturing New Orleans without a shot fired. A riot even broke out, and a man climbed the flagpole and took the American flag down. Of course, he was hung for doing so."

Many of the students began listening after they heard that last part.

"It was a museum for many years. Actually, it was a jail once before. Now, they say it's only temporary, but I think it's fitting that the city's criminals and financiers are housed in the same facility from the start. Maybe we've actually learned something over all these years."

Mira didn't know much of that history, but she was thinking of Derek inside those prison walls. Perhaps she could sneak in there while Mr. Larson took them to protest. No, she decided. Behind those walls, Derek was, hopefully, keeping himself busy with the typewriter.

Before she knew it, they had arrived at the old Jackson Square. White shells had been laid for the concrete and steel trucks in meandering driveways through loose dirt and rubble, so that the Refounders could haul away the bulldozed ruins of the Cabildo, St.

Louis Cathedral, and the Presbytère Museum. The statue of Andrew Jackson had been removed and relocated to the British Museum.

It was the first time Mira had seen the square site since returning to New Orleans. Remembering places as completely different spaces does strange things to the mind, she thought. The mind makes the eye see things that are no longer there. She saw the three-spired, cream-colored St. Louis Cathedral, which flashed into a mangled mountain of eighteenth-century stucco and wooden pilings. On either side of the construction site, uprooted oak trees had left behind deep pits now filled with red bricks, mortar, and rusted iron, but Mira blinked, envisioning two rows of live oaks and the historic Pontabla apartments with their elegant balconies. She also imagined tourists in London gazing at the ruins, wondering about ancient civilizations like Greece, Egypt, and now New Orleans.

Mr. Larson said, "Notice that the statue has been taken down. Remember that Hurricane Beckham just about destroyed everything in town, except for statues and a few choice buildings. Typically, statues are just pure stone or metal, making them almost indestructible. Whenever a statue is dismantled, it's usually the people who do it, for better or for worse. Should tell you something about how things are changing—who or what they decide to honor or to *not* honor any longer for whatever reason. You have to remember that this space used to be called the Place d'Armes when the French and Spanish were here. Let's stop here, Mira. It may be just a moonscape at the moment, but we can at least act like this is still a town square. Always a fitting spot for civic action."

Mira wasn't really interested in all the history at this point. She was more concerned with the fact that they had not even devised a plan of action for the protest. If she didn't take action soon, this "protest" would just be a long history lecture, and she wasn't risking her job for that. She pulled her penny whistle out of her pocket and played a few soft notes. The students quieted and focused on their own thoughts and memories of the eleven children who'd been accidentally gunned down on their educational field trip. Mira hoped they also realized that McMason was the monster directly responsible for the young men possessing military firearms capable of shooting through a school bus and killing eleven children in less than five seconds. A penny whistle was the best vehicle for her anger about the McMason Memorial proposal and her sorrow for the students that had been taken from their parents.

Justin Henderson sauntered over to a pile of stacked bricks, pulled a marker out of his pocket, and wrote on one of them. Mira stopped playing. "Justin, what are you doing?"

He didn't respond, looking at what he'd written on the brick. Mira walked over to him. He had written the name Jeremiah Henderson.

He said, "That's my cuz. He one of the eleven, ma'am."

She smiled and placed her hand on his shoulder, the conduct of which had legal ramifications, but she felt it was appropriate to show warmth and respect in that moment. Some things were higher than the liability paranoia of school administrators, she felt. Mr. Larson and the other students came to the brick pile.

"Who wants to write another name?" Mira asked.

They wrote the names of the ten other shooting victims on the bricks. Mira wrote on a brick, "In memory of the victims of the Ursulines Eleven. Let them live forever through us." She picked up her penny whistle and began to play again.

A blue Gulf Guard jeep drove down the shell pathway toward them with its blue flashers on. Two men dressed in blue camouflage exited the vehicle, one of whom was the Guardsman who had tried to arrest Mira the previous day for prostitution. She stopped playing and sighed.

He said, "This area is under restriction." He recognized Mira and looked at her students. He closed his eyes and nodded to her. He looked at Mr. Larson and said, "Sir, what is it you are all doing out here?"

Pushing up his glasses, Mr. Larson said, "First of all, Officer, we would like to thank you for your service to our city. We're here in protest, however."

"Protest what?"

"Well, we understand that Captain McMason just passed, but this historic site should not be honoring him."

"Who should it honor, then?" the other Guardsman asked.

Mr. Larson pointed to the stacked bricks. The two officers looked at each other and then walked to the bricks and read them. Their bodies relaxed once they read the names, and they dropped their authoritarian front and resumed their human constitutions.

Their radio beeped. "Patrol 347, do you copy?"

One of the Guardsmen responded, "Copy."

"What's your status at restricted site 145B?"

"Under control. No backup needed."

"Patrol 347, what is the nature of the disturbance?"

He looked at the schoolchildren and the two teachers, frowning. "Um, not quite sure how to respond to that one right now, Dispatch. Report will describe situation." He lifted his head from the radio and spoke softly to the other officer, saying, "If anything, *we're* disturbing *them.*"

Chapter 9

"A recitation from the Gospel according to John 21:1–19." Father Fullerton spoke from the podium.

"After the Resurrection of Christ, Jesus visited the disciples, who could not recognize him. The third time he revealed himself to them in Galilee, they were busy fishing. However, they could not catch a single fish. When they came ashore, Jesus told them to go back out and cast their nets into the water to the right of the boat. And when they did, alas! They did not have the strength to heave in the plentitude of fish. This is when Peter realized that it was, in fact, the Lord himself standing ashore, and he jumped in the water and swam to the Almighty Father. The other Disciples hauled in the net that contained one hundred and fifty-three fish, and, with the will of the Lord, their net remained strong and did not break. Once they reached the shoreline, Jesus was near loaves of bread and a fire for roasting the fish. The rest of the disciples could not deny the presence of the Lord.

"After they ate well, Jesus came to Peter and asked, 'Do you love me?'

"'Of course,' Simon Peter responded. 'Yes, Lord, I love you. You know that I do.'

"'Feed my lambs, Peter.' He asked again, 'Do you love me?'

"'Only you know how much I love you, Lord,' Peter replied.

"'Tend to my sheep.' Jesus asked Peter yet again, 'Do you love me?'

"Getting anxious as to why his Lord could even question his unconditional love once, much less thrice, Peter replied, 'Yes, I love you, my Lord.'

"'Feed my sheep,' the Lord said. 'Amen, amen. As a young man, you dressed yourself and went where you pleased. But when you grow old, you will reach out and someone else will dress and lead you where you do not wish to go.'

"For this was signifying what kind of death could glorify God. And Jesus looked at him and said, 'Come with me. Follow me.'"

As I listened to Father Fullerton, I couldn't help but smell fresh construction. A purple tapestry hung behind the priest's podium and altar, hiding the paint cans, panels of sheetrock, and flooring panels. Saws, compressors, and nail guns had also been brought from the site and locked in the seminary storage room. Even the church had to guard against rampant theft. The floor was simply plywood at this stage of construction, and white dust from sheetrock had lightly settled over it so that it looked painted until you kicked up the dust. The smell of primer, dust, and wood beams was not the best odor; however, it meant that things were in motion.

The church's attendance had never been higher. Around fifty people, all there for different reasons, filled the rows of folding chairs. Some attended out of pure devotion to the Lord. Some were there out of sheer desperation masked as devotion. Others were there simply to socialize or barter with others.

As for me, I only went to church for weddings or funerals. So here I was for Mr. Buras. To avoid any entanglements with the Redsleeves, we had not told anyone what had happened the evening before. The congregation was at a normal Sunday mass, whereas a few of us were at Mr. Buras's silent funeral.

A black family sat in front of me, and a baby boy stared at me as he sat on his mother's lap. I smiled at him, but he didn't change expressions. So I just ignored him and watched the priest. The toddler kept staring at me nonetheless. I wore the nicest clothes I owned: a faded collared shirt and jeans with two holes. They weren't clean, but it was my most presentable attire for a social gathering. Perhaps that boy was smelling me more than staring. Octave and Constance sat in the row behind me. Octave wore a tie and black sport coat. Constance wore a black, long-sleeved blouse and a black hat. She knew. Huey sat at the end of the row, his face red and his jaw swollen. Though the church was full, the chair next to Huey remained empty, probably due to his appearance. His ponytail did not appear greasy. He must have washed it for this occasion. Fitzmorris sat in the back row, wearing a black suit that was now too big. I didn't tell him about Mr. Buras, but I didn't doubt that he had learned about it somehow. Monty sat a few rows ahead. I recognized his reflective bald head. Judge sat on the other side, wearing camouflage and muddy boots. He'd either come from a morning hunt or was on his way to a midday hunt. Or maybe that was what he always wore, just the way Joshua always wore the white oxford shirt, khakis, and suspenders. Joshua, however, was not present. Neither was Choppy.

Father Fullerton stepped down from the podium and approached the congregation with open arms.

He began in his Irish accent, "It is quite fitting that Simon Peter is a fisherman. I'm sure many of you have fished yourselves or know of people that have done so…"

Monty turned around and looked at me. I shrugged then glanced over at Huey, who was looking at Fitzmorris, who was eyeballing Judge, who was looking at Octave, who was looking at me. Fullerton had left the bar before Mr. Buras died. Did he know? If so, who told him? I certainly hadn't.

Fullerton continued. "You see, a fisherman represents selfless-ness. Giving. Nourishment. It is very rare that a fisherman by trade or by leisure will hoard his catch for only himself. Instead, he feeds his family, his friends, his community. His community needs him for survival, and he goes out and travels treacherous waters so his breth-ren can live well. I grew up in a small fishing town in Ireland, and no fisherman I knew cared about capital, or money, or the likes of mate-rial needs. Instead, they were men of simple means. Their purpose is simple." He brought his palms together as if to pray. "To feed the hun-gry." His eyes darted around the church.

"Fishermen also have to be men of faith. They cannot see where the fish are. And their earthly knowledge of fishing techniques and weather can only bring them so far. They must believe. They must believe in themselves, in their purpose, in their Lord. It is not hard to believe that Peter found the fish after finding the Lord. It was the Lord's guidance and their belief that was their source of nourishment, not the fish."

Father Fullerton slowly walked down the aisle as he spoke. "Jesus asks an odd thing from Peter. He wants him to both lead and follow. He wants Peter to feed his flock, yet follow him. And Jesus does not want his disciple to feed his sheep *fish*, but nourish his people with love and guidance. To feed their souls. The only way he can do that is to follow Christ, for he cannot fully know the way, just as a fisherman needs a GPS, a map, or a constellation. In order to lead justly, one must follow the creed and live with principle, purpose, and righteousness. Likewise, in order to rightfully follow, people must lead themselves away from temptation, from sin, from evil.

"For the earth can be turbulent and violent like the sea, as many of you have seen while living here in the aftermath of Hurricane Beckham. Just as Jesus's disciples witnessed Him die in vain, many of you have seen your beloved city perish beyond all recognition." He turned around at the last pew and walked slowly toward the altar as he went on, "But this does not mean that it is gone. Just unrecognizable, no different than how Jesus appeared to his disciples in Galilee. The Lord never left them. Many of you, I know, live a life of isolation and hardship. But your Lord has not abandoned you. He never will give up on you, so you should surely not give up on Him.

"'Follow me, Peter. Come with me,' Jesus said. It is not every day when someone asks that of you, much less the Lord himself. When you take on such a responsibility, you must relinquish every selfish, individualistic desire in order to commit yourself to the betterment of your community. When you do that, you are also committing yourself to Jesus alongside Simon Peter, his beloved disciple. I know that many of you have, in fact, *chosen* to live here, which means you already possess a faith and collective purpose that few even dream of having. And, by following God, you will lead each other from this dark chapter into a new age of rebirth where your nets will be unbreakable from whatever comes. A time when your children will believe just as you do, and they can pull in the fish you provided for them."

Fullerton paused. I always hated that awkward silence in church, even if it lasted only a few seconds. And I couldn't help but think how the event of someone asking if you loved them and would follow them was rather a little too familiar. What if Peter had said no? What purpose was more important? Perhaps it's time to choose her over New Orleans, I thought.

"Speaking of children, one of our school principals is here with us. Principal Whitman, do you have something to announce to us today?"

Constance stood and walked up the aisle. Her gait, her arm sway, her stature were all under complete control. She rubbed the back of her head, stroking her skin-short hair. Constance exuded a special type of delicate tenacity that only strong black women possess. She took the podium and spoke. "Thank you, Father. I am Principal Whitman at T.S. Laurette School. Our students and our teachers have been working very hard to bring Mardi Gras back."

Everyone applauded.

Her hands firmly on the podium, Constance commanded their attention. Her stern voice possessed a benevolent undertone, like that of many seasoned educators. "It hasn't been easy, believe that. But it's important to bring it back because it's who we are, as y'all know. Many across the state and the country don't see things the way we do. They are not us. We know what we need and who we are. As you know, Red Birch Security Services banned parading and Mardi Gras altogether in the immediate aftermath of Beckham. All the krewes disbanded as a result. However, I and other educators have found a loophole. There was an exception that was made for children participating in an educational event. So we have been working on Captain McMason the last few weeks so that our students can parade on Fat Tuesday. We are still working out the details, of course, but this will not only give our students a chance to take part in such a historic cultural event, but it will give this community a much overdue sense of normalcy."

Everyone applauded and cheered again.

She nodded and waited for them to quiet. "I hate asking for donations, but I'm afraid I must. Anything you can give will be greatly appreciated. Obviously, donations of actual money are needed, but if there's anything else you can donate, it's something we will not have to buy—things like art supplies, lumber, tools. I'll have some flyers after mass that list what we will need. And we are trying to get throws that are more useful than just plastic beads. If you have an abundance of anything, please let us know, no matter what it is. My number can be found on the flyer, or you can always go to the school during the week. I'm always there." She nodded at Fullerton and stepped down, and everyone applauded a third time.

Father Fullerton took his place at the podium. "Thank you, Mrs. Whitman. And I believe we have someone else from the school here today to play some music for us." He held up his hands, palms up, signaling someone to stand.

In the first row, three children stood. Two girls, one white and one black, both about twelve or thirteen years old. A black boy, possibly eight or nine, held a trumpet. They went to a makeshift stage, which was simply plywood nailed atop two shipping pallets, off to the side of the church.

A young woman stood up and followed them to the stage, holding a guitar. Her red-brown hair curled above a blue scarf around her shoulders. It was Mira. She was here. I had to be dreaming. I didn't wake up, however. This was real.

Wearing a gray shirt and blue jeans, she joined the children at the platform. The boy shyly crept behind the two girls. Mira motioned for him to come to the front. She said, "Hello, everyone. My name is Mira Roche, and I'm from here and just recently moved back home…"

The congregation applauded.

"Thanks. Our music students will play some songs for you today." She nodded to them, and they introduced themselves so shyly and softly that I couldn't hear them, even if I had been listening for anything other than Mira's voice. One of the girls sat down at the piano.

She nodded at the children and slowly strummed her guitar. I inhaled heavily, almost gasping. I hadn't taken a breath since she'd stood up. The black baby in front of me started staring again.

The students sang together. The little boy lightly played the trumpet so as not to drown out the girls' voices. Then the black girl sang the verse solo, and Mira joined for the refrain. As the vocalists paused, the boy said "Hallelujah" through his trumpet. They all played music for a few seconds. Mira nodded to the boy, but he shyly stepped behind the girl and shook his head. Mira smiled and sang the next verse instead. I learned later that it was a Leonard Cohen song, not an actual church hymn. No one seemed to notice nor care.

I couldn't swallow. A baseball felt lodged in my throat.

Everyone in the church was fixated on the musical performance. There had not been such a pleasure since Beckham. The white girl from the piano sang her solo verse. Mira and her students sang the refrain, except for the trumpet boy, who played along with the words. Some churchgoers, however, sheepishly joined in, almost whispering, "Hallelujah."

Mira and her students sang the last verse together just the way they'd sung the first, in unison. Then, the whole church erupted in song for the finale. The boy played his trumpet louder to be heard over the singing congregation. I had been in Catholic school most of my childhood years, and I had never experienced such active participation. I joined in for the first time.

The congregation stood and sang louder, forcing the little trumpeter to play louder as well. Father Fullerton was elated. It's not often you see a priest glowing, but he sure was that day. He almost looked like a child that couldn't contain or even fully comprehend his excitement, just bursting with raw joy. He sang with us, with open palms to the ceiling as if to funnel the celebration to the heavens in case God wasn't listening. The whole church sang, "Hallelujah!"

If God was listening that day, He didn't have any plans for me, but Fitzmorris sure had a few.

Once the church let out, a lot of people went up to compliment Mira and her students. I hung around the periphery of the crowd, but I didn't have the stomach for a public reunion. I couldn't remember the last time I'd had so many emotions circling through me. Ecstatic she was here, but I couldn't help but be a little angry. She'd left me because I wanted to move here and live with purpose. Now she was here, too, living with more purpose than me. What do you say to that?

Octave and Constance walked over to her, and I felt this was my chance. I could go tell Octave I had "borrowed" that book from his store; then maybe she would see me and initiate the greeting. I swallowed and walked toward them, but Fitzmorris intercepted me and handed me an envelope.

"Ridge, I need you to do two things."

Honestly, I felt a little relieved that I didn't have to confront Mira, until I learned what he needed.

"Mail this for me."

"Where?"

"The post office."

"Downtown?"

"Downtown." He wiped sweat off his forehead with a handkerchief.

Thinking of any logical excuse, I said, "It's Sunday. They're not open."

"Tomorrow morning."

"What is this?"

"You remember what Octave's wife just said, right? Needing throws for the parade? I have a friend that owns a farm upriver. Big farm. He usually sells to big grocery stores in his parish, but I'm asking him for a large donation for the kids. To throw at the parade."

"That just happened. Did you hurry up and write that letter in your car or something?"

He held the envelope closer.

"You know I like to help, Fitzmorris, but can't you do this yourself?"

"You're closed during the day. I am not." He poked my stomach with the corner of the envelope. "That extra salt help out any?"

"Okay." I grabbed the envelope. Downtown. The hornets' nest, swarming with Redsleeves and Refounders. My truck was certainly on their records. Nothing could be worse than this. I sighed. "And what else?"

He stepped close to me, almost like he was coming in for a kiss. He whispered, "I need you to help bury Buras."

I dropped his envelope.

Renny Rooster's Pancake House

The Saturday teachers' meeting was well under way, and Mira replenished her mimosa before the champagne could get too warm. She didn't bother with more orange juice, however.

Renny Rooney allowed his customers to bring their own alcohol in for breakfast, which brought his pancake house instant success. Principal Whitman found that meetings outside of school grounds were more effective, especially when she had them in places that permitted alcohol or tobacco use. Even before the Refounding, she had realized that the teachers opened up much more when loosened up by their drink or nicotine of choice. It also improved morale and retention, so she gave her teachers the option of drinking, but did not necessarily encourage it.

Mrs. Whitman sipped her coffee with both hands around her cup. She looked at her ten teachers talking freely at the round table. Teachers teach much better when they get to know their own, she had learned. She observed them. Stephen Cooper, the English teacher, was on his third cup of coffee. His eyes sunken, he sniffled frequently, wiping his nose. He's probably struggling, the principal suspected. He opened a small bottle of Elmer's Ryan. She set down her cup and said, "Mr. Cooper, how are your classes going?"

The other teachers wrapped up their conversations and sat to attention like their students.

Cooper was embarrassed. He was in mid-pour when his boss called on him. He put his elbows on the table and rubbed his eyes. "We're on our second essay. Drafting it. They have to give me a rough draft for next week."

"Okay."

"Um, they seem to be a little less cooperative for this one." He sipped his whiskey coffee. "I'm not sure if it's the concept they don't quite grasp, or if they're just restless coming back from Mardi Gras."

"Are they disrespectful?"

"Um, not necessarily. But if things keep on as they're going, it could get to that. There's a few times when Deaton Hires..."

Whitman held her palm out as if she was halting traffic. "Wait. If we're going to discuss specific students and specific incidents, we need to do that in my office on Tuesday, not here."

"Yes, ma'am."

She picked up her coffee cup. "Also, your students may be having a hard time coping with this Refounding business. They just saw their city lifted out from under them, so think about that when you're enforcing grammar. I've thought of hiring a counselor next year to give these kids someone to confide in. I don't have the time, and all y'all don't have the time, either." She looked at Cooper. "Back to you. How were their first essays?"

"As for the actual objective of the assignment, they did well for the most part, but their grammar mechanics need work. I mean," he sniffled and wiped his nose with his shirtsleeve, "I start grading the papers at five in the morning, teach throughout the day, and stay up to about midnight grading, and I can't seem to get them all completed."

Mr. Larson leaned forward in his chair and said, "One thing that you can think about—if I may, Mrs. Whitman?"

"Go ahead."

"You know, I've mainly taught social studies and history over the years, but I did teach comp when I was in college. And one thing we did was peer-review sessions. Are you doing that?"

"What's that?" Cooper asked.

"Well," Larson gestured with his hands, "you have them critique or grade each other's drafts. I mean, you give them a prompt or some guidelines, of course, but what happens essentially is that you put more work on *them*, take some of the burden off *you*, and they come out better for it."

"Huh." He sipped again. "What if they give the wrong feedback?"

"They might at times. I mean, in the end, you want them to know it, and know that they know it. And this is a way to ensure that's happening. I actually still do something similar in my classes. When a student cannot only recognize an error but then also properly articulate how to correct it, they feel a sense of accomplishment."

"Thanks. I'll talk to you more about it later."

Mira sucked at a shred of pulp stuck between her teeth, thanking God she didn't teach English. Teaching is difficult enough, she thought, even without reading over 20,000 pages of student essays over the course of a school year. At least math had a definitive answer and process that the students could grasp. As for religion, there really was no wrong answer, but at Archbishop Fullerton, the right answers were pretty clear. She said, "Stephen, how much are you teaching them the essay format or formula?"

He rubbed his eyes. "Well, I want them to express themselves and explore new methods. I don't really like the five-paragraph rule. It really does not allow for creative growth."

Mira finished her sip with a brief sigh and set her glass on the table. "Okay, well…"

Cooper, who was now cutting into his pancake, halted with his fork in midair. "English is not math, okay? It takes an open approach. You can't treat writing like math problems."

"Um, you *absolutely* can. I passed my English composition classes just fine once I learned the simple formula for organizing an essay. And you just said that your students don't have a problem with content, just mechanics—which is *all* just an arbitrary formula in the first place."

Cooper looked at his breakfast, away from Mira's eyes. "Well, I can't just grade a paper like you can grade a math quiz. There are so many other factors—"

"There's part of your problem right there. You need a set rubric, or *formula*, to assess your students' writing to ensure that you're being fair."

Whitman put her cup down again. "All right, all right. That's enough. Moving on."

Both Mira and Stephen Cooper sipped their breakfast beverages of choice. I'm not trying to be derisive, Mira thought, but with a tone like that, he was bound for some shit. I'm just trying to help.

Whitman turned to Mira. "Ms. Roche, I liked your suggestion about adding those foreign languages to the curriculum. What brought that on?"

"When I went to City Hall on Monday, I came across some Mexican and Greek immigrants trying to talk to me."

"Fabulous. It shows the need for it, especially since I don't see them moving away once the Refounding work is done."

"I met…" Mira stopped herself from saying Fullerton's name, since she'd have to explain *how* she'd met him, and the details would be embarrassing, especially in front of her fellow teachers. "I met a nice Greek nun the other day who might be able to help us with those language classes, at least at first."

"Oh, really? I'll see if I can contact the archbishop about that."

Mira swallowed the rest of her mimosa, hoping Fullerton wouldn't tell Mrs. Whitman about her little incident in the New Carré.

"Okay, Ms. Roche and Mr. Larson." Mrs. Whitman scrolled through her Eagle. "I read this the other day on Chase Quade's blog." She touched the screen. "I just shared it with y'all. Go ahead and read that right now."

Mira opened the article on her screen and began reading:

So, now our teachers are not only permitting vandalism but also encouraging it. Even bringing them to do it on a field trip! It is clear that it will take some time to weed out the bad seeds that have plagued this region's education system since the beginning. Unfortunately, Archbishop Fullerton will probably just forgive them as a good Christian should. Maybe the Church should take a cue from the Old Testament God and actually discipline these people. It's already on the right track by instituting their new defensive order for the war against the Muslims. Now, we just need a lesser extreme action against these inept people who are unraveling the fabric of our moral society from the inside out. It's already bad enough that certain people are making a conman and that dumb loser in jail out to be heroes. What's worse is that everyone's letting some sheepish liberal muckle-buckle, who cowardly calls himself "Yossarian," dictate the whole narrative here. Some social justice warrior adopts a character's name from *Catch 22*, which is one of the most anti-American novels I've read, if you ask me, and the liberal media wants to give him a crown! And it's probably all false anyhow! Now our teachers are allowing kids to be vandals! If only these businessmen can rebuild the people like they can the buildings. [12:37AM] chasethetruth

"Mrs. Whitman…" Mira began.

Whitman shook her head and held her hand out. "I completely understand the situation. And I also understand that this is not as bad as this guy says it is. However, Quade has a nationwide audience, and the last thing we need is to give him a reason to give us any attention. I feel that if he gives us attention at all, it's bad. So let's do things by the book for the rest of the year. As much as I encourage…unorthodox pedagogy, we need to keep ourselves clean for a while. Understood?"

Both Mira and Larson said, "Yes, ma'am."

"That goes for everyone here."

Cooper set his empty mug on the table. "Shoot. I just had an idea for a future assignment, too. I'd have my students read that blog and have them write responses to it. That will certainly light some fires."

"That's fine, just as long as it's just for your class, not for social media."

"Yes, ma'am. That's fine."

"How's my city leaders doing this morning?" Renny Rooney walked up to the table and wiped his hands on his kitchen apron. He was bald and short.

Cooper pointed at him. "You mean, 'How *are* my city leaders'?'"

He laughed and raised his hands as if guilty. "I'm a man of many words even if they ain't the right ones all the time." He picked up the empty plates.

Whitman smiled. "Everything was delicious. Thank you, Mr. Rooney."

Mira sipped the pulp from her champagne glass. "Oh, I almost forgot." She looked at the principal. "So, that permit for St. Joseph is in progress. I should be able to get it on time."

"Fabulous."

Mira looked to Rooney. "I'm having them do a math project, but with cooking. And we'll be providing a feast for the community. Would you like to help us?"

"I'd be honored. Absolutely."

"That's great news; thanks."

"Just keep in touch. I'll see y'all next week."

Relieved, Mira wiped her mouth with a napkin, grabbed her half-empty bottle of champagne, and stood. She was successful in getting her students excited about math conversions by incorporating cooking; however, she was never successful at the actual cooking, Italian cookies being the only exception. The feast would already be free, but it might actually be enjoyable now that Rooney was on board, she thought.

Chapter 10

While in line at the post office, I figured it might be a good time to continue reading that book, *Cold Chambers*. I had left off with D-Day, when the Allies made camp near the beaches. The main character, Lt. Travers, had hoped that the war would soon be over now that some phenomenon had rendered gunfire inoperable. The chapter opened up with him writing a letter back home:

Dear Mother,

I had witnessed something remarkable. We all stormed the beaches expecting an onslaught but found peace instead. This, I thought at the time, was the turning point for us. Not just for the war, but for man. Perhaps this war was the war that would end all wars. But now, reports are coming in from the Pacific front about assaults with swords and from Stalingrad about citizens attacking the Germans with stones and "Molotov cocktails." My superior officers have been having meetings all afternoon, and I fear we, as a human race, will miss this opportunity to change our bloody course. Ironically, military men are not trained well for peace even though their ultimate goal is to attain it. I suggested to Sergeant Adler that we explore every diplomatic option before restarting the war machine. He was not very receptive. He said that we couldn't let our guard down because, for all we know, this could be a Nazi ploy. Instead, I told him that this was a sign from God telling us to stop the war, and it might be our one chance. He was not receptive to that, either. No one can interfere with the war strategy. Not even God himself.

"Do you know who I am, lady?"

I snapped back to reality. There were about five people ahead of me in line.

The postal worker at the desk said, "No, sir, I do not."

"I'm a Duffosat." This young man wore a white Perlis shirt and had that wavy blond hair that rich mama's boys tend to have. He sighed then raised his voice. "We practically built this city ourselves. What more do you want from me?"

"Sir, I'm sorry, but that is the policy of this location. We must inspect your package's contents to rule out any possibility of contraband or undisclosed funds."

"I'm not letting you look through my package! This is America, goddamn it!" The desperation was evident in his tone. "Let me see your manager. Where is he?"

She stepped into an office behind the counter. The person behind me grumbled. "This man crazy. He not see us all waiting?"

Sergeant Powell walked up to the counter, and I closed my book and tried to hide it as best as I could. Apparently, his duties included not only the confiscation of books but of all other contraband, as well. "What is the problem here, young man?"

Duffosat was more diplomatic with a mercenary in uniform. "Is it really necessary to inspect my package in order to send it?"

"I'm afraid so, sir. So, if you would, please make a decision because all of these people are waiting."

"No! That's just it. I'm not leaving this spot until I can mail this with a guarantee that it will not be opened and gone through. Don't make me call my dad."

The girl behind me in line sighed loudly.

He turned around and said to us, "It's not me. I'm actually doing y'all a favor. We shouldn't have to put up with this shit. So you're fucking welcome."

Powell had ushered in two armed Redsleeves that stood on either side of Mr. Duffosat. "Okay, fine." He snatched the box from the counter. "I'll leave." The two mercenaries followed him out.

Sergeant Powell remained at the counter for the next few customers. I held the book low, as inconspicuously as possible without looking suspicious. I'd have to guess that *Cold Chambers* was blacklisted. I then also realized that I was mailing an envelope without knowing its contents. Would Fitzmorris set me up? My hands started to sweat.

Once I stepped up to the counter, the book slipped out of my hand and hit the floor with an echoing thud. Powell did not respond to the sound and walked back into the office. I handed the postal worker Fitzmorris's letter, hoping that she would not ask me what was in it.

"This will be all?"

"Yes, ma'am."

She handed me a form. "Print your name, state your purpose, and initial."

She pulled out a black machine and held it above the envelope. A thin green laser scanned the envelope. My hands were still sweating. In the *Purpose* column, I wrote "Personal letter" in hopes she'd just accept that.

"Okay, thank you." She put the envelope in a pile next to her.

I picked up my book from the floor and walked outside to find Joshua smoking a cigarette with an envelope in his shirt pocket.

"Don't you just love it?"

"Love what?" I asked.

"That pretty-boy being put in his place."

"Oh, that."

He took a drag on his cigarette while pulling both of his suspenders forward. "I actually was in line behind you but needed to step out for a cigarette. About the only time I'll take sides with McMason's minions about anything. I grew up with people like that. They think everyone owes them something or should be grateful for something they never did. Like that fucking guy there." He inhaled his cigarette hard. "He said that his family built the city themselves. First off, I'm pretty sure that the black slaves and the starving European immigrants did most of the *building* in this town. And that church groups and Mexican workers did a lot of the rebuilding after past hurricanes. He's riding on the coattails of his family name and probably hasn't done shit except cocaine and attending prestigious schools that he didn't even qualify for. If anything, his ancestors used more energy to *dis*able the people than to *en*able them. Notice that he started freaking out when he realized that he had to follow the rules like the rest of us. He started to panic once he realized that dropping his family's name didn't help him. Fuck that guy and his coattails. That might be the only thing McMason's done that's not horrendous. Disempowering the gentry and isolating them." Joshua inhaled his cigarette, tugging on his suspenders.

"Well, he was right, though. They shouldn't go through our packages."

He shrugged and exhaled like a smokestack. "Fuck that guy and his coattails. What you doing here?"

"Mailing something for Fitzmorris. I think it's a letter. They don't inspect envelopes, do they?"

"No. Just packages. I've been sending letters to a friend back east who works for the Pentagon. Trying to dig up dirt on our monster benefactor. Trust me, if they read our mail, you probably wouldn't be talking to me."

"Your bruises are looking a little better."

"It still hurts to eat. He hit me good."

"Speaking of eating, I'm starving. Is there anyplace I can get some food down here?"

"Yeah. Rooney's Grocery is just up the street here. Good sandwiches. I'd probably have gone hungry by now if it wasn't for Renny Rooney, with the way Fitzmorris's store has been lately," Joshua looked at his watch.

"Why didn't you tell any of us?"

"I told Huey once when he was bitchin' about not having stuff to cook with. That went well." He took a long drag on his cigarette until it burned down to the filter. He pulled another cigarette out of his pocket and placed it between his lips. He checked his watch again. "You might want to go there now before the lunch rush," he said around the bobbing unlit cigarette. "That's where most of the people working down here go. It's pretty much all there is here. Rooney's and Fitzmorris's store are all we have at this point. And Fitzmorris is almost out of the picture, it seems. Well, let me go send this while it's still early."

He extended his hand. His fingers, long like a basketball player's, were inky from all the papers he'd been lugging around town. The bulge in his wrist reminded me of how much this handshake would hurt, and it did.

I walked down an unrecognizable street, looking for Rooney's Grocery. My empty stomach made me bold in exploring the Monster's "lair" of downtown. Many of the tall buildings on either side of the street were cracked and crumbling. I passed a street corner of piled concrete chunks, palm tree trunks, streetlights, and moldy carpeting. A stray cat sitting on the ledge ducked into a window of a stone office building. I had a feeling that this street was the old Howard Avenue.

I looked over my shoulder and saw the Superdome peeking around a condemned building. The gold siding had flaked off to reveal a gray structure, and the white plaster on the roof had peeled off in long strands. I don't remember much about my mother before she died, but I remember her undying passion: the New Orleans Saints. She'd been a season ticket holder until she had me. Trying to learn football at a young age, I found the Saints confusing. I understood how "Panthers" or "Vikings" would be a team name, given their fierce nature, but the Saints? I thought it was a stupid name then. And that obscure French symbol on the side of their helmets didn't help matters much. I asked my parents why we had such a lame team name.

My dad said, "Son, you're missing the big picture. They're not saints to our opponents. They're saints to us. People's faith in the team transcends to their having faith in the city, in each other, in themselves. We could never have recovered the way we did after Katrina without them. You see, New Orleans is a unified city because of the Saints. There's the rich man's New Orleans and the poor man's New Orleans. There's the white person's New Orleans and there's the black person's New Orleans. There's the natives' New Orleans and there's the transplants' New Orleans. There's the woman's New Orleans, and there's the man's New Orleans. The artist's New Orleans and the businessman's New Orleans. Don't you see? Everyone has the Saints, no matter who they are."

I nodded and said yes, but back then I still wanted some vicious man-eating creature or legendary warrior as my mascot. Now the Saints are a Canadian team and the Dome just idles in eerie silence. I'm glad my mother never lived to see this day because it probably would have killed her.

A door opened to my right, and a garbage bag clobbered me to the ground.

"Oh, holy hell! I'm sorry there, guy. People usually aren't standing there at this time, and I just chuck the trash to the curb to haul away for later." He helped me up. "You lost or something?"

I brushed the dust off my pants. "No, I'm looking for Booney's Grocery."

"You mean Rooney's Grocery."

"Yeah, that."

"Well, I think it just found you, mister—"

"Ridge."

"Ridge? Pleasure. Renny Rooney."

We shook hands. He smelled of fry oil, and sweat streamed down his bald head.

"You open?"

"Just about."

I followed him into the side door of his grocery, and the wondrous odor of food made my stomach pull at my ribs. I followed him through the small kitchen. Pots of red beans and crawfish pasta simmered on the stove. Something delicious fried in the hot oil of his fryer. Loaves of bread sat atop a long shelf above a table.

Inside the store, actual groceries filled the shelves. I was amazed by what I saw: cooking oil, vinegar, flour, sugar, and salt. Yes, salt. Out in the open. What is this place? I asked myself. Another shelf had rice, grits, oats, pasta, and cornmeal. On a small table, bell peppers, broccoli, and tomatoes were laid out on a towel.

Rooney dried his head with a small towel. "I need to get back to the kitchen. Just look around for a minute. Here's a menu."

The menu was handwritten and photocopied. It was Monday, so red beans and rice were the lunch special. Specials for other days included crawfish étouffée, stuffed bell pepper, white beans and rice, black-eyed peas and andouille sausage; shrimp, catfish, roast beef, and hot sausage po-boys; crawfish pasta and jambalaya. I may have been drooling all over the floor, but I was too focused on the menu to notice. I put the menu down on the counter. Small bags of seeds of bell pepper, broccoli, and tomato rested by an old computerized register. I wanted to ask him how he got all this stuff, but I didn't. The less he knew about me or my community, the better. I was awfully curious, however.

Maybe it was a survival instinct kicking in, but I needed everything regardless. I grabbed two of each vegetable and set them on the counter next to the seed bags, of which I took one of each. I grabbed a bag of rice, flour, sugar, oats, cornmeal, and pasta. I didn't even know what to do with the cornmeal or the flour, really, but that didn't stop me. I also set a bottle of cooking oil and one of distilled vinegar on the counter, which didn't have much room left. As for the salt, I piled up five one-pound cartons on top of my groceries. I pulled the menu out from underneath the flour and selected a shrimp po-boy.

I paced as this man Rooney was finishing up in the kitchen, my stomach climbing up my throat. Then something hit me: All of this would *cost* something, and I only had a few dollars on me. I looked over at the front door. It was locked from inside, and a key was needed to open it, so I couldn't gather up what I could and run out. Again, I don't know if it was just survival instinct, but it sure made me think that theft was perfectly justifiable. I guess our whole society balances on our level of hunger: a scale that distinguishes us either as progressive individuals or as cutthroat savages. The line is much thinner than most people realize. Once that line is crossed, all of our progressive inclusiveness reverts back to brute clannishness.

Rooney came out of the kitchen. "Holy hell! You're cleaning house or what, guy?" He dried his bald head again and began tallying up everything on the counter.

"Hold up."

He looked up at me.

"I actually don't have enough to pay for all this."

"You're silly. What ya got?"

"Not enough," I said, knowing that I had about a thumb's worth of salt and an AA battery in my pocket as currency. Dejected, I sluggishly put the groceries back one by one.

"Hang on there, guy. From the look of your belt, I'd say you need them."

We both were silent for a few seconds.

He opened up a large paper bag. "Bring those back here. I'll tell you what we can do, guy."

Part of me was ecstatic that he was giving me these commodities, but I was also frustrated that I would be indebted to yet another grocer.

"The Mardi Gras parade will pass near here, and I'll have a serving station. Normally, I'm fine manning the kitchen alone. But I'll need someone to help prepare stuff ahead of time for that. How about you come early Mardi Gras morning and work for me?"

"I can do that. So they approved of the parade?"

"Yeah." He eyed me intently. "And here." He reached into a fridge beneath the counter and put a wrapped sandwich in the bag. "That's a muffaletta. It's a few days old, and I don't like to keep 'em any longer than that."

"I…I really can't thank you enough, Mr. Rooney." I grabbed the bag of groceries. No one hadn't done anything kind for me in so long. It felt weird. It felt right.

"Now, you listen." He pointed his finger in my chest. "This is a gentleman's agreement. I'm not sure if you young men ever heard of such a thing, but this is a binding contract."

"Oh, I'll be here. No question." I squirmed away from the pressure of his fingertip.

"All right, then." He walked from behind the counter toward me. We shook hands, and then he unlocked the front door.

"Thanks again. Really." I also put my book inside the bag.

"Oh, I'll work it out of you." He held the door open.

I passed outside, and a small crowd of people was waiting on the curb. Professionally dressed women and men wearing suits. Refounders, I thought. All clearly younger than me, probably straight out of college. None of them saw me because they were all engrossed in their devices. The logo of a flying eagle's silhouette marked the back. These must be the new phones that Octave had mentioned. The "Eagle," I think he called it. A few Redsleeves waited, as well, with folded arms. They stepped slightly aside as I passed them. They each had visible sidearms and stunners. I felt their eyes following me, over-analyzing the situation to create problems to resolve. None of them initiated anything, though.

Archbishop Fullerton Cafeteria

Mira was quickly getting used to having Mondays off as she awoke fully rested without the strain of a lesson plan to create and dictate. Instead, she made herself a cup of green tea and toasted a bagel while thinking about herself, not her students. Mira had learned to cherish these sweet, yet rare, times when her mind was hers and hers alone. It was the way she used to think before she'd discovered teaching and made the unconscious decision to devote her life to attaining even one ounce of progress within society. She could read a novel in those days. She could play music whenever she wanted. She could go for a walk and think about trees. She could do things that people do.

She decided to visit Derek. Visiting hours did not start for some time, so she would bring an instrument and play with some of the street performers until then. She set her mug on the kitchen table and walked over to her instruments. She crouched and examined the crack in her acoustic guitar, thinking that soon she'd save up enough to buy a brand-new style of guitar that had more pitch and tone variations. She lifted the old guitar and had only played a few notes with her thumb when a string broke. Lugging this around the city might get a little cumbersome anyway, she thought. Her route to and from the jail would be considerably longer because she wasn't cutting through the New Carré again for anything. The guitar didn't have a shoulder strap, either, so she set it back down on its stand. She picked up her penny whistle from a small pillow. The winner, she thought. Light, easy to carry, and not suspicious. No one expected it, even most street musicians, but it was always welcomed. She stroked the smooth surface and set her fingers in the holes. She put her lips to it.

As she flexed her diaphragm, her Eagle powered on and rang. The new phone could be manually turned off; however, if someone called or texted, it powered itself on, just in case of an emergency. She hated that feature.

City Hall Calling...

"Hello?"

"Yes. Ms. Roche?"

"This is she."

"Hello, my name is Dennis Galloway at City Hall. I understand you need a food permit?"

"Yes, that's correct."

"Where are you having your event?"

"Archbishop Fullerton High School."

"Okay, everything has been processed. We just need to send an inspector to approve of the kitchen conditions."

"Okay, that's fine."

"It's really nothing. We just need to know that there aren't any blatant health code violations. When will be best for you this week to meet him?"

She thought for a moment. Knowing she'd be too busy teaching the rest of the week, she said, "Mondays are really the only days I can take time out of the classroom."

"Oh, well, are you available this morning, then?"

If there was a way to sigh in silence, Mira did so, putting the penny whistle back on the pillow. "Yes, I can be available today."

"All right then. I'll send someone out to the school—say 10:30?"

"Yes, sir, just tell him to meet me at the front gate."

"I'll let him know."

"Thanks, Mr. Galloway. I'm glad you got my message."

"I didn't receive any message. I got a call yesterday morning from a colleague who told me you needed this ASAP. You called my office?"

"I did a few times. I stopped by a week ago."

"Oh. Sorry, I guess no one told me."

Mira rolled her eyes. "That's fine. Thank you, sir."

"Okay, you have a good day, Ms. Roche."

"You too, sir." She pushed the cancel button. "That *fucking* guy didn't even give him the message," she whispered to herself. Mira thought that teaching and cursing didn't mix, at least for female teachers, so she had suppressed her tendency to curse even outside of the classroom, making it taboo even in private. But there were exceptions.

Realizing that she would not have time to go to the jail before the inspection, she ate her bagel and prepared to shower. She reactivated her Eagle.

Inspector coming at 10:30 today to view kitchen, then approve permit[8:46AM]¬

OK. I'm at a conference. Check in with the staff beforehand.[8:47AM]¬ Principal Whitman

The kitchen staff worked on Mondays, preparing most of the food for the week without any interruption. Mira checked her Eagle as she walked through the front gate of Fullerton. 10:16 a.m. If the inspection didn't last long, she might have time to visit Derek before noon, she thought.

The school campus, eerie and still, was silent in the absence of students. There was something haunting about empty school buildings, Mira had always thought, especially when she was young, as if something gravely wrong had happened there. It was either haunting or mystical, she couldn't really decide. Maybe there's not much difference between the two, she mused. The students were challenging, sure, but they kept the place alive and moving. Birds fluttered from the small, newly planted birch trees, and squirrels bounded across the grassy school grounds.

She entered the kitchen door, and two staff members jumped. They both wore white chef shirts; an older black lady stood leaning on a steel table, while a younger and slightly overweight white woman had been crouching down near the wall next to the fridge. "Hi. I'm sorry. I'm a teacher here," she extended her hand, "Mira Roche."

"Mary Brown." Her black hands were slick with sweat and her yellow eyes weary.

"So, I'm just letting y'all know that a City Hall inspector is on his way."

"For what?"

"I'm having a project for the kids to cook something for the St. Joseph's Altar, and I need a permit for that because it's technically 'an event.'"

Mary adjusted her black hairnet. She exhaled, glanced at the other cook, and shook her head.

"Is there a problem, Ms. Mary?"

She shrugged. "When you say that they coming?"

"Should be here at eleven."

Mary looked down at her Slipguard work shoes, shiny from the oil in the air. "Okay, then. What you say your name was?"

"Mira. My students call me Ms. Roche, of course."

Mary smiled. "Oh, so you're the Ms. Roche I hear so much about."

Mira raised her eyebrows.

"My daughter's in your class. Effy."

"Oh, yes, of course. She's a pleasure to have in class. Really."

"Thank you. Well, we need to tidy up before that inspector come. We'll talk later."

"Sounds great, Ms. Brown. I can help."

Mary looked at the other cook and said kindly, "We'll clean it faster if you don't."

After 10:45, Mira decided to wait in the shade of a tree for the inspector. She scrolled through her Eagle to make the time pass.

Try the new Bloody Welshy today! Just like a Bloody Mary except with the new Elmer's Ryan White Whiskey instead of vodka. Same deals on Blood Marys today$^{10:00AM}$¬ Welshy

Whiskey wasn't her thing anyway, even if it didn't look like regular whiskey. She scrolled through her other notifications.

> UPDATE: DUE TO RECENT VIOLATIONS, THE 10 P.M. CURFEW WILL BE STRICTLY ENFORCED. IT IS OUR DUTY TO ENSURE YOUR SAFETY. THANK YOU FOR YOUR COMPLIANCE. 9:00AM¬ Gulf Guard of America

She sighed, scrolling some more.

> San Juan Studios begin filming a post-apocalyptic thriller in New Orleans, supporting the rebuilding process 11AM¬ chasethetruth

Mira wondered where they were filming.

Chapter 11

People tend to never miss an opportunity to bullshit, no matter the occasion or situation, except at times of someone's death. Other than trying to make the deceased's life sound more important, there's not much to talk about. We tend to share awkward moments mostly in silence with others in the midst of fear, sorrow, curiosity, celebration, and grim acceptance.

That's how Choppy and I were as we waited for Judge. We shared my last hand-rolled cigarette on the levee, as quiet as Mr. Buras's corpse that lay rolled in burlap and salt in the bed of Choppy's truck. The sun had not risen yet, and Lake Pontchartrain was simply a dark void except for the rhythmic waves that slapped against the shore. Choppy and Mr. Buras had been close friends, and Buras had told him once that he wished he could be buried in his hometown in Plaquemines Parish, which was all but eroded except for a small portion of Belle Chasse. So Choppy suggested that he'd like to fulfill his wishes despite Plaquemines now being the open sea. That mariner's bond, I guess. That's another reason why I kept my mouth shut as we sat on that levee. No matter what I said about Buras, Choppy probably already knew it.

Choppy handed the cigarette to me. The moon shone in his white stubble, and his eyes, nose, and mouth were all one with the obscure darkness of the dawn, as if he were wearing an old Mardi Gras mask with holes cut out of flesh-colored plastic for the mouth, the nose, and each eye.

"Who's taking care of Ol' Sulphur?"

"Octave." Choppy licked his lips. He stared out to the horizon, where the first haze of dawn spilled into the sky. "Here he is."

A boat's headlight approached from the dark water, quiet and slow from afar, yet fast and loud up close, like an airplane in the night sky. The rumble of the boat's engine overtook the sound of the waves. I rose and walked down the levee to my makeshift dock. I had planted a post near the water and hung a kerosene lantern on a nail. I walked over to a second post, which, like the first, was locked in a tire with concrete, lit a candle, and quickly covered it with a bottomless rum bottle, creating a hurricane lantern of sorts.

Judge brought his fishing boat to a halt between the two lighted posts and killed the engine. The waves resumed their rhythm. I walked over to help him onto shore, but Judge hopped off the boat effortlessly.

"Don't have much darkness left." The smell of dipping tobacco wafted in my face as he spoke. "Where's Choppy?"

"Over here." He stepped down the levee.

"Are y'all bringing guns?"

I hadn't yet told anyone that my gun had been confiscated. Acting as if I did have one, though, I said, "Wasn't going to."

Judge spit. "Good. We don't need to give the Redsleeves any more reason to search the boat if they spot us out there. I have my work shotgun and that's all legit. But here," he gave us each three shotgun shells. "Just in case."

Choppy wiped his nose. "Ready to get on wit' it, yeah?"

As we walked over the levee, commotion erupted near Choppy's truck. Small feet tapped against the bed and the ground next to it. In the emerging dawn, I could see the back of the truck jerk, as if someone or something had jumped out of it. A slight rustle in the briars, then nothing.

Judge spit. "Coyotes. Don't take 'em long. If we'd a waited much longer, wouldn't be much left."

The moon gave Mr. Buras's body a slight outline. He lay like a mummy: ankles tied together, arms crossed over the chest, body covered in salt and wrapped in burlap.

Choppy lowered the tailgate and grabbed Mr. Buras's ankles. He pulled him out just enough that I could grab his shoulders. I expected his body to slump when we lifted him from the truck, but rigor mortis had stiffened his body like a wooden board. We lugged him up and over the levee and onto Judge's boat.

The boat's ice bin was big enough to store Mr. Buras, but we had no ice to keep him cool.

The sun wasn't quite over the horizon, and the overcast sky helped keep us shrouded in darkness for a while longer. The wind and spray off the lake were cool and refreshing. It smelled fresh, of salt and slightly of fish—a smell any Louisiana boy relishes. The north horizon was gray and watery. I turned to look at the south and witnessed a grim shadow of downtown New Orleans. The cityscape emerged as a black shadow before a dark ash sky. The buildings, solid gray in silhouette, looked like tombstones. A single red light blinked on top of each building to warn McMason's helicopters. Other than that, the city was shrouded in darkness.

Lake Pontchartrain exuded a timelessness that felt cyclical. Native American tribes and post-Beckham clans. Old pirates and modern pirates. Mercenaries and WWII trainees. The sun had risen by now, yet the clouds kept the sky gray. As we entered the Rigolets, the cross-waters of the lake and the Gulf of Mexico, we approached Fort Pike, which had long been abandoned. The redbrick structure had withstood the onslaught from Hurricane Beckham, but weeds now grew through the cracks. The narrow gun slits were the only windows into its dark emptiness. I did sense an odd presence as we drove past, as if we were being watched. We drove through the intracoastal waterways, full of brackish marshes and shore birds. The type of environment Bienville had found centuries before. I wanted to believe that future mariners could see these wetlands rich with pelicans and blue herons, alligators and dolphins, crabs and speckled trout, otters and manatees. But I knew it was only a matter of time before it would vanish. We witnessed a doomed land being consumed by the Gulf of Mexico as if a giant nibbled at living flesh in a toying, tortuous manner.

I was tired and wanted to nap, but I refused to sleep. I wanted to see this "land" with my own eyes. There was no telling if this marsh-land would become a pumped-in beach or another oil rig. If I lived that long, of course. We New Orleanians were no different than the wildlife of the Louisiana coast: just surviving, day to day, without knowing whether something higher and beyond our control had it in for us.

We approached the remnants of the old Plaquemines Parish. At some point, we coasted along a row of leaning telephone poles that had once demarcated the old Highway 23. People used to drive auto-mobiles where we now motored over open water.

Judge spit in his coffee-can spittoon. "This is Belle Chasse, accord-ing to the coordinates. My mom was Navy and lived at the base out here somewhere."

He accelerated, and I sat lower so as not to fall over the side. Judge spit in his can and nodded at me. I slumped down and lay on the deck. The sun slipped through the clouds, and I watched them turn from silver to gold. Judge called out over the drone of the engine and the spray of the sea, "It's gonna be a while. Go ahead and knock off if you want."

The boat bobbed up and down as it cut over the waves, like a crib swaying. A squadron of white pelicans soared above. My eyelids closed.

Her red dress hugged her hips as they swayed from side to side. Mira's reddish-brown hair was longer than usual, midway down her back. She never used to let it get longer than her shoulders, which she nor-mally kept covered from the public eye. Several brown birthmarks scattered about the soft skin there; I called it her "constellation."

Mira waved a paper napkin from above her head, and I fol-lowed behind doing the same. A long train of people snaked around the grand ballroom. I never knew why people called these "sec-ond lines." Typically, there was only one line of people. White New Orleanians customarily second-lined at weddings, whereas black

New Orleanians second-lined for funerals. Never knew why, just that it was tradition. A celebration that blurred the lines of beginning and end.

Fitzmorris was there, but not second-lining. He stood off to the side, wearing a vintage tuxedo and a top hat. He was smoking a tobacco pipe. At the time, it seemed normal even though he would never do such a thing.

As we paraded around the room, we passed several food-serving stations. Some had crawfish étouffée, shrimp-mirliton casserole, and small po-boys. I found it odd that Renny Rooney managed to be at all of them.

After the second line was over, Mira and I went outside to a courtyard and sat next to a fountain. She crossed her legs toward me and her dress fell down her legs. She pulled her hair in a ponytail and rested her head on my shoulder. My fingers felt the soft dress bunched at her waist. It was like the old days. I hadn't lied to her yet. I hadn't left her yet.

We leaned in closer for a kiss, but she drew back, looking beyond me and breathing heavily. Someone cocked a gun behind me, but I just kept reaching for her lips. She pushed me into the fountain, and the gunshot rang out above as I tasted salt.

Wet and cold, I woke from the bottom of Judge's boat. Some Gulf water had splashed over the side when he'd slowed the boat down. I rubbed my eyes. "Are we here?"

Neither Judge nor Choppy answered. I stood. A law enforcement boat slowly approached us. Five men stood on the deck, wearing blue camouflage. Judge said, "Gulf Guard of America. Both of you are my fishing crew. Got it?"

We nodded.

"Go sit on the cooler bench."

"Hold up. You talking 'bout where Wade is?"

Judge spit into the water. "They might suspect something's up if you both keep glancing at it."

Choppy and I reluctantly obliged and took positions atop Mr. Buras's hearse.

The GGA patrol drifted alongside our starboard side.

One of the Guardsmen crossed his arms and called out, "Good morning."

Judge called back, "Good morning, Officers."

"Where you hurrying to?"

"I'm a Contract Harvester for the Louisiana Wildlife and Fisheries. Agent number 30893. In charge of eliminating invasive or destructive species."

The officer leaned and spoke to another Guardsman, who went inside the cabin.

"Okay, ID number 30893, what brings you out here this far?"

"Hunting the barracuda. Their population exploded after Beckham, and they're disturbing the ecosystem's balance."

The officer uncrossed his arms and went inside the cabin of the GGA patrol boat. We waited in silence for a few minutes except for the sloshing of the boat in the waves. I detected an odor similar to spoiled fish, but I knew that it wasn't. I looked between my thighs, trying to envision Mr. Buras's body underneath me.

The officer returned to his deck. "Your ID number and harvest registration check out, Mr. Justin Portico. I'm gonna have to come aboard and check your license, however, just to verify that is who you are, of course."

Judge swallowed. "Sir, I will gladly provide you with that information. However, I do need to point out that boarding my vessel is against federal regulations. This is the jurisdiction of Red Birch Security Services, Inc., not the Gulf Guard of America."

Clearly annoyed, the officer spoke with one of his Guardsmen, pointing his fingers.

"Have you seen any other boats out here?"

"Sometimes."

"In contact with any of them?"

"No, sir."

"Okay, you can go about your harvest, Mr. Portico." He looked over to his other men and gestured with erratic motions, still clearly annoyed. The boat turned inland and sped away, spraying seawater behind it.

We sat in silence for a few moments with the boat hull slapping the waves beneath. With his index finger, Judge scooped the depleted dip from his jaw, wet and slimy like a fat dead slug, and flung it into the water. The breeze halted and the stench of Mr. Buras's body drifted up to us. Judge started the engine, checked the coordinates, and cruised along the saltwater above a drowned parish, once famous for its fishermen but now inhabited only by the fish.

Judge said, "It'll be a little while still. Ya'll just relax."

I sat on the deck and pulled my book out of my small bag. Slumping down to avoid the wind, I began reading:

Without gunpowder and firearms, it seems that the war machine is reverting back to its old standard of steel and stone. The war machine had been perfected long before the advent of exploding gunpowder. The war machine is not like other machines. Whereas others wear down over time, the war machine gets more efficient and productive the longer it runs. If the smallest piece breaks, a regular machine fails to operate. The war machine, however, has a way of replacing the resistant pieces with more agile pieces quickly. How foolish and naive I was to actually believe we, or I, for that matter, could stop it. What disturbs me more than anything, though, is that our scientists are exploring different ways to kill. Genocide was much easier with machine guns and bombs, but without them, it's becoming more of a science that needs exploration. No telling what they'll develop next as an alternative. Our brightest minds are working day and night to bring forth mastery in the world of death, not life. No wonder we are a doomed race.

In church, we always were taught that this world was a place of love and peace. A place where a constant state of peace

is interrupted from time to time with war and unrest. Mother,
I am sorry to say that I don't believe such things anymore. We
are, and have been, since the beginning, in a constant state of
war interrupted by sporadic periods of peace. Peace is only a
brief opportunity for the war machine to sleep and recharge…

I closed my eyes and drifted off to sleep again. My new reading
hobby hadn't overtaken my habit of sleeping. Slumber was quite an
effective and fulfilling way to pass the time in the absence of electric
entertainment. Now I had to adjust to spending my free time otherwise. Sleep's most satisfying in the complete absence of dreams.
My body felt the boat halt, and I awoke. I stood, the wind cool
on my face. In the distance, a spinner shark lunged playfully out
of the water.

Judge pinched some dip from a fresh can and wedged it into his
jowls. "Welcome to Buras, Louisiana."

Blue water draped every horizon as if we were in the open
ocean. And, to an extent, we were. But somewhere below lay the
remains of a civilization that had once survived on an entangling
alliance between the oil and fishing industries. Now, only fish and
oil remained there. Perhaps, one day, deep-sea divers would explore
this area like they had for the *Titanic* or Atlantis. Beneath the blue
water, I guess the world hadn't changed much despite being sub-
merged. Everything just needed to eat, escape, and reproduce. As
long as that cycle continues, nothing begins or ends. Everything in
the middle is just bullshit to make it less painful.

Judge dropped anchor, and Choppy opened the ice chest that
had been Mr. Buras's temporary casket. The odor hit us in the face.
Death is bad enough without the sense of smell replacing the presence of sound. I walked over and held my breath. Choppy and I
lifted the stiff body while Judge tied a cinderblock to it.

"I didn't even know his real name."

Choppy licked his lips. "Mr. Wade. Wade Reid. Come on, nah.
Let's get 'im home."

Mr. Buras's body splashed water back on us. I could taste the salt, perhaps a mixture of the embalming salt and the natural salt of the sea. The sharks and crabs would probably eat his remains shortly, and he would be all the happier in death for it.

We were silent, each giving our own internal eulogy. He had been there to give us fish and citrus fruits, sure. However, he lived a life of respect, honesty, and simplicity. Most of all, he lived without bitterness. That's something we all hadn't yet mastered. And that was the only way to survive healthily in this world: without bitterness. We had only seen New Orleans destroyed once. Wade Reid, however, had seen his entire community wash away with several past hurricanes. Moreover, he'd watched his homeland erode bit by bit, while we New Orleans people were too full of ourselves to even notice, or care. Well, Beckham sure made us notice and care. He'd watched his hometown of Buras gradually sink into the sea like a cancer that no one took the effort, nor cared, to remedy. And that was before New Orleans was ruined. Of all the horror that Wade Reid had witnessed, it never claimed him. I feared that without him, it wouldn't be long before anguish and hate would poison our aspiring good spirits. I never really heeded any words from priests, but perhaps Father Fullerton was right. A fisherman—at least Wade Reid—is a man of faith, of selflessness, of nourishment. Now it was up to us to take the bait.

Inspection Location 2384;
Contact: Ms. Roche

The longer she waited for the inspector, the more tempting a bloody Mary became. She had tried calling Galloway, but dialing the number he had called from wouldn't connect the other way around. So she just waited in the shade. Across the street, a group of street musicians walked toward Baladucci Drive. One young man with a mustache carried a guitar strapped over his shoulder. A young woman, unhealthily thin, scraped her boots across the pavement. Half of her head was shaved and her linen dress blew freely as a flag does upon a flagpole. An older man carried a black leather case. Mira sighed as she reluctantly held back from joining them.

A city-issued purple sedan pulled up to the front gate at 11:13. Mira swallowed to help relieve the dryness in her throat, as if that would digest her anger at the same time. She kept telling herself that she couldn't be abrasive. The kids and the community needed this permit, no matter how irresponsible the city officials were. The car parked just outside the gate in the driveway, and an obese man dislodged himself from between the steering wheel and the seat. His gray shirt fit tight around his gargantuan torso, which overhung his waist and legs. His tan suit coat hung from his shoulders, not able to fit around his waist. He reached into the car and grabbed a large Styrofoam cup. Shaking the ice inside, he slurped the remaining soda through the straw. His clothes smelled of fried food. He said, "You Miss Roach?" with breath reeking of garlic.

"Yes." Mira concentrated on breathing regularly to hide her anger. She felt like she was suffocating as she held her breath every few seconds.

He looked at her for a moment. "Where's the kitchen at?" He wiped his nose with his shirt cuff.

Not even an apology, she thought as she steamed inside. She pointed at the white building across the lawn and turned toward it. Ears burning and temples taut, she walked fast through the grass. Mira didn't turn around, but she knew that he would be waddling at a much slower pace. If he had apologized at least, I'd have suggested the sidewalk around the garden, she thought, but *fuck* him; he can roll that fat ass across the grass for all I care or get some exercise out of it. Even though she rarely verbalized cuss words, she often thought them.

Inspector finally here[11:15AM]¬

Mira waited by the door. The sounds of light wheezing and shoes scraping along concrete let her know that the inspector had survived the walk. Without looking back, she opened the door for him. Sweat streamed from his forehead, and the shirt around his belly had become a wet, dark gray. He slurped the remaining beverage from his cup.

"Our kitchen's right here, sir."

"I see that." He waddled inside a few steps and looked up at the ceiling and around at the walls. Shuffling further inside, he took in the condiment bottles and supplies on the shelves. He looked down at the floor. He looked at the doors of the food cooler for a long time. Mira wondered what about the cooler would demand his attention for that long. The inspector had gotten to the far end of the kitchen when the rat darted across the floor behind him. Mira's heart leapt into her throat as she muffled a shriek, squeaking herself like a rodent. He turned around and looked at her. "You say something, Ms. Roach?"

She half smiled and shook her head. He turned to the side and studied the ice machine against the wall, scratching his sweaty, bulbous belly.

Mira started sweating herself. She looked at the lower shelf near the wall. A corner had been chewed out of a bag, and yellow grits spilled out onto the floor. A few tiny brown pellets of rat feces were visible under the wire shelf. It could pass for some kind of grain, but she knew better, and the inspector would certainly know the difference. She stepped in front of the shelf with her back to the wall. The hair on her arms stuck straight up. Her instinct was to leave the kitchen as soon as possible, but she needed that permit. The St. Joseph's Altar was more important than her squeamishness. Now it was clear why the staff had been so jumpy.

The inspector turned around and waddled toward Mira. "All right, Ms. Roach. There's some problems."

Tiny feet scampered behind her, and she inhaled aggressively and held her breath with her eyes shut. She wiped her forehead and exhaled in a controlled manner as would a training athlete. "Yes?"

"These handles here," he pointed at the small cooler, "should be facing downward. They are facing upward, and that can cause buildup of bacteria. You see, things can fall down and build up if they are upside down. But, if they are facing down, things won't catch there; they can fall down and be cleaned up later."

"Okay." Her biceps ached from clutching them as she stood with her arms folded.

"So, we need someone to come in and fix those. Also, I noticed that the ice machine is about twenty feet from the grill. It really should be farther away to ensure the ice doesn't get contaminated from people handling raw meats."

I'd say twenty feet is far enough to avoid that, she thought. "Okay."

"Someone will also have to come in and move either the grill or the ice machine and make them farther apart. That will take more time because I take it the grill is hooked up to the gas line, while the ice machine is hooked up to the water line. So some extensions will have to be made."

"And what regulation is that again?"

"Yeah, the grill and ice machine need to be at least twenty-five feet apart."

"Yes, sir. I understand that. What is the actual regulation number so I can tell the principal?"

He looked at the wall. "I, um, can't think of it right now. But it's a common violation."

Well, if it's common, then you should know it offhand, she thought. "Okay."

"And this I noticed." He pointed at the paper towel dispenser on the wall above the wash basin. "You see how the paper towels are near this AC vent on the ceiling?"

"Uh-huh." They have a good five feet between them, she noticed.

"You see, over time dust will build up and fall and contaminate the paper towels. And you wouldn't want to jeopardize the health of our students."

"So, just move it to the other side of the sink, then?"

"Well," he looked at the vent. "Actually, the sink needs to be moved, too, because the vent will make things unsanitary around the sink, and that's where you clean things. So that will be a problem, too." He nodded and shook the ice at the bottom of his cup. "We need to send a contractor out here to make these modifications before we can proceed with your application. In my experience, it may cost about two thousand dollars."

She cringed at the cost estimate, considering he'd used zero criteria. "How long will this take?"

"Well, each contract is auctioned. So simply getting a contractor may take up to two weeks. And with the extent of the services needed here, it may be another two weeks."

"A month? I'm afraid we don't have that much time, sir."

He shrugged. "I'm just the inspector."

Mira looked down at her shoes and sighed. She couldn't ask Renny Rooney to donate his whole kitchen for this event. She imagined how she would break the disappointing news to the students.

The inspector then said, "There is, however, a way for you to proceed in a timely fashion."

Mira's eyes slowly rolled up to meet his gaze. She didn't know whether to be hopeful or fearful of what he would say next.

"Look, I want this to happen for you. How about I charge you…

an 'inspection fee,' and you can get the permit as early as the end of the week?"

Despite being remapped, redistricted, and redesigned, New Orleans hadn't changed at all, Mira realized. She had never agreed with how New Orleans did business. She was glad the inspector hadn't noticed the rat infestation, yet she was not surprised that he hadn't. The inept and unqualified somehow got the arbitrary high-paying positions in the city because of probable nepotism and the ability to exploit desperate, well-intentioned people. Maybe that's how they always got away with it. The top qualification for some jobs was not only the knack for sniffing out desperation but also the indifference necessary to bill people for such desperation. And she needed that permit, more so than her ethics could protest.

"What's the fee?"

"Three hundred fifty. Cash, of course."

"Okay, but I don't have that on me right now."

He gave Mira a blank business card with a handwritten phone number on the back. "Don't bother texting. I don't respond to those. You'll have to call me later so I can collect."

"I'm sorry, your name? I don't believe you introduced yourself."

He smiled. "You just call that number and pay that fee so you can get your permit on time, Ms. Roach."

"*Roche.*"

"What?"

"My name is *Roche*. The *e* is like in café. I am not a cockroach." She held her breath and clenched her teeth so she wouldn't slip and call him one.

He shrugged and placed his empty cup on the food prep counter. "All right. I'll give you till the end of the week to pay the fee. After that, your maintenance request will be in the queue." He exited the kitchen.

Mira's phone buzzed.

How did the inspection go?[11:32AM]
Principal Whitman

It went well. We should be approved by the end of the week[11:32AM]⌐

Never doubted you, child[11:33AM]⌐ Principal Whitman

She skirted her way out of the rat-infested kitchen that could easily have been $500 to approve if the inspector had noticed.

Mrs. Brown and the other staff member were right outside. "What did he say?"

Mira, quiet for a few moments, said, "Everything went well."

Mrs. Brown sighed in relief. "He didn't say nothin'?"

"About the rats?"

She nodded.

"Nope."

She wiped her forehead. "They just started comin' around about a week ago. At first, we thought it was just one and we can go 'head and take care of it ourselves. But they lot more now. We about to call Mrs. Whitman."

"She needs to know, sure."

Mrs. Brown looked to her colleague. "Awright, let's go put the traps back."

"Thanks," Mira said.

She walked across the grass of the campus. A squirrel darted from a small birch tree, and Mira jumped back, shrieking. The squirrel disappeared up the tree. Noting the time, Mira realized visiting hours would soon close at the jail. She'd have to wait another week to see him. Perhaps she would write him another letter.

She walked out of the school gate, thinking, Now I'm not only bribing the city, but keeping it secret. Of all of the blunders and ineptitude of this New Orleans, there's one thing the city has perfected: corruption. The St. Joseph's Altar was a unique cultural event in New Orleans; however, culture does not come free. They've made sure of that, Mira thought. Over time, city officials had discovered how to capitalize on, and even extort, residents and business owners for taking part in the culture that they themselves had created in the first place. Many people paid without a fuss, but those talented officials were needed for those who didn't. While the politicians themselves were the bullshit artists, their inspectors were the bullshit art dealers. They had the talent of pricing out an opportunity for extortion just right according to demand, and of making people feel thankful for getting extorted. It was a legitimate art.

Her Eagle buzzed.

The Bloody Welshys are a hit! Don't miss out![10:40AM] Welshy

Without a second thought, Mira marched toward Baladucci Drive. Just as her father had once said that a drink helped him remember what New Orleans was about, she thought perhaps a drink was just the thing she needed to *forget* what New Orleans was about.

Chapter 12

When I hooked a fish out of Lake Pontchartrain, it felt as if the blood in my veins had been replaced by electricity. I couldn't even remember the last time I had fished, much less actually caught anything. The elation rendered me temporarily insane, prompting me to speak, even shout, at the unlucky mystery fish that yanked my line and dove for the dark depth of Lake Pontchartrain but was stopped by a sharp pain in the face. It was simply trying to survive, but so was I. Such was life, and I drooled all over my shirt as the animal within me came out.

My arms were rubber, and the redfish finally splashed the surface of the green water. I prayed that the fishing line would not break as I heaved the fish ashore. Its tail whipped, searching the bright void for something to push off. I stood over it in victory. The orange sun reflected off its blood-orange scales. Its awkward mandible, which I always thought made it look like a crudely drawn likeness of a fish, opened wide, reaching for even a single drop of water to tantalize its gills. The black beauty mark near its tail fin gleamed in the light like a pair of eyes. I paced around it in elation, having gained all the confidence in the world. It seemed that, if you could catch a fish, you could accomplish anything. My lungs filled with the cool breeze rolling off the water. I can do this, I thought. I can survive.

As the fish's attempt at breathing slowed, my breathing returned to normal and my confidence melted into oblivion. What do I do now? I asked myself, squatting over it. I had never cleaned or scaled a fish before. It could be done, I knew that. But how? Timidly, I touched the redfish. It twitched and its scales secreted a sticky substance. I wiped my hands on my shirt, staring at the fish helplessly.

A knife. I needed one of those. I grabbed the fish by the mouth and dug the hook out as it used up whatever fight it had left in thrashing around on the grass. I inserted my thumb into its gritty, lukewarm mouth and carried it up and over the levee. If my stomach had been full it might have gotten queasy, ready for anything.

Remembering where I'd left my knife, I put the redfish down on the grass and walked to my garden, which was still a work in progress. I hadn't planted the seeds yet, but the fence roll was unraveled. Finding useful posts to support the chain-link fence was harder than I had thought. I had found some broken iron fence finials with fleurs-de-lis on the tops. Naturally, I was going to use those.

I sorted through the fence pieces and shovels, but found no knife. I looked up, and to my dismay, a coyote trotted up to my fish. Grabbing one of the iron fence pieces, I charged the wild dog with my "spear." The coyote stopped short and lowered its thin orange-and-gray head. I stood over my catch waving my fleur-de-lis spear wildly. "Get away, you mangy bitch!"

It hopped back a few steps and paced in a small circle. I took a few steps closer to it, pounding my iron spear in the grass. "Fuck off!"

It snarled, but turned and fled a few yards. Turning around, it bobbed its head just above the grass. Then it looked me in the eyes with its own fearless blue ones and backed up a few steps.

"Yeah! That's right!" I ran forward and lunged at it with the spear. I missed.

There was a sudden yelp behind me. I turned around and another coyote was running into the debris grove with the redfish between its jaws. My heart sank. I turned toward the coyote that had played me for a fool, and it had run back into the debris fields.

I charged for it through the forest of debris, growling and roaring. Hell, I could have run straight into the entire pack, for all I knew. Briar patches, young pine trees, and whatever else the flood felt like displacing. With a big stick, I thrashed at a briar patch that had grown around a rusty sedan that had vines growing through the hood. Its trunk had popped wide open from bottled-up heat. I stepped up on an overturned toilet on top of a computer printer that looked more like a muddy cinderblock than anything electronic.

"Where are you?!" No sound. Not even a distant peep from a sparrow or the close buzz of a mosquito.

I moved forward, stepping on a broken Spanish tile. I stopped short just before my foot landed on an upturned roofing nail. I had heard horror stories about what people called Hyatt Hospital downtown, which was a hotel converted to a hospital. A slight hum filled my ears, and I looked just ahead. A massive wasp nest the size of a gumbo pot clung to some sort of metal post I belatedly recognized as the mast of an upside-down sailboat. The mast dug into the earth like a makeshift piling, and the hull was suspended in the air about twenty feet with a young pine tree bent across its deck. The drone got louder, so I turned around. The briar patches obstructed my view of any escape route. Just a few feet in, I was completely turned around. I couldn't even see the sedan shrouded in briars. That's when I got scared. Whatever was out there, I was at its mercy. Rumors had spread about tribes of "vagrants" that lived within this filth and scavenged the ruins for anything they could find to make meth—once-civilized folks that returned to their old neighborhoods to rebuild but turned to the wrong thing to cut the sorrow. The Redsleeves never responded to those rumors, which prompted me to believe that they were, in fact, true.

A twig snapped to my right, and my heart sank as my neck snapped in that direction. Something big enough to snap a branch was near. Could the coyotes be closing in for the final course? Another wild boar?

The drone grew louder; however, I realized it did not come from the wasp nest above, but from my left. I followed the sound, and within only a few feet, I felt the cool lake breeze on my cheeks. I reached Lake Pontchartrain without the impediment of a levee. Relieved, I now had some sense of direction to backtrack to my bar. Then I saw an oyster boat coasting along the shore to my left. So I turned left. That familiar drone faded as the boat slowly coasted away from me. I followed it, sidestepping industrial-grade freezers that smelled of rancid fish.

The boat idled and drifted toward the shore. A levee rose to my right, and the metal posts looked familiar. Home was just over the levee, and relief revived my breath. But who were these people, and why were they stopping here? Voices carried over the hum of their engine. I breathed heavily again. I needed to reveal my presence before they came ashore. My legs ached with each long, hard step, and my palms were locked on a defensive fleur-de-lis.

The voices stopped once they saw me. I waited for them to make the first contact. As I approached the vessel, which was still about ten feet from shore, it seemed like an eternity before one of them spoke. "Ahoy, bruh!"

I recognized the Manchacs who had given me the Elmer's Ryan. Gris, the young black man with dreads, and Copper, the gruff white man with orangutan-Popeye arms. Other men were on the boat with them. One man had strapped a freshly killed brown pelican across his chest.

"Ahoy back," I called out.

Copper cupped his hands around his mouth, which made his elbows cock out at an extreme angle. "Checking up on you, is all."

"I'm fine. Sold out of that whiskey already."

All the men looked at the pelican hunter, and he spoke to them. Copper asked, "You need another one?"

"If you got one."

"How about you let us come ashore, son."

I'll admit that I haven't made the brightest decisions; however, I can smell a crossroads when I come to it. By agreeing, I'd be in business with them from here on. Giving them an opportunity to make me an offer was simply a binding contract. But men make most decisions based on their stomachs, especially if they are empty. Being hungry took on a different meaning at this time and place. We weren't immersed in a bountiful land, like the rest of the United States, where companies fought each other to get us everything we could ever want.

We were on our own, and we had to fight to get anything. So, when you were hungry, you stayed that way unless you got lucky.

I wish I had learned how unapologetic the world was at an earlier age. I wish my teachers or my uncle had told me that, so I would have grown up seeing life for what it was: a blank slab that would not build a house by itself. If I'd have known that then, I would have learned something useful like basic farming, hunting, or some mechanical skill with which to barter for my essentials. But instead I believed all that malarkey about how going to college would magically build a mansion for me. They told us that somehow the twenty-first century was different from the past, but it wasn't. Savage or civilized, ancient or modern, capitalist or communist, first world or third world, rural or urban, foreign or indigenous, scholastic or corporate, the world consists of two kinds of people: those who produce and those who do not. And the latter must leech off of the producers to live, either by enslaving themselves to the producers or slyly enslaving the producers for themselves.

I needed Fitzmorris, but his store was barren. Rooney's grocery was well stocked, but the Redsleeves had me on their watch list. Mr. Buras was dead. I had other people's guns without any ammunition, so I couldn't hunt anything. Judge had plenty of wild hog cuts, but I had nothing to trade for them. Clearly the hogs and the coyotes were staking out my place and eating anything I could produce. Everyone knew by now that my bar was completely out of alcohol. If I got hungry enough, I'd have to sell my friends' guns for food. To avoid that, I made the decision to call the Manchacs ashore.

Chapter 13

What is life but a compromise of principle for some stake in this world? At least, that's what I told myself in the truck ride to Fitzmorris's store. At daybreak I had no liquor inventory, but now I had full bottles of Elmer's Ryan Whiskey, Kepler's Vodka, and Monte Ligero Dark Rum. Tobacco was in my possession, and now I had almost enough to trade for a week's worth of hot food from Rooney's Grocery or probably two weeks' worth at Huey's café. Or, if I spent it wisely, a month's worth of food and supplies. Also, a small stipend of U.S. cash for gasoline. And all that for a simple deal with the Manchac pirates. Twice a week, I would pick up a large box in a designated location not far from the crossroads and bring it to the end of Oyster Shell Road before nightfall. They did not say what would be in it, and I didn't ask. And for doing that, I received a parcel containing liquor, tobacco, duck jerky, and anything special I needed. The Manchacs claimed to hijack government supply boats en route to McMason's depot near the Rigolets, so I slept well knowing that I was making a living at the expense of the mercenaries.

The term *criminal* is simply relative. Weren't men like Jefferson and Adams criminals in the eyes of the redcoats? Was not Martin Luther King Jr. a criminal in the eyes of the segregated South? Was I not a criminal already for storing guns that had been unconstitutionally claimed by a mercenary corporation with the blessing of a highly conservative federal government? Wasn't Fitzmorris a criminal by illegally dealing salt, a basic necessity for survival? Was Octave a criminal for hiding marked books in his store? Was Joshua a criminal for simply trying to inform us of the truth? When someone is paid money by either a company or a government for a service, isn't there some social contract that is made between the parties that essentially benefits the payee's benefactor in some way? Sure, I told myself. More importantly, I believed it.

People needed to know that I was back in business, and someone at Fitzmorris's store, if not Fitzmorris himself, would spread the word. I needed gasoline regardless. I parked in the parking lot, which had only two cars I didn't recognize. I entered the store and did not see Fitzmorris. Other than a few cans of tomato paste and bottles of mustard, dust covered the shelves. I smelled buttery grits and walked over to Huey's café. Two men I didn't know were eating their meager breakfasts alone at separate tables. I approached the counter and found that *The Declaration* rack had been recently replenished. I grabbed one, and before I could read the headline, Huey stuck his head out of the kitchen door.

"Oh, it's just you." He ducked back in the kitchen.

I shook my head. Fucking Huey. Figuring that Fitzmorris would pop up eventually, I sat at a table and opened up Joshua's latest issue of *The Declaration*.

The man sitting at the next table slurped a spoonful of grits every seven seconds. I counted to be sure.

Revival of the Flesh: Return of Carnival
Editorial: January 22

Apparently, before I moved here, "laissez le bon temps rouler" was a common saying; however, the times have not been good lately. Mardi Gras is anything but normal to the rest of the nation. TV and the internet have depicted it as widespread debauchery. But no matter how many Jump-jive posts you've seen on your feed, that's not really the meaning of Mardi Gras, and no one knows that more than New Orleanians. For them, it is normalcy. Without it, things would be just too strange. Things have been awfully strange since McMason the Monster banned Mardi Gras parades upon taking command. To be fair, I guess there was nothing to celebrate.

The city's schools, only three at this time, have come together to bring back Mardi Gras. Principal Whitman of T.S. Laurette School has been the leader in the project they call "Laissez Les Bon Temps de Rebondir," which translates to "Let the Good Times Rebound." Whitman and several other educators have finally convinced McMason to allow Mardi Gras's return under the conditions that the students will be the center of the celebration. Principal Whitman says, "It's been wonderful working with the students and teachers on this project. I haven't seen such fire in their eyes. Many of them have never been a part of such a communal event as this." Her school has been active in cleaning up the aftermath of Hurricane Beckham, and the students have gathered on weekends to pick up debris in places like Lafayette Square, where they intend to have a small music festival at the parade's end. Instead of elaborate floats and krewes as in past years, the students will be riding modest floats that they've been building in class. Art and music teacher Mira Roche, who coined the new project's name, is excited to be a part of such a historic development. She grew up in the New Orleans area until relocating to Houston to finish school after Beckham and then to France to pursue an advanced degree in music; however, she returned home after only one semester abroad. Roche says, "The Mardi Gras experience changes as you grow up with it. Eventually you start to feel like you've already seen all there is to be seen. This year, though, is very different. I've never experienced a Carnival quite as exceptional as this."

The parade will end at Lafayette Square, where the proposed music festival will feature students as well as some local musicians. Roche says, "This city has always been gifted when it comes to music, and we plan to give that gift back to the city."

Parade-goers can enjoy food and drinks from local booths and vendors. The proceeds will help the schools purchase an efficient air-conditioning system. Principal Whitman says, "This may very well be the turning point for this community— when things start coming back to normal."

Supposedly, Mardi Gras started with the Catholics, which means it really started with, more sensibly, the pagans. Its origins have been disputed: The Romans started it; the French started it; Mobile, Alabama, started it; the list goes on. Whether New Orleans invented it or not, this city has immortalized it. Upon Mardi Gras's return, New Orleans will live once again. |JT|

The door opened and shut. The man stopped slurping his grits, and the place fell silent. No one even sipped a coffee. McMason the Monster stood in the doorway, impeccably dressed in his mercenary uniform. He was alone and studied the room as if looking for someone. He stroked his mustache and stretched his lower jaw, as was his custom. He folded his arms behind his back and marched slowly toward me. His boots creaked along the floorboards.

I hunched over and pretended to read Joshua's article, but the creaks just amplified. His musky aftershave overpowered the buttery grits next to me. His breath was hot on the back of my ear. His hairy hand grabbed the newspaper and pulled it from the table. He breathed deeply and said to himself, "Delivered today, dated for tomorrow. When does this regularly come in, son?"

I wasn't sure how to answer. Was he fishing for information? Was he mentally noting who favored Joshua's paper and categorizing them as potential enemies? I shrugged while thinking of a response.

The kitchen door swung open. "Get out!" Huey pointed a greasy spatula at McMason.

McMason backed up a few steps. "Hey now, Sergeant. I'm not doing a thing."

Huey lowered his spatula. "The hell you're not."

"What makes you so sure?" He folded the paper under his arm.

"You damn well know that all we got here is grits and rice. Why don't you go to that fancy po-boy place downtown?"

"Is this how you treat customers, Sergeant?"

"Stop calling me that."

"You act inferior, you'll be treated as an inferior."

"We had a deal."

"What are you going to do, Sergeant? Call the police?" McMason stroked his mustache and exercised his jaw again.

"I've done my part. I know gentlemen's agreements aren't really your thing, Randy."

"Watch yourself, Sergeant." He took off his sunglasses. "You're not that much different than me in that regard."

Huey's voice softened, but not with empathy or sincerity. With fear. "Just, just get out. Goddamn it."

McMason put his sunglasses on. "Sergeant, you may have been dishonored, but you can at least act like a soldier."

"Breaking that horse jaw of yours was the highest honor anyone could have, Randy."

McMason stroked his mustache, stretched his lower jaw, and exited.

Fitzmorris finally saw me as I finished topping off my gas tank. He stuck his head out the front door and yelled, "Ridge! Just the man I'm looking for." He pulled at his bungee cord suspenders. "Mardi Gras preparations. Got some produce shipped to me today from an old friend of mine around Alexandria. Sorting through it right now for the kids to throw. You're probably hungry, and I need the extra hand."

"Actually, Fitzmorris, I'm fine at the moment. Good news, though: I got a shipment of liquor in."

"Scotch?"

"Not yet. Got Elmer's Ryan, Monte Ligero, and Kepler's Seven, so spread the word. Could use some customers again."

Fitzmorris popped the bungee cords on his chest. "Well, hell. I may have to try something else. Did you switch distributors or something? I still can't get anything in."

"Um, nope that's all they had."

"Who's they?"

"The," I looked down at my boots and kicked the ground and said, "the distributors."

Fitzmorris looked down as he folded his arms. Then, looking me in the eyes, he said, "A national liquor wholesaler only had three brands available? What is this, post-Prohibition?"

"No. Just limited supply in this region, I guess."

"You guess? Your whole livelihood's riding on a guess?"

I shrugged and offered a crisp twenty-dollar bill. "So I still owe you for the gas."

Fitzmorris gazed at the pristine cash for a few seconds. "Everything all right? Nothing's the matter? Things have only gotten worse around here, and you don't need anything?"

I shoved the twenty into his chest. "Look, take this. I mean...I could come in for a little while and help."

"No. I think we're fine at the moment. You obviously are doing okay for yourself." Fitzmorris, however, snatched the cash.

Damn that Fitzmorris. Who the hell put him in charge of this community? Who would know a grocer could have so much power? As I drove down Oyster Shell Road, I couldn't help but feel liberated from him. His place was the only place for groceries, gasoline, hot meals, clean drinking water, and fresh laundry outside of McMason's downtown. Sometimes I felt like he acted like he was the Godfather or something. He always had things for me to do for him, of course, yet he made it seem that it benefited me, not him. He was good at what he did. Anybody could own a store, but Fitzmorris had this uncanny ability to get what he needed from everyone, to instill a need for himself, and give back just enough to seem like a Robin Hood of sorts. Even then, I thought he'd make a good conman. And if I'd known then what I know now about Fitzmorris, I probably wouldn't have trusted him from the beginning. Now, in the end, I'm stuck with him.

Town Hall Emporium

M ira's mother used to tell her not to listen to people who claimed that one thing or another made something "real New Orleans" because there was never one thing. And that's what made New Orleans real.

She realized that she hadn't been listening for some time at the meeting under the massive tent near the construction site of the Town Hall Emporium. Except for its stripes, one could have thought a circus had traveled to town. Mira had had high hopes for the crowd's resistance to naming the town square after Captain McMason. She didn't really care what it was called, just as long as it wasn't named after him. Mira thought that McMason embodied an authoritarian mindset that had no place in the future of New Orleans, especially since the city was being remanufactured before their very eyes. That was the goal, she thought—to let the Refounders know why a McMason Memorial Park would be a travesty. An enshrined vestige of a lost future that could spur a dogmatic following. To Mira and many others, McMason was spilled paint that needed mopping up before someone decided to paint the whole room the same color. But instead, the crowd argued over what the name should be and how "New Orleans" it was or was not. Mira shook her head, thinking how New Orleanians, more steadfast in their collectiveness than people in most American cities, became clannish at the wrong times.

It was apparent that many returning residents didn't quite understand what the Refounding was all about. The act of demolishing the Superdome should have been enough indication that nothing remained sacred. She empathized with them, sure. She wanted to stroll down Frenchmen Street where the music from all the different clubs merged to form its own musical gumbo. She wanted to ride the famous green streetcars down St. Charles Avenue again, gazing at live oaks older than the luxurious nineteenth-century homes they shaded. She longed for fall picnics at The Fly or City Park or Armstrong Park. She wanted to explore the eclectic cemeteries and study the above-ground tombs she'd climbed on as a little girl. But that just wasn't in the stars anymore. Frenchmen Street and Armstrong Park were buried under a wasteland of debris. The historic streetcars had been destroyed, as had the impressive homes. The Fly had been a staging area for ships and barges to unload their cargo until the Mississippi River got too shallow after its course changed, and briar patches grew around rusty shipping containers and rotten pallets. City Park was now at the bottom of Broadmoor Bay. Many live oaks and stone tombs remained steadfast, however.

And it wasn't that those other things couldn't be restored. The fact that they *could* be restored but would *not* be was heartbreaking. Mira wasn't well read on the history, but she knew that this town had endured this before. Her parents told her of Katrina and her grandparents of Betsy, and what she gathered was that the community leaders seemed to have a vested interest in restoring things as they once were. The community itself always wanted the sands of time to reverse and would usually do whatever it took to attain its pre-disaster state. The current community leaders, however, were not from the community and didn't thirst for the essence of what was once New Orleans, she thought. Under the veil of "progress," they understood their numbers and their orders. Despite its evils, New Orleans had been an addictive opiate that anchored people in sinking marsh mud for the long haul, and Mira couldn't help but think that these Refounders were an awfully sober bunch.

Mira couldn't say that about the present audience, though. The topic of naming the new square incited such an uproar that the presenters moved to the next topic. Mira didn't think any of the speakers talked for more than three minutes at a time without being interrupted by derisive shouts or babble. She was certain that, for the next meeting, they would not entice people by providing free beer.

Completely off topic, a woman stood and shouted, "Will our families be safe from all the zoo animals?"

The crowd reinforced her worry and applauded. Mira shook her head thinking, One of McMason's lies.

A representative took the microphone. "Let me just be clear here. I see that a lot of you are worried about this. There is no threat of exotic escaped zoo animals. Let me say that again if any of you didn't hear it: *There is no threat of exotic escaped zoo animals.* Yes, there was a concern in the immediate aftermath of Hurricane Beckham. That is true. However, any threat of lions, tigers, panthers, or any other wild cat has been neutralized. It is to be said that the feral pig, alligator, and coyote populations have skyrocketed. But as far as any 'man-eating' animal on the loose, it is all just rumor. Is that clear enough? Do I need to repeat that?"

The crowd did not respond. The young white man sitting in front of Mira was watching his Eagle screen and nodding his head at whatever he was streaming. He pushed the earbuds farther into his head. Some Chinese character was embroidered on his backwards cap.

The representative waited for a few minutes and then said, "Okay, then. We will now move on to the *original* topic of discussion. Mayor Crowley?"

Alex Crowley stood and brushed off the front of his suit. The woman behind Mira groaned and said to the person adjacent, "No one elected his ass. Damn feds appointed him."

"*Mmm*-hm," another voice confirmed.

Crowley stroked his lush brown hair back and his beard down. Straightening his red power tie, he spoke. "I understand that many of you are passionate about the New Orleans you once knew, but this city needs to be rebuilt, and it just makes more sense to rebuild it to fit the twenty-second century, not the twenty-first or earlier. And there's one thing that is essential to take this great city into the next century, and that's revenue. It is imperative that we generate revenue to achieve progress. One of those avenues to the future is the movie industry. The matter is simple. We need money. They need more affordable and flexible places to base their operations. We figure the city can accumulate millions in annual revenue. Additionally, Hollywood intends to hire a large local workforce, so that way, we can also keep people working in the area. It's not just actors, but construction workers, plumbers, technicians, caterers, and the like. We've successfully negotiated a contract with San Juan Studios to film exclusively in the area. So we are already active in commerce and need to continue down such a path. It has been proposed that a full-scale facility, similar to those in Los Angeles, be built somewhere on the high ground along the river. Some of you may know it as the avenue of Ta-choop-a-tailey-us."

The crowd groaned. The woman behind Mira said, "The bastard can't even say it right." She curled her program and yelled into it, "It's pronounced 'Chop-a-tool-us,' dumbass!"

The young man in front of Mira looked around, clearly annoyed, and pushed his earbuds even farther into his skull. As if he had dosed himself in an expensive cologne to mask his body odor, Mira thought he smelled like someone had tried freshening a bowl of spoiled chili with lavender oil.

Mayor Crowley did not falter. Smiling, he said, "Oh, pardon me. I have simply *read* these fascinating…old…street names. But New Orleans can really be at the forefront in this shifting industry."

A young woman holding a baby stood from across the room. "What about St. Francis of Assisi? The foundation is still strong. We can rebuild it. The city doesn't even need to pay for it! Y'all just have to *allow* us to start working."

The people seated near her applauded.

Crowley looked at the bench of presenters. "Does anyone want to take that one? Mr. Blanc?"

Mira figured the mayor hadn't the faintest idea what St. Francis of Assisi was.

Daniel Blanc, who quickly was becoming the moderator whether he liked it or not, stood and walked to the podium. "I will have to say, if we are going to get *anywhere* here today, we need to stay on point. Please hold your specific questions until the end. Once again, as I have said before, time will be allotted at the end of this session to address your personal concerns. And, to somewhat answer your question, that's a question for the Archdiocese of New Orleans and Bishop Fullerton. They handle all church matters." He nodded and took his seat.

"Okay, thank you." Crowley looked down at the podium. "We'd also like to discuss…what we're calling, at least right now, the White Sands Community and Commercial Development Project."

Eagle screens lit up, it seemed, all at once. The rows in front of Mira were full of silhouettes of people's heads, black from the white light of their Eagle devices. This very thing struck her down to the nerves, especially as a teacher. When someone gave their time and effort to communicate to a crowd, the listeners, no matter who they were, needed to show some respect—or at least give the illusion that they were listening.

Crowley straightened his red tie and rolled his neck to fit his starched collar. "The premier feature of the area, of course, will be a sandy beach to which we will ship white sand from Florida. A series of resort hotels will face that beach. There will be many other exciting new features that," he paused, cocking his head, "both locals *and* tourists can enjoy. A first-class golf course will have a range, a clubhouse, a beautiful view of the Gulf of Mexico, and plenty of challenging holes for avid golfers. We hope to bring back the famous Zurich Classic, which will bring much revenue to the city and create many jobs. Next, we are looking into establishing a Disney amusement park somewhere in this quadrant. Thrill seekers can glimpse the sea when they go up high in the roller coasters. But it won't be just another Disney World. It will be truly unique. It will also be a water park with slides and lazy rivers and snorkeling. We predict the annual revenue of this park will far exceed the monies generated from previous Carnival seasons.

"We also have another amusement option that will bring visitors by the thousands. One of the most popular sports in America is

NASCAR racing, and we intend to be a part of it. A racetrack facility has been proposed a ways inland from the future beach, set away from the residential districts so as not to vex our loyal citizens. As for our residents, the City of New Orleans is dedicated to giving them opportunities for both living and commerce. Seven state-of-the-art subdivisions will be located on the high ground, as well. Also, a sizable outlet mall will be built to provide jobs for our residents and to give them access to first-class shopping. This is exactly what…"

The kid sitting in front of Mira took out his earbuds and stood up. The back of his T-shirt read *Optimum Engine*. Mira wondered how he could sit in such tight jeans.

"Um, excuse me! You are simply just avoiding a public safety issue! What about the lions that escaped from the zoo? How can you expect us to move here when there are dangerous animals on the loose?!"

Crowley smiled, glancing down at the podium. The kid looked at the audience seated around him for support. Daniel Blanc's face turned red, and he leaned forward in his chair, fingers rubbing his temples, teeth grinding.

Mira thought to save Crowley's patronizing breath. "They talked about that already," she said quietly.

The kid snapped around. "No, they didn't!"

The older woman seated behind Mira said, "I'm afraid so, sonny. We don't believe 'em, though."

The kid sank down into his chair and untangled his earbud cords. If those earbuds go any farther, he'll hit brain tissue, Mira thought. Crowley continued. "Now to our last order of business…"

Mira looked at her program:

Speakers: New Orleans Mayor Alex Crowley, New Orleans Councilwoman Megan Watson, Jefferson Parish President Evan Allerio, St. Bernard Parish President Ken Meraux, State Representative Debra Robertson, Project NuOrleans Director Russ Canterro, Historian and Redevelopment Board Member Daniel Blanc.

Agenda:
- Greek immigrant influx, labor force, and pickpocketing
- Proposed demolition of One Shell Square and construction of Shangri-La Hotel and Casino
- Name proposals for downtown square
- Recruitment for movie industry
- White Sands Community and Commercial Development Project
- Proposal of Orleans Parish to cede certain territory to both Jefferson and St. Bernard parishes

*Please consume refreshments responsibly.
*Out of respect for the presenters, please silence your Eagles for the duration of the meeting.

She knew that the last topic would not be well received, and a beer would help her get through the rest of the meeting. She didn't even like beer. She quickly rose from her chair, scooting past two people toward the aisle. As she stared at her shoes gliding over the blue carpet, she couldn't help but notice that the audience was relatively silent. The fold-out table only had three empty plastic trays littered with cookie crumbs. Among three large ice chests, two were simply filled with icy water and bottle caps. The other was full of bottled water.

Mira looked around at the audience. Over half the attendees had left. She chuckled. The crowd had shrunk significantly now that the beer was gone. She shook her head and returned to her seat.

Crowley continued. "Over the centuries, New Orleans has been connected with the surrounding parishes. Unfortunately, we now face the fact that Plaquemines Parish is something of the past. However, our other neighbors, Jefferson and St. Bernard, are in need just as we are. And a good working relationship is what we all need to thrive. We are currently considering proposals to, in fact, cede land to these parishes. St. Bernard has nearly eroded away, and it is proposed that old areas like the—" Crowley looked at an index card, "the Lower Ninth Ward and New Orleans East be ceded to them, while areas like—" he looked at the card again, "the Riverbend, Lakeview, and Hollygrove areas go to Jefferson Parish. These areas have been designated to provide industrial plants, warehouses, and a new airport that will support our entertainment and tourist economy..."

The crowd had started babbling things like "no" and "bullshit" over Crowley's voice. Crowley looked to the moderator, who rose from his chair. Someone from the back yelled, "Let those rednecks drown! They're not New Orleans. *We* are!"

Blanc took the podium again and wiped the sweat from his forehead. "Hey now! Quiet! People, this kind of thing is not that unheard-of. As a historian, I can tell you this. A large—shut up!—a significant portion of Orleans Parish was once Jefferson Parish. As communities change, whether they grow or shrink, these types of things happen."

The woman behind Mira shouted, "Well then, what's happening with Uptown?"

Daniel Blanc's face turned as red as Alex Crowley's power tie. He held a clenched fist up to his mouth. Mira figured he was probably holding back profanity, not a burp. "We literally *just* went over that. Get off your Eagles. That's where the White Sands project is planned to be located."

The crowd roared. Daniel Blanc shook his head and walked off the stage into the back room. Mira had hoped that she could speak with either Crowley or Councilwoman Watson after the meeting about her food permit, but the volatility of the crowd would most likely deter them from joining the crowd. Mira rose and left the boisterous room.

Chapter 14

A number of cars were parked at Octave's place, which meant that some locals had either been struck with a sudden interest in books or urgently needed a haircut. Cars were even parked along the edges of Oyster Shell Road. I had never seen that many cars at Octave's. No more than three or four, normally.

Despite its being a good opportunity to announce that I had liquor, I kept driving. Octave probably wouldn't even remember, with him being so busy. I didn't remember the last haircut I'd had. If I saw Mira at Mardi Gras, looking like a gutterpunk would not make the best impression. I had a few days to clean myself up before Fat Tuesday, so I drove on.

Instead I went to Joshua's. Despite having plenty of pirated tobacco to roll my own, I still craved his name-brand cigarettes. I had never been to his place, but I did know it was in an old warehouse along Oyster Shell Road beyond my bar.

"Damn, I left that *Declaration* in the café. Maybe he has one at his place," I said to myself in the truck.

The road curved and paralleled Lake Pontchartrain, and I passed my bar. Briar patches, rusty fishing skiffs and sailboats, moldy carpet rolls, and a few surviving trees covered both sides of Oyster Shell Road. I passed several soggy piles of flesh-colored insulation, which looked like slices of whale blubber. I write that in retrospect because you eventually don't even *see* devastation after living in a disaster for a while.

A large metal building appeared out of the shadows of debris and carnage on the right side of the road. I let the truck idle to a stop. The front of the building did not have windows or even a door. Instead, six enormous ventilation fans, two rows of three, covered the outer wall. Circular screens protected the fans—or perhaps they protected people from the blades. It looked like the back side of a spaceship that had to make a crash landing. I probably would have continued driving if I hadn't seen the sedan parked out front with the remnants of an NOPD logo on the door. Monty was there, at least.

I parked next to Monty's decommissioned police car. When I exited my truck, the wind from one of the turbines nearly blew me to the ground. I crouched slightly as I walked along the wall. I turned the corner, and a door appeared at the opposite end. The building must have been forty feet long.

I knocked a little jingle in hopes that Joshua would guess that I was a friendly visitor. Politeness didn't have anything to do with it. I just didn't want a wrench or something to the face. Or, he might not answer at all.

The door opened, and the odor of smoke hit me in the face. Joshua wore a white T-shirt with suspenders and khaki pants. His shirt was ruffled around his suspenders like crashing waves or sea foam against a jetty. His feet were bare, and naturally, a lit cigarette hung from his lips. He nodded, took a deep drag, and exhaled smoke. "Ridge." He shook my hand firmly, oblivious of his own strength. You can't tell a man like that to ease up on you, so you just have to take the pain in order to keep his respect.

"I got liquor."

"Gin?"

"No. Whiskey, vodka, and dark rum."

He took another drag, and exhaled smoke as he spoke. "Will work. Elmer's Ryan?"

"Yep."

"Heard they're making a white whiskey now."

"Well, not that."

There were a few moments of silence between us until I said, "McMason might be on to you."

"Not surprised. Being the monster he is."

"He came into Huey's café and went straight to the stack. He was trying to figure out when you normally delivered. He even asked me."

"And you said?" He shook ashes on the ground.

"Actually, nothing. Right after he asked, Huey started yelling at him to get out."

"Really? Sorry, come in. Cigarette?"

"Yes, please." I followed him to a table, atop which were a half pack and two coffee cans full of cigarette butts. He pulled a glorious brand of cigarette from the pack, along with a box of matches. "For nothing?"

"For now, anyway."

As I inhaled the smoke, warmth and comfort came over me—like a wool blanket but from within.

"Well," he dragged and spoke, exhaling, "I trust that you wouldn't tell if you knew. I deliberately misdate it just to throw him off track. As much as I hate the Monster, he's not stupid. Makes me *really* hate him."

The room appeared to be an old break room from an industrial site: wood-paneled walls, white linoleum floors stained black from boot prints, a broken soda machine that was cracked open, a sink, and a small counter. A 25-pound bag of rice, which at first I thought was a pillow, sat on the shelf above the counter. A coffee pot, a rice cooker, and a food dehydrator sat on the counter next to a Barq's Root Beer can with the top cut off, full of cigarette butts. Above the sink, a window appeared deliberately tinted, but a few smudges near the lock made me realize that the glass was stained from secondhand smoke.

"Let's go out back. Speaking of the Monster, did you hear that speech he gave?"

"No." This must have been the speech he'd needed the shave for.

"Well, you'll read about it shortly. Don't feel like getting into it now. It's my day off."

I followed him out the back door and saw Monty sitting there in a plastic lawn chair, drinking a mug of coffee. "Say there, Ridge." His dark head was freshly shaven and reflected the sun.

"Hey, how goes it?"

"Oh, you know. Things good. Things terrible."

"I know it." I laughed a little.

"Ridge just told me that Huey read McMason the riot act for going to the café. Hopefully, he won't get dragged downtown."

"Naw, naw. They go way back. He might be all right."

"They do?" Joshua and I said at the same time.

"They war buddies from Afghanistan and Iraq. Like, forty-plus years ago."

Joshua and I looked at each other, surprised.

"I ain't sure why, but Huey done gave him one good. That's why McMason's jaw off the track."

"Huh. That makes sense," I said. "Hey, Joshua, maybe he went easy on you."

"Doubt it, dickface. Got a lot more respect for the man. Wish *I* could deck McMason and not end up in Revnor's Pond with seventeen bullet holes in my chest." Joshua popped his suspenders against his chest and stepped toward several golf clubs that leaned against the wall. Smoke slunk around his head, and he chose the driver.

"It got him thrown out of the army. He still say it was worth it."

"Damn right it was." Joshua inspected the golf club.

"I remember one time the cap'n went to his old place. Same thing went down."

"Old place?"

"Yeah. Huey's little coffee shop on the West Bank near the Gretna courthouse."

We were silent.

"Why you think we call him what we do? His place was on Huey P. Long Avenue. My sister used to stay down there, and I used to take that ferry right there. We used to meet up at his place and talk family stuff."

Joshua walked up to a five-gallon bucket. He bent down and retrieved a yellow golf ball from it. "That's nuts, how you knew each other like that."

"Ain't just me. Choppy used to be a deckhand on that ferry back then. And Fitzmorris worked somewhere around down there. Can't tell ya what he did, never talked about it. They both went to Huey's place, too."

Joshua took a peg from the ground and set the golf ball on the spot. He assumed a proper stance, looked down at the ball. Smoke must have been careening in his eyes, and I don't know how he could stand it. In good form, he hit the ball perfectly, judging from the sound of impact. His stroke was perfect. He looked like a rich person. We watched it fly and disappear into a long strip that was overgrown with briars.

"Are you serious, Monty?" Joshua turned around and set his feet and focused on the next golf ball.

"I ain't bullshittin'."

I blew out some smoke. "You can't make this stuff up, I guess."

"Ridge, you from here, ain't ya? You know everybody know everybody." He sipped his coffee.

I nodded and inhaled smoke into my lungs.

Joshua centered his aim with a few controlled swings in the air. "Interesting, though, that just a little coffee place like that was enough for y'all to become that close."

"It wasn't. It was that ferry wreck. Mr. Fitzmorris and Choppy, they was the only ones who made it."

Joshua swung, missed the ball, and launched the golf club into the briar patch. He snapped around, and the cigarette fell from his lips. "You're bullshitting us now."

"No, I ain't."

Joshua and I stood frozen for a few seconds.

Monty finished his coffee and rose from the chair. "Aw'ight. I gotta go soon, but I'll fill y'all in right quick. The ferry cap'n stone drunk and didn't see that tanker. Ship hit 'em broadside, flipped the bitch over, split 'er in two. People still in they cars when she went down. Choppy and Mr. Fitzmorris got shot toward the bank, and lucky for them they just outta the current and got hung up on something near the levee. Hell, they done found some bodies as far as Fort Jackson. Me and Huey waiting for that ferry when it happen, and we run out to go get 'em."

Joshua and I remained still.

"Well, that be it. I'll be here tomorra, Joshua. To talk business 'bout these kids and how they getting guns. You know dat monster of a man ain't doing nothing because he wants us to kill ourselves off."

Joshua scratched his head. "You're not wrong, Monty Cello. Yossarian told me that at a meeting the Redsleeve PR person asked the Monster about rising public concerns that he wasn't doing enough to end the Ward Wars; allegedly, he said the problem would take care of itself over time. So, yeah. On point, there."

Monty asked, "Man, who this Yossarian character?"

"He calls himself that. I only care what he tells me about what's happening from the inside. I'll follow you out."

Both men went into the break room. The outside door banged shut, and Joshua clicked the lock. Joshua emerged outside with a freshly lit cigarette. His lips puckered as he drew in hard, and the smoke curled out of his nostrils as if he was growing nicotine tusks.

"Know any of that?"

"Nope." He shook his head and stood in contemplation for a few moments. Two gray squirrels chased each other around the roots of an upturned oak tree. Their tiny claws scratched the bark the same way a Zydeco artist would play a washboard.

"Want to check out the machine?" Joshua pointed inside with his thumb.

I followed him into the break room. He snatched a pack of cigarettes and the box of matches off the table as I followed him to his printing press. He pushed open a steel door into a large space with a high ceiling and a concrete floor. Basically, it was a warehouse without the shelves or inventory. A large dock door, big enough for an eighteen-wheeler to enter, was open a quarter of the way. Near the door, a vintage electric typewriter sat on a tall bar table.

"Do you stand when you write?"

"Sometimes. But usually I have to hook my bike up to the generator and pedal while I work."

The room was empty except for a mattress of newspaper bundles, covered with a wool army blanket, in the corner. A headlamp rested on a book atop another bundle of newspapers.

"Not exactly the Hilton. But after biking all day, feels like a Serta." Joshua turned and pointed at the dock door. "That's where the trucks used to come in. Built originally after Beckham as a burn station. You saw that line of briar patches in the back? Feds cut that road out for trucks to bring debris in."

I exhaled smoke. "Like Oyster Shell Road."

"Yes. But salvageable stuff went down Oyster Shell. Scrap metal and copper mostly. Then boats took it out through the Rigolets. This road was for logs, furniture, carpets, rotten barge boards, those things. Road never had a name. Works out for me because the Monster doesn't know about it. If he did, they'd have done something with it."

"So where did it all go?"

"Right here," he pointed at the wall opposite the dock door. An industrial-size conveyor belt, about as wide as a one-lane road, led into a large door. We stepped onto what looked like a giant treadmill. "It's not on. Not nearly enough power in here to run this thing. Well, maybe, but I rewired everything to go in here."

"There's still electricity?"

"They forgot about this place, too, I guess. Like the invisible man."

"Yeah, but visible."

"Like the book."

"What book?"

"Never mind. Don't waste your time."

"What? Bad book?"

"No. Actually, brilliant book. Just reading novels in general."

I felt guilty about not reading *Cold Chambers* for a while. I let it go, since I knew Joshua wouldn't deviate from his ways and means. It seemed unnatural that our journalist had such a distaste for reading literature. That was a conversation for another time.

We entered the space that Joshua had made into his own press room. A draft blew past us as the six fans funneled the cool air through their spinning steel blades. The walls, the ceiling, the floors—all black from soot, ink, and smoke residue. The printing machine was smaller than I had expected. It was about the size of small bedroom. Ink splatter painted the floor even blacker underneath it.

"This is where they burned. Fans blew the smoke out over the lake. It took about two months just to clear all the ash out of here. Nails and screws were the real problem, though. All that lumber from old houses and fences burned down to ash, but all the nails and screws made it like a minefield of spikes."

I imagined him shoveling ash, charcoal, and blackened nails out the doorway with a cigarette hanging from his mouth, and right then, I decided that someone should write a book about us vagabonds who chose to valiantly live in the squalor that we still believed to be New Orleans underneath.

"Got it cheap. No one wants, or needs, to print anything these days. Especially with that new Hawk thing that just came out. Or eagle, owl, something." He closed his eyes as he inhaled the smoke from his cigarette. "Actually, right here in the summer, fans make it somewhat tolerable. But got to take in the cool weather. Usually set up outside or just under that big door. Need to hook my bike up to the generator when I work, since most power's wired to the machine. Not today, though. It's my one day off."

"I bet someone gave you that typewriter for nothing."

Joshua sucked down the last of his cigarette and tossed the butt into a bucket in the corner. "It was given to me, sure. But everything comes with a price."

Rio Rojo Restaurante

Being a teacher, a musician, and a stage performer, Mira had learned to put money out of her mind because she rarely had much to even think about, much less use. She stopped pacing her apartment, looked at the stack of money on the table, and sat down in a chair. She sighed and opened her Market Place profile on her Eagle. The latest guitar technology, the Queteen Quasi guitar, could act as every stringed instrument invented because of its wide pitch range and tone variations. Essentially, one musician could play the acoustic, electric, banjo, and steel guitar all in one instrument, though at different intervals. Or, one could play the fiddle, the upright bass, or even the harp simply by turning a different knob on the neck. The options were endless, Mira thought, if she played along Baladucci Drive. She could change genres without having to lug around, or secure, multiple instruments. Mira looked at the broken guitar sitting on its stand near the wall. Then she looked at $350 of the $500 she had saved to purchase the Queteen Quasi. With her salary, even with her discounted rent in the teachers' dormitory, it had nearly taken a year to save that much. Her index finger felt the smooth surface of her screen as it reached the digital *Cancel* icon. She closed her eyes and tapped the icon.

> This product is in high demand and back ordered. Canceling may result in this product being unavailable for an undetermined duration. Are you sure you do not want to reconsider your [Queteen Quasi] order before canceling?

Since payment was due in two weeks, and the St. Joseph's Altar was less than a month away, she did not have the luxury of reconsidering.

Her stomach jolted and her throat dried as she touched the *Confirm Cancellation* icon.

Mira scooped the cash from the table, counted it a third time, and stuffed it into an envelope. She then shoved the envelope into a safety travel belt that she clipped around her waist. She put on her coat, checking the bribe's accessibility to a pickpocket. In Paris, this was the norm for simply walking in public, and pickpockets had found their way into New Orleans after the Refounding. Everyone blamed the undocumented Greeks or other European immigrants escaping the dismal economic conditions of what Chase Quade labeled the "European Disunion." It's quite ironic, she thought, that when New Orleans was being "de-Europized" it began having European-style crime. Mira picked up the health inspector's business card and slammed the door behind her.

She had never gone to the Rio Rojo, but she had heard that the Mexican cuisine was quite exquisite. It was becoming an institution onto itself, and Saturday lunch was one of those times when all of the important people could congregate without being pestered. And that's where he wanted her to meet him.

Mira shivered from the cold wind funneling between skyscraper skeletons as she stepped onto Baladucci Drive. Her hair still slightly wet from showering, Mira's ears stung as if brush-burned by something much coarser than simply moving air. Even though she had showered a few hours prior, she felt dirty. She felt sick. The money belt gripped her waist, and the bribe, bulging into her belly button, felt like an ulcer deep within her gut. She envied every person passing her on the sidewalk, thinking that his or her conscience was clear. None of them, she assumed, were suckers in trying to improve the city by giving in to its corrupt ways. She passed a young black man sitting on a bucket playing a saxophone. Only a few coins were in his overturned hat. The ulcer in her stomach seemed to get hotter as she thought how much the man probably needed some of this money. Judging from his thin frame, he might miss an occasional meal, Mira thought, unlike the asshole she was about to give the money to. She just shook her head in disgust.

"Ms. Teach! Hey, Ms. Teach!"

Mira stopped. Ahead of her, Tamantha Warren and a few other girls were walking in her direction. "Hi, Tamantha. How are you?"

"Oh, we just out. I mean, we're just walking around. Sorry."

Mira chuckled and nodded, knowing it was Mr. Cooper's responsibility to teach grammar mechanics, not hers.

"Where you going?"

Mira said, "To meet a friend for lunch."

"Oh, yeah? Where at?"

"That Rojo Rio place."

One of Tamantha's friends said, "Oh Lord! They food is good!"

Tamantha said, "Oh, it is? Girl, I'm gonna have to go there, then."

"Hey, I'm *hongry!*"

"No, no, y'all. We got to go meet up with them in a minute."

"Oh, yeah, you right. Bye, Ms. Teach."

Relieved that they would not be going to the restaurant, Mira said goodbye.

Mira's Eagle marked the Rio Rojo Restaurante just a block ahead. She passed a few men smoking hand-rolled cigarettes at the side of the building. They wore tight hairnets and food-stained white aprons with the restaurant logo. They stopped talking in Spanish as Mira passed them. Then, a mustached man wearing a maroon suit came out of the door.

"Trabajamos! Vamanos!"

The kitchen staff took one last drag off their cigarettes and pitched the butts on the concrete before shuffling back into the kitchen.

She turned the corner and found about ten people standing outside the front door. She nudged her way into the restaurant. The same man wearing the maroon suit greeted her at the hostess stand.

"Hola, señorita! How many?"

"I'm actually meeting someone."

"Okay, are they already seated?"

"I don't know. Can I just look around?"

"Sure. And please, if you need anything, let me know. This is my place. Make yourself at home. Here, let me take your coat."

"No! I'm fine, thank you."

The walls were a dark red and the oak trim was varnished to a chocolate brown. The wooden tables were unclothed, revealing their dark finish similar to that of the trim on the ceiling and the baseboards. The lights had been dimmed to a dinner setting, which emphasized the candles on each table. Paintings of Mexican villas and desert landscapes covered the walls. Most people would have been uncomfortable while meandering through tables of diners. Mira, however, took it as an opportunity to get an impression of the restaurant experience no matter the strange looks she received from the people. She studied each table for a few seconds, taking note of the contentment level of the patrons, the frustration level of the wait staff, the portion size of the meals, the popular entrees, the pour size of the wine, and the strength of the cocktails, depending on their color. She strolled from table to table, analyzing one factor at a time. A table of six, four men and two women in their mid-thirties, was boisterous considering they hadn't received their entrées yet and had gone through nearly two pitchers of horchata rum punch. An older couple across from them sipped a rich red wine whose legs streamed down the glass as they each took a sip. A young Mexican waiter, wearing black attire and a red tie, came up to their table, sweating from the forehead. Mira couldn't hear what he said over the din of the restaurant, but his eyes and his gestures spoke apology for something, probably the lack of entrées on their table, Mira thought. At the next table of four, each person sat motionless, staring straight ahead like eagles perched for prey. One of them stood and waved to a waiter once he saw one. It seemed that the kitchen was having some difficulty churning out dishes. So, she thought, maybe ordering food is not the best idea. She didn't want to be there one minute more than necessary.

The inspector's table was obscured by a pillar adorned with a photograph of the current prime minister of the Mexican Sovereign

Republic. The picture showed a clean-shaven, dapper man with graying sideburns. The prime minister appeared sophisticated, confident, and stately. Just to the left of the picture, an obese man sat sideways at the table. The inspector wore an unbuttoned gray suit coat that stretched backward while his bright white shirt somehow had the strength to contain his immense belly. Mira gagged a little as she compared his sagging stomach to a blob of mayonnaise hanging from a spoon.

As she passed the pillar, Mira noticed that the inspector was not dining alone. A middle-aged woman wearing a flowy sweater decked with flashy beads sat across from him. The inspector rolled his head over the folds of his neck, coughed, and nodded at Mira.

The woman rested her chin on her interlocked fingers, which were adorned with gold and diamonds. "Oh, hello. Someone you work with, honey?" Her tone was surprisingly welcoming.

The inspector was chewing and nodded.

"What's your name, sweetheart?" Her makeup was thick, like glittery plaster.

"Mira Roche, ma'am."

"And what do you do?"

"I'm a teacher." She rubbed the bribe beneath her clothes. The money belt fit the contour of her body like a suffocating corset.

"Oh, lovely; you must be hungry. Pull up a chair. And you must be burning up in here. Take that coat off." The woman fondled the fine rings on her fingers as if she unconsciously needed to confirm that they were still there.

"I couldn't possibly. But thank you."

"Oh, I love meeting my husband's friends. Please." She motioned with her hand to the chair just in front of Mira.

Mira and the inspector glared at each other for a few long moments. He remained silent.

Two servers came with full trays, setting them on nearby tray stands. A young woman with long black hair said, "Two orders of chipotle quail con posole and two orders of the pescado frito con chayote. And your creole cubano sliders and crawfish tamales are coming right out."

The woman said, "We've got plenty. Don't be shy. Come on."

"I'm sorry, no. I was just saying hello." She glanced at the inspector again, who focused all his attention on a steaming bowl of Mexican stew. "Goodbye."

"Oh well, anytime, honey!"

She stormed out of the restaurant and kicked a beer can into the street. "All I want is a fucking city permit for my class!" She hadn't cussed aloud in years. But it felt good. She had remained strong through years of educating at-risk youth, but a just a few weeks of city bureaucracy was enough to break even a saint's patience.

Chapter 15

If it weren't for women, men would be the filthiest cretins on Planet Earth. My hair hadn't been professionally cut for almost a year. Whenever my hair touched my shoulders, I just chopped it off so that it wouldn't annoy me. Brushing my teeth was certainly not a daily habit. Ever since toothpaste became scarce, I'd been rationing it, and, out of laziness, I only brushed when my mouth felt intolerable. This being January, I hadn't bathed since mid-November. The water temperature in Lake Pontchartrain had dropped too much, and running water was not even available unless you were a Redsleeve, a Refounder, or Fitzmorris. I have to admit that not cleaning my hair and teeth annoyed me sometimes, but I'd become rather content in my own bodily filth. The odor wafting from my armpits and balls was quite comforting after a while, like I was a Neanderthal relishing my own primitive virility. So my sincere gratitude goes toward women for prompting us to at least try to be somewhat civilized.

I made my second package pickup for the Manchacs right before daybreak, during Redsleeve patrol shift change, and decided to stop into Octave's early for a haircut. He probably wasn't open yet, but I knew he was awake and wouldn't turn me away. The eastern sky had a pink-orange hue, yet everything elsewhere was dark with a few lighter objects emerging ghostly from the darkness. Following my headlights down Oyster Shell Road, I glanced to the right, where Broadmoor Bay reflected the pink sky. Shadows of Xavier University and the Falstaff Brewery Condos ran down the water's surface, giving the illusion that they were freestanding structures instead of half-submerged in brackish lake water drifting in from Bayou St. John and the broken I-walls of the London and Orleans Avenue canals.

I slammed on the brakes, and my wheels skidded through oyster shells. A herd of wild boars lounged in the road, taking turns wallowing in an enormous pothole. The idle water, the color of milk from the white shells, plastered the beasts. I honked the horn, and a few scooted to the side of the road while others sauntered about the pothole, completely ignoring me.

I stuck my head out the window. "Get out of the road! Assholes!"

The pigs' ears perked up, and they scampered into the darkness. I felt proud…until a helicopter buzzed over my truck, soaring toward downtown.

I parked in front of Octave's pirogue sign, covered the small box on my floor with a jacket, and locked both doors. I didn't have much choice but to chance leaving the box in the truck because I wasn't bringing it in the store for anyone to see. I knocked on the door, and, to my surprise, Constance answered the door wearing pajama pants and a sleeveless shirt. Her arms and shoulders, just like Huey's, were tattooed in a pattern that initially looked like either barbed wire or rose vines on her dark-brown arms. Or both. She wore a maroon bandanna over her short black hair. It was easy to forget that the school principal looked like a rock star without her professional apparel. Well, she was a rock star in her own way.

"Good morning." She sipped a steamy cup of coffee.

"Morning, Constance. I thought you'd be at school."

"It's Saturday. And it's six in the damn morning."

I nodded apologetically.

"Mm-hmm." She rubbed her arm from the cool draft. "So what is it you want?"

"Your husband home?"

"He's home."

"I was hoping for a haircut."

Constance looked at me for a few seconds. "It's Saturday. And it's six o'clock." Her tone stern.

"Who is it?" Octave asked from inside.

"Ridge."

"What's wrong?"

She stepped back, extending her arm to me, and walked back inside. Octave came to the door. "Ridge, what's going on?"

"Well, I may see an old friend at Mardi Gras and was hoping for a haircut."

He turned around to his wife, who was now seated in a chair just behind him. She shrugged and sipped her coffee.

"You won't be open tomorrow or Monday, will you?"

"No, I won't." There was a long pause. He was probably trying to work up the nerve to tell me to leave and come back later. But instead he said, "Okay, come on."

As I walked over the creaking floorboards, I passed Constance sitting cross-legged. Her eyes glared at me as if I were a problem student in her office, and I looked away. She did not.

I sat in the barber's chair. "Just make it short and neat."

"What about the beard?"

"What beard?"

He handed me a hand mirror, and I didn't recognize myself. I hadn't taken time to see my full reflection since I'd moved back. I only noticed my face above my nose in my truck's rearview mirror. Now it made sense that my face itched from time to time. My beard was wild, like an untrimmed bush, and plenty of spots where grits, mud, or whatever else had dried and hardened. "Um, yeah, definitely."

His battery-operated trimmer hummed behind me. He yawned. "Why are you up here so early? Don't you work late?" He clicked it to the right adjustment.

I had to pick up the Manchacs' package during the Redsleeve shift change. But I didn't say that. I couldn't. "Just getting a head start."

Octave sheared my hair unto the wooden floor, and the back of my head buzzed as if a million curious insects were marching around on my cranium. "I would think you'd be working with Fitzmorris. Getting ready for Mardi Gras."

"He didn't mention anything the other day," I lied.

Octave pulled my ear forward and buzzed the hair just behind it. "Well, he's busy over there. Getting all the throws in. I even heard that he somehow got a bunch of old Zulu coconuts, and he's fixing to do something with them."

"I'm actually doing some work for another grocer. His name's Rudy or something. Ready Rudy? Probably not, but something."

Octave trimmed the back of my neck, which made my shoulders quiver a bit. "Downtown? Fitzmorris is the only one I know otherwise."

"Yeah, it's downtown. He needs help on Mardi Gras day cooking food for the crowds."

"Huh. Hot food on the parade route? I don't go all that way often myself, but I may make it down there, especially since they got all that music at the end. You gonna be able to even go to the parade?"

"I'm hoping. Need the work, though. I'll be good either way, really."

He turned off the trimmer and sharpened his shears. "It's going to be just spectacular. The kids are so excited." He shifted in front of me and cut my hair in soft pinches. "Constance says some of the students have been staying hours after school making costumes, decorating their little floats. Love it. Can't wait for the music, too. One of her teachers is gonna perform with them, even. Supposedly she studied music in France."

"Oh, really?" I said, feigning ignorance. It was too early in the morning for some topics, like Mira.

We did not speak for the remainder of the haircut. Octave adjusted his trimmer accordingly, and buzzed upward on my neck, brown fuzz shedding off of me and into my lap. "Well, she's putting those kids right back to work after Mardi Gras."

"Oh?"

"They're taking the younger classes on an educational field trip on a school bus across some of the wrecked areas. Right on Ash Wednesday. Most of these kids never really knew the city before Beckham. They don't even know what their parents' old neighborhood looked like, much less where it was."

"That's good."

"Yes, fine sir, it certainly is. Now, just be quiet for a second; let me get this lather on."

The shaving cream bit at my face, almost burning it as it sank into my dry skin and prickly bristles. The cold blade slicked across my face, like the hull of a ship slicing the surface without leaving a trace. My pores gasped as if they had long been stifled. Octave dried my face with a towel and handed me a little mirror. I hadn't seen myself in that way for a long time. I could see my face, which seemed odd, ugly, and wrong at first. "Looks great, Octave."

"The charge is twenty dollars, fine sir. But I'd be willing to trade something if you don't have that."

I had the cash, sure. But it felt so good to have it, and even better to keep it. "How about I just put it toward your bar tab?"

"I don't keep a tab."

"I'll give you a credit, then."

"What am I going to buy there?"

"Oh, I forgot to tell you. I got a small shipment in, so I do have some liquor right now. Spread the word."

"Okay, then. I'm not sure if I'll ever spend twenty dollars' worth over there. But if it's all you have, we can do it."

Excited, I thought about Mira performing on stage, not about the road. Perhaps the last time I'd seen her perform was in a play where she played a character who was blue. She was always adamant about me not attending the opening show. "Everyone will be sharper after that first day," she would say, as if she wasn't the sharpest one on that stage from the beginning. "We'll learn what works and what doesn't." But I couldn't stand it. I went to the auditorium and sat in the very back so she would not see me.

As the cast took their bow, I hightailed it across campus to my dorm, since she'd said she would come over after the show. I went into my room and changed into gym shorts and a Saints T-shirt. The game, Operation Tetra, was just as I'd left it, and my game was saved.

I picked up where I'd left off, killing digital men with my fingers pulling imaginary triggers.

Of course, she knocked on the door when I was in a tight situation. As much as I wanted to see her, that game still pulled me in, away from her, as if it offered more than what she could. Mira knocked again after about five seconds, and I tried to get my shot off. The damn asshole kept dodging to the left, and Mira knocked a third time. That's when I gave in, paused it, and opened the door. She was already down the hallway a bit, but she turned around and smiled.

"Did I wake you?"

"No, I was just—"

"Playing Operation Tetra?"

"Yep."

She took a few steps toward me. "Well, should I leave you alone, then?"

"No, no." I stepped inside and held the door open for her.

As she entered, I noticed she had forgotten to wipe the blue paint off her ears.

"I am so exhausted, my God." She crawled onto my bed.

"So, how was the show?"

"It was good, I think," her words muffled as she spoke into my pillow.

"You think?"

"Mm-hmm."

"Why is that?"

"Hmm."

I walked over to the bed, where she had totally crashed. Blue paint had streaked across my pillow. She breathed deeply, rhythmically, even musical in her sleep.

Red lights flashed in my rearview mirror. It was a Red Birch Security Hummer. "Goddamn it! Again?" I said aloud as I pulled over to the side of Oyster Shell Road.

As I set the truck in park, I saw the Manchac package on the passenger seat, peeking out from my jacket. And I didn't even know what was in it. This was it. They'd haul me in for this one. It had reached the point where I had to choose one or the other to make it in this world. At least I had an idea what the Redsleeves could do to me—at least legally—if I crossed them. Captain McMason was a monster, sure; however, even he had legal and corporate stipulations to abide by. Prison, intense questioning, possibly exile would be my fate. He could not resort to torture and execution, I believed.

I gripped the steering wheel with both hands and caught my breath. The tall blond-haired Redsleeve stepped down from the Hummer and spit on the white shells. His lower lip bulged out so much, it looked like he was having an allergic reaction to peanuts. But nope, it was just a massive pinch of dip. His partner sat in the passenger seat. With the glare of the windshield, I only saw the glare of his sunglasses, as if he was an invisible man wearing wrap-around shades.

He placed his hands on his hips, close to his sidearm and night-stick. "All right, fella, what gives?"

"Morning, Officer." I said after a second or two, since I wasn't too sure of his reason for pulling me over.

He spit on my tire and stepped closer to my window. "You was driving real slow back there. All swerving 'bout. Drunk, ain't ya?"

"No, sir. I ain't."

He placed his hands on my truck door and leaned in. His dip breath made me nauseous. "Then, why you stink of it?"

"I just got a shave at the barbershop. It's probably the aftershave."

"Fella, ain't no barber open this early. How 'bout you get out the truck and stop being a li'l shit-tart." He spit on my tire again and backed up a few steps.

"Damn it." I said softly to myself.

"You talking shit there, fella?"

"No, sir."

"We've pulled you over before. Probably shoulda sent you to the captain then for being an asshole. The captain hates assholes. And you look like one. Say…what's that on your seat there?"

The jig was up, I thought. "Just a box of stuff."

"Well, let's see it."

I lifted it from the seat and handed it to him. The box had some random numbers and marks written on it. The Redsleeve started shaking it. Then his partner exited the Hummer and ran to him. Could this get any worse? It was the same bald-headed guy that had pulled me over last time and dumped all my crabs on the street.

"This thing fragile?" With two arms, he lifted it high in the air.

"Give him that back!" the bald Redsleeve said.

"Awright, fine." He handed it back to me.

The bald Redsleeve said, "Let's go. We got another call. Have a good day, young man."

I sat in my car, baffled by what just happened.

Hornsby National Bank and Trust

As Mira left the Mexican restaurant, the intended bribe money still hugged her stomach, and, uncomfortable with having so much cash on the streets, she decided to put it in the hands of the Hornsby National Bank and Trust for safekeeping. She waited in a line of about ten people. A pack of immigrant demolition workers, probably Greek, she reasoned, distributed cash among themselves. They had slightly tanned skin and brown hair. Some had mustaches. Their plaid shirts were crusted with paint, sawdust, and concrete. A young white man wearing skinny jeans and an ironed plaid shirt designed more for fashion than durability stood in line constantly looking over his shoulder at Mira and then turning away. Mira stared at him, hoping he would feel uncomfortable and stop. An elderly Latino woman and her teenaged granddaughter struggled to converse; it was clear that the granddaughter spoke little Spanish and the grandmother spoke little English. They spoke in three-word sentences. A young black man with long dreads pushed a stroller and kept apologizing for its wheels hitting the heels of the obese lady in front of him.

The corporate customer line was just as diverse. Three Vietnamese-American women were at the counter: One of them spoke with the teller while the others spoke Vietnamese to each other. Behind them, a white woman wore a sleek black dress with a slit up the side that revealed her red lace stockings underneath. Her lusty perfume filled the entire bank. She frequently flipped her long maroon hair out of her face. She was accompanied by a large suited black man carrying a security lockbox the size of a child's lunch box. As she stepped up to the counter, she spoke with a deep, manly voice. At first, Mira thought she was transgender, but in actuality, she was German.

"Das Rapunzel's Café. Deposit, please," she said. The black man handed her the box, and she pulled out four large bundles of cash and gave them to the teller.

The teller held one of the bundles sideways so that the edges of the bills faced her. She used a handheld money-counting device that cast a blue laser around the bundle and flashed red as the computer beeped. She did the same for the other bundles.

Behind the madam and her bodyguard stood a tan-skinned nun and a young white priest. The young priest wore the traditional outfit of black with the white neck collar, except his countenance was not that of a priest, Mira observed. He seemed less "God's work" and more Secret Service, she thought. He even wore sunglasses, which reminded her of a classic movie about a man being chased by computerized agents in a virtual world. The nun held a briefcase while the priest folded his arms and swiveled his head, sizing up every bank customer.

"Thank you, Ms. Konig. Anything else?"

"No. I am finish. Thank you." Her high heels clicked as she walked toward the door.

The nun shuffled up to the counter, and her guarding priest turned around with folded arms, facing Mira and the other customers. She opened the briefcase on the counter.

"Well, hello, Sister. How have you been?"

"Oh, the Lord's work is ongoing." The nun gave her seven bundles of cash that were scanned and deposited.

As Mira watched the transaction from her spot in line, things started coming together. Just as Archbishop Fullerton had a sidearm under his robe, this priest must also carry under his jacket. One of the "new" clergy. A soldier of God. It gave Mira the shakes. She was almost to the counter when the nun turned toward her. It was Sister Matrona, the Greek nun she'd met at the cathedral, and they recognized each other.

"Hello! You're the teacher, yes?"

"I sure am."

The teller said, "Next in line."

"Uh, Sister—"

"Sister Matrona."

"Right. I wanted to talk to you about something. For the students."

"Next in line, please."

"Okay. When? I have to get to the donation center soon."

"*Next in line, please!*"

"Meet me in my office at the school on Monday around ten. We don't have class, but I'll be there anyway. Grading and administrative stuff."

It didn't become clear until after Mira deposited the money into her account and exited the bank. The brothels' profits had skyrocketed, and there was only one way the church could have that much cash: the indulgence mutuals, she concluded. With the education overhaul, students didn't have to pay tuition to attend Catholic schools, and that money needed to come from somewhere. Whoredom was, in fact, New Orleans's future. Her life, her students' lives, and their families' lives relied on the lucrativeness of women's bodies. Mira didn't know whether to be sad or to laugh. Either way, it made her want to cry.

Chapter 16

A lack of honor is contagious, and each man without honor is a direct threat to the human race. We as a society lost something special when we began preferring legal jargon and signatures over handshakes. I hadn't even spoken with Renny Rooney since he'd given me food in return for helping him Mardi Gras morning, but I knew deep in my being that our gentleman's agreement was still valid. I had signed contracts before, and they'd meant nothing to me. But something inside me wouldn't let me walk out on Rooney. Sure, I could have just claimed to forget all about it and gotten that food for free, but then forty bucks' worth of groceries would have been the price for my principle. Not only would Rooney be screwed, but my own sense of masculinity was at stake. I felt more of a man than ever just simply driving to Rooney's to honor that agreement.

I wouldn't say that I'm fortunate for experiencing all that in my early twenties, but I'm glad I realized early on what manhood entails. Committing our lives to something grants us the purpose we've been searching for. Each man's commitment and purpose is different. A man without purpose is simply wasting the Earth's precious resources. Scientists have been studying everything from the core to the crust to the stratosphere and beyond, whereas the main problem with this world is that there are too many inept fools walking around. Each male has strong opinions, which he erroneously calls principles, but until he decides to commit to something, he is not a man of principle.

I parked my truck on the curb alongside Rooney's Grocery and switched my headlights off. Downtown before dawn was even quieter than the area where I lived. Not a sound from frogs, birds, or even insects. Surviving buildings were nothing but dark shells, void of life. It was here when I felt New Orleans had lost its soul: doomed, decimated, abandoned, erased.

Then something delicious wafted through the air, and I knew my mistake in thinking that New Orleans had lost its soul. I got out of the truck and knocked at the door, which resonated tenfold in the utter silence. I waited so long that I debated returning to my truck. Until a small hatch opened at eye level on the door, and a light blinded me temporarily. Someone behind the door unlatched three locks. Rooney opened the door, holding a flashlight in one hand.

"Sorry about that. Can't take any chances. I didn't know how to install security lights, but I knew how to cut a hole in the door."

Green-purple blotches pulsed across my line of vision. "I understand."

"I wasn't too sure you'd come. I'm sorry, your name—remind me." He held out his hand.

I shook it. "Ridge."

"That's right. You look different." He sniffed the air. "You showered. I appreciate that."

If he calls jumping naked into Lake Pontchartrain after lathering with rough soap "showering," so be it.

He shined the flashlight behind me. "Well, come in and lock 'em all up. Got some hot coffee to get ya started if ya like." He waved me on to follow him.

His grocery looked similar to Fitzmorris's store. The shelves were bare of supplies, not bountiful as I remembered. Apparently, Rooney was not shielded from the Monster, despite living downtown in his lair.

We walked into the kitchen. Sliced andouille sizzled in a stock on the burner. A medium-size pot sat on the adjacent burner with grits simmering inside.

"Get some fuel. We got lots to do. I'm using most of that in the jambalaya, so don't be too generous."

"Thanks." I helped myself to a bowl of grits and shoveled some grilled sausage and orange grease into it. The salty deliciousness. Oh, Lord, the salty deliciousness.

Rooney tied on a white apron stained with grease and various sauces. "Ridge, take your time. Drink some coffee. Get some grits in ya. Cuz when we start…" He paused, nodding. "You know how they say 'les bon temps rouler'?"

"Yeah?"

"Well, we gonna be rolling as soon as the good times get going." He wiped sweat off his bald head and went into the cooler.

When I finished eating, he started me preparing the first batch of jambalaya. He had me remove the grilled andouille and chill them in a separate container. He said, "We'll put that in later, once it's all done. That way they don't boil down to little hockey pucks."

Rooney turned on a radio on the shelf above him. Fiddles, accordions, and incomprehensible Cajun French resonated from the speakers. If I knew any Cajun, it probably wouldn't be all that undecipherable. It was evident that the male singer wasn't singing to someone like me. The French had founded New Orleans, but we had been Americanized since. Most of the French words spoken were simply place names and some bastardized slogans, but the American cultural bulldozer couldn't fully penetrate the swamps and cane fields of central Louisiana. The musician's confident voice spoke to his people, not to anyone else. It was inspiring.

I poured a pitcher of homemade chicken stock into the stockpot, and the red-orange grease sizzled. Shreds of chicken flopped into the jambalaya base.

Rooney's back was to me at the other burner top. He was carefully stirring boiled crawfish heads in heavy cream.

I set the pitcher in the wash basin. "What are you doing?"

"Where do you think crawfish cream sauce comes from, kid? Got that broth in there?" Never taking his eyes off the simmering cream, he reached above his head and turned up the radio volume.

"Yep."

"Okay, you need the trinity in there, so go in the cooler and get one each. Well, maybe two or three celeries."

"The what? Trinity? Like the Father, the Son, and the Holy Spirit?"

He turned around. "Green bell pepper, celery, and onion! You sure you're from here?"

I shrugged.

"Get one bell pepper and onion out of the walk-in. Get two or three celery stalks. Dice 'em up and throw 'em in. That broth will take a little while to start bubbling. And don't put in those seeds and bell centers, either."

By the time I'd cut the vegetables up and put them in the stock, Rooney was picking out the crawfish heads with tongs, one by one, and throwing them in the garbage. He turned up the radio volume again. "There's probably no science to it, but I think listening to this music when you're cooking this kind of stuff makes the food a bit better."

"It's okay, I guess." I'd never really liked Cajun music growing up. I think the French Quarter T-shirt shops ruined it for me. My whole life, I'd associated Cajun and Zydeco music with tourists; however, it is one of the last remaining authentic slivers of cultural inertia that Louisiana has left. Cajuns live within the heartland of Louisiana, and their music is its heartbeat.

"Where did you get the crawfish from?"

"I got a guy out in St. Martinville. He's harvesting early this year. Decent size for February, too."

Rooney checked his watch. "But it's time for talk radio." He spun the dial through static. "The show's pretty new. Talks a lot about what's going on down here. I think everyone else forgot about us already. All right, now dice up about four or five garlic toes. De-paper them, but I shouldn't have to tell you that. There should be some garlic left in that bin to your right. And beneath you in that cooler should be some tomato paste in a plastic cup. Stir a few spoons in there so the broth is good and orange. Don't put too much paste in there. I hate jambalaya with too much paste. It's like eating rice and ketchup. Blech!"

"I noticed that you're short on supplies out there. Are you having trouble getting deliveries?"

Rooney turned the burner to low and dipped his finger in the crawfish cream sauce and tasted it. "Getting there. Um, I can't recall having any issues getting things in. But I'm fixing to close shop for a month after today. Go visit my wife. Trying to use everything perishable. Everything else like the rice, pasta, and spices are sealed up in totes so the damn rats don't overrun this place."

"Where you going?"

"Fort Worth. She relocated there for work after Beckham. They'd have hired her anywhere, really. New York, Chicago, you name it. But she wanted to stay closer to home. Daughter needed to go to school somewhere, too."

"She doesn't want to move back?"

"Sure she does." He poured dry bow-tie pasta into a pot of water and turned the burner on high.

"What's stopping her?"

Renny set the stirring spoon down. "What's she gonna do here? She's a civil engineer by trade—and terrible at food service, mind you. She ain't got the patience for it. Not to mention, New Orleans is still a war zone out there. But hopefully that changes soon. Her firm is trying to set up a New Orleans office if all goes well with the courts."

I stirred in the garlic and tomato paste.

"You're gonna need the chicken. I gotta go in the cooler anyway to get the roast beef. I'll get it for ya while I'm in there. You don't have to keep stirring it like that. When you stir in the chicken, let it go for a while on its own. Let it do its thing. Just watch the pasta for me. It won't take too long to boil; just don't let it boil over everywhere until I come back."

I set the spoon on the stove top. Maybe I was wrong about this Renny Rooney. Was he one of us, or was he a Refounder? I was tempted to walk out on him right there and have him cook everything his own damn self. Now was the time to do it if I was going to. But how could this guy be for the Refounding? Especially being from

New Orleans? New Orleans had woven the very fabric of his identity, so anything otherwise was nothing short of fabrication.

Rooney fine-tuned the radio, and a man's voice thundered through the speakers:

"Let's just cut to the chase, folks. The City of New Orleans doesn't deserve its people, but they stick with it regardless; they are like an abused wife who still adores her husband who exploits her devotion. The difference here is that the wife is not surprised when she gets beat. You know, I might be sympathetic to people down there if they weren't so naive. They deserve what they get for sticking with a place that's quite frankly illogical to live in. And you'd think that the New Orleans government would be doing anything they could to keep people there and make them happy. Couldn't be further from the truth. I mean, quite frankly, they deserve what they got.

"Here's how I see it. The city never cared about its people, whereas the people overly cared about the city. One-sided relationship there. And literally everything about the place was a ticking time bomb. The coast, the river, the schools, the government, the crime, and hell, even the streets themselves looked like they were caving into the heart of hell. And this whole time, you know what people were concerned about? How *authentic* everything was. Like they were chasing a culture like a hawk chases a chickadee. To wear it out to death and then consume it! And now look at it. Ancient history!

"From the outside looking in, I see a city that was riddled with crime; can't really decide who's more criminal, the jailed or the jailers. The education system was just about the worst in the country. The city put its faith in the Corps of Engineers to build and maintain the river, which is like putting a pedophile in charge of a daycare center. And all the while, about a football field of coastline disappeared each damn day. And they were all just talking about who's 'New Orleans' and who's not, what restaurant is good, or what band is playing—and if you don't like said band or restaurant, then you might as well move to the arid panhandle of Texas, since it has more culture than you. You know how when you realize one of your uncles was actually a chronic cocaine fiend but as a child, you thought he was just jittery and always sweating? Well, New Orleans people never grew up to see the city for what it really was. I don't know what's worse: if they didn't see the telltale signs for disaster, or did and just ignored them. It's time to give it up. I admire their zeal, but please. A lot of the New Orleans people I know are a bunch of self-indulgent schmucks that believe they are better than everyone else.

"I can't stop hearing about the 'culture.' Culture of what? Longing for times past? I smell a paradox here. Anytime anyone wanted to change anything in New Orleans they just about got run out by the townies. Now they say New Orleans should progress and be more modern, yet when someone wants to tear down a crumbling building and put up a useful commerce center, they run them out of town for not saving and reconditioning the building because someone somewhat historic did something important in there sometime. Hell, the city's been destroyed. It *is* destroyed, and they just can't let it go. You can't have modernization without change, people! But many seem to think they are somehow higher than that simple truth.

"Let's face it, New Orleans is gone. It's [*bleep*] gone. But those people want to keep it that way. How irrational can you be? As if outside developers with no intention of retaining the New Orleans of the past are committing a mortal sin! Who in the hell do you think developed New Orleans in the first place? New Orleans was built by people with money who wanted to *make* money. Call them slave owners, call them robber barons, call them American entrepreneurs, call 'em what you want. The French didn't develop a hole in the swamp because they wanted to eventually create this multicultural Mecca that three hundred years later people could brag about and act like they created it in the first place. Anyplace that has a house on it was probably built by someone with money who didn't give a pickle-puss about 'culture.' Truth is, that's how culture is born. A bunch of assholes do a bunch of things for the wrong reasons, and one or two things turn out okay out of the mess. Then people make it out to be some kind of miracle. I swear, if I have to hear about 'culture' anymore, I'm gonna—"

"Ahhh, come on, man!" Rooney set down a bag of stuff by his stove and moved the pot off the burner. Water had been boiling over everywhere. "Seriously? How could you not notice?"

I shrugged. I was embarrassed, but also furious. Too furious to speak.

Rooney turned off the radio. "Well, gonna need you concentrating. We only got a few hours to get all this done. Yeah, this guy Chase is a bit much sometimes, and I don't agree with him all of the time. But he's the only one out there who even dares talking about the situation here."

I shrugged. "He's not the only one. There's *The Declaration*."

"What's your deal, kid? I leave for three minutes and you got your pants in a fuss."

I shrugged and turned to the simmering jambalaya.

"You got something ya wanna say, kid?"

I stirred the jambalaya. "Didn't know you were a Refounder."

Rooney grabbed my shoulder to turn me to face him. He poked his finger, which smelled of crawfish cream sauce, into my sternum. I squirmed back, and he just poked harder. "I'm gonna be straight with ya here, kid. I appreciate how the Vieux Carré Council is putting up a fight, I really do. But sometimes they forget what's most important." He then pointed elsewhere, relieving the pain in my chest. "This city don't live on out there in the goddamn buildings or in the streets." He dug his finger into my left pectoral. "It lives on in here. You follow me, kid? It's the people who make it what it is. It's the flesh and blood that gives New Orleans its heart. Not streets. Not artsy-fartsy architecture. It's *us*, damn you!"

Teachers' Office

She and Matrona were not much different after all, thought Mira. Both were women committed to the betterment of society; they just fought the good fight on different fronts. Matrona set out for the people's souls, whereas Mira set out for their minds. God knows, she thought, she couldn't be a follower of God in that sense. Both were women committed to the greater good at the sacrifice of their individualist hunger. Both were part of a collective entity with a collective end goal. Both had accepted a life of poverty, Mira unofficially. Both did God's work: Matrona clothed the naked and tended the sick; Mira educated the unfortunate. And sex, she thought. At this point, she figured she was having as much sex as Sister Matrona, since Derek remained locked away. The last time she'd had sex was with an Argentinean man visiting France, and it just hadn't felt quite right. To some extent, she had vowed celibacy also, not to God but to Derek. That celibacy, of course, depended upon his release.

It was nice, Mira thought, to have a casual conversation with another woman. Nearly all woman-to-woman interactions had been professional after she'd moved back. Mira and her principal. Mira and her students. Mira and her students' mothers; New Orleans had become a very masculine place with contractors, construction and demolition laborers, and military personnel. These professions were not exclusive to men; however, there were unarguably more of them. The tourists, too, were mostly men flocking to the New Carré for the brothels; however, every café employed at least one bisexual or gay woman because their customers were not exclusively men. There was no mention of an all-male or all-female homosexual brothel, given their business involvement with the Church.

She knew that the Refounders were hiring women to manage customer accounts for raw materials, sales departments, and SEO tactics to compete with the other resorts. Due to voracious competition, many companies had, by contract, forbade all employees to leave the confines of their workplaces and employer-sponsored lodgings. Moreover, the companies claimed that the streets were not safe for young women and scared their female employees with embellished data concerning sexual assault. Mira realized also that most women living in New Orleans post-Refounding stayed within their own walls, whatever their place in society was. The whores typically didn't leave the boundaries of the New Carré unless escorted by staff security. The nuns, ironically, also resided within the red-light district sheltered by the blessed walls of the convent and cathedral, and they also were escorted by armed men who allegedly could spill blood in God's name. As for the educators, Mira and most of her colleagues didn't have much time, or money, to spend outside of the classrooms and their subsidized dorm rooms.

Mira mentally noted the time on the clock hanging on the office wall. Nine teachers shared the office, but only one other teacher was there at the moment. Mira shared a fold-out table with two other teachers. The pile of Mr. Cooper's ungraded English essays had begun spilling over onto her allocated "desk" space. Mira had stacked several outdated professional development textbooks and poetry anthologies as a barrier to stop the endless essays from cascading onto her end of the table. Several stacking trays stood against the wall, and each class period had two slots labeled IN and OUT. Math tests and homework sheets were scattered about her desk space.

"So, Sister, I suggested offering some basic Greek language classes to the students next school year. Would you be interested in teaching here if Principal Whitman approves it? It wouldn't be full-time." Mira had to laugh at the thought of teaching not being full-time.

"I think that's wonderful. I would like to be part of this, but I would have to speak with the Archbishop."

"Oh, of course. I wouldn't expect you to quit your duties there. I know your real boss is kind of a big deal."

Matrona did not understand. A few moments of silence passed, and the legs of a chair across the room squeaked as another female teacher turned to face them.

Mira said, "I meant, I know you are devoted to God, so I wouldn't expect you to quit your duties at the church."

Matrona nodded, adjusted herself in her chair, and looked at her knees. "I will ask him. Much of my work to make the Greek support shelter is done. I would like to extend my service to the children of the city."

"Great! And if you can't, please refer someone else who would like to. Especially anyone with any teaching experience whatsoever. This wouldn't happen *this* school year, but maybe next or the year after that. These things take time...apparently."

"Do you think your school would like starting a Christian service program?"

Mira's eyes widened. "What would that entail?"

"I'm sorry?"

"What would the students do?"

"Work at the Greek shelter or one of the other support shelters. We have soup kitchens, donation centers, and rebuilding projects. And nursing intoxicated men back to health."

Mira remembered the nuns helping the drunk men near the cathedral. "Maybe not that last one. Though I'm sure you would need the extra help."

"I must speak with your principal?"

Mira reversed the cross in her legs. "Let's work out the details first so that we have a pretty set plan when we do. I'm actually a religion teacher here," she laughed a little inside, "so I might be able to do a field trip or something to get things going."

"Okay." She rubbed her knees. "I still must ask the Archbishop about this idea, too."

"I don't see how he could say no. It's...it's perfect." Mira smiled.

"Thank you. I must return to the church." Matrona stood.

"This has been great, really." Mira stood and shook her hand. "Get the okay from Fullerton, and call me. We can talk about this over some drinks…um…or coffee."

"Okay, bless you."

Mira said goodbye, pulled her hair into a ponytail, and resumed organizing her math papers. It *was* perfect, she thought. The students could learn firsthand about the importance of charity and hardship, the church could have more volunteers, and Mira could spend less time in the classroom talking about religion.

"Excuse me, Ms. Roche."

Mira turned around.

Spanish teacher Pam Lucero said, "I'm sorry; I couldn't help but eavesdrop. Am I keeping you from your work?" From her accent, it was evident that she was originally from either Central or South America. Mira didn't know where, and felt bad about asking, so she didn't and kept wondering.

"Not at all, Mrs. Lucero."

Pam Lucero was an attractive woman in her late thirties. Her skin was light-brown, and her cheeks were peppered with dark freckles. Her long hair was so black it gleamed. She came over and sat in the chair Sister Matrona had just vacated. "This is related to what you and the sister talked about." She moved her open hands up and down as if she were juggling invisible balls. "Here is my problem: I have many students from Spanish-speaking families who are just not learning anything in my class."

"Because they already speak it at home?"

"Well, I have some that speak it at home, and they are really just wasting their time in my class. Then there are others who *haven't* spoken much Spanish at home. A lot of them watch so many videos and converse mainly in English on the social networks. They are out of practice but can learn it quickly. But they don't really progress any further than the other students. What I am saying is that we might possibly reorganize things so that the Spanish-speaking students could help tutor the other students, or something like that. Students learn better from each other than they do from us."

Mira nodded in agreement. "I think it's a great idea. Have you talked with Mrs. Whitman about it?"

"No, I have not yet."

"You should. I think she'd go for that."

"Um," Lucero pulled her shiny black hair over her shoulders. "I also wanted to ask about this event you're planning for the school."

"The St. Joseph's Altar?"

"Yes. What is this?"

"It's an Italian...well, maybe more Sicilian...tradition in New Orleans. It's March nineteenth every year, and it celebrates the feast day of St. Joseph. It's basically a big potluck party, just no meat dishes. Only seafood or vegetarian, being Lent and all. Whatever's left over gets donated to soup kitchens or homeless shelters. There's much more to it, but that's basically it."

"Okay. And are we only supposed to cook Italian dishes?"

"Oh, no. It just can't have any meat in it, other than seafood, of course. Desserts are needed, too."

"Good, good. Because some of my students asked me about that. They weren't sure what they could bring."

Chapter 17

The streets bustled as if New Orleans had been resurrected just within the few hours I worked inside. It was as if the people had become one united life form—one single beating heart rather than many individual ones. When that happens, it all becomes natural. It becomes real.

Even though the Monster had permitted Mardi Gras, he had strictly prohibited masks and costumes. Considering the hard times at hand, everyone laughed and smiled. Though their smiles were genuine that day, they seemed to be wearing masks.

We had finished cooking around nine, and people had been coming up to the door. A sign on the door read "Opening station outside @ 10."

Rooney wrapped foil around the two trays each of jambalaya and crawfish pasta. "Why don't you go scope it all out?"

I turned from the window. "You're sure?"

"Yeah. You've been cooped up in this kitchen all morning. I can tell you want to see it."

"And you don't need me?"

He poured himself a cup of fresh coffee. "At ten I will, yeah. But take an hour. I need a little quiet time for myself before all the crazy." He sat down, resting his elbows on a small metal counter. He nodded. "Ten o'clock. And, dear God, lock it." He then took a long sip of the hot coffee.

Three small white children ran past me, their parents strutting behind them carrying cans of beer.

The father yelled, "Don't go near the debris! Stay in the street."

The mother yelled, "Or you'll get a nail in your foot and get tetanus."

He continued, "And then you'll be bedridden at the Hyatt. And I ain't talking about the hotel."

A black family gathered on a small concrete slab near a red building. A large man wearing a white tank top and long jean shorts rotated cuts of meat on a charcoal grill. Two older women sat in lawn chairs while two teenage girls and one younger boy sat atop overturned buckets.

One of the women said, "Say, Jonah. You better turn that before it burn."

"I'm gonna get it, Ms. Lagrasse. Damn." He closed the grill and hung the tongs on a hook. As I passed them, he nodded and said, "How y'all this morning?"

I said, "Doing pretty good. And yourself?"

He gestured with his hands and arms as if he were showcasing a large fish. "It's Mardi Gras mornin', babe! Do whatcha wanna! You heard me? Do whatcha wanna!"

I would have saluted him with my beer if I'd had one. Instead I gave him a thumbs-up. That made me want a drink badly. It was only nine in the morning, but that didn't matter much. Mardi Gras was timeless, in whatever way you wanted it to be. I walked up to what must have been the parade route. Large crowds of people stood and sat on both sides of the street. Frankly, I was surprised there were so many people in New Orleans then.

I know now that it wasn't only people living here, though. I learned later that Captain McMason had allowed for special event visas and charged top dollar for them. So some of the spectators were exiles craving anything New Orleans.

"Wait, do you know where they are?" A young red-haired girl adjusted the huge sunflower in her hair. She wore the kind of dress that the "new" hippies were wearing, one that looked like loose fermented skin.

"No, I don't see them." A young man scratched his neatly groomed mustache and raised his new Eagle, searching for a signal. He wore skinny jeans over designer cowboy boots. His thin brown tie was purposely loose around his neck, not even within the collar of his white shirt, which had light-blue embroidered lines. He pushed the brown fedora down on his head and adjusted his eyeglass frames—which lacked actual lenses. If a 1920s newsman and Lubbock, Texas, had decided to have a baby, he would have been the recessive result.

She put large orange sunglasses on. "Call them, duh."

"I don't have reception."

At first I thought that these two were refuting McMason's ban on costumes, but then I realized this was how they normally dressed. I marched back to Rooney's. It's odd how a bunch of strangers can make you feel so alone.

I knocked on the door and he answered eventually.

"Horseshit! Is it ten already?"

"No, I just came back early."

About an hour had passed before I realized we had sold a whole tray of both the jambalaya and the crawfish pasta. We had arranged the trays horizontally on the fold-out table in front of us so each of us could serve from both. Underneath the table, two storage containers were at our feet. One had foil-wrapped roast beef po-boys with Swiss and Creole mustards. The other had muffalettas made with the Rooney family's olive salad recipe and premium sliced provolone, Chisesi's ham, and Genoa salami.

In between us, a small lockbox sat on a crate. I suggested that we place the money box behind us to save space; however, Rooney refused to put us, and his profits, at risk by ever turning our backs to the hungry, desperate masses. He said, "You turn your back to the wrong person, and they'll shoot you in the back. There's food and cash right out in the open. Ain't gonna risk it, kid." He also had a loaded pistol under his apron, just in case anyone was that brazen.

The line for Rooney's food stand could have been nine miles long for all I knew. The customers kept coming and coming. The cash just rolled off my fingertips into Rooney's bank box, which rested on top of a laminated pink PRA permit.

I don't think I've seen that much money before or since.

Once the parade started up the street, the line died down and we caught our breath.

Rooney wiped the sweat off his balding spot, which was sunburned. "Eat yourself something when you got the chance. Ain't got much left. We've been doing good." A few seconds of silence passed between us. "So, you say you're from here. Where about?"

"Well, I guess both River Ridge and Esplanade Ridge Avenue." I unwrapped a roast beef po-boy and dug in. The savory debris juice and zesty Creole mustard combined to make my own Mardi Gras Mambo in my mouth.

He chuckled. "What, the two halves met in the middle?"

I swallowed the large bite. "No. Born and raised in River Ridge but later moved to Esplanade."

"Return flight, huh?"

"What?" I took another bite.

"Parents moved back to New Orleans?"

I didn't feel like digging into my dark insides by telling him about my parents' deaths and how my uncle had raised me. So I just said, "Yes," once I stopped chewing.

"Yep. Same thing. You've heard of white flight? Well, later there was a white return flight. My grandparents moved from the Marigny to Kenner. I guess an Italian family of six kids outgrew their tiny, crumbling shotgun house. I guess even that place was the Hilton compared to the Italian ghetto in the French Quarter where my ancestors first lived. My mom and I later moved to Mid-City, Bayou St. John area."

"Rooney's Italian?"

"No, that's my father's last name. He flew the coop and left my mom to raise us on her own. Not sure what he was, but whatever it was, it can't dilute that Italian blood."

"Never really knew my family history."

"I'd like to say you're probably a mutt of Irish, Italian, and German like a lot of people who were born and raised here. But I think so many people from across the country moved here and stayed after Katrina, it's kind of a genetic crapshoot now." He perked up and said over my shoulder, "How you doing, sweetheart? What can we get you?"

Rooney's storefront was meager and rough, yet industrious and alive. It could easily have been an Italian grocery in the early 1900s, just from the look of it. I took a big bite of the sandwich. Rooney cleared his throat. I looked at him, and he motioned for me to turn around.

Mira cautiously smiled at me. Her eyes locked on mine while my mouth was full of po-boy. I had to swallow and chew in increments.

"Tough to swallow, isn't it?" she said.

Zesty Betty

After writing the week's lesson plans and the month's progress reports along with grading what seemed to be 150 religion homework assignments and 153 math tests, Mira was ravenous. It was almost four in the afternoon, and she hadn't eaten since breakfast. Her stomach needed something heavy to balance out her numb brain cells. Something fried, she thought, or maybe rich and savory. Or both. Fried catfish and some baked macaroni would do her just right. Or a chicken-fried steak with gravy and mash. Yeah, that. All of it, she thought.

She stuffed the graded papers in manila folders in the trays marked OUT and searched on her Eagle for eateries that were still open. Rooney Rooster's closed at three. His grocery only served fresh po-boys for the lunch rush. Though Rooney's Grocery probably had some cold, wrapped muffalettas in the cooler, Mira craved something hot and greasy. New Orleans was in the midst of a state of demolition and redevelopment, so the social eatery scene was at its nadir in the city's history. Most, if not all, restaurants and joints were only open for lunch or were closed on Mondays. Or both. There was the Rio Rojo, but it was a little too pricey for Mira's salary, plus she didn't want to risk seeing her favorite city inspector again. She didn't want Mexican food anyway. She wanted something New Orleans, and that was harder to find than ever.

Mira tapped the sandwich icon on her Eagle screen and an image of a buzzing radio tower. Her phone scanned the social cloud for signals emitted from transmitters required of food establishments. Five results were found in the entire New Orleans area, most of which she knew were closed, either for the day or for good. One place that was open was the Zesty Betty, a great soul-food café that had been closed since Beckham. It had not shown up before, so Mira tapped it.

> Grand reopening today! New owners! New menu! Doors
> open at 4!^{3:52pm} ZB

Mira bolted out of the office and locked it behind her. She needed to get there fast, she thought, because surely there would be a line. She asked herself out loud, "How did I not know about this?"

Her ankle ached as she strutted down Baladucci Drive. Her wishful mind toyed with her pleading stomach, teasing it with images and remembered smells of smothered chicken and white beans and rice, shrimp and mirliton stuffed bell peppers, and fried eggs topped with crawfish étouffée. She didn't notice the empty hole in the sky where the Superdome had stood just a few weeks before. Maybe there was hope for New Orleans to preserve some semblance of itself, after all, she thought. If this restaurant came back, they'd keep some of the culture alive at least. And maybe there would be more places that came back. Yes, she thought. We will prevail. We will survive as a culture, one bowl of gumbo at a time. She decided to order that, too.

The green awning came into view down Prentiss Street, extending from the original concrete building that had somehow survived the hurricane. A few people walked ahead of her and went in. At least there isn't a line outside, she thought. However, when the bell rang upon entering, Mira was already at the back of a line of ten people. The smell of fresh food filled her nostrils and nearly made her stomach twist. The line was moving relatively fast, just as it had before. Nothing fancy. Just great food, true to the city. The place was alive with chatter and the clamor of silverware and plates. Mostly white customers, which was quite different from before Beckham, she observed, but Mira reasoned that was the nature of things. The chalkboard menu read simply, "Full menu coming soon!"

An older man in front of her turned around. "Hello, miss. I love that shirt! Where did you get it?" He had a silver head of hair, combed over to his right ear.

Mira looked down at the lettering on her T-shirt: "NOLA Exile."

"I love it. Where can I get that?"

"I got it online. I lived in France for a while, so it was quite fitting. I'm not sure of the company or website, but if you just search for 'NOLA in Exile,' you'll find it, I'm sure." She thought to herself that his hair would be one hell of a ski slope for miniature thrill seekers.

"Thanks! I'll definitely check it out." The man ordered and moved off to the side of the counter.

Mira stepped to the cashier and said, "Great to see y'all are back!"

A young white woman, wearing a clean white apron said, "Thanks, welcome!"

"Please tell me y'all have the stuffed bell peppers."

"We do! Anything else?"

"Everything else." Mira laughed and reached into her purse for her wallet.

"Well, here's our new menu." The clerk showed her a laminated printout. "We're still working on having a digital menu. You know, more trees, more air."

"Agreed." Mira took the menu and read it:

Red Beans and Quinoa. A traditional New Orleans favorite with a skinny twist! Served with a side of baby kale. $12

Eggplant-Stuffed Bell Pepper. A hearty treat for your stomach and heart! Served with sweet-potato mash (made with almond milk!). $10

E-Tofu-ée. Get your étouffée fix and spare a couple of mudbugs in the process! Served with spicy corn mash. $11 – add more tofu for only $4 more

Phombeaux. Get your favorite two New Orleans soups all in one bowl! Served with warm wheat rolls. $6

Vegan Pastalaya. Our homemade sun-dried tomato base gives this famous dish a zest even andouille can't match! $12

Kale Creole. Just because it's healthy doesn't mean it's not spicy! Served with sweet zucchini bread. $15

Not Ya Mama's Poor Boy. It would make sense that a poor boy would be skinny, and so that's how we make ours! Choose any below. Served on a fluffy woven bagel loaf or a kale torti-lla. $10 – go gluten-free for $2 more
> – Creole Tomato (Gramercy, LA) and Pesto
> – Red Bean (burrito only)
> – Farm-Fresh Eggplant (Kiln, MS)
> – Oyster Mushrooms and Sweet Onions (Reserve, LA)

Mira's mouth ran dry. "Um, I'm confused."

"Okay, how can I help you?"

Mira wanted to ask where the *real* food on the menu was. But she asked, "Well, I remember the menu being…different."

"We're new ownership. It's our goal to preserve traditional Louisiana cuisine but give people a little healthier option."

"Uh-huh." Mira looked around her.

One customer said, "This is so great. New Orleans is back, baby!"

Another customer at a different table said, "Finally, I can eat the food here and not feel so shitty."

Bewildered, Mira shook her head. She felt an ache in her stomach that went beyond hunger. She looked at the walls surrounding her with kitschy posters and signs saying, "Naturally Nawlins" and "Nouvelle Orleans" and "Who Dat? We dat!" This wasn't New Orleans, she thought. It was a mirage of New Orleans, except it worked the opposite: Normally the false image disappeared when you looked closely to reveal the real one. But this time, the real image of New Orleans had vanished. For the first time in her life, for just a few moments, she actually felt like she could commit arson.

"So, just the bell pepper then for you?"

Mira put her wallet back in her purse. "I'm sorry. I…I'm sorry." She turned for the door and weaved through the line of customers that now ran down the block. Now that she couldn't have any soul food, she might as well have a drink for the soul, she thought. A vodka tonic might do it. A hundred vodka tonics would *definitely* do it.

Chapter 18

Silence can be tranquil or agonizing, but this was somewhere in between. Clearly both of us had plenty to say, but this wasn't the time to hash out years of separation. I had always dreaded our reunion because I envisioned an explosion of emotions and frustration. Her silence, however, concerned me. I needed to break it before it broke me. As we walked toward the parade route, I said, "Hey, remember that day when we skipped school and hung out at the river?"

As we walked, she looked forward and smiled. She looked at me and nodded. "You mean when you first kissed me? Then, yes."

"Let's go."

She stopped. "Go where?"

"The river."

"What river?"

"The...Missing River."

"A little too soon."

"That's what everyone's calling it."

She looked at me apologetically. "We can go." She pushed her reddish-brown hair behind her ears. "Where is it?"

"I think that's south."

She looked down, forward, and behind. "I think you're right. I think this is St. Joseph Street. I remember the bricks."

Long ago, the street had been cleared by the Gulf Guard of America, back before the Monster took over. Brown bricks piled on either side of the road were the remains of nineteenth-century warehouses turned apartments. The treacherous street itself consisted of uneven cobblestones, probably upturned from bulldozers and Bobcats. Two buzzards circled above us.

After about two blocks, we saw what had once been the Convention Center, now severed by a loose dredging ship the way a knife cuts through butter. To the right, the ship's bow buried itself in an old hotel. The keel and propeller dug into the street, which must have been Convention Center Boulevard. To the left, the Convention Center building stretched for a few blocks, but it had been flattened to our right. The ship seemed to have pushed all of the debris and structural elements of the center with it, making the walk to the river quite easy. We had had homecoming dances and proms at this place, which was now just crushed concrete and steel.

I say this in retrospect. Neither of us even thought twice about that decimated history as we walked through the ruins. It was just what you did when the city of your childhood had been uprooted before your very eyes. All of your precious memories dissolved into malaise and obscurity. An upturned steamboat sat crushed into the Convention Center's back side to our left, and the coastal wind picked up as we neared the Missing River. The old ship's paddle wheel spun in the wind like a windmill.

The salty Gulf air blew into our nostrils. I'd never felt the sea breeze in New Orleans before. I'd first smelled that essence when my parents took me to Ship Island. It's one of the only memories I have of them, and what I remember the most is throwing a temper tantrum. I was more interested in playing a pirate video game than enjoying the ferry ride or the beach. In the game, you got points if you found Jolly Rogers in a series of mazes. I got fussy when they took it away from me so that they could actually spend time *with* me, not with me simply around them. We joined a tour of some boring old building, and I scratched a Jolly Roger into one of the bricks, or tried to, anyway. It was more like an upside-down egg above an X. When they realized what I had done, they yelled, and I cried. They had to drag me back to the ferry along the sandy boardwalk.

I didn't have to go to the beach for a sea breeze anymore. We couldn't see the Gulf, but it was coming. And it was just as insatiable and ravenous as the Monster and his indirect army of Refounders.

Off to our right, the Crescent City Connection Bridge stood in abso-lute isolation. The connecting roads had collapsed, so just the steel frame stood over the Missing River like a pair of astronomical anten-nae. A large black plume wafted over it for a minute, as if it were burning, but then I realized it was a massive flock of birds. Now, the bridge was nothing but a bird sanctuary.

I hadn't seen the river since Beckham had pushed north and sab-otaged the Old River Control Structure so that the Mississippi and Atchafalaya Rivers could finally consummate their marriage and become one. I hadn't realized how deep it had been. A small bayou crawled below 200-foot river-mud bluffs that had dried out in dif-ferent colors: the "bank" was lighter, like sand, while the base of the Mississippi Gorge was a wet black clay that could swallow a man whole. Both of us had been desensitized to tragedy for some time, but losing the river was different.

We just gazed into the dark channel barely deep enough for a pirogue, not uttering a word. When it comes to tragedy, severity and words are proportional. The words come later, but upon witnessing history, there are no words. And the proof lies in what you are read-ing right now. All of this insight and observation came to me in a jail cell many months later. It was a geological event: a testament to the fickleness of the Mississippi River and how it had made the delta around us, and thus how much it could take back. It was a histori-cal disaster: one of death and devastation of biblical proportions. It was a cultural purge: All of what New Orleans had built itself to be, for better or for worse, had been washed away, finalizing its place for either complete ruin or the totality of Americanization. It was a socioeconomic milestone: public policy revamped concerning the role of the feds and the corporations concerning flood protection and historical preservation, along with the legitimacy of corporate bigwigs to constitutionally confiscate communities from the people. The Mississippi River had been New Orleans's umbilical cord, keep-ing it alive all these centuries. Now that it had been cut off, was the city we all knew and loved just a prenatal dream after all?

Something enormous splashed from below, and we stepped closer to the edge of the Missing River. At first, it seemed like some mutated monster had crawled from the water. It was half shiny gray and half green and scaly with a pair of stubby arms. It rolled itself up out of the water, thrashing about as if suffocating. A giant catfish, the size of a small walrus, was trying to eat an alligator that was too big to swallow.

"Ugh," Mira turned away while I looked on, mesmerized.

The catfish's eyes, the size of pool cue balls, flicked back and forth. It rolled its mouth from side to side, working tirelessly to suck in the gator. Its fishy mustache writhed like spiny antennae. Its gills expanded for any drop of water in the oxygenized void. The gator's tail churned the wet river mud around them. Its hind legs searched frantically for leverage, something to scratch or push off of. Its front claws slashed through the gills from the inside out.

So, we are all just beasts. Even with them, hunger goes beyond mere sustenance. Power. The need for dominion. It all runs within our veins, no matter whether they pump warm or cold blood. We just think we're better because we try and do it with green leaflets of paper before we resort to teeth and claws.

I said, "Well, it gets what it deserves."

"The what?"

"The catfish."

"Why?"

"That thing's probably eating up his insides."

"Well, maybe there's nothing left for it to eat. It's gonna die for sure if it doesn't eat it."

"You got to at least admire the fight in the gator."

"Yeah, well he's gonna die anyway, right?"

"Well, yeah, but that's not my point."

She folded her arms. "If both die, it's a win, then?"

"Well, not exactly…"

"Fighting for your life when you're already dead seems silly to me."

Back at the parade route, crowds cheered.

Mira cleared her throat and spoke nervously. "Derek, I need to get back to my students, make sure they're ready and have what they need for the show." She inhaled and exhaled deeply, her hands on her hips. She gazed to the left toward Algiers Point, which looked like more of a peak now. She folded her arms again and looked at me, but not at my eyes. "Um, after the festival, would you be interested in going with me to—"

"Yes! Absolutely, yes!"

She shook her head in surprise. "But I haven't said to what yet."

"I'll come with you."

"Okay," she looked down at her shoes, blushing. "Meet me behind the school after the last show."

Teachers' Office

Derek,

Sometimes I wonder if it's worth it anymore. Not the students, they're always worth it. New Orleans, I mean. I was so excited when I heard that the Zesty Betty reopened. Remember how good that food was? Well, I went, only to find a bunch of yippies running the place, and they had changed the menu to vegetarian. Red Beans and quinoa! Seriously? And what makes it worse, they acted like they were the real thing. My mom used to talk about this all the time. But I'm not sure if it is real anymore. Sometimes I feel like I'm in a hallucination where everyone's tripping on acid, seeing things that I can't. Or maybe more like a stage production where everyone wants to join the production but doesn't care about how to produce it.

These days, the only thing that reminds me of New Orleans are my students. As long as the students keep being true to themselves, New Orleans will come back. If not, we'll all have to give in to the whoredom, one way or another. We'll all have to play our part in the production of the original New Orleans that we all, in a sense, played our part in destroying.

Then the Greek tragedy of New Orleans will be complete. Ha, see what I did there? Except the Greeks aren't tragic at all. Maybe they'll give some cultural sense to the city before companies claim that, too. I'm actually trying to collaborate with a Greek nun at the church to give the students some real service experience instead of boring Bible babble. I think that...

Several girls screamed in the hallway. Mira swallowed the air she had intended to breathe. She dropped her pen and waited a few seconds for any other sound to indicate the nature of the problem. No gunshots. Mira stood, but before she could step into the hallway, three girls ran into her office.

Renisha Gresham said, "Ms. Mira, there's a big rat in the hall!"

Mira breathed a sigh of relief, thinking how crazy it was that rats could ever be *good* news. Then she said, "Well, close the door. Don't let it in here." She sat down in her chair.

Mr. Cooper called out down the hall, "It ran outside. It's okay!"

One of the girls said, "Well, at least that man good for something." Then she noticed Mira and said, "Oh, I'm sorry, ma'am."

Mira shook her head.

The third girl cocked her head, asserting in a high-pitched tone, "What you apologizing for? That man be trippin'!"

Mira said, "Ladies, the less you complain about your teachers to other teachers, the better it is for everybody."

She said, "Oh, all right."

Renisha Gresham and the two other girls pulled out their Eagles and engaged in their screens.

Mira felt that, if they had some concern to discuss, she'd be okay with having them stay in the shared office. But it seemed like they were just lingering. "So, Ms. Gresham, what did you think of today's lesson?"

All three looked up from their Eagles, and then the two looked at Renisha, who looked down at her phone. "Um, it was good."

One of the girls looked out the door. "Hey, they meetin' up with us in the cafeteria."

Renisha said, "See you tomorrow, Ms. Mira. I'm sorry."

Mira waved, smiling. Works every time, she thought. Mira picked up the pen and went back to her letter. She looked at the clock. She had twenty-six minutes before class. She bit down on the pen, thinking of what she needed to tell Derek. She didn't want to say too much about the inspector and the permit fiasco until it was resolved. It was also highly likely that the warden was reading these letters, too. She tapped the pen on her table/desk, thinking. Just a conversation where I can touch him, she thought, without sticking my arms through steel bars would be heaven.

She wrote:

Have you at least heard about McMason? What does that mean for your testimony? And, more importantly, your amnesty? I'm going to try to...

Someone knocked on her open office door. She looked up.

A young black man wearing a grease-splattered chef shirt and pinstriped black pants leaned in the door.

"David?"

"How you doin', Ms. Mira?"

She put her pen down, shrugged, and sat back in her chair, tugging her interlocked fingers across her stomach. Her high school sweetheart, with whom she had just rekindled a relationship, was being held prisoner. She had barely escaped sexual assault in the New Carré, had been wrongfully accused of soliciting, and would have been arrested if not for the Archbishop. She was being extorted by the city inspector for trying to have a student-family activity. And obviously, this was the first time she'd seen David since he had raged from her classroom. For almost a year, she hadn't known if he was alive or dead. But "Okay" is what she told him.

"You ain't givin' these kids a hard time, nah?" He chuckled.

"I do what I can." She dug her fingers deeper into her stomach. "How's your mother?"

He stopped smiling, licked his lips, and looked at the floor. "Better," he said. "Yeah, she better."

"That's good. What brings you here?"

David looked her in the eyes. "I came to talk to Mrs. Whitman about taking that test in the summer, so I can get that diploma. Ya 'eard me?"

Mira smiled and looked down at her hands. "That's...that's wonderful, David." She looked him in the eyes. "What do you want to do?"

"Maybe start up a community center or something like that to help these kids get back on track."

Mira nodded, smiling. "Like a cooking school?" She pointed at his attire.

"Nah. But maybe. I'm just cooking at the Belle for the time being."

"*Cooking* at the Southern Belle?" Mira raised her eyebrows.

"Yeah."

Mira eyed him inquisitively.

"Awright, awright, Ms. Mira. I get it! We's a whorehouse. But they shut all that down come nine to eleven and from three to five. The rooms get cleaned and the girls get a break. Kitchen's open and we do a good job."

Mira was quiet for a few moments. "Lunch at a brothel? I'm not too sure…"

"Nah, nah. Come on in. I work all week. These new people down here like that southern food."

"Like what?"

"Like…chicken-fried steak and mash potatoes an' gravy, corn-bread, and pork ribs."

Mira's stomach growled. Less than twenty-four hours prior, she would have given anything for some real southern cooking. "And… your red beans maybe?"

"They all right."

"Better than the Zesty Betty?"

He closed his eyes and nodded, holding back what seemed to be disdain.

"Okay. Maybe I will," Mira said.

He chuckled. "Awright then." He started toward the hall.

Mira picked up the pen and looked at her letter to Derek.

"Ms. Mira?"

"Hm?" She looked up.

"I…uh…I 'preciate…how ya cared 'bout us dat much."

Mira smiled, looking at her desk.

A few moments of silence passed between them.

"Well, come holla at me at the Belle."

Mira looked up at him. "I just might."

David nodded. "A'ight, Ms. Mira."

"Bye, David. Tell your mom I said hello."

"Right, yeah." He walked into the hall.

Mira breathed deeply and set her palms on the desk. Then she pulled her hair into a ponytail and picked up the pen again. She looked at her letter and reread it. She smiled and underlined: <u>As long as the students keep being true to themselves, New Orleans will come back.</u>

Chapter 19

I must have heard the motto "laissez les bon temps rouler" a zillion times in my life, but I never knew what that meant until the Mardi Gras after Hurricane Beckham. Officially, it translated to "Let the good times roll," and I had always felt that it was simply an eclectic way of saying "let's have some fun." But I was wrong. It runs much deeper. It was a time to let go. Let go of our individualism and join our collective Earth. Let go of hardship and woe, welcoming blessed moments of joy, incarnated as our state of being. And those good times would roll until the wheel of fortune stopped, bringing us back to a grim reality. But, for that good time, we are immortal, willingly held in a cage of eternal jubilation. Whether it's self-liberation or self-denial, I still can't decide. That's how the Mardi Gras crowd regulated itself. Of course, drunkards and bullies found opportunities to ruin a few people's good time; however, gatherings on such a grand scale typically turned to rioting elsewhere in the world. But not during Mardi Gras in New Orleans. Even for that time, with everyone desperate and hungry, revelry without incident had to be the work of some kind of gris-gris.

I walked back to my truck near Rooney's Grocery to retrieve an empty Dr. Tichenor's mouthwash bottle I had filled with Elmer's Ryan because Mardi Gras, as with any celebration, wouldn't be the same without a little booze. The line had all but faded away, now that the parade had rolled by a few blocks up. Rooney sat in the chair, cross-legged with both hands on his knees. Four trays were stacked inside each other, with a massive ball of used aluminum foil inside the top one.

"Thanks for letting me take a break. You want some whiskey?"

"I thank ya, but no. Gotta keep my wits about me. That's a lotta money in that box there. In fact, just watch the table for a minute, kid, while I go lock up most of this cash inside."

"Okay."

"All we got left is a few sandwiches. They cleaned me out of the pasta and the jambalaya once you left. Next year, I…or we…will have to double up. Here," he handed me a few bills and change. "Just in case anyone needs anything while I'm inside." He took the armored safe box and unlocked the front door, never turning his back to me. I guess no matter how much magic is in the Mardi Gras air, enough cash around could make anyone untrustworthy.

Sitting in the chair behind the serving table, I unscrewed the top of my Dr. Tichenor's flask and took a generous swig. No glass was ever permitted on the parade route, and I wasn't going to break that rule. A car horn sounded from the parade route, and cheers followed. The door opened, and Rooney came out with the lockbox.

"Anybody come?"

"Nope."

"I tell ya what, kid. I only got about…" Rooney bent down and counted the remaining po-boys and mufalettas in the container underneath the table, "five left. I think I'm gonna pack it all up."

"You sure?"

He held out his hand for the whiskey. I handed the bottle to him and he took a modest sip. He groaned and said, "Top shit right there. Um, yeah. I haven't eaten since breakfast, so I'll have one and maybe save one for tonight. You want one?"

I never passed up free food. "Yeah, sure. A muffaletta. Thanks."

He handed me one. "So that's two left. I might just take 'em down to the parade and give 'em to someone who needs 'em. Go ahead and enjoy yourself, kid. I got it from here."

I stood and shook Rooney's hand. "Thanks for the work and for the food."

"To be honest, I thought you'd forgotten about the whole thing. Never know with you kids these days." He wiped the sweat off his

bald head. "Now get the hell outta here, and go get her before someone else does."

By the time the second float passed by, the potatoes and carrots bulged
from my pants pockets, making it seem like I suffered from bulbous
hip cysts. A black family in front of me had nearly filled a laundry
hamper with vegetables. The preteen son held up a green fishing net,
and the students aboard the floats couldn't resist testing their accu-
racy. Perhaps next year, I thought, I'd do the same thing. As a small
child, your Mardi Gras high depended on the size of your bounty. As
a teenager, it depended on how much alcohol your liver could process. As a young adult, it was a strange balance between the two. This
Mardi Gras, however, everyone was high on purpose—the purpose
of restoring some sense of self-preservation. I felt the reinforcement,
the reassurance that things were moving in the right direction.

A small high school band marched behind the second float.
Some of the kids wore band uniforms, others wore street clothes.
They marched with high knees, like a brass army. People whistled
and cheered them on as they played. With the small population and
low enrollment, only one or two students played each type of instrument. A red pickup hauled a trailer with a big fleur-de-lis cardboard
cutout stapled on the side. The students had cut letters spelling "The
Saints" on the side, but had cleverly pinned the bottom of the S so it
hung down, leaving the message "The aints." Depressing, sure, but we
had to accept the team's departure someday.

A man next to me sighed, "Awww. That's messed up," in an appre-
ciative, playful tone.

There were about a dozen middle school students inside the trailer,
each wearing a Saints shirt or jersey. Two of them were white while
the rest were black. A small black boy wearing a Drew Brees jersey
gripped a red potato like a quarterback and signaled to the boy with
the fishnet to "go long." The boy turned around and smacked into me.
"Sorry 'bout that," he said but kept running. The young quarterback
pumped the potato a few times before launching it over my head into

the fishnet. The crowd around me cheered, and the boy jumped up and down on the float as if he had thrown the winning touchdown.

After float three, a familiar black truck rumbled down the street. A high-pitched squeal silenced the crowd. It set my nerves afire, and I'm sure others felt it, too. As the truck approached, a large cage in the truck bed came into view. Two wild boars were tied at the feet, thrashing about in the cage and screaming. Judge was hunched forward with both hands on the steering wheel. I stepped around people to get to the truck. When he saw me, he shrugged apologetically and rolled the passenger window down. If he puts any more dip in his mouth, I thought, his bottom lip will burst.

"Didn't know I'd get into *this* mess." He spit in a Mardi Gras cup between his thighs. "You want in? I'm going to the park."

"Okay, yeah." I opened the door and got in. "Never been in a Mardi Gras parade before."

"Well, believe me, this wasn't part of the deal. I told a friend I'd trap a few hogs for him because he was planning on roasting them and selling the meat at the music festival." He spit. "Shoulda just shot they ass and field dressed 'em. But he wanted all the guts, too, and I wasn't risking them spoiling. You, um, got a problem?" Judge said, looking at my bulging pockets.

"Oh, just throws," I said, pulling the vegetables out.

"Oh. This guy could use those in the pig roast. He might be willing to give you some pork in return for 'em."

"So, he's roasting them?"

"Well," he spit into the cup, "not enough time to slow roast 'em. I think we're gonna have to just butcher 'em quick and grill 'em up. There used to be place off Judge Perez that did pork good dat way. We should be awright. Maybe you can help me clean 'em."

"Okay sure." I pulled my Dr. Tichenor's flask from my back pocket. "Want some?"

Judge sat with his back to the seat, more relaxed now that he had some company. "Nah."

I unscrewed the cap and sipped from the bottle.

"Hey, man, you wanna mix that? I think there's a cup under the seat. And a soft drink might be back here." He reached behind his seat and retrieved a canned Coke. "I ain't got no ice. But now you won't look like such a bum."

"Thanks. I haven't had a whiskey and Coke in a while." The cola was hot and fizzed violently as I poured it into the cup. A generous pour of Elmer's Ryan followed. The essence of the bourbon filled me to the core, and I sat back in the car seat feeling luxurious and imagining myself as a parade rider of the old days. I held up the cup to inspect what was on it. It was from the iconic Rex parade, the big krewe that used to roll on Mardi Gras day. An illustration of a white steer with the words *Boeuf Gras* was on one side of the cup and some Latin motto was imprinted on the other side.

"What does 'Pro Bono Publico' mean?"

"What does what mean?"

I showed him the cup. He shrugged and spit out the window.

"And what's with the cow on this cup?" I asked.

"Beats me, brah."

Judge turned off toward the park as soon as the parade veered right. The route had another large horseshoe to do before doubling back to the parade's end point. He parked, and I stepped out of the truck. An older Vietnamese-American man walked quickly across the green space. On the opposite side of the square, a small wooden stage stood under a white pop-up tent. The square was enclosed with abandoned stone high-rise buildings. The perimeter of the square was lined with living trees that had been colonized by vines of yellow wildflowers. The silhouettes of the branches against the buildings behind them made the stone seemed fractured throughout. Down the street, I recognized St. Patrick's Church, which looked like the ruins of an Irish pygmy castle. I realized then that this was the old Lafayette Square.

I said to myself aloud, "Huh, the big buildings must have blocked the wind from the trees."

"Ridge!"

I turned around to find Judge offering me the handle of a long, thin knife.

"What's this?"

"You wanted ta kill a hog. Here's your chance." He spit on the ground. He pointed at the hog's neck. "Clean and quick across."

I hesitated, looking at the bound pig thrashing in the cage. It knew what was coming. It knew it was already dead.

Judge said, "After they run you up a tree and ate your garden, you got a soft spot?"

The hog squealed.

Judge said, "People starting to come to the park. Come on!"

I shook my head.

Judge spit again. "I thought you weren't such a pussy after we threw the old man in the sea." He took the knife, and slit the hog's throat. The dying hog's legs twitched from the nerves, and the other hog began squealing.

A man may pull a trigger with his stomach, but something else inside must command a knife.

Toddy's BuzzBar

Mira awoke late Saturday morning, craving the chance to play music with other adults. She jumped out of her twin bed, picked up an oversized gray sweatshirt from the floor, and put it over her tank top. She pulled on the pair of jeans with holes and wine stains. Common rituals like brushing her hair, eating breakfast, brushing her teeth, or showering were ignored. She needed to be out of her tiny room and away from her coworkers and students. Street musicians were out by now, she figured. So she wiggled her feet into old tennis shoes, put her penny whistle in her pocket, and slammed the door behind her. Mira did need one other thing this morning besides music with strangers. A coffee, she thought, would tune her temples to the right note. Toddy's BuzzBar was near the corner of Alex Crowley, and they kept their French roast fresh at a reasonable price.

The late February air was sharp, calming, and invigorating, the kind of briskness that could tempt a nonsmoker to light up a cigarette for the hell of it. Her sandals slapped against her heels as she strode up Baladucci toward the river. To her surprise, the regular musicians were not present along the street. Perhaps they were getting their morning fix first, too, she hoped. The street bustled, however, as if it were a weekday with business folk and construction workers. Mira reminisced how Saturday mornings in New Orleans were once peaceful, with most people sleeping off their Friday night. Now there was too much work to be done for any fun, apparently. She continued on to the corner of Alex Crowley and turned right. A few people gathered outside of Toddy's BuzzBar. Two men and a woman, white and in their early twenties, sat at one of the metal tables. One of the men, wearing a black sweater vest over a checked shirt, projected his voice loudly. The other two listened intently. He adjusted his thick black-rimmed glasses and crossed his legs in brown corduroy pants short enough to show his sockless ankles in Kesh boat shoes. He was saying, "…and that's why we are so unique and culturally strong…"

Mira walked around to the door. An old black man sat on an exterior bench near the door. His elbows rested on his knees, and his fingers were interlocked. A lidded paper coffee cup rested on the bench next to him. He wore a tight black coat and high-water pants. He also was not wearing socks with his scuffed tuxedo shoes. His eyes were tired and bloodshot but keen. He wiped the coffee from his beard and rested his elbows on his bony knees again, staring forward blankly as if he was ignoring the outspoken kid next to him, but he was probably *listening* keenly as well.

Mira opened the door and breathed in the strong, pleasing aroma of roasted coffee and fresh bread. A white man in line wore a yellow hardhat with office attire. The black female employee handed him a portable pail of coffee about the size of a paint can.

"I'd send one of them in here, but heck, can't trust these damn *yo-gees* not to get drunk on the job." He pulled a roll of bills from his pocket and flipped through them.

"Will that be all, sir?"

He looked up at the menu. "Um, no. Small Columbian, and throw a shot of Elmer's Ryan in."

The employee stared at him, and he stopped flipping bills and looked back at her.

"Oh, I'm sorry." She turned to make his alcoholic coffee. "I thought you…you were playin'."

"It seems like a legitimate order to me. I don't understand."

"Here you go." She handed him his drink. He paid cash and left with his single coffee and the big jug of coffee for his workers. He brushed by Mira, clearly irritated.

"How can I help you?"

"Medium French roast, please."

The employee turned around and poured steaming coffee into a paper cup, but the pot emptied a bit early. She turned and handed Mira the cup. "Enjoy it. It's the last of it." With a permanent marker, she then drew a line through "French Roast" on the coffee menu.

"Last of it? Like, for good?"

The employee sighed. "I'm afraid so."

"Oh, no. You're closing?"

She nodded with disappointment.

"I'm sorry, I'm just a little surprised. It's always packed in here. I wouldn't think business was hurting."

"It wasn't. We got bought out."

"By who?"

"Greylock's."

Mira sighed with disgust. "Ever since I moved back to the States, you can't go anywhere anymore that has a healthy local coffee culture. If it's any consolation, I won't be patronizing the place after they take over."

"Well, it gets worse. Their actual coffee shop is a few blocks up Baladucci. They're knocking us down and paving it over so their employees won't park in the customer spots."

Mira looked at her in disbelief.

"I ain't playin'. We're gonna be their employee parking lot."

"Well, that's disheartening. I'm sorry."

"That's okay. Thank you so much for your loyalty."

Mira stepped out into the city, which felt much colder than before. She completely understood that what the Refounders were doing was entirely self-beneficial, no matter what they told everyone. It was necessary to save New Orleans. There was just no alternative. Unfortunately, it took more than determined people to rebuild a city, she thought. Money was just as essential and normally had a greater voice than a steadfast community. She knew that this transition would not be easy, and she would have to adapt accordingly. But now they were messing with her Creole food and local coffee. This would be a lot harder than she'd expected.

Chapter 20

Both revelers and Mother Nature had decorated the surrounding trees for Mardi Gras. Vines of yellow wildflowers adorned the green leaves, and people had cleverly hung purple drapes, completing the Carnival color triad. I didn't know what kind of trees they were, but it seemed that the branches looked crinkled, as if the trees struggled to support their faithful leaves and the power of their floral crowns.

People had started to set blankets and folding chairs on the grass before the stage. My seat on the steps of the statue granted me a great view of the music, which I hoped would start soon. Two speakers on each side of the stage seemed to be connected to a generator backstage.

I spent the next half hour leaning up against the statue among green vines. I looked up. I had never really noticed the statue much. It was of a man standing in a rather compromising pose. The twisty green vines and white blossoms blanketed the inscription of who it was and climbed up to the stone man's body and wrapped around his neck, as if a thicket of cotton had choked his life away.

I leaned back and closed my eyes for what I thought would only be a few minutes.

I awoke to applause. Father Fullerton and an older white man approached the microphone.

Fullerton, attired in traditional clergy dress, began, "God bless you all. Thank you for coming to this wondrous occasion. A milestone for you and New Orleans. A round of applause for the hardworking principals that put this together."

Thunderous applause followed as Constance Whitman, an older white man with a gray beard, and a young black woman walked onstage.

Fullerton said, "Please come to my church on Oyster Shell Road for ashes tomorrow." He nodded at them.

Constance stepped up to the microphone. "Our first act today comes from my students."

The students who had sung with Mira at the church took places on the stage. A young, heavyset black girl took the microphone, a white girl sat at the piano, and a black boy, no more than the age of seven, walked up with a trumpet. They played Al Johnson's classic "Carnival Time." People in the audience clapped along or danced to the beat. The purple banners blew eloquently and the green leaves fluttered in the breeze. The yellow flowers in the trees glowed gold from the sun. Children laughed and ran in the grass. Adults swayed and danced to live music. The taste of whiskey on my lips. Les Bon Temps Rouler. For that moment, we were all one human heartbeat.

A young Vietnamese-American girl, quite cute and petite, approached me with a bowl of what looked like pulled pork. She smiled and handed me the bowl, "Hi, feeling better?"

I was a little taken aback until Judge walked around from behind her. He wasn't dipping. "What's going on, Sally?"

I shrugged. "Did you still need me to help clean up?"

The girl looked at Judge.

"Clean up what?"

"You asked me to help clean, remember?"

He laughed. "No, brah. I asked you to help clean the hogs. Gut 'em and skin 'em. But you proved not to be the best help."

"Oh. Sorry."

The girl said, "Try some."

Judge said, "I didn't think her dad could pull it off, but he butchered 'em and cooked 'em up in no time. Freshest pork you'll have."

I took the bowl of wild pork and ate a spoonful. A little tough and gamey, but savory and delicious.

Judge said, "Well, see ya, brah."

The girl rolled her eyes. "I'm Amy. Justin's not the best with introductions."

"Who's Justin?"

"Me." Judge said.

"Oh. My name's Derek, but people call me Ridge."

"Nice to meet you." She shook my hand.

Both of them walked toward the stage past a man wearing a fedora and a tan trench coat. Cigar smoke danced above his hat, and the cigar smell wafted far across the grounds into my nostrils. I was disgusted, but not with the smoke odor. It was the audacity. The opulence. Legal cigarettes were too expensive for most people here, much less a big cigar. Only a Refounder had the money for something like that. He might as well have taken cash from our hands, rolled it, lit it, and blew the smoke in our faces. The man put the cigar in his mouth so he could clap as the band finished the song. Everyone cheered, and I set my Styrofoam bowl of wild boar on my lap so I could join in the applause. I then proceeded to wolf the whole bowl down by the time the next song, "Mardi Gras Mambo," began.

Constance and Octave walked in front of me, holding hands.

"Hey," I said, taking a sip of Elmer's Ryan from my Rex cup.

"Oh, hello, Ridge." Constance hugged me.

Octave shook my hand. "Fine sir. Happy Mardi Gras!"

"Congratulations on this event. It's great; thank you."

"No, thank you. If you and everybody else stayed home, this wouldn't mean anything."

Cigar smoke drifted toward us as the wind changed directions. Both Constance and Octave looked at the man in front of us. She shook her head, probably thinking the same shit that I had.

"Ms. Mira's been working with them a lot after dismissal. They've been jazzed about this for a while."

I smiled and looked down at the ground.

"She gonna play something later."

I couldn't really muster up a response, even though I wanted to hear her sing so badly I could taste it. Instead I changed the subject. "You know, I'm surprised no celebrities wanted to come to this."

"Oh, they tried, yeah."

"And you said no?"

"Damn straight, I told them no."

"Oh. Why? Wouldn't it be…like…good exposure?"

"Exposure for whom?" she said.

I hesitated. "Us?"

She shook her head rapidly. "Then everyone in the damn country will be talking about them. Like they're saving us or something. I saw it with those telethons after Katrina, like they're the stars and we're just the extras. People talked about how emotional it was for Harry Connick to sing 'What It Means to Miss New Orleans' or how crazy Kanye was for speaking the damn truth. I mean, their hearts are in the right place, but this is no TV show, child. These kids are going to determine how this city turns out, and they can't be thinking that they can't do it on their own. You understand?"

"Yes, ma'am, I understand."

"And don't tell me that we're missing out on charity money. You know where all that FEMA and Red Cross money went?"

"No."

"Mm-hmm. Exactly."

The odor of cigar smoke intensified as the man in the trench coat approached us. He held his cigar in one hand and removed his fedora with the other.

"Ms. Whitman, kudos on putting this together." It was Renny Rooney.

"Mr. Renny, I didn't recognize you."

"Yeah, had to change out of those greasy clothes. Been sweating since six this morning. This kid here knows. Big help today, kid."

Octave said, "Didn't pick you for a cigar smoker."

Rooney put his fedora back on. "Not often. But bought one for today. Wasn't cheap, kid."

Constance said, "I bet not. With that thing, we're all here thinking you're the richest man in all New Orleans."

"I wish. But I had to do something to calm my nerves before passing through the checkpoints."

"Where you going?"

"Gonna visit my wife for a while."

"Who's gonna be manning the joint?"

"Nobody. I'll reopen the week before St. Joseph's." He put his cigar in his mouth, reached into his coat pocket, and pulled out an envelope. "Kid, a little lagniappe for helping me out." He handed me the envelope. "Probably shouldn't open that out here."

"Thanks." I put the envelope in my pants pocket.

He said, "Well, I wish I could stay longer, but I need to make the afternoon ferry for Slidell. I'd like to be in Texas before midnight." He shook hands with Constance, Octave, and me.

"Good luck, Mr. Rooney. We'll be here when you come back."

He dragged off his cigar and attempted to blow the smoke away from us. "I have no doubt. Happy Mardi Gras, y'all."

Constance and Octave said goodbye to me as well, and they walked off toward the stage.

"Mardi Gras Mambo" ended, and the crowd applauded.

I lost my breath when Mira approached the microphone. "Thank you, everyone. We only have one more song for you, and then the students from the other school will take the stage. A round of applause for our young, upcoming musicians."

The crowd applauded again.

"Well, it wouldn't be Mardi Gras without 'If I Ever Cease to Love.' We made a few changes to it, so I hope you enjoy it." She nodded to the white girl at the piano.

The piano girl played the introduction, and the young trumpeter joined in.

And the singer sang:

In a house, in Jackson Square, in the French Quarter,
In the street, in the neutral ground, in the road,
Turn to the left on the right hand,
You'll see my true love's abode.

I go there courting, and cooing like a dove,
And swearing on my knees, if I ever cease to love,
May alligators grow on orange trees,
If I ever cease to love.

If ever I cease to love, if ever I cease to love,
May the moon turn into green sour cream,
If ever I cease to love.

I took a swig of Elmer's Ryan. Things were good. Better. Mira was back. I had whiskey. What I didn't have, however, was a bathroom. I looked about the square and found four blue Port-o-lets at the back corner on the riverside.

The crowd applauded when they finished.

Mira said, "Thank you. I'll let my talented students take this last one. It needs no introduction or explanation." She talked to her students and gave them a thumbs-up before stepping backstage.

The piano girl played a few keys and the singer uttered the opening lines to "Do You Know What it Means to Miss New Orleans" into the microphone. I don't think there was dry eye in the whole square. Even men nonchalantly wiped the corners of their eyes with their shirtsleeves, acting as if it was merely a light winter sweat. I lounged against my statue, sipping more Elmer's Ryan. Mira had touched more hearts in that afternoon than I had in my whole life. I had moved back to New Orleans when I did with a purpose: to bring back the city. To prove to these jerks that we could find ourselves from within, not from without. And here Mira was, in the forefront of resurrecting Mardi Gras from its ashes and reinforcing the New Orleans music lifeline. Me? I had just turned coats on my community for a weekly bribe of commodities. What a saint I was.

The piano girl played light keys as the young boy approached the front of the stage, carrying his trumpet. He lifted it up to his lips with some difficulty, but then effortlessly generated jazz sounds as timeless as the Mississippi. The audience cheered. The boy played louder over them. Out of sheer jubilation, everyone yelled and whistled as if they were all at a football game. Still, the boy crescendoed louder and louder, as if his larynx was larger than he was. The crowd could not cheer over him.

As the crowd cheered and cried, it finally hit me. I needed to piss something vicious. The lines for each Port-o-let snaked along the dead grass patches. My eyes searched for alternatives as well as where the Redsleeves were. I hadn't really thought about it until then, but Redsleeves had been kind of off the radar. I had heard rumors that the Monster was originally from New Orleans, so maybe he had loosened his grip on us for Mardi Gras day. Either way, it had to happen now. I couldn't wait in those lines for two reasons: I'd spill the juice box and I'd leave Mira waiting. I drank the rest of my whiskey and felt the burn in my gullet and the strain on my penis muscles holding back what felt like a tidal surge. I walked quickly with a slight limp so as not to loosen the floodgates. I entered a brick-layered corridor between two white stone buildings. Several dead cypress trees and round stone tables were scattered about, and I couldn't help but imagine business and lawyer folk smoking cigarettes and eating lunch there, back before Beckham.

But I scooted around the corner of one of the large buildings and let loose. My eyes may have rolled back into my ears at that point. I said to myself, *Now* it feels like Mardi Gras.

But then I heard distant chatter, and I tensed shut. It burned. I sidestepped around to the corner to investigate. Two young white men wearing feathery Mardi Gras masks were also looking about for a place to pee. They must have seen me venture off from the Port-o-let lines. Relieved that they weren't Redsleeves, I scooted back over and proceeded with relief.

I finished up, exhaling deeply. When I approached the corner of the building, two different men faced the two masked men, and I ducked back behind the corner. They were dressed in civilian clothes, but one of them had a shaved head and wore mirror sunglasses.

He held up his Red Birch Security badge to them. "Are you boys aware of martial order 5711? You ain't supposed to be wearing those masks."

One of the men said, "Is that what this is about? Masks?"

The other "undercover" Redsleeve said, "We can't allow it. Might give y'all an opportunity to commit crimes."

"But it's Mardi Gras."

The bald one said, "This ain't no masquerade ball, son. Off with 'em."

The quiet man took his mask off.

The talkative one protested. "No, put that back on. They can't tell us we can't!"

"The order was clearly stated ahead of time, son. You're either insubordinate or a dumbass. Which is it?"

"I'm an American."

The other Redsleeve whispered into a wrist radio hidden under his oxford shirtsleeve. Just as soon as he finished the call, he said, "You're a dumbass" and swung a hard punch into the defiant man's nose. I heard his nose crack even at a distance. He dropped to his knees and wet himself. The other man cried as the shaved-head Redsleeve cuffed his hands behind his back. The other "undercover" Redsleeve grabbed the defiant one's shirt collar and shoved him face-first into the building, cuffing him. A black van with a red stripe up the side drove down the corridor and stopped. The back doors opened, and a uniformed Redsleeve jumped out and assisted in tossing the two detainees into the van. The undercover Redsleeve spoke into his wrist radio again, looked up at one of the windows above, and gave a thumbs-up.

The black van sped off away from the square, and the two undercover Redsleeves straightened their clothes.

The bald one said, "You stuck that asshead good, rookie," slapping him on the back as they both walked back to the festival.

So, clearly, McMason was here. He was everywhere. He had banned masks, but his men were the ones in disguise. I waited in my spot for a few minutes before walking back toward the festival. When I was close to where the altercation had happened, I saw a blood spot on the wall just under the remaining letters on the chalky marble building: "—— Wisdom. —— of Appeals."

The Faubourg Wastelands

Her penny whistle poked the top of her thighs as she walked down Alex Crowley looking for a group of musicians to get lost with. She waited for the Gulf Guardsman to wave her and the other pedestrians across Baladucci. Several businessmen and women, dressed professionally, stared at the screens of their Eagles while carrying on conversations via digital technology but simply muttering to the actual people next to them. A clean-cut man in a purple-striped shirt looked up at Mira from his Eagle and looked back down into his digital identifying inertia. As the GGA held back the traffic, he waved the people to cross the street. Men sitting in idling cars banged on the sides of the car doors, hoping to catch the women's attention.

She said, "Ugh! Do they really think we like this?"

Another woman yelled, "Goddamn *yo-gees*! Go hop the first boat back to Macedonia, if you ask me."

Mira enjoyed the lack of attention, thinking that maybe it was worth dressing down and having lunch at the Southern Belle Café one day. Dressing like a bum seems to give you a sense of voluntary invisibility, she thought.

Three white gutterpunks gathered on the corner of Alex Crowley and Persimmon Street with instrument cases at their feet. Overjoyed at the possibility of playing music with them, Mira nearly jogged over to them. A tall boy with a meager beard crouched to peel a piece of fabric off his worn shoes. Another boy, short and fat, squatted with his back against the stone wall of a vacant building. A redheaded girl sat cross-legged and rubbed her milky knees, which had as many freckles as her face.

Mira smelled them as she got close enough to say something. "Hey, y'all, can I play along?"

The tall boy stood up from fixing his shoe sole.

"We're actually heading to a gig right now. Just waiting on our ride."

"Oh?"

He scratched at his aspirational beard. "A man came to us yesterday when we were playing. He said he had work for us."

The redheaded girl stretched out her legs and rubbed dirt off her calves. "In the old Marigny."

Mira's eyes brightened. "Oh! Are they finally bringing it back?"

"I think so. Yeah."

Right then, a big pickup truck pulled up to the curb, and a thin white man with a graying goatee walked up to them. He wore a long-sleeved shirt tucked into blue jeans. With both hands, he pulled his jeans up to his belly button. "You kids ready to work? I'm Dac." He shook everyone's hands. He pulled his Eagle from his back pocket and looked at the screen for a few seconds.

They put their instruments in the bed of his truck.

Dac was still looking at his Eagle. "Hm. They told me they had three of you, not four."

"I just walked up, sir."

"Well, hell, we can use you, too. Some good service work in the old Marigny area. Pay ya thirty bucks an hour for the next few hours or till the job's done. Now, that ain't bad for a day of good clean work. Who can agree with me on that?"

The girl said, "Oh, I thought you were paying us for a music show."

"Oh, I never said that. Looks like you need the work regardless."

Mira peeked into the bed of the truck. There was a large tankard of clear liquid and what appeared to be gardening tools.

Dac pulled up his jeans again. "We need to clear out some areas so the crew can get in there and do their thing. Move forward. You in?"

Since Mira's base salary translated to under ten bucks an hour, especially after accounting for the extra hours needed for class preparation and grading, she had to consider it. She had never done the actual computation; however, she doubted she made thirty dollars in a school day. The opportunity to take part in revitalizing the Marigny also excited her. Something didn't add up, though. Good "service work," as he called it, wasn't often synonymous with good money, if any at all.

The man stared at Mira. Clearly, she was costing him precious dollars by the delay.

"Yes."

"Well, let's get after it."

Mira had never been to a landfill, but she thought that the old Marigny ruins couldn't be much different. She rode in the backseat of the big pickup, with the redheaded girl and the short boy. Dac rolled down the windows as soon as they all piled in, probably to disperse the heavy stench of human funk. Mira appreciated that.

Dac drove through a freshly cleared road. Bulldozers had pushed muddy vehicles, splintered barge boards, and rusty kitchen appliances to the side of the road almost a story high. The debris piles were highest near the roads, as if Dac and his crew had parted a sea of the rotting relics of a former civilization now woven in briars and blackberry bushes. The truck turned around a bend in the road, and a flock of city pigeons scattered explosively.

"Holy pissin' shit!" Dac slammed on the brakes. "Phew. So, I'm glad to give you kids some work. Need to help our own. Not like these damn *yo-gees* givin' up on their own damn country. But when I see some red-blooded Americans out of work, then it's my civic duty. Who can agree with me on that?" His knuckles were white as he steered the truck.

The bearded boy in the front seat said, "Thanks for giving us the work."

"No problem, y'all," Dac said with a disingenuous tone.

The redheaded girl shifted what little weight she had to retrieve something out of her brown corduroy shorts. Her hair cascaded around Mira's shoulder for a second, and dandruff flaked down

Mira's arm and right leg. The girl pulled out her Eagle Gold, which was the newest and most expensive model on the market.

Mira said, "Sir, that's the second time I've heard the word *yo-gees* today. What's that mean?"

"Yogurt-heads. Greeks." Dac then went on a verbal tirade against the Greek immigrants and how they would "destroy" this town and America if we weren't careful.

Mira tuned him out and instead wondered how she had ended up in a pickup truck with three stinky gutterpunks and a bigoted redneck foreman. Perhaps she was wrong about the anonymity of dressing like a bum. Initially, it had seemed that people just didn't see you or tried their best to *act* like they didn't. But, she realized, you were highly visible to the wrong people: those who wanted to use you for something.

Dac pulled into a large clearing and parked the car. "This is it."

They all exited into stagnant, stale air that reeked of moldy carpets, ruptured sewer lines, and rotten raw shrimp. On the paths they had driven, objects and debris had been haphazardly pushed out of the way. That was not the case here. The area where they stood appeared eerily manicured. The grass had given way to a chalky dust. A muddy and rusted Dodge Charger, looking deliberately muddied and aesthetically rusted, sat idle in the clearing near a few metal drums and wooden crates. To the right of the Charger stood a corner store without a sign. It didn't appear open, nor was the building three-dimensional.

Dac handed them each a pair of blue latex gloves. He pointed at the tall gutterpunk. "Help me unload." The tall boy and Dac lifted five canisters filled with sloshing liquid and set them on the ground. Then they unloaded a large air compressor. He grabbed a few plastic hoses with metal nozzles on one end. Dac said, "Here's how this goes. You hook up the air hose to the compressor. Attach the black hose screws on the canister, and you spray it by opening here. Like a little metal steering wheel."

Mira grabbed the hose. "So what are we doing, exactly?"

"Film crews can't really film with all these varmints around, can they? How would you like it if a bunch of rats were all around where you work?"

Mira breathed deeply. "I'd hate it."

"Yeah, well, there you go. Ya'll start sprayin' in the middle, then go out from there. You need to get inside all the junk piles, too. That's where the rats hide. Drive 'em out. And don't get that poison on you. It's potent like a tobacco-spit pie. Just make your way out from the shoot site till I say stop."

"So, it's a movie?"

"Yeah."

"Which movie?" Mira remembered a post on her Eagle about it. But she didn't have the device with her.

"Don't know. What does it matter? You got a job to do, sweet pea. I'll be back in about half an hour to check in with y'all."

.

Chapter 21

At dusk, Mira led me through a neighborhood of new homes, nearly identical, similar to a mainstream suburb; however, it didn't feel like one. Each house bustled with people coming in and out or sitting on the front stoop. Some grilled on the front lawn. Others stirred giant pots of succulent gumbo or briny yaka mein. As it had been before Beckham, the neighborhood was mainly black. We were two of the few white people walking around.

I said, "So what's this parade you're talking about?"

"It'll be different. I've only heard a few things; it's still kind of secret. Pretty sure Captain McMason doesn't know." She looked around. "My students tell me the officers don't really patrol this neighborhood much."

"I'm surprised how new it looks."

Mira pulled her hair into a ponytail. "It was one of the first neighborhoods to come back. Church groups came by the hundreds."

"Where did they go?"

She shrugged and waved to a young black teenager standing over a large cooking pot atop a small wood table. "Hey, David."

"How you doing, Ms. Mira?" He opened up the lid of the pot, and steam rolled up into the sky to reveal red beans. "It ain't Monday, but it's all we had for today."

"Ridge," I said, offering my hand.

"David." He shook it. His hands were rough and strong, especially for a high-schooler.

"David's in my math class." She looked to him and said, "You cooked these?"

"Yes, ma'am. Sometimes my mama gotta work nights, so I know how. They ain't as good as hers, nah. But they all right."

We grabbed some paper bowls and plastic spoons. David lifted the cloth over the rice. "Ya'll take whatcha want." The beans weren't soupy; instead they embraced the rice like a red-brown cream sauce. I stirred it together and didn't hesitate for it to cool down. I sopped a spoonful into my mouth. Savory saltiness from the pickled meat, hearty earthiness from the beans, and the sharp zing of green bell pepper. All in one mouthful.

"Yeah, they all right."

"Best I've ever had." I said.

"David, this is delicious!"

He looked back to the house. "They all right." His mother and little brother walked toward us.

"Where did you get the pickled meat from?" I asked.

"Sometimes it's on the list."

I nodded, assuming that he referred to Red Birch Security's Food Program, and I couldn't help but think that my name in their system might be a smaller price to pay for food than I thought, especially since I was already in their system with the gun confiscation.

"Can't get salt out here like talkin' 'bout it. They just all right."

Mira said, "Hi, Ms. Patty! How are you?"

Ms. Patty was short, about as tall as her son David's shoulders. "Ohh, I'm good, Ms. Mira! My son's a rock star." She shook the younger boy's shoulders in front of her. "He never play like that at home. Got a li'l Satchmo in the family."

The little trumpeter smiled bashfully and sipped a canned soft drink.

David said, "Yeah, you right. I'm a start callin' you Li'l Satch." He rubbed the top of his brother's head.

Mira bent down slightly to be on the boy's level. "Raymond, you played so well today!"

"Thanks, Ms. Mira." He sipped his soda, looking at his tiny shoes.

Mira said she didn't want to overstay her welcome, so we walked farther down the street to a cross street, where more people had convened.

"This should be fine," she said.

"Are the students going to be in this one, too?"

"Not this one."

I needed to pee again, and looked around for a spot. About a half block down the street, a number of men were coming to and fro from an inside fence corner.

She nodded. "You need to pee, don't you?"

I said, "Yep. Reading my mind again."

"I'll be right here."

I rounded the open fence and saw a few men pissing near the corner. I waited behind two other men. In the dusk light, I could still make out some things tacked on the fence boards at perfect aiming height. As I stood at the fence, I saw a printed image of Captain McMason that had been laminated to withstand an onslaught of urine. Portrait style, as you'd see in a military office displaying the chain of command. He did not smile, his jaws tight behind the yellow streaks running to the ground. I unzipped and let loose. I'd never pushed out harder and focused more on aiming, as if this would avenge all the people of New Orleans. Of course, when I finished, his cold face remained steadfast. Another piss portrait was off the corner, but the pictured subject was not a Redsleeve but a civilian that I didn't recognize. A white man, probably mid-thirties. I read the caption beneath the image: "Chase Quade." That son-of-a-bitch spewing all that anti-New Orleans poison from the radio. I hocked a big loogie and spit on it.

I returned to Mira. "I just pissed on the Monster."

Her eyes wide, she asked, "McMason's here and you peed on him?"

"Oh, no, no. Someone put his picture on the fence. Chase Quade, too."

Relieved, she exhaled. "Well, that's nice."

"Do you ever listen to that crackpot?"

"Who?"

"Chase Quade."

She shook her head. "Who's that? A musician?"

"No, he's a shock jock on the radio."

"Derek, if it doesn't involve teaching music or math, I'm out of the loop."

"He's an asshole who hates on New Orleans."

She paused for a few seconds. "Does he, though? Or is he just criticizing it?"

"No difference."

"Sure there is."

"I mean, you're either all in or you're out. Period." I really wanted a cigarette right then.

"Well, *you're* in past your ears, I guess. I think the parade's coming."

Cheers resounded down the street, and a small brass band approached. The band was not official because the members varied in age and simply wore casual clothes, unlike the neighborhood brass bands of yesterday dressed in conductor-like uniforms. Several people danced behind the band, mostly black but some white. Five black men, wearing vintage-style suits, were at the center. The suits had long tails, and the men wore tall top hats. No suits were the same color, however. An older man with white stubble wore bright orange. A younger man with long hair wore bright green. The others wore sky-blue, a peach color, and hot pink. They all strutted and spun in the street like dance-crazed tropical barons.

We stood on the street curb, cheering them as they whisked their way effortlessly down the parade route. A pickup truck pulled a small float without any riders on it. However, it had a backdrop with a spotlight illuminating a mannequin bending over with a big plastic butt "mask." A microphone stood next to the fake butt. The backdrop read, "Cutting to the Chase." I laughed hysterically. "Mira, that's about the radio guy."

Mira pointed at the float, looked at me, and nodded.

A giant papier-mâché head was mounted on the second float. It had red eyes, a jutting bottom jaw, and a bushy mustache made from old brooms. Two paraders, dressed in red long-sleeved shirts and black vests, high-stepped on either side of the float. Each held a push broom, frequently grooming the big mustache with it. Directly following this float, several more men high-stepped along, also dressed in red shirts and black vests. The inscription on the back of the float read, "Oh Captain, My Captain."

The next float passed, and most people stopped laughing, but they still cheered at the message. The facades of several city landmarks were built on the float, such as St. Louis Cathedral, the Cabildo, One Shell Square, the Hibernia building, and a few shotgun-style homes. But each building had a cross erected on top of it. The float inscription said, "Tomb It May Concern?" I understood the message. Unlike Chase Quade and McMason the Monster, the Refounders remained ambiguous. A faceless collective fighting for the promise of our land.

Then I caught the scent of Mira's hair as she stood in front of me. I slowly approached her from behind and placed my hands on her hips, hoping she'd accept my touch. She tensed for a moment and then leaned into me. My chin on her shoulder, and her balance trusting my own, I forgot about New Orleans in that moment. Chase Quade, McMason, Fitzmorris, the Refounders, the Manchacs. I forgot all of it for a little while. Just Mira and me, the way it once was before I let New Orleans stand between us.

Greylock's Coffee Company

When Mira had left her apartment that morning, she hadn't cared about taking a shower, but, upon returning, she wanted nothing more than to wash off the smells of chemical repellant, moldy debris, and gutterpunk. She noticed that more people had silently scoffed at her on the walk back to her dorm. The doorman had initially stopped her before recognizing her.

She swung the door open and shut it hard behind her. She immediately disrobed in the kitchen, placing her dirty sweatshirt, socks, and jeans directly into the trashcan. The apartment had a chill that made the skin on her unclad legs, arms, and shoulders erupt in goose bumps. Her Eagle sat on the short kitchen counter, and its notification indicator blinked red.

Warm your insides with our homemade hot apple cider and a generous pour of El Capitan Spiced Rum!12:03PM¬ Welshy

Ms. Roche sorry but she sick wont be in class1:31PM¬ Renisha G mom

Drinks at Welshys tonight, everyone?2:45PM¬ Stephen Cooper+5

Hello, Mira Roche. This is Jack Levens, the regional executive at Greylock's downtown. I heard about the St. Joseph Festival you're planning. I'd like to meet with you next week to discuss ways I can help3:12PM¬ Unknown

Mira's eyes brightened at the last message, and it gave her something to hope for while she showered. A feeling she always loved. But first, she sent her colleagues a response:

In[6:38PM]

Mondays were not only "administrative" days but also laundry days, and Mira was relieved that she had one clean dress left in her closet for her late-morning meeting with Mr. Levens. She woke and dressed early so that she could have a coffee at Toddy's BuzzBar. They could close any day now, depending on when they sold out of coffee. They had been open over the weekend.

To her dismay, however, the door was locked. A handwritten sign had been taped to the glass door: "We are sorry to say that we are now closed. We want to thank all of our loyal customers for making us what we were. The owners and the staff here at Toddy's are forever grateful for your local support."

Mira frowned and walked to Greylock's instead, which was the bottom floor of the regional corporate office in a building farther down Baladucci Drive. More businessmen and women strolled the streets in this section, fewer Greek demolition workers and begging gutterpunks.

The Boston-based chain coffee house was located on the ground floor of the last tall building on Baladucci Drive, and Mira had a strange feeling. She had been there before somehow. It was a feeling like in a dream when you're in a familiar place that is not that place at all. Perhaps how a ghost feels in an old converted building.

"Hello. Can I help you?" A cheerful young woman greeted Mira from the register. She wore a magenta shirt and a black apron over black pants. She also wore a black visor.

Mira shook herself out of her daze. She looked up at the digital menu and felt rather lost. She scanned the six columns of beverage offerings, and the word *coffee* came up only once in the "Pastries" section for "coffee cake."

The young clerk said, "Something I can help you find?"

"Coffee?"

The young clerk's face went blank.

Mira said, "Can I just get a small medium roast coffee?"

"You want it, like, black?" The cashier grimaced.

"Sure, to start with."

"Okay, hold on a minute." She walked a few steps away and spoke with a manager.

A slightly older man, yet younger than Mira, approached the register. "Ma'am, all of our pricing is applicable to our specialty beverages. It'll be an upcharge for plain coffee. Can we get you one of our frozen lattes instead?"

"No. Just give me a small medium roast. I don't mind it being extra."

"No problem," he said. He then guided the cashier through the intricate digital maze to produce a cup of "plain coffee." He walked away and continued his previous task.

"Will that be all?"

"Yes, thank you." Mira paid by scanning her Eagle.

"Thank you. Your receipt should be on your phone."

Mira looked at the receipt:

> *Purchased $6.17 from Greylock's*
> *-Tall Boston Latte*
> > *-Minus latte*
> > *-Add plain coffee*
> > *-Add hot*

She had about twenty minutes before her meeting with Mr. Levens upstairs, so she sat at a small table near the window. She looked around the establishment for a caddy or counter containing cream and sugar but couldn't find one. Instead she just blew the steam rising from her paper cup full of black coffee that seemed to have the transparency of black tea. Mira figured that she'd probably get charged for a dash of cream, since she'd had to pay extra for black coffee, but she needed to cool it down.

She asked the cashier, "Can I get a few ice cubes in here?"

The cashier said in a low tone, "We have iced coffee here. Is that what you meant to order?"

"No. Iced coffee is…never mind. Just a little ice to cool it down a bit."

"Oh, sure." The cashier handed her an empty paper cup half full of ice.

"Thanks."

She landed the only available table left in the place. She sipped the overly bitter and weak-bodied coffee. Every table was occupied by mostly younger people who, to Mira, seemed indecisive that morning on whether they should dress professionally or casually. She also noticed that all the men and women at the café were intensely socializing, yet not speaking to each other. Even people seated across the table from each other. They all spoke to each other via their Eagles, their typing fingertips racing at the same pace as their multitasking brains. Mira thought to herself that her generation must be the first in human evolution when the closest of friends never learned the color of each other's eyes.

Next to her, a middle-aged man wearing a green fleece vest and wind pants told another similarly aged and dressed man, "I mean, the only way to save this city is to buy local, support local businesses. If we don't, then we lose everything."

The other man said, "Absolutely, Gil. Some people just don't get it."

Mira chimed in, "Yeah, Toddy's just closed. It's a shame."

Gil turned to her. "I'm sorry. What?"

"Toddy's BuzzBar. Little local coffee bar that just got closed down," She stopped herself upon realizing that this was the corporation that had bought it out.

He shook his head and said dismissively, "Never heard of it." He sipped his frozen "coffee" that was somehow orange in color. He then held up the cup and said, "The old standby hasn't failed me yet."

Mira just let it go. She didn't want to get too worked up before her meeting. Instead, she just sat back and tried to figure out what this place had been previously. She swore she had been there before. Pieces of the puzzle were flowing in, just not gelling together.

Pitching her half-full coffee into the trash, Mira boarded the elevator to the twelfth floor. The elevator doors opened, and she walked into a business foyer with a few waiting chairs and a secretary's desk.

The secretary, a brightly red-haired middle-aged woman, warmly greeted her with a piney Alabama accent. "Hi, may I help you?"

"I'm here to see Mr. Levens."

She touched the digital buttons on her desk. At first glance, her desk surface looked to be simply glass; however, it was actually a computer screen. She shifted windows off to the side as if sorting through actual pages. "Did you have an appointment, hon?"

"Yes, at eight thirty."

"Eight thirty," she repeated thoughtfully. She swiped the digital pages with her fingertip. "You gotta bear with me, okaaaay? This ain't the kinda desktop I'm used to."

Mira chuckled silently.

"Okay. Ms. Roche?"

"Yes."

"You can come along with me, hon." She rose from her chair. She was much more thin and fit than Mira had expected. She wore a flowery blouse, beige capri pants, and sandals. Her calf muscles flexed with each step. Mira thought to herself, Must be a cyclist.

She followed the secretary around the hallway into a bustling workspace of forty or fifty people standing on either side of three long tables. It was not a conventional office space. These employees didn't even have chairs, and the tables weren't quite high enough, so they had to hunch. The tables were equipped with screens so that each worker had a horizontal one at chest level and an upright one mounted like a traditional computer screen. The digital planes were similar to the secretary's, but these very young men and women, practically right out of college, were fluent in this digital discourse. Every worker had earbuds dug into their ears. A little black box, the size of a cigarette pack, was clipped on the back of their pants with a cord running under the table into a mainframe somewhere. Their screens flashed quickly with digital chats, technical algorithms, and map locators. Mira felt that if she stared at one of their screens long enough, she'd suffer a seizure. Their eyes fixated on the digital tasks in front of them, the staff in this room wouldn't have noticed if Mira had strolled through naked. She wished she could make her students concentrate like this. But seeing their blank faces drawn into the electronic pull of digital inner-verse, she redacted that. Mira's students' attention spans frustrated her, sure, but at least that confirmed they were 100% human. Also, it was eerily silent for an office. No business chatter or keyboard patter. The digital planes were touch screens and made no sound. Other than the secretary's sandal bottoms slapping her heels with each step, the dull din of the mainframes under the tables sounded like a robotic monster in slumber. It felt like she had stepped out of a coffee shop and boarded a Douglas Adams novel.

The secretary slowed her pace and walked alongside Mira. "These talented youngsters are our entrepreneurial optimizers. They don't actually work for us…well, they do. They technically work for another company. Optimum Engine. We contract them out to do our marketing and network optimization. Highly competitive here now, hon."

Mira nodded. It was impressive, she thought, but in the same kind of way a fascist military parade was impressive. Diligent, structured, and efficient means with an ominous end. She remembered when she had first moved back to New Orleans in Beckham's aftermath, when people said bad things about the "Refounders" as if that word was some kind of slur. Growing up, her dad had thrown out "Yankee" like a slur, and yet he never knew anyone north of Tennessee. However, she'd never really met anyone who fit the "Refounder" description, nor could she get anyone to elaborate on who those people were. But these people, concluded Mira, were certainly Refounders. The old lazy days were giving way to laissez-faire, while the tech corporate culture was moving in. If Optimum Engine wasn't the actual Refounders, it certainly employed their economic mercenaries. A digital army firing their technical triggers, yet lacking the collective gut to literally pull a trigger. If the Refounders hadn't taken possession of New Orleans yet, it was only a matter of time, except that it wasn't via stifling sugar plantations or stuffy warehouses. They would do it with digital sweatshops and unsuspecting young talent.

Chapter 22

The effect a guaranteed breakfast has on a man's psyche is uncanny. My belly full of duck jerky and oats, I carried *Cold Chambers* along with two knuckles of Elmer's Ryan in a coffee mug up to the levee. I had yet to become accustomed to the burn of morning whiskey absorbed by the sustenance in my stomach. I needed more propane, but Fitzmorris wouldn't be open for another few hours, and I wasn't looking forward to seeing him. I stepped over the fencing roll I had taken to protect my vegetable garden—which was now a small frog pond. Unable to beat the beasts, I had just left them alone to wallow and overpopulate. We can only do so much.

The dim orange sun had just begun to brighten to yellow. A squadron of four brown pelicans soared over the lake in search of their breakfasts. One shifted in flight, almost looking as if it had a sudden seizure, but dove with laser precision. It resurfaced upright, shaking the living fish down its gullet. Near the shore, a patch bubbled erratically as though a small pocket was boiling in the expanse of tepid water. I remembered Mr. Buras telling me that those were "feeder" fish trying to escape a redfish or some other kind of predator. Nature is beautiful and serene only when you're the spectator, I guess.

I sat cross-legged on the top of the levee and opened the book to where I had left off.

It must take worldwide bloodshed and continual folly for a man of God to question the motives and character of our Lord. In this world, fathers who simply allow their sons and daughters to make wrong decisions and expect love and respect in return are essentially bad fathers. He has come to us directly in the past, so why does he not now? This war has taken even a worse turn. Reports are coming in that the Japanese have turned the tide in the Pacific. They're calling Guadalcanal a full-on massacre. The Japanese have gone back to their Samurai roots, even if not their code of ethics. Not one man was spared. Even those surrendered were beheaded on the field of battle. Now the Japanese are launching air-strikes against Australia with weather balloons loaded with disease-riddled fleas.

Now, our government, out of sheer desperation, has turned to the Indian reservations for help. Roosevelt has promised them reparations, more fertile lands, and other incentives to organize their best fighting men. Obviously, they see the Indians as they have in the movies and expect them to ride bareback and shoot arrows and scalp people. But it's the twentieth century. We couldn't expect a white man from Minnesota to fight like a Viking, so why should we expect an Indian to fight like a Comanche? My superiors have heard of my missionary work on the Navajo reservation, and I am being promoted to Sergeant over a regiment of Native soldiers. It has been excruciating enough to be a mere participant in this folly, much less a leader.

What if we've been wrong? The Bible says we are "chosen." Perhaps out of pride we take that as being chosen to live or to lead. But what if we are marked instead? Chosen to perish.

I looked up from the page and stared at the distant ruins of the Causeway Bridge and the Lakeway building. Meant to perish. That was harsh to read. Maybe both the catfish and the alligator were supposed to die. Maybe that was their purpose. Maybe their own struggle is as irrelevant as an insect's will to live. I had to ponder on that for a minute before continuing. I closed the book and went back inside. I needed to get it over with. It seemed that Fitzmorris didn't much trust me anymore, and fair enough, considering I was secretly working with the Manchacs to get what he couldn't supply. But I needed propane and drinking water, and he had the monopoly on those two things.

I finished the Elmer's Ryan and set the coffee mug on the book atop my register box. I pulled the drawer open to find something enticing to trade with him. The Manchacs gave me U.S. cash, but most everyone in our little community along Oyster Shell Road still bartered. Last time I tried paying cash, Fitzmorris just about sent me away. I hadn't seen him since, so I didn't know what to expect. Rummaging through my box of various items, I spotted the silver necklace pendant that I had found in the lake some time back. It had been tarnished from the brackish water. I had forgotten about it. Now there was a woman I could give jewelry to. Perhaps Fitzmorris had some kind of metal treatment to make it shiny. It must have been meant to be, because the pendant was a music note. I decided to bring it so that he could suggest what to use, if he had anything. I dug and dug through my junk register for any type of medication. Fitzmorris would just about hand me the keys to his store for the right stuff. I found a red disk-like pill, a pink oval, and a cream-colored long pill. They could have been anything from ecstasy to vitamin C, for all I knew. I put them in my pocket. He might know what they were or take the chance. I pondered on what else he might need and pulled my pants up and tightened my belt. It struck me. I had an extra belt somewhere. Surely he would rather a belt than those hideous bungee-cord suspenders.

As I arrived to Fitzmorris's store, I noticed not much was different. Bare grocery shelves. No customers in either store or café. I took it that both Huey and Fitzmorris were surviving on gasoline sales. I knew neither of them would cower to McMason and register for his federally funded food relief program. Seeing this state of affairs, I didn't regret joining the Manchac pirates because otherwise I wouldn't have anything to sell or barter with. Eventually I would have had to join the Manchacs or McMason, and that was an easy decision.

With a small backpack over my shoulder, I entered to find Fitzmorris and Huey seated at a table in the café, sipping coffee.

Fitzmorris stood. "I have something for you."

"For me? What?"

He pulled his bungee-cord suspenders to adjust to his standing position. "I don't know. Here." He motioned for me to follow him to the back. His pants were baggy, though not by choice. He wasn't eating much these days. The belt would be a good barter, after all.

We entered the warehouse and walked to a large brown box with "Ridge" written on it. "Joshua left this for you. He said he stopped at your place but you weren't there."

"What is it?"

"He didn't say, but it's very heavy."

"Hmm. Has he been in yet today?"

"He hasn't been here for a while."

Huey had followed us to the back and he graciously chimed in, "I told y'all. He's got no commitment. Sooner or later, he'd jump ship when things get tough, just like the rest of 'em."

Fitzmorris rolled up his sleeves. "Well, it might be because he's afraid of McMason coming after him."

I crouched to examine the mysterious package. "Yeah, one time I was in here, and McMason came looking for him."

Fitzmorris asked, "When was this?"

"I don't know. Sometime before Mardi Gras."

"Oh, then you haven't read the latest *Declaration*?"

"Nope."

Fitzmorris adjusted his glasses and walked over to a storage shelf and grabbed the newspaper. "You can take that with you. I don't even want that in the store anymore. I don't want to give the Redsleeves any reason to be hostile."

"Oh, it's that bad?"

"You'll see. Bring your truck around so I can get rid of this heavy thing. Lord knows what's in there." He slapped the newspaper down on the box.

"Okay. Also, I need propane and water. And do you have any-thing that will make this shiny again?" I pulled the necklace out of my pocket.

Fitzmorris stared at me for a few seconds. "No. We're down to one meal a day, and you care about some flashy jewelry?"

"It's not for me, it's for…never mind. I have some pills here to trade you, but I don't know what they are. Do you? Or I have an old belt you can wear instead of those bungee cords."

Defensively, he held out his hands like an offensive lineman. "I don't barter here. I only take cash here, like any legitimate business."

I was taken aback. "Since when?"

"I don't care what you do, Ridge. I'm a businessman."

"Okay, well, how much do I owe you for the propane?"

"I don't have any more."

"Well, I have a few bottles to fill up with water."

"Those will cost about five dollars a bottle."

"You're charging for that now?"

"Do you see this place? What else I'm going to sell? I've been cut off from all my suppliers because the trucks keep getting hijacked, and no one wants to do anything about it. I've filed a report with Red Birch and haven't heard back. I've contacted the Gulf Guard of America and the Coast Guard, and they say it's out of their jurisdic-tion. It's those damn pirates, I tell you."

"You can sell salt, can't you?"

He threw up his hands in defense again. "I don't know what you're talking about, Ridge."

It was evident that Fitzmorris suspected I was in cahoots with someone, so he played it straight with me, whereas I knew very well he was still trading under the table. "Okay, okay, I'll pay you for two bottles' worth. I'll bring my truck around."

Annoyed, I drove around to the back. I filled two empty liquor bottles with water and paid him $10.

"I'll also take a pack of Kikenney Lights."

"That'll be twenty dollars more."

I handed him the money. He shook his head and went to the store for the cigarettes. He helped me lift Joshua's package into my truck, and I slammed the tailgate shut. "Thanks. Maybe I'll see you around the bar."

"I'm afraid you won't."

I went home and lugged the box inside. It must have weighed forty pounds. I opened the box to find Joshua's typewriter. I hauled it up out of the box. The letters on the keys had been nearly worn off. I also found a book in the box, *H.K. Mencken: Selected Writings*, with a note attached reading, "Give to Octave." Why was Joshua bequeathing his personal belongings? I know they'd told us in school that this was a telltale sign for people contemplating suicide. But there was no other note or anything else with the package.

I pondered on that while I poured myself two knuckles of Elmer's Ryan. I then lit a Kikenney cigarette. It didn't taste like the tobacco that had been in a pirate's flatboat for three weeks. I could see why Joshua smoked these all day, just not how he could afford it at $20 a pack. My eyes glanced over the latest issue of Joshua's paper. I picked it up and began to read:

Grievance
Editorial | February 3

When I started this newspaper, I decided to call it *The Declaration* because upon arriving in New Orleans I was cross-examined by McMason's mercenaries like a foreign national. I had to "declare" my purpose then in vague, altruistic words. Now, my purpose cannot be more clear. It is a declaration of independence from, as well as a declaration of war on, Captain Randall Prescott McMason. If this is the last you hear from me, then someone must launch an investigation because McMason would not only be guilty of being a monster but also of being a murderer. My commitment is not in question.

It is not unusual for the media and any law enforcement to be at a cold standoff, because they could destroy each other if one of them crosses the neutral ground. With each mastering their own respective weapons, the old cliché of the pen and sword comes to mind. The pen is only metaphorical, of course, since a sword cuts deeper than a pen can. The "pen" can only be mighty if it yields action.

That cold war between me and the Monster reached its boiling point when his mercenaries attacked me. They wore plain clothes but their typical oafishness and lack of concern for human decency gave them away. They knocked me off my bike and threw it in Broadmoor Bay. They punched my face and kicked my ribs. Typical of their lack of brainpower, they left my fingers healthy to type this and spared my legs so I can deliver it. I got another bike. Fingertips trigger all weapons, whether they be firearms or typewriters, and just as long as mine are agile, I'll keep firing shots. I've been compiling a dossier on the Monster since I've come to town. I have sworn secrecy to my sources out respect for their safety. I have been waiting for the right time to expose all of the egregious actions perpetrated by this mercenary, and now is the time for retaliation.

By deploying his thugs on me in a failed attempt to silence me, the Monster crossed the line. I therefore, declare war on Red Birch Security Company and its champion, Captain Randall McMason, for:

Slaughtering surviving animals at the Audubon Zoo. Undisclosed sources told me that they found several animals still in their sheltered cages. They anonymously called the Gulf Guard of America, which was relieved by Red Birch Security a few weeks later. A report was then made that several lions and tigers had escaped the zoo and would have threatened the citizens if not for "the valiant efforts of Red Birch deputies, who had no choice but to do what they had to do." My contact, however, claims that each animal was shot in its cage, whimpering from starvation.

Burning Mardi Gras floats. In the wake of Beckham's arrival, several iconic floats from Rex, Orpheus, and Bacchus were moved to a more secure location. The brick building Uptown was an unmarked factory; however, its brick and stone walls survived, thus shielding the floats from the onslaught. Last winter, a fire was reported in the brick building. McMason blamed it on the vagrant elements making fires for warmth. My contacts claim, however, that they had sealed the place tightly for fear of vandalism and looting. They are adamant that the place remained locked at all times. With the decommissioning of the NOFD and with the Red Birch Fire Division in charge, no proper arson investigation followed.

Creating an environment of fear and the need for security. Picket lines, "food relief" programs, confiscated books, censored art and media, and armed mercenaries patrolling the streets make it martial law. The Monster and his men also turn us against each other at our most desperate hour. Patrolmen propagate the illusion that the Ward Wars are encroaching upon other areas, which they are not. In the meantime, they tell the black community in "The Ward" that other people do not care about the violence within their neighborhoods—which is also not true. All the while, local grocers are destitute since the Manchac pirates hijack supplies unopposed. This is just a tactic so that you will come crawling to the Monster for help.

Exacerbating the Ward Wars. It seems odd how the violence gets worse when a privatized security company becomes in charge. The Monster's men are practically absent from neighborhoods, and when the residents have called for more presence, they get only poor excuses about resources spread too thin due to budget cuts. In the initial aftermath of Beckham, the average death toll was 3 per week. Now, after one year of the Monster in charge, that has increased to 5 per week. At this rate, 96 *more* black youths will have died under McMason's watch than under that of the Gulf Guard of America. And despite disarming the populace, guns seem to proliferate in The Ward. It's as if McMason wants the deaths to increase, like some kind of "Final Solution."

I man my battle station with my "pen." I'm officially admitting my full commitment. If I end up in Revnor's Pond or "someone" says I've lost heart in the fight and moved away, please launch an investigation because the Monster is behind it. There are only two ways I will stop: if I stop breathing, or if McMason resigns. So I'll keep triggering my pen. McMason, you know where to find me, and I may just have a sword if you've got any spine left under that beastly jawbone. |JT|

Boston Bold and Strong, LLC, Regional Headquarters

T he red-haired secretary led Mira from Optimum Engine's control room to a more traditional space of private offices with
doors heavy enough to conceal any final business decision. This must
be the executive office, Mira thought. They entered a vacant conference room with a twenty-foot table with a beautiful dark wood finish.

"You just take a seat here, my dear," the secretary said. "Mr. Levens
will be in shortly."

"Thank you." Mira did not sit in one of the plush leather chairs.
Her attention steered her toward the window that occupied one
whole wall. It was the first time she had seen the city from a high ele-
vation since Beckham. Initially, things looked as they had before: the
brown, ribbon-like curves of the Mississippi; tiny little tourists stag-
gering in the streets of the French Quarter to her left; the extensive
Convention Center hugging the banks of the river; the metal frames
of the Greater New Orleans Bridge standing tall and kinked like an
umbrella frame. It was a strange feeling for Mira. Perhaps she had
entered some time and space portal through Optimum Engine. Then
the optical illusion broke down into reality: the brown ribbons were
solid clay, not rushing water; tiny little tourists still staggered in the
New Carré, where the sides of the modern buildings were of concrete
and the facades of bricks and fake wrought iron, like a movie set but
permanent; the Convention Center's shell seemed intact except that
a canted rusty ship bisected it like a gag hat with an arrow appear-
ing to have pierced your skull, yet real; the bridge simply stood alone
and unattached like a giant TV antenna crusted with brown rust and
white bird feces Jackson Pollocked on the steel beams.

From this height, it was quite evident that the past had passed, the future marched forth, and the present was anything but a gift. The tall levees, fit tight against the channel, were as obsolete as the Great Wall of China. The Mississippi's deep channel, a millennium's worth of scoured earth, held historical relics mucked deep in its brown intestines. A preservation team below operated a crane to lift a sunken cotton ship. Mira remembered reading about scientists who'd found what they thought was a skeleton of a small whale, but it turned out to be that of an enormous catfish. The old river was nothing but a small bayou surrounded by towering cliffs of clay except for the outer curve of the crescent. The deepest point of the river, once over 200 feet, had formed an oxbow duck pond. To Mira's far right, on the opposite bank, there had been a town called Westwego. Now a big pond, commonly called Revnor's Pond, marked the deliberate breach made by a wealthy New Orleans landowner to save his East Bank properties.

The sight due south, however, was the most unsettling. She could see the Gulf of Mexico. It was only a blue-gray haze haloing the horizon, but it was now in sight from an executive's window. Near the opposite bank's levee stood several massive sand dunes with pointy cones that looked like ancient pyramids but were staged for the future with loads of sand meant for grand beaches central to the Refounding proposal. Mira's grandmother had grown up downriver in Boothville and had to relocate to New Orleans once her home began to sink into the sea. She said that New Orleans people would not notice the tragedy of coastal erosion until it was too late. She had been right. However, the real unforeseen tragedy, Mira felt, was that the new business bourgeoisie of New Orleans were quite aware of erosion, but did not dare stop it. Coastal erosion was now an economic opportunity, not an environmental tragedy.

A man's voice behind her said, "It's quite beautiful, isn't it?"

Mira turned to find an older white man with silver hair wearing a red tie and white shirt, sleeves rolled up to mid-forearm, tucked into dark-green slacks. She looked back at the sand dunes and the halo of the distant Gulf.

"Wouldn't you say?" he said.

Maybe a beautiful diaspora, Mira thought. She nodded, "It sure is something."

"Jack Levens." He held out his hand.

"Mira Roche." She shook his hand, noticing that the white hairs protruding from above his knuckles were abnormally long. His hand was one of the softest she'd ever shaken.

"Please, have a seat at the table. Did you have a coffee downstairs? Would you like one?"

She said, "Sure. Thank you."

He pulled his Eagle out of his pocket, tapped the screen twice, and set the Eagle on the table. "Please," he offered with his palm up for her to be seated. "Did you have trouble parking?"

"No, sir. I walked. What was this building before? I've been here before, I think." She sat down with her back to the window.

Jack Levens sat, put his bony elbows on the table, and cupped his hairy hands. The sunlight reflecting off his silver hair made it blinding white. "That's something we're working on. Trying to improve the parking the situation. And this used to be the Loews Hotel, to answer your second question."

"Ah. Swizzlestick Bar and Café Adelaide. That's it. Great places."

He touched his fingertips together. His voice became soft. "Essential New Orleans institutions, some would say. A very productive contributor to the culture of the city. We want to be a part of that. So, once I heard from a colleague at City Hall that you had proposed this St. Joseph festival, I wanted to see what I can do to help. These kinds of things—festivals—show that the spirit is still alive in New Orleans. And we'd like to help with that."

"Well, you've already dressed the part."

"I'm sorry?"

"The red tie, white shirt, green pants."

He stared blankly at her.

"Like the Italian flag."

He paused for a few seconds. "I guess I'm not following."

"Well, St. Joseph's Altar is an Italian thing. Well, I guess techni-cally Sicilian…but yeah. It's something the Italians have been doing for a while in New Orleans."

Jack Levens sat back in his chair, crossed his legs, and clasped his hands on the overlapping knee. His voice was even softer when he said, "Oh, how interesting."

A young intern entered the room with two steaming mugs of fresh coffee.

Levens said, "Thank you, Taylor. And maybe some cream and sugar for our lovely guest."

Mira said, "Thank you."

"Please elaborate, Ms. Roche."

"We—as in my family—used to have a big St. Joseph's Altar at my nonna's house. My mom's from a loud Italian New Orleans family. A lot of people would come and bring food. Meatless dishes of course, with Lent, but seafood's okay. But we all—well, the women of the family anyway—would prepare a few main dishes and desserts and wear aprons with our names embroidered in the white part of the Italian flag. They put me in charge of baking the Italian cookies once I was in high school. It was great. Once my nonna passed, though, my mom and aunts and uncles didn't want to take charge, I guess. Oh, I'm sorry… As far as the event goes, teachers and students would be encouraged to make either a vegetarian or a seafood dish, being Lent and all, to share. A priest will come and bless the food—oh, no, that's something I didn't think of. Just add that to my list. But what-ever food is left over is donated to a homeless shelter or distributed to the needy in some way. I think maybe we brought it to St. Vincent de Paul's. I think."

"Okay, so it's almost like an Oktoberfest, but Italian?"

Mira slurped slightly. Her coffee had cooled down just enough and was full-bodied and delicious. "Um, no. Not this one, at least. Mr. Levens—"

"Call me Jack."

"Jack, let's be honest here. My students are clearly *not* Italian."

Levens nodded, lowering his eyes to the table.

"So I can't push that on them. It's more about getting the kids and the parents to do something fun together. Of course, I'd want them to make something that requires some kind of measurement or unit conversion. That's kind of how this all started. I teach math and religion."

"Naturally."

Mira smiled. "You know, Jack, I hadn't even thought of that until now."

He returned her smile and sat up in his chair. "So, how far are you in planning this event?"

Mira sighed. "Still trying to get a permit from City Hall."

"How long would that take?"

"Forever."

"Oh, so it's not going very well."

Mira closed her eyes, took a deep breath, and shook her head. She took another sip of coffee.

"Oh, I see. Well, if you had your St. Joseph's Altar at a private business—let's say downstairs in our café—no city permit would be necessary." His voice changed to that of a salesman. "We have clean bathroom facilities for your students and parents. We have a top-notch kitchen capable of producing a wide array of dishes. Not to mention Italian dishes. We have first-class servers so that your students can simply enjoy their experience and celebrate the feast day! Why put them to work? Why put yourself to work? Our staff and cleaning crew can break everything down and clean up for you. Doesn't that sound nice? You're probably putting in many late hours as it is, teaching. Why not let us to do the work for the day?"

Mira had not expected this. It certainly would relieve her of much heavy self-inflicted pressure. And time was running out. "But Jack, if that happened, couldn't my students still help cook the food, at least? The whole reason for this originally *was* to actively involve them. I'd hate to lose that."

Jack Levens's tone switched again to that of an attorney. "Unfortunately, we cannot allow the children to use our kitchen equipment. Too much liability. The kitchen would be too dangerous. Gas burners, sharp knives, slippery floors. And that could even jeopardize our permit, if we allow anyone other than our specially trained chefs to use our facility. So I'm afraid that's non-negotiable." Levens leaned forward on his elbows again, and his voice became the softer, more caring tone of an altruist. "However, you did say that this St. Joseph's Altar is essentially a charitable event. How about if we raise money for the school? We can open it to the public and sell tickets or plates. Certainly, your school could use a new soccer field or a technology lab or improvements to the cafeteria? Does it not?"

Mira was careful about how to respond. If she said yes to his last two questions, it could be misunderstood as an agreement to his business offer. Every decision, she always had felt, was a compromise of hard cash and raw principle with varying proportionality. She'd have to sell out either way, she thought. She could bribe the inspector and perpetuate crookedness. Or she could hand over her school plans to a voracious corporation quick to buy the altar from St. Joseph in the same fashion they'd taken the Buzzbar from Toddy. Mira needed more time.

"Well, Ms. Roche?"

"Can you give me some time to think about it, Jack? It's an awfully generous offer, but I need to talk to my principal before making a decision."

"Oh, absolutely! You don't need to give me an answer right this second." He smiled. "Lord, what kind of monster would I be then?"

Mira drank down the rest of her warm coffee. "Thank you for the coffee. It was delicious."

He stood. "Oh, it's our pleasure. Our success didn't come from serving bad coffee."

She stood to shake his hand, noticing that Levens's coffee mug was still full. He had not taken a single sip of it.

He took her hand with his hairy-knuckled one. "Thank you so much for stopping by. I'm looking forward to hearing from you."

"Thank you, Jack. You have a good afternoon."

Chapter 23

Fitzmorris wasn't overreacting. Joshua could have just as well dug his grave with that article. And, with him giving away his personal items, it made me think that Joshua knew that when he wrote it. I had to go see him. Leaving the typewriter and book on the bar, I grabbed my keys and locked up.

I parked at Joshua's press house. The turbines on the outer wall stood still. I walked up to the door and knocked a friendly knock. No answer. I knocked again and waited. Still no answer. I finished my cigarette and threw the butt on the ground. I checked the door handle and found it unlocked. I went in.

"Hello?" The place smelled of cigarettes and ink. The floor was sticky. Sunlight leaked through the safety grill and turbine arms, casting a soft gray about the whole interior.

Then something jerked from behind my right shoulder. Startled, I slipped on the floor. Above me, Joshua stood holding up a golf club as if to bludgeon me with it. He relaxed his arms. "Ridge?" He walked over and switched on a hanging light bulb. Stubble sprouted from his cheeks and chin. He was shirtless, but he still had suspenders on. A deep-purple bruise covered his right ribcage. He had a black eye and extensive scrapes down his arms.

I found myself lying in a pool of black ink. Just as I began to lift myself from the floor, Joshua forced the bottom of his 9 iron onto my sternum. The edge, however, had been roughly sharpened into a jagged blade.

"Why you here?"

"I got your package from Fitzmorris. After I read the latest, I wanted to see you."

He took the club off my chest. "Well, here I am." He walked a few feet and sat on a bucket.

"What happened?"

"Redsleeves ran me off Oyster Shell Road and jumped me," he gestured with his hands to show off his bruises. "They broke my bike and threw it in Broadmoor Bay. They also took the stack of papers I was delivering to Constance's school for a little project."

I approached him and offered him a cigarette and a lighter.

"My life saver," he said as he snatched them. He lit it, and his eyes rolled back in ecstasy as he inhaled. He looked at the lit cigarette in his hand as if he recognized an old friend. The smoke curled upward, looking like a spring suspended from the ceiling. "Yeah, it was time. Someone had to say it. Figured they'd react to that, too, that's why I gave you all some things of mine." He rose, deeply inhaling the cigarette, and waved me to follow him. "Because…" He pointed.

His printing machine had been destroyed, and ink rivers crawled across the floor and pooled in low areas.

"Took all my cigarettes. They even broke my rice cooker, Ridge. Iron Reporter wouldn't have stood a chance."

"The what?"

"My typewriter. Called it that since childhood." Smoke billowed from his nostrils. "It was my father's. My father should've been an English professor, for both our sakes. All he wanted to do all day was talk about books, but my grandparents told him to be a surgeon instead. So he became a surgeon for everyone else, but to me, his only son, he was the professor. Outside of schoolwork, he would assign me book reports of his own. On top of that, when I handed it in to him, we'd have…I don't know…an oral exam or discussion about the characters and the author's intent. We eventually moved into a big house; he dedicated the largest room as his personal library. I hated it. It was just a constant reminder of all the books I hadn't read yet." He took a deep drag on the cigarette, down to the filter.

I handed him another. He nodded and lit it immediately. "Tell Octave he can keep or sell that Mencken book. Can probably recite the whole collection by now. It's what made me do what I do." He chuckled quietly. "Hadn't thought of the coincidence until now, calling it the Iron Reporter." He walked back to a bucket and sat down.

"So, what do you want me to do with it?"

"Keep it for now. If this blows over, give it back. But for now, keep it safe from the Monster. It's all I kept from my parents' Maryland estate after they died." He rubbed the bruise on his ribs and exhaled smoke. "See, Ridge, I wasn't always such a Spartan. Grew up a rich little turd. Spent much of my teenage and young-adult life doing drugs and drinking because I could get away with it, as rich people do. I was off with friends in Europe when I heard that they had been killed in a car accident."

"Lord, I'm sorry." I lit another cigarette.

He shook his head and set his cigarette between his lips. "That's the worst time to realize that you've been pissing your whole life away. When the people that have worked their whole lives to give you everything are gone. I decided then, I'd live for a purpose. Sold the estate and everything, really, except the typewriter. Donated most of the money. Bought the printing machine cheap, assembled it myself. Don't spend anything, really, except on these beauties." He held up his cigarette.

"So, you've been rich this whole time?"

He thought for a few seconds and nodded. "Yep. Suppose so."

"I always wondered how you could afford all those cigarettes, but never thought you were rich. You fooled me."

"Clever rich people will do that. I came here once before Beckham with friends on a five-day bender in the Quarter. One day I stepped into a little coffee house. Picked up a newspaper and someone had written an article about the future of the city and the people in it. Never really felt that kind of solidarity anywhere else. Shit, before that, I thought New Orleans was all boobs and beads. But the people here love it, and I thought they needed someone to remind them why. Not many places have any human spirit left. Once the fire goes out, we all die. So, here I am." Joshua smoked and cleared his throat. He pointed at me with his lit cigarette. "You're the only one that knows about this." He pointed at the vandalized printing machine. "Don't you tell anyone. Waiting to see if anyone implicates themselves. I trust you're all right, though."

"Okay." I took a lovely drag off my cigarette. I reached inside my pocket and took out the precious pack of premium cigarettes. I threw it to Joshua. "You need these more than me."

"Obliged. Pay you back, if this all blows over. But…" he shrugged with skepticism.

If the Redsleeves hadn't confiscated my gun, I'd have lent it to him. I had several guns in my storeroom still; however, I couldn't give him someone else's. Fitzmorris had an extra revolver, I thought, but he clearly didn't trust me anymore. He knew I had been working with the Manchacs. He had this knack for sniffing out clandestine criminality. Of course, I would find out why soon enough.

But what do you say to someone whose purpose is so steadfast that he has graciously accepted a grim fate? If he wanted to live, he could stop or leave, but he wouldn't. If McMason wanted to remain professional, he could resign if the allegations had merit, or he could simply dismiss Joshua's inflammatory words as libel. That wouldn't happen, either. Both men, I think, had signed in blood a mutually destructive contract.

So instead I said, "In the meantime, what am I supposed to do with your typewriter?"

Joshua placed the half-smoked cigarette between his lips and said, "Ridge, you always kind of struck me as a writer. Why don't you write something and see what happens?"

The Southern Belle Café

Mira stood at the corner of Baladucci and Stefinson, thinking about whether she should try the lunch at the Southern Belle. She could be mistaken for a prostitute, as she well knew. She could get sick from unsanitary food preparation. Or, she could have something delicious that would hopefully lead to a nap. It's amazing what we'll go through for good food, she thought. Mira put her Eagle in her purse and brushed dust off her dark-blue dress. As she stepped into the New Carré, goose bumps spread across her skin, and a sharp chill shook through her shoulders. This time the crusader blockade wasn't there because the GGA had cleared the street for delivery trucks. Only a lone older man stood atop a plastic crate on the banquette reciting Bible passages into a megaphone.

Stefinson Street bustled with feet at nine in the morning, but not of men mongering for whores. Garbage and commodity trucks cruised down the thin service alleys between brothels. A white legal courier whizzed by Mira on his bicycle, the leather document bag hugging his back. A black man wearing light-blue overalls waited for Mira to pass.

"Awright." He said while looking at something down the street.

"Thanks."

As soon as she passed, he tilted his hand truck back, loaded with five cases of Corona longneck bottles, and pushed it inside the Mexican Mariposa Café as if the boxes were simply filled with air. Once next door, she looked up at the sign: The Southern Belle Café. The magnolia flower, painted under the lettering, resembled something else far more familiar to all women. She brushed fresh dust off her dress. Once Mira's nose detected the zesty smell of the kitchen, she couldn't resist entering. She took a wooden chair at a small table against the wall in the back corner.

The café was actually quite quaint, she admitted to herself, for a twenty-first-century whorehouse simulating the Old South. An antique rifle and an eight-point deer head hung on the opposite wall above a grandfather clock. The tables and chairs had been stained to look like red mahogany or cherry. Small white-lace table-cloths lay diagonally on the tabletops with silver pitchers for cream and crystal sugar jars. On her table, a dainty coffee cup sat on a saucer, both with matching blue-checked borders. A portrait print hung on the wall displaying a white woman with brown hair pulled back into a bun and a purple dress revealing cleavage in the old, yet ongoing, tradition. If Mira hadn't known she was in a brothel, she'd think it was some old tea parlor or an Uptown socialite's sitting room.

A young woman resembling the woman in the portrait approached her smiling. Her lips were red, and her pink dress was long and poufy—she looked like she was floating along the floor. "Hi there, hon," she said with an accent Mira suspected to be North Louisiana.

Mira returned her smile. "Good morning."

The woman nodded. "Is it cold out?"

Mira, slightly surprised at the question, said, "No, not really."

"Thanks, I worked last night." She turned and walked toward the fainting couch near the opposite corner. She fell back into the couch and let out a deep sigh. She kicked off her heels and put her feet up, fully showing off her ankles as her back sank into the soft, velvety couch. She pulled her hair out of the bun and shook it out. She reached up underneath her dress, revealing her milk-white legs, and removed her Eagle from the black garter belts. She saw Mira watching her. "Pardon me." She covered her legs and began messaging on her Eagle Gold.

"Good morning! Joining us for breakfast today?" A different woman with a twangier accent.

Mira turned to the waitress at her table. She was a bit shocked at the attire comparison. The white waitress's hair was braided in pigtails. She wore a long-sleeved, tight plaid shirt and tight jean short-shorts.

Mira's pause provoked the waitress to say, "Or, d'ya need a manager for an application?"

"Oh, breakfast! Sorry about that."

"You're fine, sweetie. I'm Tammie." She set a small laminated menu on the table. "Take your time. How 'bout coffee?"

"That sounds wonderful."

"Regular, chicory, or café au lait?"

"Café au lait?"

"Yes! It's half chicory coffee and half hot milk. I'm not from around here, but I think it's kinda a New Orleans thang."

"Uh…yes. It is. I…haven't had a café au lait since high school."

"Oh, you're from 'round here then!"

"Yeah, we used to go to a beignet place in City Park all the time after school."

"Oh, how fun. Where's that?"

"At the um…bottom of Broadmoor Bay."

"Oh."

"So, yes. Café au lait, please." Mira smiled. "Oh, is David working in the kitchen tonight?"

"I think so."

"Tell him his old teacher is here."

"Sure. I'll be right out with the café au lait." Tammie bounced back to the kitchen.

The woman on the couch said, "There used to be place up in Mon-roe that had café au lait. But it's a lot better here." She went back to messaging.

Mira thought, Yep, North Louisiana. Nailed it. She also couldn't help but think that, of all the efforts the owners had put into the place to replicate the essence of the South—the good essence, at least—the employees seemed genuinely chatty, which certainly added some authenticity to the Southern Belle Café. Mira slid the menu toward her and read it.

All Dishes Served with Grits and Gravy-Smothered Biscuits.

Eggs Benedict. *A New Orleans Brunch tradition served daily.*

Gulf Crab Omelet. *Lump crabmeat and sautéed green onions.*

Smothered Chicken-Fried Steak *with 2 eggs any style.*

Shrimp & Grits. *Gulf shrimp sautéed in garlic and picante sauce.*

Chicken & Waffles. *Served with our specialty maple gravy on the side.*

Bacon or Sausage *with 2 eggs any style.*

Ham Steak *with 2 eggs any style.*

Tammie returned with a white mug and set it down on the table, the frothy head dancing within its ceramic walls. "Did ya de-ciide, sweetie?"

"All of them."

Tammie laughed.

"You know, I've never had chicken and waffles. I'll think I'll do that." Mira handed the menu to Tammie.

"All-riight!" Tammie bounced her way back to the kitchen.

Careful to not burn her tongue or jeopardize her taste buds, Mira blew on her café au lait and cautiously took a sip. As soon as the smooth beverage hit her lips, she thought of high school and all of its oblivion. Everyone was too busy torturing themselves over petty things to appreciate the fact that they had little responsibility. But that petty pain was pain nonetheless, and who could ever understand at that age that the angst-y steam was just cooking up their future personalities. Despite its perks, Mira thought that she wouldn't go back to those days for anything, since ignorance is not always bliss, especially when you're too ignorant to be blissful.

The click of her breakfast plate on the table snapped her back into reality. She looked up at David, smiling. He wore a white chef shirt, pinstriped pants, and a nylon bandanna. "Ms. Mira."

"Hey, I made it!"

"Yeah, I see dat. You playin' hooky today, Ms. Mira?"

Mira cocked her head and gave him a look.

"Nah, bad choice a words. You ain't teachin' today?"

Relieved, she said, "No school on Mondays. Budget thing."

"Shit, I wish *I* could have dat three-day weekend."

"Yeah, I would, too, David." She began cutting her chicken tenders into smaller pieces. "So, I get the waitresses' farm-girl outfits, but they don't seem to go with the whole motif here." With her fork, she dipped the chicken in the gravy and popped it into her mouth.

"When they first opened, they just had 'em wear dresses, too, but like, I guess, more 'commoner' dresses back then. We had mostly black waitresses then because that's who need jobs. But someone complained, playin' up that whole kitchen slave mistress thing. So, they hired more white girls and made 'em dress like dat."

Mira swallowed her food. "Right, morality. Such a strong suit for the customers here." She sipped her café au lait, which was delicious. "Have you thought of calling Principal Whitman to see if there are any openings in the school kitchen? You'd have benefits."

David's eyes drifted over to the pink-clad prostitute as she slipped her feet into her heels and stood from the fainting couch. She smiled at him, and he licked his lips after she walked by him. His eyes drifted back to Mira, and he laughed. "There're plenty benefits here, too, yeah."

Mira decided to ignore her former student's sexual innuendo. "You know I'm organizing a St. Joseph's Altar. Would you and your mom be interested in bringing a dish to it?"

He thought for a second and leaned on the opposite chair's back rest. "What kinda dish?"

"Anything y'all want. It would be nice to still be a part of it."

He smiled and looked down at the backs of his hands resting on the chair.

"I understand if you don't. It's up to you."

David looked up at her. "Let me see what she say."

"Thanks. Just think about it. That's all I ask."

David laughed. "Awright, Ms. Mira. I need to get back to the line. You enjoy."

"I am. Bye, David."

As David walked past a table at the far wall, Mira recognized the obese customer seated with his back to her. An Elmer's Ryan Whiskey mirror mounted low on the wall reflected the face of the infamous inspector. Mira had not contacted the inspector since she'd backed out of bribing him in front of his wife at the Rio Rojo Restaurante. But she needed to talk to him because if she couldn't get the permit soon, she'd have no choice but to accept Jack Levens's offer. She finished her meal and paid the check. Mira approached the inspector's table and stopped just behind him, thinking of what to say. He could see her torso in the mirror, but her face was out of view.

He perked up and seemed eager to speak, so Mira waited for him to initiate the conversation.

He wiped his mouth with the cloth napkin, still facing the reflection in the mirror. "Oh, y'all are starting to wear different dresses, I see. Won't matter because I'll be taking it off anyway. How's about an appointment at eleven, sugar tits?" He swung around quickly, and his slimy smile faded when he recognized Mira.

Mira was shocked, enraged. She had wanted to punch him in the face even before this indecent proposal. She might have if she'd had a drink or two. A professional educator and musician, yet somehow, people couldn't resist assuming she was a prostitute. It's true that most men judge a woman's looks before anything else, Mira sadly acknowledged. They even judge their own wives the same way, she thought.

His wife! Mira realized.

"How would your wife feel about that?"

He breathed deeply and said nothing.

"So, I can expect that permit this week? Time's running out. I'll need that ASAP. Thanks."

He looked down at his bulbous belly. "Okay, fine."

Chapter 24

Mother, the conditions here in the Levensworth Prison are better now that spring's here. Sometimes my cell would get so cold it would freeze like ice and drip. Most importantly, my spirits have improved, for I have put moral principle first in attempting to resign my post and withdraw from the war effort. In return, they imprisoned me since it is clear that a man who refuses to fight and advocates peace is far too dangerous during wartime. I have read what the newspapers are saying about me. That I'm a coward, a traitor, a Nazi sympathizer.

It is much quieter and calmer in a cell than on the battlefield, but it can be quite maddening, as well. Writing these letters helps pass the time. No other prisoners are around me. I guess solitary confinement is my punishment for civility. Certainly, as long as the war continues, I will be incarcerated in this place. The question remains whether or not I will be able to go home like the other soldiers once an armistice is reached. I think sometimes...

"What are you reading?" A slightly familiar voice said from the other side of the bar.

I hadn't heard anyone come in. Folding the corner of the page down to mark my place, I looked up and said, "*Cold Chambers.*"

The vaguely familiar young man wore jeans and a light-brown pullover. His eyes widened. "Oh, that's a good one. I read that when I was in grad school." He sat at the bar stool across from me. "Ages ago, it seems."

"So, what do you want?"

"That's a good question. To go back to those days, I guess. When my whole existence revolved around reading books and making sense of them. In a *good* way."

"Right. But what do you want to drink?"

He sighed in self-reproach, speaking softly to himself, "Of course that's what you asked." He sighed, reaching into his back pocket. He placed his wallet on the bar. His eyes scanned the bottles behind me. "Do you have the new Elmer's Ryan white whiskey?"

"Nope. Just the regular Ryan."

"That'll do. Have you had the white Ryan?"

"Nope. Some things don't find their way out here."

"No, I suppose not."

I served him two knuckles of whiskey in a glass and then poured four knuckles' worth in a coffee mug for myself.

He sipped and rubbed his forehead. "So how far you into it?"

"Into what?"

"*Cold Chambers.*"

"A little more than halfway, I guess."

"Is he in jail yet?"

"He just got there. It's fascinating…" My heart sank when I finally recognized Sergeant Powell, the Lead Civilian Content Protector.

"Yeah, it is fascinating." Powell finished his whiskey in a single gulp. "Interesting premise. Makes you think about things, doesn't it?"

I was still in shock and just stared down at the bar.

"If you like WWII novels, you should check out *Catch-22*. It's one of my all-time favorites. Kind of feels like I've been living it lately." He rubbed the back of his neck. "Whenever you're ready."

I looked up at him, then looked down at my book. I closed it and slid it over the bar toward him.

"No!" He slid it back to me. "I meant another whiskey."

I poured him another two knuckles and drank about two knuckles' worth of mine.

He gazed at the door and then took a Kikenney cigarette from his front pocket. "Thanks." He lit it and coughed violently. He wiped his eyes, cleared his throat, and said, "Takes some getting used to, huh?"

"Are you trying to *start* smoking? I mean, I smoke too, but if I could do it all over again, I wouldn't."

He quietly laughed. "If that's all you'd do differently, then you're doing great." He sipped his whiskey. His voice hardened, yet he spoke at a low volume. "I'll say this: Being broke is not the worst thing to come out of a life decision. When you're broke, you can't see it any other way. I was penniless coming out of grad school; tons of student loans to pay back, no school or company would hire me with an English degree. In that situation, you'd think the bad life decision had already been made." He inhaled the cigarette and nearly fell off the stool in a coughing fit.

"I can see how being broke can make you start smoking."

He looked at me, chuckled, and said dismissively, "Never mind, man. Do you know the journalist for *The Declaration*?"

The image of Joshua poised for attack with a golf club in the dark flashed in my mind. "I've read some of his stuff."

"Does he ever come in here? I heard he does."

"Sometimes."

Powell reached in his pocket and gave me a small piece of paper, folded. "If you do see him again, give him this message for me." He slid the paper to me, then finished his whiskey. He stood, set cash bills on the bar, and said, "Have a good day."

"Wait, what's your name? So that I can tell him."

Powell stared at me for a few seconds. "You just tried giving me a book that you're in the middle of enjoying, without me even asking for it. I think you know very well who I am." He turned and left.

I unfolded his note. It said, "Thank You."

The door opened, and I quickly folded the note again. But it wasn't Powell returning. It was Octave.

I said, "You just missed your best friend."

"I don't care. Constance just called me. Something terrible has happened. She needs you at the school. Right now."

Renny Rooster's Pancake House

By Saturday, Mira hadn't received the city permit and began to worry. Blackmailing a blackmailer might not have been the best idea, she thought, despite how good it felt. She felt too uncomfortable to follow up with City Hall, so she waited in urgent agony.

It was also Mira's turn to choose the location for their faculty meeting. She chose Renny Rooster's Pancake House by default. She had always selected Toddy's BuzzBar, but that was now the future site for employee parking of Greylock's, despite all the blighted properties surrounding it. She didn't want to go to the new mega coffee shop. Not only did she not like their coffee, but she also wanted to avoid seeing Jack Levens. He had been sending follow-up messages, and she had yet to respond. The Zesty Betty probably served eggless omelets or coffee-less coffee. The Southern Belle Café, though quite delicious, was clearly not appropriate for a schoolteachers' workshop. Surely, multiple teachers and a principal meeting in a brothel would magically register on Chase Quade's radar. She did consider Welshy's Pub, but only liquid breakfasts of bloody Marys, bloody Welshys, and coffee stouts were available. Though entirely fine with that, Mira felt it might not be the most professional move to choose a bar for a nine a.m. meeting with her principal and fellow educators. Bringing a little something to sip with breakfast was one thing. Going to a bar was another. So, Renny Rooster's was the place. Not a bad place, Mira thought, but it would be nice to go somewhere else for a change. She remembered how her parents had tried to choose a breakfast place on Sunday mornings. It was lunchtime before they could make up their minds, weighing every possible place, where it was, what was on the menu, or most importantly, what was not. But in a post-Beckham New Orleans, eating establishments were scarce.

Principal Whitman steadied her coffee mug just a few inches from her lips. "Mira, what's the status of St. Joseph's Day?"

Mira steadied her screwdriver in front of her lips and sipped greedily. "Um…still in process. I'm afraid I'm still waiting on the city inspector for approval. For official approval."

The principal's eyes widened, and she set her mug down. "Mira, it's almost March. Why's this taking so long?"

Mira paused and shrugged. She couldn't tell her about the extortion, her attempt to succumb to his extortion, and then her reversal in blackmailing the inspector. I'll tell her about it after we get it, she thought, because then it will be an interesting story instead of a controversy. "Um, we have a Plan B if necessary."

"Yeah?"

"We could possibly have it at the new Greylock's downtown."

Whitman's face showed brief relief.

Mira continued, "But the whole thing would not be a hands-on experience for the students and their parents. The staff there would do everything and might even charge admission to the public."

"Oh." Whitman furrowed her brow and sipped her coffee.

"He did say the proceeds would go to the school, though."

Whitman paused for a few seconds. "Who is *he*?"

"Jack Levens. He's a big executive over there. We met in his office about this. He called me."

Whitman shook her head slightly, closing her eyes.

"I should have told you. I'm sorry."

Stephen Cooper said from across the table, "If I can butt in, this sounds a little fishy. He may be trying to commercialize or even *own* St. Joseph's Day. These companies are ruthless."

Whitman sighed and folded her tattooed arms on the table and looked at Mira. "This is your project; I'm putting that call on you. But don't let this man make you think he's saving us from failing, hear? We got the whole damn church on our side. So we are not desperate for money."

Mira nodded. "Yes, ma'am."

Whitman scrolled down the outline on her Eagle screen. "Anything worth mentioning?"

The teachers pondered and then waited, out of courtesy, for the others to speak.

Mira poked at the straw in her screwdriver. "David stopped by my office on the way to your office."

Whitman's eyes widened. "Oh?"

"Sure did."

She paused for a few seconds. "And?"

"It was okay."

Whitman lifted her mug toward Mira as if to toast her from across the table. Mira raised her glass to Whitman, and they saluted each other.

The other teachers looked around at their colleagues. Cooper said, "I'm sorry. I think we all missed something."

Principal Whitman said, "'Nother time, Stephen. Different time, wasn't it?"

Mira said, "Yes, ma'am."

Whitman sighed, "So, anyone else?"

Mr. Larson balanced his crooked spectacles on the bridge of his nose. "Does anyone know what's going on with Renisha? She hasn't been to class all week." His glasses corrected themselves to crooked.

"She messaged me on Monday and said she was sick and wouldn't make it to class on Tuesday," Mira said.

Ms. Lucero said, "She no come to my class all week."

Whitman said, "Someone needs to call her or her parents this weekend or on Monday. She's missing too much schoolwork. Stephen, how's the paper grading going?"

Cooper sat up in his chair. "Better." He looked over to Mira. "I guess I owe you an apology and a thank-you."

Puzzled, Mira gave him a curious look.

"I tried out a more mathematical rubric like you suggested, and the students seem to be more aware of what I'm asking from them.

And it gives me something concrete. So, sorry for blowing up at you about it. You were right."

"That's okay, Stephen. I kind of felt bad myself. Felt like I was calling you incompetent in front of everyone."

Cooper said, "Water under the bridge." He shifted his weight in the chair toward Principal Whitman. "So, I'm on the second round of drafts on the rhetorical essay, and my due date is next week…"

Mira's attention drifted off when her Eagle buzzed on the table. Her eyes scrolled up to Stephen and the principal discussing final essay portfolios. She discreetly pushed the "New post. Cut to the Chase?" button.

NOLA? More like "No, Louisiana." One of the behemoth companies rebuilding New Orleans just sent cease-and-desist letters to hundreds of companies that have been selling products containing the popular acronym NOLA, claiming that they have trademarked it. It happened when one of the company's lead executives was dining at a local lunch joint when he saw a young woman wearing a shirt that said NOLA EXILE. Of course, one of the conditions of the terms is that they would be allowed to sell the products as long as the corporation would receive royalties. Well, we all know who the goddamn royalty is going to in this scenario. Allegedly, they quietly trademarked the NOLA label as soon as the Refounding proposal was brought forth. So, they planned for this. They just needed a production to make of it to slap their big-money dick in everyone's faces. Really, I do think it's kind of shitty, but let's cut to the chase, folks. Are New Orleanians that drunk or hungover all the time to never have seen this coming? The NOLA brand could literally sell itself no matter what it was. Hell, I could have had two loaves of bread next to each other. One was freshly baked that day, and the other was all moldy, but if I stuck a sticker on the moldy one that said "Special NOLA Bread," people would buy the moldy one

in a heartbeat because it made them think they were somehow investing in the culture. It was only a matter of time
before a savvy corporation would cash in on all that emotional equity. They think they're being grassroots, and in
doing so, they've created the most centralized commercial
consumer market in America, maybe second only to Disney
World. For all it's worth... [Read more?]$^{10:38AM}$¬ $_{chasethetruth}$

Her brow furrowed, her teeth clenched, and her eyes stayed glued
to her Eagle screen. That person in line at the counter of Zesty Betty
must be who he's referring to, she thought. She must have been the
person wearing the shirt in question.

A message window popped up as she was reading.

Ms. Roche, I just wanted to follow up with you about your
St. Joseph Altar. We would need to know soon because we
need to make appropriate orders and preparations. We at
Greylock's are excited that you'd consider us to take part
in such a traditional New Orleans event. I look forward to
hearing from you soon$^{10:45am}$¬ $_{Jack\ Levens}$

Mira stared at the message from a senior executive from a corporation desperately trying to establish its place in the New Orleans
Refounding. Would Levens trademark St. Joseph's? Perhaps the
buyout money was masked as a "charitable donation?" She couldn't
even trust a random person in line at Zesty Betty, much less a
hungry Refounder.

She responded.

Mr. Levens, I'm sorry, but I must respectfully decline your
offer. Thank you for taking interest.$^{10:48am}$¬

We're up here, child$^{10:48am}$¬ $_{Principal\ Whitman}$

Mira blushed and put her Eagle away in her purse. "I'm sorry, ma'am."

"So other than St. Joseph's, Mira, how are your lessons going?"

"They're going well, actually. I had some ideas for next year, though. I thought we could do more in giving the students a sense of professional progression. Like maybe group up the students based on their interests and give them specialized instruction for those interests. Maybe even involve some professionals or tradesmen—anything from welders to engineers. It doesn't have to be a whole overhaul, but just one class. What do you think?"

Her fingers entwined around her coffee mug, Whitman looked Mira in the eyes. "I think it's a great idea, but let's focus on this school year because…I'm afraid I won't be your principal next year."

The teachers went silent and still.

"I've accepted the New Orleans Archdiocese Education Superintendent position. So I will oversee all the schools during this transition going forward. I must say that I have been very pleased with all of you this year. We are, in fact, the most successful school this year so far. And I want to thank all y'all for that. The students do, too, even if they don't know it yet."

Chapter 25

Civil unrest sometimes hangs in the air like the hairy humidity does just before the downpour; not everyone can smell it, but the storm's coming regardless of who's ready and who's not.

The Redsleeve in the picket line booth waved my truck through. I skeptically slowed down and watched him. He was preoccupied with something else. At first, I thought they had extended the Mardi Gras season another week. People walking in every direction without any respect for the car traffic. A red patrol Humvee at nearly every corner. The school was up the street a few blocks, but the red lights from patrolmen and a massive crowd of protesters stood between my truck and the school. I pulled the truck off to the side and stepped out onto the street. I felt the fervor. I felt it heavy in the air. I felt it steaming up from the storm drains. I felt it trembling in the concrete beneath my feet. I completely forgot that the Manchacs' box was on my passenger-side floor.

I approached the protesters, who stood on the stairs of the old building, spilling onto the curb and into the street, but a stocky Redsleeve with sunglasses stuck his sweaty palm on my chest.

"It's not safe in there, boy! Best get going." His other palm rested ready on his hip near his holstered pistol.

I observed the crowd. They were angry and resistant, yet unarmed and steadfast. Mostly black people of all ages. I concluded that if I was one of the Monster's men, it would not be safe. It was clear that the Ward Wars had escalated too far, and these people wanted McMason to stop it. I rolled my shoulder and slipped by the Redsleeve.

"Your funeral, buddy!"

The people in the crowd faced outward toward the Redsleeve

line that had formed to stop the spread of their numbers. I passed an older black woman with dark freckles on her cheeks. She yelled at the mercenary officers, "Oh, yeah, y'all show up, nah! Damn Reds, where you been at?"

I pushed my way through the crowd into the front door. Well-dressed men and women gathered in the foyer. Teachers, I presumed.

"Ridge!" Constance emerged from the commotion. She wore a blue business suit without the jacket, so her sleeveless white blouse revealed her extensive tattoos. Something she never did at the school.

"Thanks for coming."

"What happened?"

She motioned for me to follow her. The din of protesters softened as we walked farther down the hallway. Her high heels clicked down the linoleum floors, bouncing off the painted cinderblock walls. Then she said while looking at her shoes, "Some of our students were killed today."

I stopped.

She stopped and looked at me, her eyes bloodshot. "Fourth graders."

"My God. I'm so sorry."

"Got caught in a crossfire on the way to a field trip. Someone unloaded a machine gun at a few boys in a parked car across the street. Didn't see the school bus pass right in front. Eight killed instantly. Another six in the hospital."

"Well, what can I do?"

She continued down the hallway. "Well, you see, those children have brothers and sisters at this school. Many of them seem to know who may be responsible. They want revenge. One of those students is in Mira's classroom. Do you remember the little boy playing the trumpet at Mardi Gras?"

"Oh, no."

"Yes, Ridge. We lost him today. His brother, David, is in Mira's class. He tried to escape once he heard, but Mira shut the door before he could."

We came to Room 104. The heavy metal door reduced the voices behind it to an angry and desperate mumble. It sounded like a typical unruly class except that there was no laughter. None.

"She's locked herself in there with them. I dismissed school almost two hours ago. Their families are here to pick them up. She's not listening to me."

I stepped up to the door. Through the window, I could only see the tops of her shoulders and the back of her head. She had her back to the door.

"You'll have to get right up to the door, nah. These doors are soundproofed to prevent distractions. But she should hear you if you get up close."

I tapped on the window. She didn't budge.

"Mira?" I said to the glass. Her head twitched slightly, so I knew she'd heard me at least. "It's me. It's Derek."

She breathed deeply and looked to the ceiling, probably more out of embarrassment than relief.

Just over her right shoulder, David saw me through the window. "Open the door!" His lips said. He was far enough away that I could just hear his stern voice.

Constance said from behind me, "Ridge, say what you can say. She's got to understand, our end goal as educators is to let them go, no matter how much we hate ourselves when we do. We can't hang on to them." She wiped her cheek. "I gotta get back out there." She walked down the hall, tattooed arms crossed, head down, heels echoing down the hallway.

I licked my lips. "Mira, please come out."

She turned her head sideways, "No."

"Please."

"No. I will not fail them."

"Fail them? How?"

She sighed and shook her head, her ponytail waving like a pendulum.

"How?"

"You…just can't understand."

"Well, I understand that you've done more for this community in less than a year than I have my whole life."

She leaned her head forward.

"I made New Orleans my whole…identity, my whole purpose. I thought I understood what purpose was until I saw you in that church, and on that stage on Mardi Gras day. I had always thought that…that New Orleans was my place in the world. But now I wonder if New Orleans ever knew I was even here to begin with."

She turned her head sideways again. "Well, I'm sorry that I made you feel that way."

"Don't ever be sorry for how you make me feel, Mira."

She sighed. "Not now, Derek."

"I…I fucking chickened out. I did. I should have come with you to France."

"Oh…my God. *Not now*, Derek. Are you kidding me right now?"

"No. I'm not kidding."

She turned her head a little more to me. "If I open this door, one of these kids could die. You understand that? You don't, do you?"

"Locking them in the room won't stop them from being mad about what happened. Even if I had a brother or sister, I couldn't imagine what they would feel. I might feel the same."

More angry voices sounded through the door. Mira's body shook as she firmly ignored their pleas.

My throat dry, I licked my lips and swallowed. "If I could, I'd go back and go with you. I'd do that today if you said so, but I can't follow you inside the classroom. Please come out. Will you come with me?"

She turned and faced me. Her tired eyes met mine. She leaned her forehead against the window, and I leaned mine against it as well. The glass fogged and cleared with every breath. Multiple footsteps echoed down the hallway. Some heavy and some light and frequent. The footsteps stopped behind me.

Constance demanded, "Ridge."

I turned my head. Several family members had accompanied her.

"Where's Tricia, Mama?" A little black girl, her hair wrapped in a bun, tugged an older woman's sleeve.

"She in there."

"But school's over, Mama."

The woman glared at Constance. "Sure is, baby."

Constance looked at me. "She needs to let them out. Their families want them to come home."

I turned to Mira, who looked at the families in the hallway.

"Their families are here. You see, they'll be okay."

Her eyes shifted to mine.

"You can't save the city from in there. Come out. Come with me."

Her eyes looked down. The lock unlatched.

Her students ran from the classroom as if the pressure building behind that metal door was quite literal. Their families were there to catch them. They hugged and cried.

David crept around the door, spotted his mother, and gave her a hug as she cried. He then let her go. "I'm sorry, Mama," he said in a tone more apologetic than sympathetic. "I gotta make this right."

"What you doin', my son?"

"I'm sorry." He backed up and ran down the hallway toward the side door.

"Oh no, you ain't! Don't let the Lord take you, too!"

Mira sat at her desk with her head down and folded her arms. I walked up to her and wiped her cheek. She stood and hugged me tightly and sniffled.

Chapter 26

New Orleans always had the power to leave one speechless, yet it wasn't always because good things happened. Occasions like this—the tragic death of school children—sometimes forced you to have an inner dialogue with yourself and your city, questioning your place in it. For Mira, it could have been a feeling of futility. The accidental shooting of a school bus full of fourth graders was tragic enough, but it wouldn't stop there. Some of her older students, like David, stopped coming to class, lost in a vengeful rage. Parents had seen their young children taken from them, and they now feared their older sons and daughters would meet the same fate, as students became soldiers trading in their futures for the type of fury that cleared the paths to prison bars and blood. This was something the city had faced long before Beckham, when one single murder could lead to dozens more. For decades, entire generations had been erased in the midst of rage and gunfire. And when things like this happened, we'd just shut it out in order to keep going, keep living, keep believing in New Orleans even though deep down we knew we had done nothing and *could* do nothing to stop the violence that had swallowed generations of young men and women and would continue to swallow them like some mythical, ravenous beast that no one could see or defeat.

Many of us believed in the New Orleans parable, engrossing ourselves in its narrative, indulging its elements, embracing its imagery, imitating its characters, and yet we missed its lesson altogether. Growing up in New Orleans, I had little choice but to attach every ounce of New Orleans identity with my own. But it's not easy when you realize how your so-called struggle, your purpose, meant much less than what you'd imagined from your pedestal. When you realized that New Orleans was actually something different entirely, and you'd been too busy eating po-boys and drinking highballs, like an unwise gardener bragging about the flavor of his fruits and forgetting to water the roots. How we had been simply *using* New Orleans, exploiting its culture, ignoring the real city and its real struggle. But, on occasion, the elephant tore the room's walls down in a rage, and we would rush to another room for refuge so our New Orleans vision could continue without all the fuss, hoping the elephant would not follow. But it always did.

In short, I felt at that moment that I had never lived in New Orleans. Rather, I had lived off of it, like a leech sucking the lifeblood from a sick leviathan, oblivious of my voracity quickening my beloved host's demise. A leech always thinks it's part of the pod.

We walked back to her apartment without speaking to each other, but we each spoke to ourselves. She inserted the key in the lock, rubbed the back of her neck, and turned around. "Would you stay for a minute?"

"Sure." I attempted to kiss her.

She pulled back and poked her strong finger in my chest. "But... none of that. Not tonight. Not like this."

We went in. "Don't mind the mess." Her sofa and living room table were covered with stacks of school papers. Her guitar leaned in the corner. I followed her to the window, and she opened the shade. Protesters gathered around the Superdome ruins. The news had spread that three more victims had died in the adjacent interim hospital in the old Hyatt Hotel. I remembered when it only took eleven Saints on the field to unite the city. Now, it had to take the spirits of eleven innocent children for everyone to stand together.

I cuddled Mira from behind, and she breathed deeply as she touched my wrists. She wanted my arms, not my words. Honestly, she'd get much more warmth that way.

I awoke on the couch a few hours later, just before dusk. I climbed up and over a snoring Mira, whose slumber was not remotely disturbed by my movements. I found an envelope and a pen and wrote her a note saying, "Had to open the bar. Please come visit me tonight."

Protesters still lingered around the Superdome. I found my truck undisturbed, and, to my surprise, the Manchacs' box remained on my floor. I had completely forgotten to make the drop yesterday. Driving down Oyster Shell Road, I kept glancing at the box, pondering what it could be.

Instead of parking in the back as usual, I parked in front of my bar so any patrons would see I had opened late. I opened the front door and immediately noticed something was wrong. It was drafty inside. I walked up a bit and noticed the back door was open, and then I heard something in the back. Back where the guns were. I grabbed an empty glass mug off the bar and turned into the cooler. Gris spun around, pursed his lips, pointed a pistol at my chest and fired. I fell back onto the concrete floor, breathless. Two clicks sounded above me, and then the gun crashed on the ground. His boots stomped out around me. The gunshot echoed within the cooler's insulated walls. I lay on my back for a few minutes, waiting for my vision to fade, for the end. But I regained my breath. The fall had simply knocked the wind out of me. I stood up, shaking from shock, yet still had enough wits about me to wonder how he had missed from such close range. I examined the door frame behind me. There was a large slug in the metal wall. I inspected each room and made sure no other intruder was there. I locked myself in and sat on a bar stool.

Then it hit me. My gun, which had been confiscated by the Redsleeves, used to pull left. I walked into the cooler and picked up what was certainly my gun. I'm not sure what frightened me more: that Gris had aimed perfectly with the intent to kill and would have succeeded if he had used anything else, or that a pirate had a gun that had been confiscated by the Red Birch Security Company. Guns were not something that could easily be stolen from them.

I went out to my truck, grabbed the box from the floor, and returned to the bar. I opened the box with my knife and found bundles of brass, pointy military-grade bullets. I felt sick. I took the box through the back door, marched up and over the levee, and threw the box in the lake. I watched it sink into the frothy brown water and then vomited.

Across the water, I saw a skiff speeding toward the western shore, toward Manchac Pass. It had to be my attempted murderer en route to his pirating horde to tell them of my hidden gun cache. They'd return in numbers and make my bar their new south shore outpost. I needed to at least hide the guns. They'd return in the night, I was sure. I needed a plan.

Downtown

As soon as they all exited the pancake house, Principal Whitman approached her and asked, "Are you going to see Derek today?"

Jack Levens calling...

Mira silenced the call and put the Eagle in her purse.

"Oh, that's okay. Answer it."

"No, it's not important. Um, I'd like to, but there are no weekend visitation hours."

Whitman shrugged and blinked.

"Yeah, apparently everyone there needs the weekend off. Well, except the warden and the guards."

"Well, who the hell else needs to be there?"

Mira shrugged and held her shoulders up for a few moments. "So, I'm going to miss you. You've been a great boss. The best, actually."

Whitman smiled. "Well, how 'bout we go for a walk?"

Mira, surprised, said, "Sure."

The city streets still buzzed with activity that late Saturday morning, so they walked out into North Hart Street to avoid a pile of cobblestones and bricks that had been stripped from the banquette. Two Greek laborers carried a brick in each hand and neatly stacked them against the near wall. One of the men stood up and wiped the blood from his cracked, blistered hands onto his white T-shirt.

"So, Mira, do you like teaching? Is it something you think you can stick with?"

"Yes, ma'am. As challenging as it is, I can't imagine doing anything else."

"So, in general, you'd say that *education* is your career of choice?"

"Yes. I went to France thinking I should be a musician. But when I was there, I just wanted to be part of something much bigger. I realized that I needed to reach people, and the music wasn't enough. That's why I came back. It's been hard, but I don't regret it."

Whitman smiled as they walked up on the banquette, out of the street. "I became a teacher for the same reason. Not the same situation. Same reason," she sighed. "I had a son once. Got pregnant, dropped out of high school, thinking that was the best thing then."

"Oh, I had no idea."

Principal Whitman nodded. "The best job I could find was the old Rally's on Louisiana Avenue, so I didn't have much. But I gave him everything I made. Well, he got killed one day coming to pick me up from work. Someone thought he was somebody he wasn't. The cops blew it off like just some other dead *nigga* in *Nu'ar'lens*. Pardon my words, child. And the people in the neighborhood wouldn't say who did it, though I had a good idea who did. You can't do something like that and expect a tight community not to know. I went out and bought a gun to hunt down the son of a bitch that took my only boy from me. I waited in my car one night with the gun in my lap outside his mama's house. He came out, walking his pit bull. I had the opportunity but couldn't do it. Then I thought escape was what I needed, not vengeance. So I enrolled in a GED center the next day, then went to college after I got that. Got myself out of that neighborhood and got a small place much farther down Constance Street, near the corner of Octavia, where I met my husband. But child, my goal was to get the hell outta New Orleans, so if I ever had any children again, they wouldn't meet the same fate. You understand? Well, I was wrong, Mira. I didn't want escape. I wanted revenge the whole time, and I got it by being the toughest teacher these kids would ever have. That way I could stay with them and keep teaching them when I wasn't there. You see, we can throw information at them and test them all we want. We need to reach them to teach them. If not, then we're just *informing* them, and not very well, either. Hell, they can learn math and writing skills out there in the world the hard way.

Really, we just need a reason to get these kids in a room together and force them to believe in themselves again. That's why I don't put up with any crap from these students—'cause we don't have time for it and neither do they. You understand?"

"Yes, ma'am. I agree."

"You teach like I used to teach. In the end, you put them first. Some teachers out there are too wrapped up in themselves or in their subject matter to even notice the students in front of them. Like the kids are obstructing them from their work; however, they are obstructing the students. I thought I did all right in keeping that kind of grouchy teachers out of Archbishop Fullerton. Next year, though, I'll be making sure that *all* our schools have good teachers."

"I'll miss you. You'll be great at that position."

"I'd like to bring you with me. I need a Curriculum and Community Outreach Coordinator."

"Oh?"

"You wouldn't be teaching in the classroom, which would be the downside. But I can get anyone to teach religion or math. I need someone to help me teach everyone else outside the classroom a damn lesson. Everybody who ain't a teacher thinks they're an expert on education, and I'm sick of it! Ya hear me, child?! This Chase Quade character....ugh! I wish he could find something good to say about us. And the school board ain't got anyone with a teaching background. Bunch of politicians, what they are. I need a groundwork person. The army that finds that high ground wins the battle. You understand? I need you to come with me to find that high ground, and we'll build it if we can't find it. Playing it safe can be dangerous in education, especially when the kids aren't learning anything because everyone's too worried about their own damn jobs 'cause they ain't doing they jobs in the first place!"

Mira smiled at the principal's slip into *Nu'ar'lens* lingo.

"You know, child, we got rules in this world because we need to keep the worst of us from taking over, but the rules can keep the best of us from being great. Some of the best teachers I've ever met are the ones that break the rules when they need to. And some of my best students—within reason, now—broke the rules, too, so they could grow into their own." Principal Whitman stopped walking and looked Mira in the eyes. "Will you come with me?"

Mira was speechless, afraid. She wanted to do this. She wanted to follow Principal Whitman on her valiant quest to save New Orleans from itself once and for all. She strongly felt that no matter how much the Refounders renamed the streets and stamped out the city's cultural inertia, it would not change the menacing machine of reactionary anger and desperation that consumed the dejected and neglected New Orleans youth if they did not prioritize mending the long-fractured education system, which had been functioning as a means of containment rather than development. But she somehow couldn't muster the courage to say so. Whatever held her back would not materialize at will, and she hated herself for it.

Principal Whitman smiled and said, "That's okay, child. Tell me when you're ready."

Chapter 27

Night fell, and I loaded all of the guns in the small cab of my pickup. I struggled to keep track of whose guns were whose and what was what, but they were plenty: six handguns—four pistols and two revolvers…well, three revolvers now that I had just reacquired mine; three rifles, or what seemed to be, anyway; and five shotguns, one sawed off, one double-barreled, and the rest regular for all I knew. Fitzmorris had kept track of whose guns were whose, or at least I hoped he had. Fitzmorris would have a plan. Oyster Shell Road was dark and lonely. A Redsleeve Hummer wasn't creeping in its usual spot behind a pile of bar patio umbrellas. Maybe they were on shift change. Or maybe they were focused on the protests downtown. Either way, I watched my speed and my driving so as not to give them any reason to pull me over and discover my truck's arsenal.

To my dismay, Fitzmorris's store was also desolate. What would I do now? Octave didn't like guns and refused to own any, even in a world of chaos and desperation. The Redsleeves had been to Joshua's and would return soon if they hadn't yet. Judge lived out in the marshes of what was left of St. Bernard Parish because he couldn't leave his beloved Chalmette, even for solid ground. I wasn't sure where Huey lived. Choppy lived somewhere in The Ward. Hell, I didn't even know where Fitzmorris lived. I assumed he stayed in the store somewhere like I did with my bar. I drove around to the back of the building. A bullfrog croaked somewhere in the darkness, and a few fireflies glittered away from me. A horrid stench nearly made me gag as I approached the door. Under the full moon, I saw a dead possum being devoured by a pack of rats that didn't cower even slightly at my approach. I searched for a brick or a pipe—anything that could bust the door open. A spade shovel leaned against the wall. That might do the trick, I thought. I grabbed the doorknob to check how tightly the door was latched, but surprisingly, the doorknob turned. It seemed a little odd that Fitzmorris would simply leave his store open for vagrants. But then again, maybe he didn't have much inventory left to loot. I stuck my head into the dark space behind the doorway and called out, "Hello? Fitzmorris?" No one answered. I ran my right hand along the wall until I felt the light switch. I flipped it up and down and nothing would turn on. I then remembered that Fitzmorris ran his place by generator. Since I had no flashlight or lighter, I just had to feel my way in. I had no idea where he kept the ammunition, but I figured I wouldn't be able to find the secret stash anyway, if I knew Fitzmorris well enough. I pulled my arms through the straps of the backpack loaded down with pistols and grabbed a shotgun in each hand. I stepped into the dark storage room, walked a few feet, and set the guns and the backpack down.

I was only a few steps from the exit when something like a sand-bag hit me in the face, knocking me to the ground. Dazed, lying on the floor, I felt what seemed to be very heavy pillows being thrown on top of me. My lip was busted and it burned intensely as I tasted salt. A thin male silhouette stared down at me. A voice that I didn't recognize said, "What are you doing?"

I got a hint of foul body odor that had been masked by the dead animal outside. It was the gutterpunk. I shifted and tried lifting the heavy bags from my body. The guy knelt down on the bag resting across my torso. I said, "I'm Ridge! I know you! I know Fitzmorris!"

"I asked what you're doing here, not who you are. I know who you are; that's why I hit you with a bag of salt and not a hammer."

"Where's Fitzmorris?"

"I still have the hammer right here."

"The Manchacs found the gun stash. I was hoping Fitzmorris would know what to do."

"Why would Fitzmorris keep your guns for you?"

"They're not just mine. Some are his. They belong to others, too.

McMason accessed the federal registry and marked them for confiscation. We all reported that our guns had been stolen or were missing from Beckham. I've been holding the guns at my bar, and Fitzmorris has the ammunition so that we could split the power."

The gutterpunk stood and removed the three thirty-pound bags from my body, one of salt, one of sugar, and the other of flour. "Why don't you call the Redsleeves and say you just miraculously found them?"

"Can't do it. McMason and the Manchacs are working together."

The gutterpunk was silent for a few moments. "How's that?"

"Listen! The pirates are going to come back to my bar tonight and probably loot everything in my place. I need to leave these here. Where can I find Fitzmorris?"

"He locked up early to take part in the protests downtown. I don't know where he lives. He usually gets here around four in the morning."

"Damn it! Well, whoever you see first—either Huey or Fitzmorris. Tell them that it's finally happened. And to come as soon as they can."

"You're going back there?"

"I gotta put up a fight." I remembered that one of the rifles still had one bullet.

Perhaps vengeance could be my penance. God may not have agreed, but I never really was a God-fearing man despite my Catholic upbringing. I sought forgiveness from New Orleans, not God. Too concerned with myself, I had enabled them in their mission to exploit us, which made me one of them. And this was the only way to divorce myself from the Manchac pirates. They had simply been stealing liquor from me, but elsewhere they were stealing lives. I owed it to the victims of the shooting and their families. I owed it to Mira and Constance. I owed it to Fitzmorris. And I owed it to New Orleans, whatever that meant anymore. A hodgepodge of blunders and plunders had developed New Orleans, and only one was forgivable.

I walked around in the bar and my apartment for anything I needed to hide from the marauders that were sure to come. I didn't have much. I left the liquor bottles where they were. Any blood money they had given me I piled on top of the bar for them to easily reclaim. I put the remainder of the tobacco in my pocket, however. In my living quarters upstairs, my sheetless mattress lay on the floor with a stinky blanket on top of it.

I knelt down and rubbed my finger along the faded blue stain on my pillowcase. Mira hadn't been able to wash the stain out and was embarrassed that she couldn't. I, however, was quite content with the stain remaining. I pulled the music-note pendant from my pocket. The Manchacs would certainly take that. I opened the copy of *Cold Chambers* and wedged the silver piece inside the spine, figuring the pirates probably wouldn't take a book. I stood and sighed. My life felt a little empty as I realized I only cared for an old stained pillowcase, a silver piece, and a half-read novel. Other people my age had many things in their lives to care about, to hold and keep. My first loves, however, I had done wrong: Mira and the city of New Orleans.

The Manchacs were on their way. I was sure of it, and I needed to make it right. I had little choice, really. If I ran, they'd find me sooner or later. It was time to stop being such a coward. I walked downstairs and peeked out of the window blinds at a dark Oyster Shell Road. After I covered Joshua's typewriter with dry towels under the bar, I lit a cigarette and allowed the smoke to calm my nerves and churning stomach. I'd kept a shotgun and the rifle. I loaded three shells into the shotgun and slipped my arm through the rifle's shoulder strap. I walked around behind the bar and poured a whole finger's worth of Elmer's Ryan whiskey in a glass. I tore off a piece of paper, wrote "Come to the levee," and left it on the bar in case Fitzmorris came in time. A shotgun in one hand and a glass of whiskey in the other, I kicked the back door open and marched up the levee. I lay on my stomach at the levee's peak and practiced firing positions with the rifle. The moon was not quite full, but it illuminated the lake just enough for good aim. It lingered above the watery horizon like a lazy eye in the sky.

I watched the lake meticulously, waiting for them to enter the lighted lane the moon granted me. After what seemed to be forever, my back ached, so I rolled over and slunk down the levee with the rifle cradled against my chest. My eyelids got a little heavy. Perhaps it was the whiskey; perhaps it was the nautical symphony of Lake Pontchartrain; perhaps it was just my tendency to never learn from my previous mistakes. Whatever it was, I gave in.

The Faubourg Wastelands

Principal Whitman walked back to her car on Baladucci Drive, but Mira continued along North Hart looking for any street musicians or gutterpunks to play music with. She'd brought her penny whistle for just such an occasion. She kept pondering why she hadn't taken Whitman's offer when she knew she wanted it. Really, she *wanted* to follow Principal Whitman, no matter the job. Perhaps, she thought, she'd be dealing with a platoon of odious, philandering inspectors. She couldn't blackmail all of them. She was already taking a chance with just the one. She figured she had to choose Whitman or the scores of her faceless future students. She had to choose the elation, as well as the grit, of teaching over the influence, as well as the drudgery, of administration. Mira didn't see the fine line that her principal walked concerning the difference between the big picture of education and being on the front line in the classroom. To her, it was all the same. It was true that the first army to reach the high ground won the battle, but a war couldn't *ever* be won if the front line failed. She taught her classroom with transparency and always held open-door meetings with colleagues and students. As an administrator, that policy would not be possible, she speculated. She never bullshitted her students. That rule had worked for her thus far, so she wanted to carry on that approach. However, she knew that any administrative and political infrastructure was largely reliant on bullshit to keep the walls from crashing in on themselves, and it would just take more bullshit to pick up the pieces. When she began teaching, Mira had surprised herself with how much patience she had for her students' antics and eccentricities. Bullshit, however, she had zero tolerance for. Neither did Principal Whitman, which led Mira to think that both of them could actually bulldoze those walls. It was all a matter of emerging from the wreckage alive. Perhaps that's what Whitman had in mind after all, she thought.

She walked into the intersection of North Hart and Persimmon and turned left. Mira felt lost. She never knew north from south, but she at least sensed where the lake and river were. With the streets renamed and the buildings rebuilt, she had no idea where she was going in relation to the old city. The newly built apartments along Persimmon were lived in, but the street was ghostly quiet and still. These must be the Refounders' housing for their female employees, whom they kept behind the stucco walls through fear-baiting. Pondering that assumption, Mira felt unsafe. She had been assaulted while immersed in a gaggle of perverts, but now she was lost and alone in a city under martial law. Unlike McMason's Redsleeves, Mira felt safer with Gulf Guardsmen in the streets. Living under the oversight of an occupying army, no matter if it is domestic, unsettles everyone. However, the Gulf Guardsmen were not mercenaries but civil soldiers who had pledged to ensure the security of the citizens of the Gulf South, and were not committed to corporate profit as the Redsleeves were. But Mira now stood in an empty street, *somewhere* in an unstable New Orleans. She had always felt that the Refounders exaggerated stories about men preying on young unsuspecting women, keeping them wedged between the concrete and the glass ceiling like spineless organisms mashed flat under a microscope.

Mira heard the tires of a car behind her, and she turned to see a pickup truck driving in her direction. About ten feet from her, the driver slowed to a creepy crawl toward her. She felt a shake starting up her thighs. Mira recognized the plaid-clad man in the driver's seat. It was Dac the exterminator, and he was interested in something other than her ability to spray rat poison. Without knowing where this street would lead her, Mira quickly walked in the opposite direction, past where the truck lurked. Mira glanced over her shoulder: Dac had hit the brakes, and his red taillights stared back at her like a demon's hungry eyes. The muscles in her neck tensed, and Mira walked another half a block until she heard him drive away.

Mira had not told anyone what she had seen or done in the Marigny ruins. She had a strange feeling that city government, the Refounders, and perhaps the Gulf Guard of America knew about it. She was actually embarrassed to tell Principal Whitman or Derek because she'd put herself in a compromising situation for sheer curiosity and some cash. If only *The Declaration* was still around, she thought.

And then there was Chase Quade. He was the anti-*Declaration*. At least the former newspaper helped keep us together and gave us confidence that our fight was worthwhile, she thought. Quade, on the other hand, seemed bent on breaking any sense we had left of ourselves and our city. What infuriated Mira the most about him was the fact that he seemingly understood New Orleans well, and that made him powerful. He did tell *some* truth, a conniving and hurtful kind of truth, but truth nonetheless. But there was something beyond his selective truth. From his words and demeanor, Mira suspected that he deeply had it in for New Orleans, as if he were getting back at the city for something it had done to him, that his mission was to take anything "old New Orleans" and crush it. And that's what made him dangerous, she thought. The Refounders are breaking ground outside, while Quade is chipping away at our foundations from within.

Mira walked until she found Baladucci Drive. She bit her lip and pulled her Eagle from her purse. She scrolled through Chase Quade's home page and found the Join the Chase! button. She sighed and selected it. Since she already received notifications, her account automatically logged her in. Then, relieved at seeing the Remain Anonymous option, Mira checked it and wrote in the Gimme Something to Chase message box: There's a pest control company that's hiring gutterpunks off the street to spray toxic chemicals (without protective gear) in the old Marigny area, has to do with filming a movie. But the rats have been getting flushed out and have been infesting our homes and schools. Please investigate.

She sighed again and sent it, hoping to harness his venom for something good.

Chapter 28

Even though it's easy to do, never sleep with a gun in your lap. Copper stuck the rifle's barrel in my gut. "Sleep good?"

A man behind me laughed and slipped a cloth hood over my head. He tied my hands behind my back and pulled me to my feet. I turned my head slightly and through the cloth saw dark figures looting my bar. I heard glass break somewhere inside and more boisterous laughter.

The man behind me kept laughing hysterically.

"Give 'em here. Take da gun. Grow up."

The laughing man let go and the serious one gripped my left arm. I felt a sharp pinch in my lower back. "Bes' c'mon, son!"

I stepped slowly down the levee and paused. I felt the blade prick my back again, so I walked on further, unsure of where the Pontchartrain began and New Orleans ended. The hum of a boat motor joined the splashing waves and sea breeze. What sounded like a wooden board banged against the ground, and I felt the nick in my back again, so I walked over a flimsy wooden board that dipped down before leveling up again. With my next step, I fell forward, and the side of my face hit the floor of the boat. Over the din of the boat and the footsteps, I heard that familiar laugh erupt behind me.

"Dis 'em?" a deep, raspy voice asked.

"Yeah. Das him."

"Why ya laughin'?"

The laughing man breathed deeply to collect himself. "He was 'sleep. Dat boy ain't got no sense." He chuckled some more.

I felt a boot in my gut. The deep, raspy voice commanded, "Squirm o'er till you can't squirm no more." His voice sounded both robotic and animalistic, word by word.

I slithered along the bottom of the boat until my head bumped against the side. My face rested on the boat floor, and the foul bilge water tasted astringent, metallic, and fishy. I stretched my neck upwards, but after a little while, my neck stiffened up, forcing me to relax it, which landed my mouth on the floor again.

Then I felt a boot in my lower back. "Where dey at, pony boy?

"Who?"

He kicked me harder in the back. "Don't play wit' me."

I paused, trying to conjure up some rational lie while being held prisoner on a pirate ship.

He kicked me again. "You keep playin', you gonna find yo'self tied ta dat motor."

I said, "I threw them in the lake."

"Oh, is dat right?"

"Yes."

"Why?"

"Because the Monster was coming to take them all away after the school shooting. They were stolen. That's what I was coming do this afternoon."

The men standing above me muttered among themselves.

Then, in a mechanical but menacing way, the leader commanded, "Send 'im to Massachusetts."

Chapter 29

I remember hearing someone say once that when you get taken prisoner, you either did something really wrong or really right. But as I sat there, bound to the docks of the Manchacs' port, I couldn't help but feel it was a little of both. I should have expected this outcome when I agreed to deliver those boxes in exchange for the very things they knew I needed. Sure, I tried to stand up to them for the right reasons, but that can't turn back time. There's no way of knowing whether those boxes were all full of bullets or if those were the ones that landed in the hands of the Ward Warriors. There's really no way to prove it, but that doesn't matter to me. Many people, including Mira and Constance, have told me not to blame myself for those kids' untimely deaths, since we don't know that for sure. Bless them for making me feel better. But it didn't work then, and it won't work now. I felt the same way then on those swampy docks as I do now as I type these very words in the temporary jailhouse. I'll be the first to admit: I killed those eleven schoolchildren. Not the Manchacs, not the Ward Warriors, not McMason. It was me, and there's nothing that will convince me otherwise.

So I waited in the dark for my fate; I was at their mercy. I had expected a watery grave, but the captain wanted me in Massachusetts for some reason. What connection did the pirates have with Massachusetts? It was quite clear that McMason and the Manchacs were working together. But were the Refounders really so brazen that they would work with them as well? But really, those questions came retroactively. Right then, any sense I had of a future had been shattered. I had always thought that getting up day after day to go to school or work was mundane, monotonous, and miserable. But really, it's a gift to be in such a position. Try being at the mercy of pirates when at any moment you could be stabbed, shot, drowned, or enslaved. My whole life, I'd taken the next life stage for granted. In high school, I expected college. Then I expected some sort of career. And even with my fickleness about committing to Mira, I still thought of family and kids with her. That was quite a wondrous thing. I won't ever take that for granted again. The only thing in the future I could hope for now was a quick death.

When we reached the base camp, the humid night hung over the cypress swamps like an execution hood. The Spanish moss lightly blew with the wind, looking like gray cartoon ghosts. Clouds restrained the moonlight, and a few patches of stars trembled. In a way, I was glad they had already taken the hood off and that we had arrived wherever they were taking me. The choppy waves of Lake Pontchartrain had rocked my stomach to the point of vomiting on the boat's floor, which had added yet another vile flavor to the bilge filth all over my face. They stood me up, but my knees buckled, sending me crashing back down.

Their captain said from behind me, "Dry 'im out for now."

They led me down the warped wooden pier that ran along what I assumed to be Manchac Pass to my right, and to my left lived a warm swamp so rich and raw it could have been the intestinal bacteria of some giant that had eaten us by mere accident. Each post along the pier had a light on top, except that the Manchacs didn't have them on, as if they had developed nocturnal vision over time. We passed a pile of putrid pelican carcasses. Their long necks had been twisted around a time or two, and the long wing feathers had been plucked from their bodies. The men led me to a metal post that had an over-hanging arm with a metal cable and hook attached. Gris untied my wrists while the other man stood in front of me holding a machete. He tied my wrists together in front of me and hung my arms on the hook. He then cranked the lever to raise the hook. I felt the muscles in my arms stretch tight. Just as it seemed my shoulders were about to pop, he stopped raising me. It was an awkward state between standing and not standing, hanging and not hanging—I would hang if I bent my knees, but I couldn't fully stand, either, which immobilized my legs.

"Hang tight, son, until dey come for ya," Copper said.

"Still can't figure how I missed," Gris said. "I gotta admire dat fight in ya, though."

Looking at my bent knees and the warped wooden boards of the pier below, "Yeah, well, here I am."

The Manchacs were masters at torture, since they didn't even bother doing it themselves. They let the swamp do the work for them. The mosquitoes found me immediately and nearly sucked themselves silly. The only defense I had was blowing at them. As miserable as that was, the deer flies were far worse. They bit my bare arms, bit my torso through my shirt, and then worked their way up to my face, which they seemed to prefer after a while, being the insatiable divas of devilry that they are. Each deer fly bite felt as if someone had pushed the tip of a thumbtack into my flesh. My eyes had adjusted to the darkness a little after several hours, and red welts peppered my arms as if leprosy had befallen me. My arms itched incessantly, and rubbing my stubbly chin on my biceps was my only reprieve. Rats descended upon the pelican carcasses. The first time I screamed at them and stomped the boards, they scurried to the supporting boards underneath the pier. When they learned I wasn't a threat, they voraciously picked apart what was left of the dead pelicans, shrieking with gusto in the night. Until cottonmouth moccasins began striking at them from the gaps between the boards.

A seaplane flew in from the east just as the first sun haze broke the horizon. It landed on the water with ease, as if Manchac Pass were a concrete runway. I had only seen planes like this in movies before: wings extending from the top of the plane, propellers on the nose and each wing, pontoons extending down from the wings, the fuselage hammocked between the pontoons like a catamaran. It was fairly large, like something you'd see in a movie set in the Caribbean islands, not like a small crop duster in Iowa. The plane glided to the dock and a crew of Manchacs met it. They unloaded unmarked wooden crates and burlap sacks of contraband. The pirates laughed and joked with each other. They either were in good spirits or liquored-up. Or both. They all walked by me and conducted their business while completely ignoring me. I couldn't really see any of their faces because the sunrise was nothing but a blot of purple leaking across the eastern sky. Also, I was facing the swamp and had to crane my neck around to see them. At this point, I felt that the less I saw, the better, in the unlikely case that I'd come out of this alive.

The men cackled in the dark like faceless apparitions haunting the swamp. They began bringing different crates and sacks into the plane. Then the footsteps resonated louder as they approached me and stopped. One of them cranked the lever, lowering my arms. The other slipped my tied wrists from the hook. My legs struggled as they led me toward the plane. The Manchac behind me grabbed the top of my pants and chucked me headfirst into the plane. The laughter stopped as the door sealed shut and the engine started. It was still very dark inside the plane, but I managed to sit up and scoot my back against something soft but unyielding, like a large sack of flour or sugar. Someone sitting across from me coughed in the dark. There were no seats in this plane, just open space for commodities or people, a delineation the Manchacs didn't make. The vibration of the plane and the white noise of the propellers made me sleepy. Sleep, I found, was a great way to deal with a horrible situation. It was the only way not to deal with it. Fully aware that I could awaken to the sharp instant before sudden death, I slept anyway.

St. Henriette Cathedral

Mira went to the cathedral in hopes she could speak with Sister Matrona about St. Joseph Day arrangements, since contacting her had proved to be difficult. The Catholic Church had added a vow of simplicity among its usual vows of chastity, poverty, and obedience to prevent the use of social and technological devices. But even a convent wasn't cloistered enough in the twenty-first century. The modern world could penetrate any stone wall and coerce its way to the holiest of hermits, for better or for worse. So the best way to reach her was either to call the church phone or just knock on the door.

The New Carré streets were probably the worst just before dawn, Mira assumed. That's when people are the most desperate, no matter who they are. In those predawn hours, dejected people wandered aimlessly through the streets like lost campers in the wilderness and would lash out at anyone for whatever they needed most. Prostitutes who had not made their nightly goal swooped at any potential customer like voracious seagulls combing the beach for anything digestible without knowing, or caring, what it was. Drug and black-market tobacco dealers who hadn't met their quotas bullied people to buy their lagniappe contraband. Good ol' boys and tourists sulked in the streets, denouncing themselves as degenerates and pronouncing their newborn sobriety. Police officers were exhausted from the night, high-strung and ready to throw cuffs on anyone they deemed odious and problematic to society. Or they were looking for a woman to take the load off. And they all preyed upon one another like a cannibalistic circus. Mira had witnessed this on Bourbon Street in high school, so she decided to head to the Cathedral around nine, when industry swept the streets clean of debauchery with booze deliveries and garbage pickups.

Empty churches were awfully ghostly, Mira always thought, and she had never decided whether they were the bad ghosts or the good ones. Possibly indifferent ones, which would be ironic for a so-called "house of God," she felt. However, one thing present that Mira didn't question was the amplification of sound. A whisper reverberated against the stone walls and arches. She walked up the main aisle, each step announcing her presence. The pipes of a large organ loomed above the crucifix as if steel teeth would bite down on the Messiah at any moment. Elaborate murals on the ceiling depicted robed and disrobed man-angels and a long-bearded God busily interacting, yet it looked more like a Saturday night at the Man-shack than a biblical passage. To the left front of the church, a statue of Holy Mary was tucked away in the corner, trapped against the wall by burning candles. On either side of her, solid cypress pews stretched out and gradually curved toward the front of the church like a hundred petrified wing bones from a colossal pterodactyl. The newly built walls, painted the color of ancient scrolls, catalogued the Stations of the Cross as wrought-iron figures retelling the demise of Jesus so His believers could learn that their beloved dogma was founded upon a heinous act of gore and intolerance.

Mira suddenly realized she hadn't yet covered the Stations of the Cross in class. She pulled out her Eagle so she could enter a reminder for herself, but the device was rendered useless except for the clock on the screen. "Hmm," she said. She turned and walked back out through the heavy ten-foot oak doors. Her phone still didn't have any service. To her left were two confessional booths and four padded chairs across from them. The right passage, however, seemed to lead back into the offices and back chambers. She walked through that corridor, yet to see or hear anyone.

The transition from the mystic aura of the church to its homey business quarters was always discombobulating to Mira. She entered a blue-carpeted room and approached an oak desk covered in paperwork. A lukewarm mug of coffee held down a stack of papers riffling in the wind from a cracked-open window. The wood trim about the room was stained dark brown for a more rustic appearance than of new construction.

"Hello?" Mira walked through the hallway that led to a few rooms and an adjoining hallway. She passed the hallway to her right and continued down the main hall. As she passed that hallway, faint singing broke the ghostly silence of the church. It sounded more folksy than clerical. Mira paused for a moment but continued, peeking in each doorway. The singing faded as she walked further down the main hall. The first door led to a clergy lounge. A big stainless-steel refrigerator stood adjacent to a set of wood cabinets. On the counter, a coffee maker groaned and breathed steam. There was also a large table with a basket in its center containing an array of hot sauces such as Tunica and Tabasco. She mused, *At least they don't have to take a vow of insipidity.*

She turned back past the other hallway and heard the song again. She went back to the foyer, hoping that someone had returned to the desk. No one had. The papers just fluttered about under the coffee mug, as if trying feverishly to escape from the oppressive heat and overwhelming weight of the mug.

"Hmm," she said and walked down the hallway toward the singing voice. She could also hear a stringed instrument plucking along with the chorus. It was only one man singing, not the whole church choir. The lyrics seemed nostalgic about a town that had fallen on hard times. Mira peeked into the chamber. A casually dressed Archbishop Fullerton, seated on a stool with his legs crossed, plucked his heart out on a beautiful mahogany mandolin. He closed his eyes as he sang.

Mira ducked back against the wall. The lyrics resonated inside of her, and even though she did not know the ballad, she shared its sentiment. Something tugged at her thigh, and she reached into her jeans pocket and discovered she had her penny whistle. Apparently, she had left it there on Saturday. She always wanted to be prepared for any opportunity to play music with strangers, but she had never expected that day would come with the Archbishop of New Orleans. She smiled and rubbed the finger holes. He played the mandolin without singing for a few seconds, and Mira put the mouthpiece to her lips. She didn't know the song, but she let her diaphragm determine the tune. He might be playing for somewhere else, she thought, but I can play for New Orleans. She blew and let all her sentimental memories guide her melody. Eating brunch Uptown with her parents. Drinking coffee with Derek in City Park after homecoming dances. Lounging on the grassy bank of Bayou St. John after school dismissal...

Fullerton stopped playing for a moment before resuming. Still with her back to the wall, Mira accompanied the calm notes and nostalgic tone of Fullerton's strings. But the archbishop's tone became more sorrowful, and he sang with more intensity. He sang of civil unrest, gun violence, and army tanks. He sang how the community had no choice but to accept the reality of their losses and press forward.

After strumming the strings to signal the song's end, Fullerton asked, "Hello?"

Mira timidly stepped into the doorway. She smiled awkwardly. "I'm sorry, I hope I didn't impose."

"Oh, not at all! Quite enchanting, it was." His Irish accent and dialect had a welcoming effect.

"I didn't know you sang so well."

"Well, I'm no Luke Kelly, I'm afraid. But yes, that's one of my dearest native ballads. Brings me back to Ireland. It's called 'The Town I Loved So Well.'"

"From the lyrics, I thought you might be singing about New Orleans."

"Oh, my! That's brilliant. Well, I was just about to sing 'Dirty Old Town.'"

Mira sneered.

He laughed. "Oh, it's actually quite flattering. Not about New Orleans, but a wondrous elegy of a place. So, to what do I owe the privilege of your presence, my lady?"

"I was actually trying to get in touch with Sister Matrona. Is she around?"

"She's been spending much of her time at the Greek shelter. Let's see if she signed out. Come with me." Fullerton led her to the unoccupied desk. "Aha! *That's* where my coffee wandered off to." He held down the blowing papers and took a sip of his coffee with the other hand. He closed the window and thumbed through the papers on the desk. "There you are, my lovely." He picked up a paper. "I believe she is off at the relief shelter this morning. Diligent server of the Lord, she is."

"Do you know when she'll be back in?"

"I'm afraid I do not know. I try not to hover over my sisters too much. She will be here sure tomorrow morning."

"I'm teaching tomorrow. I just need to talk to her about St. Joseph's."

"Oh, but of course! How is the planning going?"

"Well, I'm still waiting for the permit."

"Hmm, that's quite ludicrous, if I may say."

"Did you ever talk to Czar Gibbons?"

"I did very long ago, I'm afraid." He grabbed a piece of paper and a pen. "Here, write down a message for Sister Matrona."

"Thank you. You don't have a direct line for her, do you?"

"No, I'm afraid the one phone is all we have."

Mira pulled her Eagle out of her purse.

Fullerton chuckled. "I'm afraid that won't work in here. We have a special device that jams service. To keep ourselves in line with our vows of simplicity."

Mira nodded, thinking it was odd that the Church thought that a digital window to the outside world could be more detrimental than members of the clergy carrying firearms in public. "Thank you, Archbishop. It was lovely playing with you." She wrote a note for Sister Matrona and left the little church office.

Chapter 30

My body shook itself awake because it thought it was falling, but the plane had dipped as it changed direction. I slid down the fuselage a bit until the bottoms of my feet pushed me back into position. The sun shone through the window brightly, still a bit orange above the horizon. Storm clouds loomed over the fiery orb, however, like an enormous saturated sponge just waiting to be squeezed. The sea waves below thrashed in alternating colors of gun metal and fire. We were not flying at a high altitude. The Manchac slept soundly despite his head bobbing about from the turbulence. I looked ahead to the cockpit, and the copilot was asleep as well.

Where the hell was I at this point? Could I just jump and take my chances in the open water? Maybe I'd have a chance. Yet the odds probably weren't in my favor, since I couldn't tread water for long with my hands bound together. If this was the Atlantic Ocean, I'd probably get hypothermia before I could be rescued anyway. I just sat back and sighed, wondering how much longer the plane ride along the East Coast would take. That still baffled me, since I imagined the East Coast was more populated and built-up, unlike much of the Gulf Coast that was still a mucky wasteland, brewing organisms that possessed a knack for making human life intolerable.

The Manchac sleepily muttered, "Don't you worry, kid, you almos' there." He took a swig from a liquor bottle.

"We're going to land soon?" I looked out the window at the open sea; the plane was noticeably closer to the water. How long had we been flying?

He laughed. "We ain't, but you is." He handed me the bottle. "Want some?" I grabbed the bottle from him. Nevis Single Malt scotch. The brand I had been special-ordering for Fitzmorris. He had been right this whole time: The *Manchacs* had been hijacking the supply trucks, not the Monster's henchmen. I shrugged and took a generous gulp until I choked from the burn in my throat.

The pirate snatched the bottle from my hands. "Whatcha think, it's yours, boy?"

I coughed. "Yeah, I do."

A high-pitched alarm buzzed throughout the plane, and a red light blinked in the cockpit. The copilot rose from his chair and touched a button near the red light, silencing the alarm. He stepped around the wood crates and burlap sacks toward us carrying a buck knife. "Hands," he screamed over the buzz of the propellers. I lifted my arms, and he cut the rope around my wrists, exposing the red and raw skin underneath. Then he opened the side door, letting in a rush of wind.

"Welcome to Massachusetts!"

The two men lifted me and tossed me from the plane. I felt my body fall and my organs lift into my throat. I couldn't breathe, but I knew that I needed to suck in the biggest breath of my life before plunging into the deep water. I waved my arms wildly and kicked my legs as if that would somehow stop my fall. I closed my eyes and forced my lungs to accept air.

I don't know how far I fell or how deep I sank. Through my time spent in free fall, I wished for the water, yet I thirsted for air as soon as I plunged into the salty depths. The water temperature instantly changed from warm to cold. My feet and butt hit the soft, slimy bottom. The silt swallowed my feet as though my ankles had been locked into a concrete block like in a Mafia movie. I pulled my feet upward with all my strength. When they broke free, I raced to the surface. All the while, the pressure inside my lungs built, and the waving sun streaks charged across the surface like the chains of an electrified cage.

I made it, drinking in that delicious, humid air. I treaded in the choppy water, my body completely at the mercy of the rising and falling waves. I could only swim so far in the roller coaster of the sea, and the tides pulled me away from the strip of land ahead of me. No trees. The only thing I could see was a circular redbrick building with a green grass roof. It didn't make much sense, but it looked vaguely familiar. And though the water wasn't necessarily warm, it was much warmer than I'd expected the Atlantic Ocean to be.

Then a motor boat pulled up alongside me, and two men pulled me aboard. The boat redirected and sped toward the brick structure looming over the sea.

Chapter 31

Once I could wade through the shallows, the men in the boat pushed me out just as fast as they had pulled me in. Without exchanging words, they sped off around the island. My deer-fly welts burned as the saltwater clung to my arms. I sloshed in my wet shoes up the beach. Two white men stood on the beach, barefoot.

"Hey der, brah," the tall, lanky man said. He was shirtless and suntanned to an orange-brown crisp. His shaved head reflected the sunrise in a halo just around his crown, and three long scabs streaked across his scalp. His thick red beard cascaded over his rotted teeth. An indecipherable tattoo stuck to his left torso. He folded his arms and diverted his attention to the man next to him, saying, "I tellin' ya, brah, they pickin' up Met."

The other man was much shorter but just as thin. Blond stubble spiked from his broad chin, and he sported a mop of dirty-blond hair that had naturally lightened, looking as if he had paid handsomely for highlights at a salon. He wore a faded T-shirt, and his face and arms were pink with so many freckles he looked like he had been driving through the mud. He scratched his forearm and shook his head. "No."

"Come on! How do you not see it, brah?" The bald man waved his arms around and bounced his shoulders. "Lavario ain't produced shit since dat SEC Championship his first year. He got the talent, brah, on dat team. He just don't know how to use it."

"I get that. I know Lavario's got to go."

"Then why not Met? He's the fuckin' best offensive cordinator in the PAC 12, brah. You don't think he'd lift da team up?"

"Why would he leave? He doesn't even need to recruit. The country's best players want to go play for him."

The bald man pulled a hand-rolled cigarette out of his pocket and lit it. He shrugged his shoulders excitedly. "Gotta reach for dem stars, baby!"

"All I'm saying is, I wouldn't be upset if we got Met Reilly, but I'm not getting my hopes up."

Needless to say, I was rather confused.

The cigarette dangled enticingly from his lips. He gestured widely with his hands and rocked his body while saying, "Aw, brah, ya ain't got no heart." He beat his chest. "You gotta believe! Met comin' aboard, and we goin' get dat title. You watch!" He pointed at the other man with his cigarette.

Awkward as it was, these men were not tying me up or holding a gun to my head, so I sat down on the sand. They continued to talk sports, and naturally I tuned them out. I peered out into the open sea, not knowing if the American mainland or the vast Atlantic sloped beyond the horizon. I dug my toes deep enough into the beach that I felt the cold sand underneath. My eyelids were heavy. The sea does it to me every time. I shifted my knees up and hugged them with my arms. I laid my forehead on my wrists.

The bald excitable man pulled my T-shirt collar hard into my throat, so I stood, drowsily. My feet felt spongy inside my waterlogged shoes. A different boat approached the beach. "'Bout time, brah!" He smoked his cigarette behind me. I learned later his name was Coot.

I smelled the smoke, and my lungs ached for one. I turned around and asked, "Do you have an extra?"

Both men were surprised I asked. He eventually laughed. "Shit, you 'bout to get all the tobacco you can get, brah." He pointed at the boat that was accelerating toward the beach near us. It was like one of those boats I'd seen in movies about D-Day. It ran up on the beach and dropped a draw gate on the sand. Bushels of tobacco wrapped in brown paper with rope tumbled onto the beach. They looked like rolled-up sleeping bags.

Coot gestured, his arms out wide to indicate inquiry. "What da hells, huh, brah? You joyridin' shit?" he asked the tobacco runner.

A man called out from the boat, "Boys in blue. Had to speed off course through most of the night to shake 'em."

"Brah, they ain't supposed to be 'round here."

"They is."

The blond man hoisted a bushel over his shoulder and started along a trail through the grassy sand toward the distant brick building.

I looked back at Coot, who motioned me to follow the other man as he inhaled his cigarette. He exhaled and became irate, switching his good ol' boy demeanor for that of an eager assailant. "Listen, bitch. You don't start bringin' dem in da fort, I'm gonna drag ya 'cross the fuckin' island by your wimpy-ass balls and toss ya to the sharks my motherfuckin' self!"

He didn't have a weapon of any sort, but I wasn't about to call his bluff. I noticed the tattooed tear just below his eye, so I figured testing a murderer wouldn't be very prudent.

So, I said, "Okay. Follow him?"

"Hell, brah, it ain't like you'll get lost. Go on!"

I scooped up a roll of tobacco and hoisted it over my shoulder like the other man, who I reasoned was of the same status as me: had. My legs tired from the loose sand under my spongy feet, and I had to rest a few times along the way. The blond man had already passed me on his way back to the beach. To my right was a natural beach, meaning it was quite mucky and gross. For a half mile or so, putrid jellyfish and stingray carcasses decomposed on the beach as armies of ghost crabs relished their rotten flesh. Driftwood, seaweed, and whatever type of sun-bleached trash you can think of littered the sand. The body of a dead manatee had washed up the beach too, bloated like an elephant-skin balloon. The fishy smell of the sea submitted to the rancid stench of the rotting sea-cow corpse. I was surprised at the lack of seagulls, or any other shorebirds, fighting feverishly for a morsel.

To my left was a marsh that was quite healthy, considering it was detained behind beachy walls and a salty ocean. Cattails and long green grass swayed joyously in the ocean breeze. The marsh was about the width of a grocery-store parking lot. Beyond that, the sea rounded the horizon to somewhere. Because here was nowhere. If there ever was a time in my life that I went to some place in the middle of nowhere, this was it.

The fort was eerily familiar. Déjà vu wasn't the correct way to describe it. Déjà vu is more a sense of the repetition of an experience, and if you ponder on it long enough, you can figure out the source of illusion. Not this time. I couldn't shake the feeling that I had been here. Like some Civil War–era past-life experience or something. I had never been more north than Hattiesburg, much less Massachusetts.

Cathedral Confessionals

As Mira walked through the church foyer, she noticed a young black woman, possibly even a teenager, sitting in one of the confessional chairs. She covered her face with her hand, but Mira recognized Renisha Gresham.

"Renisha?"

Embarrassed, Renisha said, "Oh, Ms. Mira, how are you this morning?"

"Is everything all right? We've been worried about you."

Renisha averted her eyes. "Oh, I'm good." Her voice deflated.

Mira crouched.

Before Mira could reiterate, Renisha said, "I'm pregnant. What do I do?"

These were the times that Mira felt uncomfortable, since pregnancy depended entirely on the social situation surrounding the mother. For a married couple, it called for jubilation and congratulation. For a teenager, however, it could warrant sympathy, derision, or even ostracism. Mira didn't want to appear to be on either side and tried her best to seem neutral.

She always took pride in the fact that she never bullshitted her students. She decided this was not the time to start. "I don't know, Renisha. I've never been pregnant, much less in your situation. But I can help if you want me to."

Renisha breathed heavily and wiped her eyes. "This ain't even my religion, but I didn't know who else to talk to. I know the Lawd ain't too happy."

"I'm not sure that a nun or priest would be the right person to talk to, either."

"Why's that?"

"Because they probably won't be so sympathetic. They don't know what you're going through…for obvious reasons. *I* don't know what you're going through."

"So, who does?"

"Principal Whitman."

"Oh nah, Ms. Mira, she scary."

"Scary how much she cares about all y'all. Talk to her."

"None of your friends got pregnant in high school, Ms. Mira?"

"One did."

"What she do?"

"They expelled her." As soon as Mira uttered those words, she regretted them. That was a possibility Renisha hadn't even thought of. Now that the Catholic Church had taken the reins on public education, their stance on abstinence until marriage clearly needed to be revisited. The Church didn't have to *approve* of premarital sex, just forgive it. "Oh, Lawd! My mama gon' kill me."

"Talk to Principal Whitman. She can empathize, and she can help you make sure something like that doesn't happen. Okay?"

"What if I just went and got a job, Ms. Mira? A man down the street said they hiring."

"Wait. Hiring for what?"

"He said they need waitresses right nah, and I had the potential to make a lot."

Mira shook her head, understanding that Renisha had no idea that a slimy pimp was trying to suck her into his underworld. Renisha would be a prime target. She was young. Too young to be a prostitute. However, she could be a waitress and make quick cash for a few years, just enough time for her to discover how to make more money even quicker. At that point, she'd be of age, of course. These brothel recruiters were bad men, but that didn't mean they weren't excellent at their jobs. They had an uncanny ability to sense the desperation and confusion in Renisha as she simply passed them in the street. And they could offer flashy and comforting words to blur her overall judgment. But all these sexploiters saw were Renisha's black shiny hair, her ebony skin, her budding breasts, and her wide hips. In the end, all these men cared about was Renisha's vagina, which would essentially be just another bottomless money jar for them. Mira pointed her finger at the girl and commanded, "You listen here, Ms. Renisha Gresham, don't you dare accept a job from anyone in this part of town. You understand me, young lady?"

Renisha cocked her head back in surprise.

Mira had never spoken to a student that way before, and she suspected that Renisha would instinctively want to fire back. Renisha's eyes sparked, but she paused, perhaps sensing care in her teacher's authoritarian tone.

"Will you come next week?" Mira asked more calmly.

"Awright, Ms. Mira. I guess."

"Principal Whitman is in her office on Monday. It's a perfect time to go and see her."

Chapter 32

Once the tobacco bushels had been set inside the fort, the grass needed to be harvested, according to the Asian-American man taking inventory of cocaine canisters. He had to be as short as four foot six, but he probably could have snapped my head between his bicep and forearm if he felt so inclined. I waited for further instruction on the grass, but he continued weighing the canisters and marking the weights down on a notepad.

He was surprised to still see me standing there. He then yelled, "Doza!"

A sweating Latino man entered. He wiped his brow with a hand so enormous it was unclear whether it was a marvel or a deformity.

"Take him and another out to the green field," the Asian-American guy said, handing Doza two burlap sacks.

"No machetes?"

"Talk to Hefe."

"El Jefe?"

"Yeah, Hefe. Armory."

Doza motioned with his paddle hand for me to follow him. "Vámonos!"

Still wishing that I could take off my shoes and let my spongy feet dry out, I begrudgingly followed him, dragging the bottoms of my shoes on the brick floor. He handed me the burlap bags. We walked through the brick archways surrounding the place. An open space opened up to the right beyond the archways, and an unorganized mess of empty wine and rum bottles occupied the tops of scattered of wooden crates. Cigarette butts and dope roaches littered the ground. Lumps of burned-down candles sat atop the crates, and red and white wax had dripped down the sides of the crates and hardened to look like either melted vanilla ice cream or spilled blood. A young black man napped in a dark corner, and Doza woke him with a heavy palm to the chest.

"Get up! Vámonos!"

The black man was probably about my age, and he carried himself like a captive rather than a captor. He licked his lips and met my eyes briefly with distrust. I felt like he wasn't sure if I was a prisoner or a pirate. He came along with us.

Due to its architectural design, the fort was drafty throughout, and its interior felt quite cool. The ocean breeze squeezed through the gun slits, funneled through the cannon slots, and circulated through the building. The open space to our left was oddly neat and clear of any debris or sign of activity. The open-air center of the fort consisted of a coarse dusting of white sand over a blanket of brown, dead grass. A brick furnace the size of a pizza oven was off to one side. What looked like a brick silo was actually a bricked-in spiral staircase with an arched doorway leading into it.

Doza led us to one open room with several large army-grade green steel boxes and gun safes. A handwritten sign on a pallet board leaned against the brick wall near the entrance saying, NO SMOKEING. A white man sat on a metal drum and used seven stacked pallets as a desk. Several large objects that looked to me like artillery shells stood upright on his "desk," but it was clear they were just empty liter bottles that were labeled "Rhein Rubin Hefeweizen." Unlike the white man on the beach, this white man's skin retained its milk. His hair was a bright yellow and his eyes were blue. He let out a bubbly belch.

"Whatcha need, señor?"

"Machete. Two." He signaled with two fingers so long they could have been mistaken for a swamp rabbit's ears.

He nodded and opened a beer bottle with some kind of seashell.

"How you do that?"

"Do what?"

"Drink hot cerveza."

"Payin' homage to my ancestors. When we steal a boatload of tequila, I'll let you in on it, burrito-breath." He handed him two machetes that he retrieved from one of the metal boxes.

"We call you a…sauerkraut."

"I like 'Hefe' better," he said before swallowing a hefty gulp of Hefeweizen.

"You no jefe of me." Doza pointed at himself with thumbs the size of grilled sausages.

"Fine. Don't call me that, then."

Doza effortlessly clenched both machete handles in one hand. He waved the black man and me to exit the fort onto the beach as he followed behind. He gave us each a burlap bag. The sun beat down on us, and my feet still felt like mush as we plodded through the sand toward the green marsh. Wind blew horizontally carrying sand with it, which felt like someone rubbing sandpaper on our skin. The rank smell of the dead manatee made my empty stomach churn.

Several wooden pallets were stacked on top of each other in a bridge-like or pier-like fashion. Doza shooed us to walk over them. The bottom pallet sank into the marsh mud about six inches as we walked over them. Once we reached a thicket of tall marsh grass, Doza handed us each a machete. He pulled out a revolver that he had concealed this whole time, the size of his hand making it look like a toy cap gun.

"Trabaja! Cut!"

We slashed the grass blades at their base and stuffed them in our bags. As we worked, I tried to get some information from the young black man sweating beside me. He only spoke to me in two- or three-word responses.

"How long you been here?"

"Long enough."

He grasped two or three blades of grass at the tips, pulled them tight, and whipped the machete at the water level. I imitated this method, and my yield improved. After we harvested the grass in arm's reach, we were required to step out into the marsh and keep cutting. We sank up to our ankles and would have to struggle freeing our legs to step further.

"What are we doing this for?"

The sound of the slashing grass grew louder. He began breathing heavy.

"What's your name?"

"Man, just cut."

So we cut without a word under the warming sun. A squadron of white pelicans circled the island, remaining at a distance. Occasionally, one would divert and dive-bomb into the sea for a meal. I hadn't realized that pelicans were prolific up in the Northeast. Mosquitoes either. They bit us on our exposed arms and even through the thin fabric of our shirts. The red deer-fly welts on my arms didn't deter them from taking their portion of my blood.

A few gunshots broke the pleasing ballad of wind and waves. Both of us ducked down in the muck. Doza, holding the revolver holstered in his belt, looked over toward the fort. We did, as well. Two lookouts stationed on the grassy roof had fired their rifles at the pelicans. Far out of their range, the squadron simply turned toward the horizon, unscathed.

Just as I tried standing from my squat in the marsh mud, I saw a snake coiled up in the grass near me. I yelped and flung my body away, but my feet were stuck to the bottom, so I just fell into the marsh. I shook the slimy water from my face and spit out the acrid flavor of wetland. My unnamed companion sliced the snake's head off with a sharp splash.

"Stop horsing off, puto."

I wriggled up to my spongy, wet feet. "Thanks."

"A'right." He turned his back and kept cutting.

After we filled our sacks of freshly severed marsh blades, Doza let us rest inside the shade of the fort. He returned the machetes to Hefe and brought two cups, a jug of water, and a few strands of fish jerky. Despite the water being sandy and metallic, we consumed it greedily, as we did the fish jerky. I hadn't realized how hungry I was until then. I stripped off my sodden shoes and rubbed my wrinkled, soggy feet, which had blistered at the ball and heel. My bare feet, finally able to breathe, cooled my body down.

Corrections

Since it was relatively near the St. Henriette Cathedral, Mira walked to the Temporary Corrections and Finance Department building. Maybe she could talk the guard into letting her see Derek, since she couldn't seem to make visitation hours. They really needed to have visitation hours on the weekends, she felt. She wanted to talk to him about Principal Whitman's job offer. She knew he would be supportive and tell her she'd be great, and that's what Mira really wanted to hear anyway. However, the front gate was closed with a sign reading, "Facility temporarily closed to the public due to medical emergency."

On her Eagle, Mira looked up the contact number for Warden Wally Warwick and called it. When he answered, she asked what the hell was going on inside the jailhouse.

The warden said, "I'm afraid that some inmates caught an illness that's very contagious. The whole building's quarantined, even the Financing Department employees are working from home. We got two of our four prison guards working twelve-hour shifts since the inmates gave it to them already."

Skeptical that incarcerated men had somehow contracted an outside virus, Mira said, "Some of them? That means some aren't sick? I'm trying to see Derek."

"I can't really say who's sick and who's not. For all I know, they all may be sick by now."

"Well, did you do anything to isolate the sick ones? Or did you just let them all get sick?"

"We have limited space and resources as it is. I'm afraid we don't have much space to move them."

"If you only had a whole second story not in use. Right? What do they have?"

The warden said, "I can't really disclose that information, ma'am."

"Have you called the Health Department…or anyone?"

"If you'd like, the guard post at the south end of the property has correspondence letters. Perhaps your loved one wrote you one."

"Okay, I'll check…but—"

"Listen, miss, we have the situation under control. The prisoners are not at peril; I assure you of it. We're doing everything we can to not have an epidemic on our hands. Would you want the whole city to get sick?"

"No."

"All right then. You're welcome."

Her hands shook and her eyes blinked. A tirade brewed inside Mira's gut, and she hung up with Warden Wally Warwick just before it bubbled up through her throat. Derek was under his thumb, and she still was uncertain about his situation now that McMason was dead. She didn't want to do anything to jeopardize a potentially early release. Perhaps she already had by hanging up on the warden, but that would have been less abrasive than any other alternative, she thought.

Mira walked over to the far end of the property and used her key to open the correspondence box allocated to "Detainee 30-90." She removed the solitary letter and opened it with her finger.

Mira,

I heard about McMason. He only ruled over us for a short time, yet it feels like it was forever. It's almost hard to imagine a world without him. Can't say I feel sorry that he killed himself, but I can't say that I'm glad for it, either. In the end, I think we can all agree that it's probably best for everyone. At least everyone that matters.

As far as the deal goes, it's been amended. I'd like to talk to you about that whenever you come to visit. You know I can't speak too freely in these letters.

I'm so glad they transferred Fitzmorris to another wing. He's been annoying the piss out of me. Other than being locked in a stone cell, he hasn't changed a bit.

Being stuck in here, I'm a little behind on the developments out there. Red beans and quinoa does seem a bit ridiculous, but it beats eating red beans from a can. As bad as the food is in here, I've gained weight. I had gotten used to being so hungry before, but I guess I hadn't realized how thin I'd gotten. I'm sure it seems tough seeing the city changing before your eyes. I have a small window that's more for ventilation than anything else, and I can only see a small patch of sky. Just keep fighting the good fight. If you do, maybe the good will come *without* a fight. If you don't, there won't be any good left to fight for.

At least, that's what I'm trying to get across in this damn book. Reading books was never really my thing, much less writing one. Jail simply replaces your freedom with time. If I ever get out of here, I'm never writing another damn word ever again. Thanks for sending that book, though. I've read it cover to cover already, and it's very helpful. I'm having trouble with the first chapter, though. There's something out there that's central in all of this. There has to be. I have the draft near the end, yet it's the damn beginning that's killing me.

Could you go back to the bar and get something for me? I'm not sure how much the Manchacs trashed the place, and please go with someone because no telling who or what has made themselves at home. I hate to ask you to do this, but I don't really have a way to contact anyone else. There should be a book near my mattress upstairs, if you can get that for me.

Stay strong. I believe in you, and so do they, even if they don't know it yet.

Derek

It was nice hearing from Derek; however, she still had no clue about his health. Clearly he'd written this before the outbreak because he hadn't mentioned anything about it.

Chapter 33

In theory, we were free to do whatever. In theory. I hadn't experienced being in jail then. Now, as I write this, I know better. In a "civilized" jailhouse, you're handcuffed and led by an armed guard into a cell, which mostly keeps you safe from everyone else except for your cellmate. And yourself, to an extent. You're led to different places for different purposes. It's almost like you're a child again. You're not trusted or allowed to make decisions for yourself, because allegedly your decisions landed you in jail. Once you're let out among the other prisoners in the chow hall or the weight room, that's when you have to worry and stay alert.

This island they called "Massachusetts" acted as one sandy cell, containing the captors and captives within the impenetrable walls of saltwater. It was evident that the Manchacs on the island didn't think much of me or any of the other prisoners. They knew we were there, yet they didn't worry enough to be cautious. You'd think we prisoners would have united and attempted to overthrow these hooligans, since we weren't bound or constrained. In theory. There were only three other prisoners, and the Manchacs outnumbered us threefold. There was barely enough food left over, and we competed for it. We even competed for places to sleep.

I learned that the hard way. One night, a squall popped up, and I found a little nook that was dry from the rain spraying through the gun slit. The white guy, the football fan who had hauled tobacco with me upon my arrival, asked if I could help him move a crate of sugar. We just moved it a few feet over, and I straightened the corner with my foot. When I turned around, that bastard had holed up in my dry spot. I could see why the black fellow that cut grass with me didn't trust me.

The fourth prisoner was a young woman with brown skin, possibly Caribbean. I never got a good look at her because she was mainly "protected" in the northern wing of the fort. She didn't do any hard labor like us men, though she had her own kind of labor to serve. She was the Manchacs' sex slave, to keep them satisfied enough to not venture off to the mainland to tomcat around and leave the island unsecured.

A fifth prisoner entered our ranks one night, but he was treated entirely differently from the rest of us men. Two men each held him just below the shoulder, and his feet just dragged against the sandy stone floor. He was shirtless, wearing only brown pants. He held his head low, and they wrapped his hands together with plastic wrap. They pulled him across the center space and into the brick staircase. Both Manchacs returned to ground level. All night, we heard him wailing and moaning with sporadic shouts of sheer outrage. The sure signs of torture. I wasn't sure what they were doing to him, since I'd noticed that most of the Manchacs drank wine, snorted coke, and played dominoes for most of the night. The conditions here weren't like the Manchac swamps where I had been hung up and fed upon by insatiable insects. He was up there alone, but he was in constant peril nonetheless. Wasn't sure what he'd done to deserve such treatment. Hell, I'd actually armed myself to battle the Manchacs, but I failed miserably. Perhaps if I had not fallen asleep, this would be a different story.

Each morning and evening, the young black detainee had the task of bringing the unknown prisoner rations of jerky and sandy water. It seemed that the pirates knew about as much as we prisoners did about their new captive—that is, virtually nothing.

Coot asked, "He ate anything?"

The black prisoner said, "He did, but he just threw it up and started cursing. Talkin' 'bout him needin' a smoke."

It was decided to give him a cigarette that evening. Upon inquiry, the black prisoner reported that he had smoked it greedily and hadn't touched the water or the jerky. The prisoner then stopped screaming in the night, though he still moaned from time to time. He ate some of the jerky the next night. I had lost track of how long I had been on that forsaken island. It all sort of blended together in an exhausted flurry of labor and malnutrition. Until the murder occurred. Then I began mentally keeping track of how many sunsets I saw.

It was midday with quite pleasant weather. The black prisoner and I were having a difficult time taking apart the wooden boards of a few heavy crates that had arrived early that morning. They gave us small hammers and blunt wedges that didn't work very well.

Coot snorted a bump of coke and lit a cigarette. "Say, bruh," he spoke to the Asian-American man with the huge biceps, whose name I'd learned was Longleaf Lee. "Kazenski's who they need. That O-line, garbage!" He rubbed a bar of soap on his hands and lathered his head. He brandished a sharp knife and shaved in lines back from his forehead down to his nape.

"We need a quarterback first to justify that, though." He leaned back against the brick wall, waiting for us to liberate the booty.

"C'mon, Rongreaf Ree! Don't ya get dat da offense is as good as dat line is? Hell, my grandma prolly could complete a pass from her Laplace grave with guys like Kazenski on the line!"

Longleaf Lee wiped the sweat off his face with his sleeve. He shook his head and sighed as he waited on us.

I set the hammer down and was picking at a splinter in my palm when an alarm echoed through the fort, sounding more like a game-show buzzer than a siren. In a few seconds, the alarm silenced, but the Manchacs ran toward the armory to retrieve several guns. Coot hadn't yet finished shaving his lathered head, and a streak of blood trickled down his face. He cornered us and held out his bloody knife. Longleaf Lee ran to the armory and brought back a sawed-off shotgun and a rifle.

He gave the rifle to Coot. "Boat's headed our way."

"Hell's yeah, bruh. I'm a-gettin' antsy babysittin' Amos and Andy ova here. Need some o' dat action, brah!" He shrugged his shoulders and sheathed his knife. Checked the chamber of the rifle.

Longleaf Lee said, "Don't you do anything unless they make it inside. Complete discreetness."

"Disk-*what*?"

"Jesus, Coot, don't do anything unless we have to or anyone tells you to. Just shut the fuck up for a few minutes." He looked at us and pointed the sawed-off at us. "Same goes for you two. Get down behind that crate." We did.

After a while, Coot looked through the scope and started jumping up and down. "Brah! Got some ass comin' dis way! Wooo!"

"If you don't settle yourself a bit—"

Coot snapped back, "You're gonna what, brah?"

Longleaf Lee paused for a second. "It's not me you have to worry about. You know that. Just get your shit together, you coon-ass."

He took a long drag on a cigarette. "I ain't lyin' though, bruh. Dat ass be dank! Come peek through dis motha'fuckin' scope. I'll watch da kids."

Longleaf Lee handed him the shotgun and looked through the scope for a few seconds while Coot guarded us. Lee turned to Coot and smiled.

"Hell's yeah, boy! Take your shit back. Gimme dat rifle back." They switched back into their original positions. "I wanna see dat hot pussy, brah!"

Eventually, we heard music. Songs varied from rap to country. I peeked above the crate and saw a small yacht through the gun slit in the brick wall. Two bikinied women drank from beer cans, their breasts bouncing like the waves beneath as they walked barefoot on the deck. One of the men threw an anchor and jumped in the water. One girl shifted the blue trucker hat over her blond hair and leaned forward on the railing, which made her cleavage bulge. Staring, Coot licked his bloody blade. The man in the water waved the woman to come swim. He also pointed at the fort. She took off her hat and gracefully dove into the water, her butt quivering in midair from the power of her hamstrings. They swam to the island and waded up the beach. With the loud music, I couldn't hear what they were saying, but it was evident that he wanted to go explore the fort. However, she stopped and stared at the fort. He kept waving her to move forward, but she kept shaking her head. She folded her arms and looked back at the boat. The man just stood on the beach and cocked his head in disappointment as she swam back to the boat. He looked at the fort curiously and then trudged back into the water.

Longleaf Lee said, "I guess blondes aren't all that dumb, after all."

Both Manchacs stretched their necks to watch the young girl's wet, lean body climb up the ladder to the deck.

Right then, the young black prisoner broke into a sprint for the exit. The joy riders danced to the loud bass bumps shaking the bricks and mortar. I paused for a moment, torn as to whether or not I should follow. Coot dropped the rifle and chased after him with his knife drawn. Longleaf Lee clubbed me in the face with the butt of his shotgun and stepped on my throat. From the ground, I could see the black man and Coot wrestling just under the exit. The black man screamed for help over and over, yet the partygoers on the boat just cracked open another beer and kept dancing. From their perspective, they couldn't see the pirate and the prisoner grappling under the entrance archway. Then the black man shrieked as Coot drove his knife through his torso. Each time the man gasped for air, Coot forced his blade further into his flesh. His feet and knees convulsed as if his life were literally being shaken out of him. Then his body went limp, and Coot pulled his knife free and cleaned the blood off on his shirt. He pulled his fresh kill inside the chamber I lay in.

Coot said, "You next, brah?" He then spit on my face.

The boat stayed for an hour or so, then the boaters retreated into the cabin and left. Everyone on the island just waited in silence for them to leave. My fellow prisoner's body, however, continued to twitch and writhe on the floor next to me. As if his soul was attempting to bust free from its earthly shell for the heavens.

It was then that I understood what real pirates were like. They were thieves by trade, and murder and rape were tricks of such a trade. Seeing them brutalize the young prisoner that way, I wanted more than to atone for the eleven victims of the Ursulines Avenue shooting. I wanted to avenge them.

The other prisoner and I had to go dump the dead body on the western point of the island near a deep underwater trench. As soon as we approached the water, shark fins sliced feverishly through the surface. We heaved his body into the water, and a violent explosion of sea foam and blood was all that was left of the young black man, who had just wanted to be free. I didn't even know his name. The only way off this godforsaken island was to willingly become one of them, and I would do nothing of the sort.

On the march back to the fort, I discovered a washed-up paddleboard in the marsh that was wrapped in dead cattails and seaweed. I longed to escape, too, but didn't know where the mainland was or how far it was. I avoided suspicion by not taking a second look at the paddleboard. I didn't even know if it was seaworthy. I just had to have faith in it and be patient for my opportunity.

Crates of ammunition and various military-grade firearms came in a few days later. A man wearing fishing attire stepped off the boat and walked into the armory. This man's gait was noticeably rigid, as if he were military.

"So, has he talked?" the new man said in a rather familiar voice.

Hefe gulped down the rest of a beer. "Who?"

"The reporter."

"Hey, that's your prisoner, not ours. We're just doing your captain a favor."

"And this shipment is part of that favor."

"Well, then, what you want to know?"

"Yossarian." The man folded his arms.

"Yossarian is the reporter's name?"

"No. Yossarian is the reporter's informant. You got orders to extract this information out of him."

"Listen, our captain and your captain need to talk. We don't interrogate *our* prisoners, much less yours. That's your job."

"Oh, that's how it's going to be?"

He picked up a full bottle of beer and popped off the cap. "Beer?"

The man shook his head and nearly bumped into me as I was stacking the bullet boxes. I recognized him then. It was the bald Redsleeve that had pulled me over months ago and confiscated my gun. The very gun that one of the Manchacs tried murdering me with. On Oyster Shell Road, he made it seem like having a registered gun was a crime, and yet he was trafficking McMason's artillery to pirates that supplied the Ward Warriors to continue a territorial battle, which McMason had been entrusted to deal with.

"The Captain will not be impressed."

"So, no then." Hefe shrugged and sipped thirstily.

The Redsleeve walked up to me. "You're that barman with the pickup truck. You know who Yossarian is, son? That name ring a bell?"

Suddenly, it all finally clicked. Looking back, I should have figured it out sooner. Joshua was here on the island as McMason's prisoner. I remembered Joshua hitting golf balls and mentioning he had a meeting with someone nicknamed Yossarian. The tobacco withdrawals, his hands and fingers taped together, him being referred to as "the reporter."

I then understood what I had to do. I said with a confidence in my voice that I hadn't heard in a long time, "I know the reporter. He trusts me. Give me time, but I can get it out of him."

I was immediately given the duty of bringing him food and water starting the next morning. My comforts on the island, as little as there were, immediately improved. Instead of finding a dry corner to sleep in, I was allowed to sleep on a wooden plank with a camping pad, most probably stolen along with everything else on the island except for the sand. Normally, I would have slept very well, considering the healthy portions of fish and Elmer's Ryan in my stomach, but I was restless, thinking of what I had to do.

I turned over on my left, facing the brick wall in hopes of blocking out the hooting of Coot and the drunken banter of the other pirates. I noticed something crudely carved into the brick like meaningless graffiti. I traced it with my finger and found it to be an X with an oval in the middle. It was a rough but distinct enough drawing of a Jolly Roger.

It all came together. This island was not in the state of Massachusetts. I hadn't been in New England at all. This place in the middle of nowhere suddenly became a place somewhere. This was the abandoned fort on Ship Island, south of Gulfport, Mississippi: Fort Massachusetts.

Feralton

That Sunday, Stephen Cooper gripped his steering wheel so tight that the skin of his white knuckles nearly turned clear. Growing up in an affluent suburb in New England, he had never seen an area so bleak. His eyes couldn't help but lift themselves from the chalky shell road deep into the jungle-y wreckage on either side of Ferrell Boulevard. His inner core worked overtime to absorb the historically horrific imagery. The sympathy for such tragedy, the fascination of devastation, and the selfish pride for bearing witness to such ugly awesomeness forged into a self-inflicted, yet involuntary, inner paradox. His drive for benevolence, which had directed him to New Orleans, clashed with his thirst for an unmanufactured human experience. The extent of loss endured by the city and its people made Stephen ill, yet his empty sense of struggle counted this experience as nothing short of a personal win.

"Watch out!" Mira yelled from the passenger seat.

Stephen gripped the wheel and braked as a coyote ran across the road. "Where the hell did he come from?"

"I'd give it gas; they usually run in packs."

Stephen hit the gas hard, and the white shells clattered against his wheel wells.

"Thanks for coming with me," Mira said, "and for taking your car."

"That's fine. I needed to see this all for myself. So, what was this area before?"

"Derek and Mrs. Whitman used to call it Oyster Shell Road before the Refounding. But before that, it's hard to say. It's probably some part of Uptown."

Mangled debris of cracked toilets, smashed laptops, and tangled kudzu vines gave way to road construction signs and cleared lots. Road workers had piled oyster shells every half mile into what looked like ancient Indian mounds.

FUTURE SITE OF BALD CYPRESS CONDOMINIUMS: TAKING APPLICATIONS NOW!

MALL OF NEW ORLEANS: COMING SOON!

STAR-MART: YOUR NEIGHBORHOOD GROCER

OLIVE GARDEN AND CICERO'S PIZZA RESTAURANTS: NOW HIRING! CALL NOW!

Even after the point of construction ended, the signs continued. They drove by an abandoned gas station as the road turned north. A pack of feral hogs had made it their home. The door had been smashed through. Three hogs lay in the shade of the two gas pumps. Broadmoor Bay opened up on the right side of the road, and a huge sign stood on two pilings in the water:

DEMELIO, LLC. DRAINAGE PROJECT:

FUTURE SITE OF GREENWOOD GOLF VISTA

Someone had nailed a handwritten sign underneath it: SAVE THE BAY! SAY NO TO DEMELIO! Two snowy egrets tiptoed around the sign posts, catching cacaos and water beetles.

As they approached a brick building, Mira realized that it was Principal Whitman's home. The barber pole had been removed from the exterior wall.

"Stephen, that's Mrs. Whitman's house. Pull over, please. I have to tell her something."

He pulled onto the shoulder near a pile of construction equipment and materials. "What do you—"

"I won't be long. You can wait here."

She walked to the door and knocked. Principal Whitman answered wearing a faded Dillard University T-shirt dark from sweat lines. Her sleeves of tattoos always surprised Mira because Whitman covered up her arms at school.

"Well, hello, child."

"Hey, I'm sorry; is this a bad time, ma'am?"

Whitman moved to the side, and Mira saw several packed boxes about the room.

"Oh."

"Yeah, they evicting us from our own damn house. They going to make this whole area a…"

"A golf course?"

"Well, that's over in the bay. They going to drain all the water out first. Don't ask me how. But where we are, child, it's going to be some kind of sports park with volleyball and baseball and disk golf and other stuff that we don't do. I didn't really read that part of the letter, just the part where they said we had to get on out."

"I'm sorry to hear that."

She sighed. "It was nice being out here for a while in the quiet. But it's probably better for me to be in the city with this new…position." Whitman raised her eyebrows.

"Right," Mira paused for a moment, "and I accept your offer."

Whitman's eyes lit up. "Excellent! You could've picked up a telephone and saved yourself a trip to Feralton."

"Well, Derek asked me to get something from his bar. Is that what they're calling this area now?"

"They don't, but we do. I don't know who thought of it. But as soon as they renamed Oyster Shell Road, I heard people saying it. You see, we spell it f-e-r-a-l, not like the street. With the hogs and dogs and whatever other nasty mongrels out this way. And we think Carrolton Avenue was near here before Beckham. So it fits."

Mira nodded.

"How's he doing?"

"I haven't talked to him in so long. We've just been writing to each other. You know, I went yesterday after our walk, and they have it all locked down. Apparently, the prisoners have some contagious disease."

"Hmm. You know, diseases don't usually start in prisons; they usually come in from outside."

"That's what I said."

"He'll be awright. He survived that island, he can survive anything. Well, let me get back to packing. I'm ecstatic to hear you're on board. We'll talk more later."

"Wouldn't have it any other way, ma'am."

The two women said their goodbyes, and Mira returned to the car, smiling.

Stephen asked, "What was that about?"

Mira didn't know if she should tell Stephen about the job offer. If she did, it would spread through the school like an oil slick over the sea. Instead she responded in a way that would make him uninterested. "Don't worry about it. Women stuff."

He nodded and pushed the gas pedal, continuing their journey to Derek's abandoned bar. The building was intact in appearance. As Mira approached, however, she noticed termite dirt trails running up from the ground like brown veins. An eviction notice had been posted on the front door just under a large hornet comb. She said aloud, "*This* is what he chose over France."

"This is where he used to work?"

"And live. I'll need you to come with me this time, please. Lord knows what, or who's, made themselves at home in there."

They walked around to the back and waded through waist-high grass to get to the back door, which had been kicked open. She shrieked at the site of a banana spider at the center of a web that filled the top half of the doorway. The spider had the same colors as fancy running shoes, black and neon green-yellow. It was big enough that Mira could make out tiny hairs on its abdomen and legs, like the silver five o'clock shadow stubble of an old man. She looked at

Stephen, who stepped backwards and shook his head. She frowned and picked up a long stick in the grass and waved in the lower part of the doorway. When she didn't see the web disturbed, she crouched down, said, "You really know you love someone when...," and darted inside. Stephen Cooper crawled quickly through the doorway, breathing heavily.

The inside was trashed. The mirror behind the bar had been shattered. Broken glasses and bottles covered the bar top. The register was missing. The floor was littered with broken chairs and tables. She stepped around a pile of white feathers and two gnawed-off bird legs.

"Stephen, you can stay down here. I think I can go upstairs myself."

He nodded and wiped the sweat off his temples.

She dropped the little stick and picked up a wooden chair leg. She slowly walked up the dark staircase into Derek's office and bedroom. An old mattress had been cut open, and the stuffing had been pulled out. She saw a familiar blue stain on his pillowcase, which also was cut open, as was the pillow.

Oh, come on. Well, now at least he'll use a different one, she said to herself.

She found a novel titled *Cold Chambers* and picked it up. Something fell on her foot. She jumped thinking it was a spider or a roach. But it was a silver necklace. She picked it up and saw that the pendant was a music note. She smiled and put it in her pocket. She descended the stairs, and said, "Okay, I think we can go."

Stephen walked up to her and handed her a humidity-stained envelope. "I found this. Someone must have slid it under the door."

She gasped and snatched the letter from him. She read:

Derek,

This is the first letter I've written since I was probably thirteen, and I have no idea if it will ever get to you. It's not like the old days when I could text you or Facebook message you. Instead, your bar is the only reliable way to find you, and the fact that you or anyone really hasn't been there for some time is awfully disconcerting. Has something happened?

I guess it is pointless to ask you that since you are nowhere to be found. It's not just you. The *Declaration* reporter has not put out an issue for weeks. To think that people here are vanishing for no reason is outright frightening. I didn't want to think that you had left of your own accord, even though you certainly have more potential than owning a bar in a town that has reverted back to the dark ages. In a strange way, I wish that you *had* left on your own accord because it seems this world won't allow us to be apart for long, and we'd find each other one day. Somewhere, Somehow. This is different, however. It seems that something else is at play here beyond our control.

In fact, that's how I know that something has happened. Because fleeing without a goodbye is something a coward would do. And Derek, you are not a coward. Perhaps moving back to New Orleans wasn't the experience or result you expected, and starting fresh elsewhere wouldn't be all that unjustified. As long as I've known you, you have not been running away. When I left for France, I thought you were embracing the Refounding proposal as an excuse to live your own life without me. I thought you were a coward then, but I was wrong. I took it personally, and I'm sure you noticed that, the way I cut you off. And though you hurt me, I understand why you did it. There was something inside of you that you just couldn't run away from. For me, it was music and France. For you, it was home for better or worse. I later understood that you wouldn't have been happy if you had come with me. You would have felt empty in France. You have always loved and supported my passion for music. You didn't dissuade me or even show any disapproval for my decision to go. I must have hurt you by deciding to move, when I really thought it was best for us both. And it still may have been, but it's pointless to harp on that now. I used to think it was indifference on your part, and I hated you for that. I believe now, however, there was something much more, much deeper, that drove you not to interfere with my passion. It was your strength, not weakness or cowardice. You forgot yourself and thought of me. God, I sound like a crazy person for admiring you for leaving me. Or maybe I left you; I don't know anymore. And maybe we would have been happy together in France. But that didn't happen; nonetheless, we were bound to go our different ways. If you had questioned my decision to go to France, I'd have done what you did. I'd have gone anyway, with or without you. Just as I may have driven you here to New Orleans by questioning your intentions. I myself couldn't stay away from New Orleans. I'd be lying if I said that you were the only reason I moved back here. I'd also be lying if I said you weren't a reason at all. I can't imagine what you first thought when you saw me. There was no way for me to contact you, and believe me, after a few drinks some nights I tried. In fact, if you read this, I'm sure you can tell I had a few vodkas to work up the nerve to get this out.

We are very alike, you and me. It brought us together. It broke us apart. It brought us back together, or at least in the same place. But now something else, I fear, has taken you from this place, and I can neither reach nor follow you. As you know, I've never been much of a praying woman, but I find myself praying more these days. For my students and their families, for the city, and now for you. That's what uncertainty and fear do to us, don't they? They give us faith, but in such a torturous fashion we end up admiring ourselves for hurting so. Such an odd world this is.

Our reunion was very brief, yet intense, and that in itself made me believe that you still felt something for me. I can't read your mind, Derek. I never could, even though I used to say I could. Maybe you even believed me sometimes. I just said what I would be thinking, and, luck would have it, I was right more than half the time.

And so, as I have faith that you someday will come back to me, I believe that you feel the same way. Wherever you are. Just whatever is preventing this is temporary. My God, I hope it's temporary. So I will wait for you to return to me, just as it seems that you've been waiting for me to return to you. Lord, sometimes it feels as if we've been waiting for each other our whole lives, and I'm sick of waiting.

Come back to me, Derek.

I love you.

Mira

Chapter 34

After dragging the harvested marsh grass inside the fort to be dried and mixed in with the tobacco, I needed a cigarette. And not one that had been blended with sand and cattails. I needed a real one.

Longleaf Lee opened a large cabinet, unveiling cartons of Kikenney cigarettes. He gave me some.

A familiar voice blasted from a radio in the armory: "So, I don't really understand what these protesters are protesting. Randall McMason didn't bring Hurricane Beckham to New Orleans. It's not his fault that a bunch of thugs want to kill a bus full of kids. This is a city culture that McMason inherited. McMason isn't giving them guns. I don't know how they are getting them. I bet the parents in these communities know more than they put on. It all starts at home. Here's a thought: Instead of disrupting the city by surrounding the Superdome and blaming the very people that are trying to keep them safe, they should deal with this at home because that's where the problem originated, and that's where it's going to end..."

Longleaf Lee said to me, "I wish he didn't play that so loud. I hate that guy."

I nodded in complete agreement. I couldn't help but get a little furious inside. Here Chase Quade was, claiming that McMason wasn't at fault for any of the violence in New Orleans, and there we were among stockpiles of guns and ammo from McMason's artillery later to be sold to whoever wanted them. And the Ward Warriors wanted them, and they sure as hell were getting them. I lit one of the cigarettes and inhaled deeply. I just needed to keep myself together a little longer.

As I gathered Joshua's rations, Hefe stopped me. Even in the morning, his beer breath was atrocious. "The sooner you get that guy to say whoever this Yossarian is, the better. We're all getting sick of their shit. Do whatever you got to do. Torture him. Coddle him. I don't give a swimming shit shark how you do it."

"I got this." I filled a jug of cold water from the underground cistern, which had less sand in it than the catch basins on the east side of the island. It was also free of mosquito larvae, which was a real luxury after weeks of drinking the prisoners' water. I grabbed the cigarettes and an extra strip of fish jerky. I marched up the circular staircase. With the open sky above me, it seemed like I was inside the barrel of a gun made of brick. As I reached the top, I walked across a short concrete bridge, and the gulf breeze roared around my ears. The overgrown grass itched my bare feet, and plenty of sand somehow still found its way up to the roof of the fort. From above, I saw that the fort was shaped like a D, and the two lookouts sat at the points where the curve met the straight end.

Joshua sat on a hot concrete slab that had once seated a large cannon, hanging his head with his back to the short brick wall. They had drilled anchors into the brick and chained his torso to it. His wrists were bound together. His skin was blistered red and peeling from sunburn. I set the jerky and water down in front of him. He didn't move, so I wondered if he was asleep. His bare chest rose and fell, and the bruising had faded from deep purple to a dull tan with some deep wells of black. When I put the cigarette in front of him, he reached for it.

I said, "Joshua."

He looked up at me. Both his eyes were bloodshot, and the skin around them was blue and swollen. His broken nose was crooked on his face. His bruised bottom jaw hung open, revealing several missing teeth. Despite all that, his look of aghast horror struck me most. "I sh-should have bludgeoned you with…that damn nine iron that day."

"No. Joshua, I'm on your side. I was taken prisoner just like you."

"Doesn't look like it."

"The Manchacs say that you're McMason's prisoner, not theirs."

He shifted on the concrete and rattled his chains. "Wrong again."

"Here," I said, lighting a match, "this will make you feel better." I lit my cigarette. The wind blew the match out, so I lit another, but Joshua studied the cigarette between his fingers. Then he flicked it back to me.

"Joshua, please. You can trust me. I want to make a break for it soon. I found an old paddleboard in the marsh over there. We can paddle our way out of here; Mississippi's like ten miles that way."

He rolled over into a fetal position.

"Joshua. They think I'm trying to get information out of you. But I'm trying to get out of here."

He remained motionless, silent.

"Well, I'm leaving the food and water for you."

I lied to Hefe and Longleaf Lee for several days, claiming that Joshua was starting to talk more freely. When they pressed me about whether I'd asked about Yossarian, I just stalled, saying that I needed more time to build his trust. But in truth, Joshua wouldn't speak to me, much less confide in me. The Gulf had been relatively calm for a few days, which frustrated me because I couldn't in good conscience leave Joshua behind. The Manchacs grew suspicious when Joshua reverted back to howling from tobacco withdrawal. They checked on him and found him more emaciated than before and adamantly refusing anything but water.

Hefe yelled at me, "What in shit you been doing, boy?"

"I think he's just sick. We should bring him indoors."

"Sick of you, it sounds like. He tell you who Yossarian is yet?"

"No, not yet."

He shook his head. "Just stick to what you're good at from now on. Okay, dirtbag?"

"What's that?" I asked.

Hefe cracked open a beer. "Getting in everyone's way." He called someone on a modern Eagle, which surprised me. "No word on

Yossarian. He's not talking. Well, yeah, we get that. What? Torture him? How we gonna do that? He's torturing himself, for shit's sake. Oh, really? Well, we're not going anywhere and the sea's open, so if that's what you want to do, then fine."

I waited till a few hours after sundown to sneak up to Joshua. Hefe had passed out by then, entrusting Doza to watch the armory for the night. From the increasing volume of the other Manchacs' voices, they were getting drunk. I crept up the brick staircase, feeling the smooth bricks and the gritty mortar against my palms. Except for the circle of stars above me, it was pitch black. Once I reached the top, the canopy of stars was quite beautiful, but in times such as that, you really have no care for aesthetics.

Joshua sat with his knees tucked into his chest, his arms hugging his legs together. His body was sweating, convulsing, and shivering.

I knelt down near him. "Rumor has it that McMason's coming here himself."

He did not respond.

"And they're on to me. I think they know that I haven't been questioning you like I told them I would."

He just breathed heavily, shivering.

"I can't make you trust me. But I'm leaving tonight. You're going to die here, Joshua. Whether you do it yourself or they do it. You deserve better than that. The world deserves better. And I may be swept out to sea, but I can't be here anymore. Not like this. I have a hacksaw blade up my sleeve; I can set you free. Will you come with me?"

He breathed deeply. "No."

City Hall

Anticipating that she would be waiting a long time, Mira arrived at City Hall on Monday morning as they opened the doors at eight o'clock; however, no one arrived at eight o'clock to open the doors. Mira sat down on a wooden bench in front of the main building, which consisted of three shipping containers positioned in a U. Her Eagle buzzed, and she read the screen that said Cut to the Chase!

"Oh boy."

I'm just going to start by saying 'thank you' to my readers and followers because you are my eyes and ears, and I couldn't do what I do so well without you. I received an interesting anonymous tip from someone in New Orleans, which was refreshing since I mostly receive hate mail from there. Well, as gracious as you know I am, I followed up on the tip and did some digging. I think this will sum up everything: A group of Hollywood studios have clandestinely purchased the mass ruins of the old Marigny, Treme, and Bywater in order to preserve authentic post-apocalyptic scenery for their future movies and shows. In doing so, they have contracted humane pest control services that merely drive away rats, not kill them, and the rats have now infested the schools as a result. Run with that, folks, until later this afternoon when the official article posts. 8:08AM ⌐ chasethetruth

Mira had mixed feelings about her involvement. She was glad to at least address and confront the issue, but she detested Chase Quade personally. When she looked up from her Eagle, a young black man had just unlocked the door.

He flattened his blue tie with his palm and extended his hand to Mira. "New intern?"

Mira shook his hand. "No, sir. Mira Roche from Archbishop Fullerton."

"From himself or from the school?"

"High school."

He nodded. "Dennis Galloway. Who are you here to see?"

"Well, actually…you."

"Oh." He rubbed his freshly shaved head with his free palm as they still were shaking hands. "In regards to?"

"I need a food services permit for my school. And I need it ASAP."

Galloway's face showed confusion. "I remember. Everything should have been taken care of. Let's go to the office." Mira followed him to the permits office. "As I recall, all was in order except for the inspection, and that's really a formality more than anything."

If formality and extortion were the same thing, Mira thought.

Instead of entering through the main door, they entered his office directly from the back corner. "I'm sorry, that mess in that main waiting area gives me anxiety. They said they'd digitize all those documents in there."

"They say a lot of things, don't they?"

"Damn straight, they do."

He set his keys on a desk so neat and clean it looked like an office stock photo. He then looked at his keys on the desk and put them in his pocket. He rubbed the desk surface with his forefinger and sat down in his black leather chair. "Please, have a seat, Ms. Roche. It shouldn't take much time to sort this all out."

Mira sat down in a chair so clean she felt bad sitting in it.

Galloway opened a drawer and retrieved a folder that contained documents so crisp they could lacerate a bricklayer's fingers. "We're supposed to have a network system whenever we move into the new building. But for now, this is what we're working with. Here you are." He studied the paper on his desk for a few seconds. "Yeah. Everything's approved." He passed the page to Mira, and she read each of the approved signatures from Dennis Galloway, Mayor Alex Crowley, and the inspector. The inspector, of course, didn't print his name in the proper line, and his signature was simply a squiggle. She still didn't know the man's name.

"So, I can take this with me?"

"Yes, ma'am. We have copies."

A part of her wanted to expose the inspector for being a corrupt dirtbag, but the signatures on the page were like magical enchantments that extinguished any frustration or animosity that she had built up. "Great! Thank you, Mr. Galloway."

He stood and rubbed imaginary dirt from his tie and extended his other hand. "Good luck."

Mira shook his hand, put the permit in her purse, and then left the New Orleans Permits Office shipping container. As she exited the security clearance booth, her Eagle buzzed.

New Orleans will unveil commemoration plans for the city monument. Mayor says it will not honor Captain McMason[8:37AM]⌐ Patriot Public Radio

Chapter 35

I didn't say goodbye to him. I walked to the staircase, furious with his stubbornness. But just as I began my descent, flashlight beams orbited the brick walls and footsteps clamored. I ran back up the stairs and hid behind a rusty cannon. Captain McMason and two Redsleeves emerged and marched staunchly toward Joshua. McMason looked down him but got no response. He jutted out his jaw and stroked his mustache. He pointed at the two men, telling them to leave him alone with Joshua. I heard his voice, yet no actual words. McMason paced back and forth, his arms folded. Joshua just sat with his head down. McMason crouched near him, lit a cigarette, and blew the smoke in Joshua's face. Again, no response. McMason shook his head and began to stand.

Joshua lunged at McMason's neck and knocked him to the ground. Joshua rolled on top of McMason, choking him for a few seconds. McMason, however, was at full strength, and he wiggled free and crawled out of Joshua's reach. McMason pulled a pistol from his boot and fired a bullet into Joshua's heart. His body slammed against the brick wall and fell over. McMason stood, straightened his uniform, and stroked his mustache. His Redsleeve guards ran up the stairs, and McMason pointed at Joshua's lifeless body, yelling something. Then the three of them descended the stairs into the central area of the fort.

Several Manchacs and Redsleeves gathered in the open space with firearms drawn. I could hear their words below me.

McMason said, "The prisoner is dead. The deal is off. We're repossessing our arms. I expect to have Red Birch's property in mint condition on the boat within two hours."

Coot screamed out, "Brah, y'all go near dem guns, I'm-a gut every las' one a ya like I did that niglet! Shit! I'm serious, brah! I'll split ya like a muddafuckin' floundah!"

Each group gathered with their own as the argument intensified.

Longleaf Lee yelled, "We don't owe you shit!"

McMason said, "The hell you don't. Who let your ringleaders escape from Angola in the first place? You are all free because I let you be free."

In the starlight, I could see the two lookouts aiming into the crowd, waiting.

That's when I made my move. I climbed over the grassy hump of the roof and leaped onto the soupy sand near the shore. I hurt my ankle, but my adrenaline was my morphine, and I hobbled along the shore in the dark. The moon shone down enough for me to make out the outline of the paddleboard. I trudged after it into the marsh, and something large thrashed away from me. I pulled the board out onto the beach and stripped off the dead vegetation. As I placed it on the sand, I heard what sounded like a fireworks show, except that the sky was not painted with red and blue lights. The Manchacs and the Redsleeves were cancelling their business contract the old-fashioned way.

I paddled on my stomach toward what I hoped was the North Star. Lucky for me, it was. After a few hours of rocking up and down in the open sea, I wondered if I had made a mistake. What was worse? Getting shot dead and being fed to the sharks? Or falling in the water and being eaten alive by sharks? Or drowning? I just hugged the paddleboard tight as I felt it rise and fall on each wave, then I'd paddle a few strokes. I kept the North Star in front of me; however, I couldn't be sure if I was actually moving in that direction. For all I knew, I was just drifting off to Florida while simply facing north. I got awfully seasick, too. I vomited what was left in my stomach and continued to vomit bile on the paddleboard. I knew if I panicked for even a second, I'd fall off in the darkness, lose the paddleboard, and drown.

So I focused on Mira the whole time. It sounds cheesy and cliché, I know. I've seen it on TV several times when someone gets stranded in the snow or on an island, and they make it through thinking about their loved one. Well, if there's anything on TV that's true, it's that. I thought back and recalled every detail from every memory, starting from when we met on Esplanade Avenue to when I walked her back to her apartment weeks ago. I even created memories that we would have in the future if I survived this voyage.

Then I saw a light ahead skimming across the water and stopping at intervals. Once the spotlight landed on me, a boat sped toward me. It stopped about ten feet away. A white foam buoy bobbed in the water between us.

A man yelled from the boat, "Whatcha doing there, son?"

I didn't recognize his voice. It was raspy and very, very Mississippi. I didn't know what to say. Honestly, I expected a bullet in the back more than anything.

"That-there's my crab trap! Dis is how I make a living."

I looked up at him. "Help me."

There was a silence that followed, though he kept the vicious light on me. "Aw hell." He steered the boat alongside me. He set the light on its side and set a pistol down. He pulled me aboard, and I sat in a chair. "Holy J. Christal, I thought you were the bastard that's been poaching my traps. I just a soon shoot ya if ya was."

I told the Gulfport Police what I have just recounted to you. They, of course, didn't believe me. Pirates and mercenaries? But they gave me hot coffee, brand-name cigarettes, and tiny homemade pecan pies, so they were my heroes, whether they believed me or not. I suspected, however, that their disbelief was a front, since they probably felt it was all out of their league for their small department if it were true. They contacted the FBI and the Gulf Guard of America.

By the afternoon, a clean-shaven older man in a suit visited me. He did not have a Mississippi drawl, so that concerned me a bit. He shook my hand. "Derek? Sorren Gibbons. Gulf Guard of

America, Investigative Division. Well, I've heard you had quite the beach adventure."

"Yeah, sure."

He interlocked his fingers as he rested his arms on the table between us. "So, I need to hear it from you. Did you witness Captain Randall McMason murder Joshua Trahan?"

"Yes."

He paused a few seconds. "You know he recently made a statement that he had been in a shootout with the men you call the Manchacs. He said he had tracked them and tried to arrest them and they opened fire. McMason himself was shot in the shoulder and the knee. And he said that he sent a team to ambush their main camp in Lake Maurepas. So, if you're speaking the truth, then this is quite a conspiracy, isn't it? Are you willing to testify in court against him?"

"I don't know."

"You don't know. Why not?" His knuckles beamed white.

"He could send someone in to kill me."

"Any way you look at it, Derek, I'm here to take you into custody." He chuckled.

"Why?"

"A large cache of guns that had been reported stolen were found in the warehouse of the Oyster Shell Road Variety Store. What do you know about that?"

My throat went dry.

"That store is close to your bar. You must have gone there for all your groceries and needs. Any other type of business dealings you did with the owner of that establishment?"

I looked down at the woodgrain table in front of me.

He sighed and set a file on the table. He showed me a photocopy from the folder. "Who's this person?"

I shook my head.

Gibbons clicked a pen and drew glasses on the photocopy. "Now?"

"Fitzmorris."

"What Fitzmorris? He have a first name?"

"No, sir. Well, he probably has one, but I don't know it."

"We've been watching this man whom you know as Fitzmorris for some time. His name is Ben Kaustis and he's a known conman wanted for embezzlement of funds from Longman and Fitzmorris Financial Services in Gretna, Louisiana."

"Oh."

"So why did you bring a stash of guns to him? Our operative witnessed you do this, so let's just be straight here. Huh, son?"

An odd feeling of both relief and condemnation came over me. "It was the pact we made. Me and Fitzmorris."

"Pact for what? Y'all starting a militia or something?"

"We were afraid that the Manchacs or some other criminal group would overrun the area if we didn't have any guns. It was Fitzmorris's idea. I had a PRA business permit, so I could have guns at my place. He had the wholesale license, so he could legally have ammunition."

"So he conned you into storing all the guns at your place?"

"I guess."

"Look, Derek, we don't need you to help us get Fitzmorris. We've already taken him into custody. We need you to testify against Captain Randall McMason. And if you do, we can negotiate a lesser sentence or perhaps even immunity. Depending on your safety at that point, of course.

I hesitated and babbled a bit.

He stood up. "So, you're saying that you got captured by pirates, witnessed a high-ranking official murder a reporter, and then paddled your way to freedom so you wouldn't do something about it? Maybe you're just a coward." He walked to the door and said, "I'll be back later." He opened the door and looked back at me and said, "If you ever, in your whole life, wanted to do something great with your life, here's your chance."

He slammed the door and left.

Prison

The morning of the St. Joseph Altar, Mira called Warden Wally Warwick.

"So are the prisoners still sick?"

"Um, no they're fine now."

"So I can visit Derek today?"

"During visiting hours."

New Message from Principal Whitman.

Mira said, "Thanks. My boss is calling. Bye."

First assignment. Mayor wants music and youth involvement at his park ceremony$^{9:11AM}$ ⌐ PrincipalWhitman

She had a few hours before meeting Sister Matrona at the church for preparations, and she sorted through a box for some clean clothes. She found some jeans and a white, long-sleeved shirt. And at the bottom of the box, she found her Italian apron from her family's St. Joseph's Altar. Her first name was etched cleanly inside the white part of the Italian flag patch, and she put the apron on over her clothes. She adorned her neck with the music-note pendant and grabbed Derek's novel, *Cold Chambers*. Just before leaving for the jailhouse, Mira opened a plastic container of extra Italian cookies from the full batch she'd made the previous day. She wrapped two frosted and sprinkled cookies into a paper napkin and put them in her purse.

The guard checked the contents of her purse and flipped through the paperback novel just to confirm she wasn't smuggling in any escape tools. Accompanied by another guard, she walked through the hall in front of other cells. Mira didn't dare peek into the other cells as she passed them; however, she could smell them. One smelled of rabid body odor. The next one of clothes left in the washer too long. Then, of bleach and chicken feed. Then, of acrid gun metal and marsh muck. Those odd smells did not distract her from the sound of rapid typing gunning down the hallway.

"I'll stay right here, ma'am. For your privacy, you know."

"Oh, are you sure? I mean, great. But…"

The guard nodded, smiling comically. "He's not gonna do anything."

"Thank you."

The *tick-tick-tack* of the iron typewriter resonated louder as she approached the last cell. Derek typed furiously on a particle-board table.

"Hello!"

When he saw Mira his hard eyes softened. He smiled and stood. The chair legs squealed across the concrete floor. He approached the double-rowed cell bars, which prevented their lips' embrace. They held hands between the bars, feeling both warm skin and cold metal at the same time. They leaned their foreheads on the bars in an attempt to be as close as the bars would allow.

He said, "Hi. How are the students?"

"Good. How is the writing? Sounds like it is going well."

"Okay, I think. I didn't know I had so much inside of me."

"Well, keep writing. Not all of us can save the city behind locked doors."

Derek smiled and nodded. "Did you go to the bar?"

"A mess. There's an eviction notice on the door."

"I figured."

"But here," she said, handing him the paperback book.

"You're wonderful. Thank you. You found something else, I see."

Mira thought of the letter she had left for him long ago. "What's that?"

He pulled a hand free from her gentle grasp and tapped the pendant.

"Oh, right! How did you get it? You know…don't answer that." She reached into purse for the Italian cookies.

"Oh, did you find anything else at the bar?"

Her fingers rubbed against the smooth paper of the letter as she searched for the soft tissue encasing the cookies. "Nope."

"I know that apron."

"Yeah, finally this is happening. It's been a nightmare. All for a school event."

"You did it, though. So everything's in order for today?"

"I need to go see Sister Matrona first."

"Who?"

"Oh, I guess I may not have mentioned her in the letters recently. She's a nun at St. Henriette Cathedral that's helping me a lot with things. Her Greek relief camp is getting the leftovers. And hopefully, Archbishop Fullerton remembers he agreed to do the blessing. But yeah, all the students and their parents are making covered dishes. We've got shrimp-stuffed mirliton, fried catfish, collards, and a whole lot more."

"Who's making the Italian cookies?"

She pulled the cookies out of her purse and gave them to him.

"Yes! Don't get a lot of freshly baked sweets in here. Your mother would be proud." He set them atop *Cold Chambers*. "I'll have those later."

"Oh, how are you feeling? Have you been sick?"

"All of us got food poisoning a couple weeks ago from some bad beef in the kitchen."

"The warden had this whole place quarantined. Said all y'all had a contagious disease."

Derek shook his head. "No clue. They say a lot of things."

"They do, don't they. So…what's going on with the deal?"

"They said that they're investigating Red Birch Security Company even further, and that's going to take some time."

"So, you're just going to be in there till…whenever?"

Derek laughed. "They said they'd drop all the charges and set me free just as long as I don't live anywhere near New Orleans. They're afraid I might disrupt the Refounding efforts given my… 'rebellious nature.'"

"So what now?"

"I told them I'm not going anywhere. This is where I need to be, even if I'm locked up."

Mira sighed. "Derek, I just took a promotion from Principal Whitman. I'll be here for a while."

"Once I testify against the company, they'll give me three years if I decide to stay here. That way, the Refounding efforts should be well on their way."

"Damn it." Mira leaned forward, her forehead resting again on the cold steel bars.

"Hey, I belong here with you. So here I am. I'm not about to go live somewhere else now. Did that before."

Mira let out a deep sigh and closed her eyes. "Why can't we just have normal lives like everyone else?" They were silent for a few seconds. "So…the city statue isn't going to be of McMason, thank goodness. It's going to be a fleur-de-lis."

"Really?" Derek smiled. "That's it!"

Mira saw sparks in his eyes.

"What's it?"

He looked back at the typewriter. "What I needed to finish."

"I disagree. It's really just beginning. Right?"

Derek looked back at Mira and squeezed her fingers. "Right." He smiled.

Chapter 1

At the time of writing this book, the New Orleans City Council had approved the commission for a statue of a fleur-de-lis in the park to honor the city and its residents. They had considered commemorating Captain Randall McMason; however, that ended once enough damning evidence on the Monster surfaced. His supporters had claimed he was honorable in establishing order for the region and having food relief programs in place. They also said it was simply a piece of history worth remembering but not repeating, which is a valid point. But statues aren't erected to correct errors in judgment; however, they often illustrate such errors over the course of time. McMason was a murderer and a conspirator. We'd have millions of statues everywhere if murder and conspiracy were worthy of immortalizing. And still, people would murder and conspire even with the constant reminders.

Thanks to the tireless investigative reporting of the deceased Joshua Trahan, the public is aware of such infamy. I hope, for him, that Heaven has an unlimited supply of cigarettes and golf balls. Also, we should thank whoever "Yossarian" is for risking everything to bring this out in the open. Joshua took that person's identity to his grave, so probably no one will ever know who Yossarian is—or was.

I used to explain the fleur-de-lis to outsiders as an ancient regal symbol of hope. But I couldn't have been more wrong. There's nothing ancient about it. It's constant. It gives people hope for the future, a hope that everyone feels. A selflessness, even if only for an instant, that calls for solidarity. It gives them faith in themselves and in others. It gives them a unity when it seems everything else wants to break them.

Certainly some people know what the symbol originally meant, but everyone knows what it means today and for tomorrow. It's an eternal beacon that everyone can see, that everyone can follow, that beckons us to one another. It encourages people to rebuild their houses and inspires new businesses. It's the symbol of spirit; without it we'd all have sunk under the swamp long ago. Things always change. We can't change that. After Beckham, almost everything was hard to come by, but even in those dark days, spirit was never in short supply in New Orleans. That will never change.

Acknowledgments

Thank you to the staff at Maine Authors Publishing, who helped turn the dream for publication into a reality.

Thank you to Lindsey Reynolds, Julia Coe McKelvey, Geoff Kenmuir, Eric Camarillo, and Melanie Greaver for their great feedback and suggestions on my drafts.

Thank you to my New Mexico Highlands University professors Eddie Tafoya, Brandon Kempner, and Kristie Ross, who comprised my creative thesis committee. Even though much of my creative thesis didn't make it into the final manuscript, these professors showed me what worked and what wouldn't.

Thank you to Ann Glaviano for inviting me to join her New Orleans–based writers group many years ago. Critiques from the group members were vital for this story's early progress. I also want to thank Chris Smith and his writers group at the Jefferson Parish East Bank Regional Library for the encouraging feedback once the story took shape.

Thank you to almost every coffee shop in southeastern Louisiana, northern New Mexico, and southern/central Maine.

Thank you to my parents, Gregory and Marie Breerwood, for shaping me into the man I am today and for their unconditional support for my endeavors.

I owe my wife, Madelyn Breerwood, tremendous gratitude for believing in me all these years and supporting my writing passion.

None of this would have been possible without the unwavering spirit of New Orleans and its people.